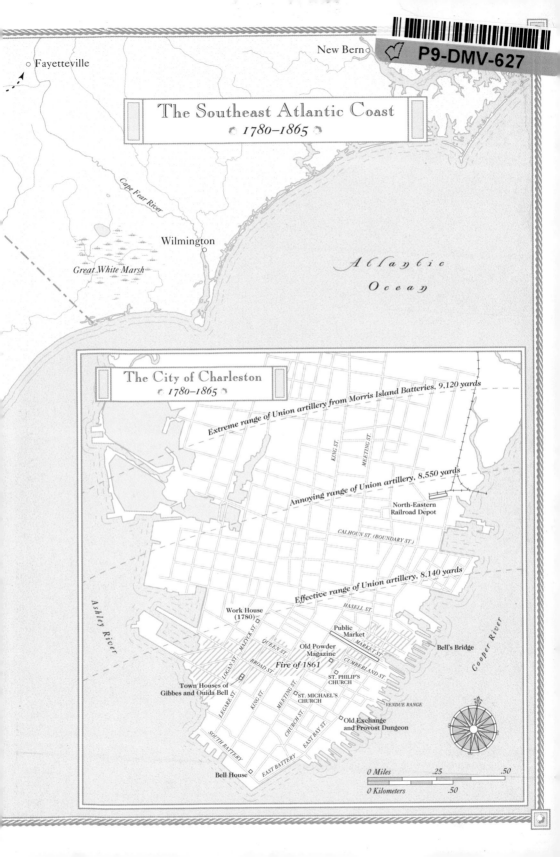

CHARLESTON

Also by John Jakes

ON SECRET SERVICE*

The Crown Family Saga
AMERICAN DREAMS*
HOMELAND

CALIFORNIA GOLD

The North and South Trilogy
NORTH AND SOUTH
LOVE AND WAR
HEAVEN AND HELL

The Kent Family Chronicles
THE BASTARD
THE REBELS
THE SEEKERS
THE FURIES
THE TITANS
THE WARRIORS
THE LAWLESS
THE AMERICANS

*Published by Dutton

CHARLESTON

A NOVEL

JOHN JAKES

DUTTON

DUTTON
Published by the Penguin Group
Penguin Putnam Inc., 375 Hudson Street, New York, New York 10014, U.S.A.
Penguin Books Ltd, 80 Strand, London WC2R 0RL, England
Penguin Books Australia Ltd, Ringwood, Victoria, Australia
Penguin Books Canada Ltd, 10 Alcorn Avenue, Toronto, Ontario, Canada M4V 3B2
Penguin Books (N.Z.) Ltd, 182-190 Wairau Road, Auckland 10, New Zealand

Penguin Books Ltd, Registered Offices: Harmondsworth, Middlesex, England

Published by Dutton, a member of Penguin Putnam Inc.

First Printing, August 2002
1   3   5   7   9   10   8   6   4   2

REGISTERED TRADEMARK—MARCA REGISTRADA

LIBRARY OF CONGRESS CATALOGING-IN-PUBLICATION DATA

Jakes, John.
Charleston : a novel / John Jakes.
p. cm.
ISBN 0-525-94650-0 (acid-free paper)
1. Charleston (S.C.)—Fiction.   I. Title.
PS3560.A37 C48 2002
813'.54—dc21   2002021251

Printed in the United States of America
Set in Sabon
Designed by Leonard Telesca

PUBLISHER'S NOTE

This book is a work of fiction. Names, characters, places, and incidents either are the products of the author's imagination or are used fictitiously, and any resemblance to actual persons, living or dead, business establishments, events, or locales is entirely coincidental.

In memory of two good friends at
The University of South Carolina

DR. GEORGE C. ROGERS, JR.
Department of History

DR. GEORGE TERRY
Thomas Cooper Library

The scholarship of George Rogers
drew me to South Carolina's dramatic past.
The library directed by George Terry
helped me study it.
I hope both of them might have liked
this retelling of some of that history.

CONTENTS

AUTHOR'S NOTE

Charleston, its residents like to say, stands where the Ashley and Cooper rivers form the Atlantic Ocean. At the time of the American Revolution, Charleston was the fourth largest city in the colonies, and the most elegant. She was loved and admired by Americans and Europeans for her ambience and charm, her culture and gentility.

The foundation of Charleston's wealth was a series of dominant cash crops: indigo, then rice, then cotton, each dependent on slave labor. Charleston's white elite lived in constant fear of those it kept in servitude to insure its prosperity.

Ultimately the city, the state, and political thought became slaves of the economic system. In the struggle to preserve it Charleston moved from an open society founded on religious tolerance and the free flow of ideas to a closed society threatened by, and hostile to, the outside world. At the end of this road lay secession and bloody civil war.

This is a tale of three eras, three Charlestons, and one family that endured fires and epidemics, hurricanes and earthquakes, bombardments and military occupations—nearly a century of history that was by turns courageous, turbulent, and tragic.

Through it all, and much more that followed in the next one hundred years, Charlestonians white and black remained proud survivors, and went on to create the beautiful cosmopolitan city that greets the visitor today.

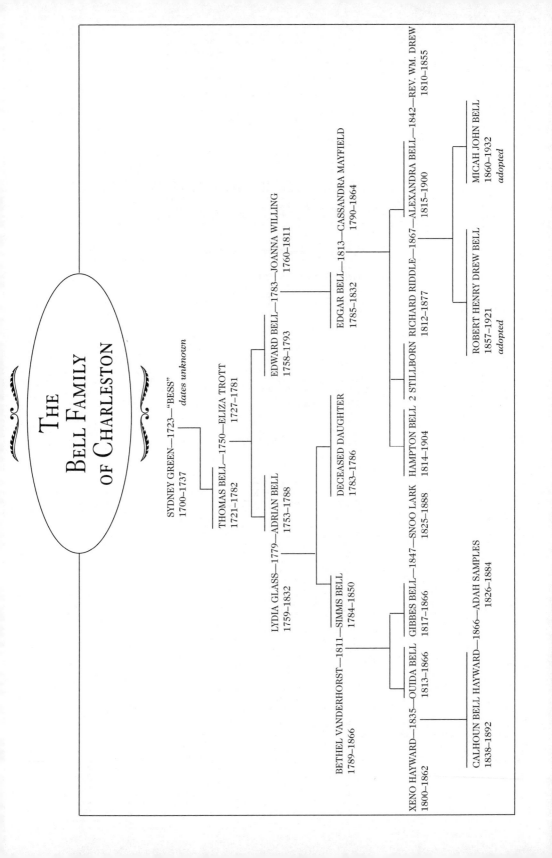

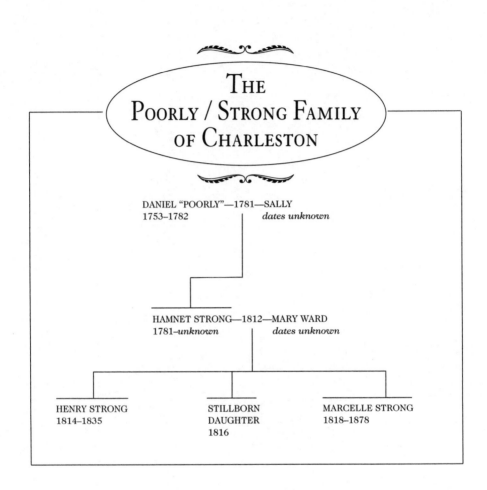

THE
POORLY / STRONG FAMILY
OF CHARLESTON

DANIEL "POORLY"—1781—SALLY
1753–1782   *dates unknown*

HAMNET STRONG—1812—MARY WARD
1781–*unknown*   *dates unknown*

HENRY STRONG   STILLBORN   MARCELLE STRONG
1814–1835   DAUGHTER   1818–1878
                        1816

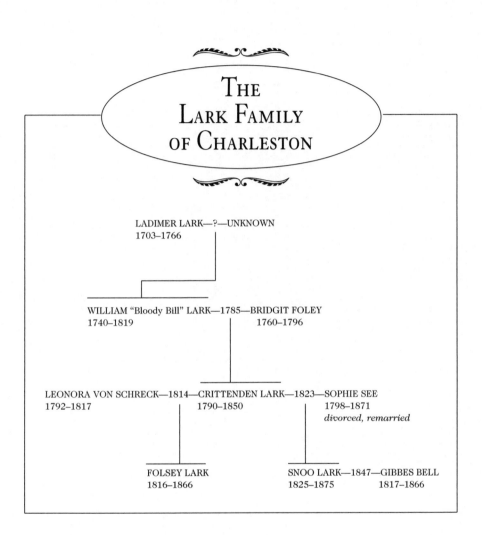

THE
LARK FAMILY
OF CHARLESTON

LADIMER LARK—?—UNKNOWN
1703–1766

WILLIAM "Bloody Bill" LARK—1785—BRIDGIT FOLEY
1740–1819   1760–1796

LEONORA VON SCHRECK—1814—CRITTENDEN LARK—1823—SOPHIE SEE
1792–1817   1790–1850   1798–1871
                                                                  divorced, remarried

FOLSEY LARK   SNOO LARK—1847—GIBBES BELL
1816–1866   1825–1875   1817–1866

The people of Charleston live rapidly, not willingly letting go untasted any of the pleasures of life. . . . Their manner of life, dress, equipages, furniture, everything, denotes a higher degree of taste and love of show, and less frugality than in the northern provinces.

> Johann Schoepf,
> an eighteenth-century visitor

The institution of slavery shaped and defined Charleston as much as, if not more than, any other force in its history.

> Robert N. Rosen,
> *A Short History
> of Charleston*

The waters run out of the harbor twice a day, leaving the mud flats uncovered, and with a hot sun baking down upon decaying matter, there is an odor—not unlike that of Venice—to let one know that all the beauty is built upon unsure foundations.

> George C. Rogers, Jr.,
> *Charleston in the Age
> of the Pinckneys*

South Carolina is too small for a republic and too large for an insane asylum.

> Charleston Unionist
> James L. Petigru,
> on the eve of the
> Civil War

PROLOGUE
1720

Families are sometimes the children of chance. The family of this story had its beginning at the intersection of Broad and Meeting streets, in Charles Town, on the coast of Carolina, one rainy autumn afternoon in 1720.

Charles Town was by then fifty years old. It had been established as the center of a proprietary colony organized and financed, with the king's permission, by eight wealthy Englishmen known as the Lords Proprietors. The chief organizer, Lord Anthony Ashley Cooper, chose the name Carolina—*Carolus*, Latin for Charles—to honor his sovereign, Charles II.

That rainy day—no more than a steamy drizzle, really—a man and a woman hurried east on a footpath on the north side of a rutted mixture of sand and crushed oyster shells masquerading as a civilized street. Their destination was the Cooper River piers, where the man hoped to find menial work and cheap lodging. He was already discouraged by the sight of so many slaves, blue-black Africans, with whom he would have to compete.

He and the woman had journeyed in from a little trading station on a tributary of the Santee River. The store and stock pen of the station had long served one of the busy trails leading northwest to the Cherokee towns, but the Cherokee slave trade was dying as more ships sailed in from West Africa. The man and woman had abandoned the place because of poverty, loneliness, and the woman's delicate condition.

On the southeast corner of Broad and Meeting stood a small Anglican church built of cypress. From somewhere within the palisade surrounding the church a bell rang the hour. The man stopped to listen. He'd always loved the sound of bells—ship's bells, handbells of street criers, and especially the mighty cathedral bells of his native England, which he'd left as a boy. This bell was thin by comparison but sweet all the same.

Sydney Greech, late of Bristol, Barbados, and the sloop *Royal James*, was now twenty. He had a certain lean good looks, though his eyes possessed a hardness born of his recent career at sea. The best that could be said about the young woman was that she still had a prettiness not yet ruined by harsh living conditions or the kind of debauchery in which she and Sydney liked to indulge. She called herself Bess; no last name ever came down to later generations.

A widow at seventeen, Bess had met Sydney in 1718, when he stumbled into her late husband's trading station, lost and starving. Finding each other by accident, they lived together and took care of the business until deciding to leave it for the bustling town.

The sonorous peal of the church bells moved Sydney to say, " 'Spose we should be officially married someday."

" 'Spose we should, since I'm carrying your babe."

"Not very familiar wi' churches. Truth is, never stepped inside one."

"I did, once. But I got something else on my mind about marrying."

"What?"

"Our name. Don't be mad now, Sydney. It's been in my thoughts every day because of the baby."

"What exactly?"

"Greech. It don't sound pretty on the tongue. It don't sound important. It sounds low."

Incensed, he flung down her hand. "Goddamn you, woman, it's the name my dear mother gave me, I won't—"

There he stopped. Sydney wasn't a brilliant or educated young man, but neither was he completely insensitive. He saw the hurt in Bess's eyes, the tears mingling with rain, and reconsidered. "Oh, I guess maybe there's something in what you say. What ought we do about it?"

"Change our name to a better one that fits the kind of life we'll have from now on. We're going to do well in Charles Town, I know it." As if to reinforce that statement the baby kicked vigorously. She had no doubt it was a boy.

As the last bell notes floated into the rainy sky, Sydney rubbed his jaw. "All right, then. You know I love bells. *Bell* is a pretty word all by itself. Bells are strong, made of fine metal. Bells do important business in this world."

Excitement showed on her grimy face. "Yes, they do, Sydney."

"Well, do you like Bell for a name?"

"Oh, yes, very much."

"Then Bell it is," he said. Thus he settled the issue and set a stormy future in motion.

BOOK ONE
CITY AT WAR
1779-1793

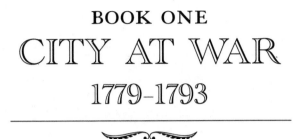

*All their cavalry was annihilated. Our works came up to their ditch.
Fort Moultrie and the entire harbor were in our hands. They could
not entertain the least hope of succor.*

> Diary of Captain Hinrichs,
> Hessian Jäger Corps, at the siege of Charles Town
> May 1780

*The city looks like a beautiful village. . . . It is built at the end of the
Neck between the Cooper and Ashley rivers and is approximately a
good English mile long and half a mile wide. The streets are broad
and intersect one another at right angles. Most of the buildings are of
wood and are small; but near the rivers ones sees beautiful buildings
of brick, behind which there are usually very fine gardens. . . . If one
can judge from appearances, these people show better taste and live
in greater luxury than those of the northern provinces.*

> Diary of Captain Ewald,
> Hessian Jäger Corps, British army of occupation
> May 1780

*The safe rule, according to which one can always ascertain whether a
man is a loyalist or a rebel, is to find out whether he profits more in
his private interests, his mode of life, his way of doing things, when
he is on our side or on that of the enemy.*

> Diary of Captain Hinrichs

1

The Summons

One night in early November 1779, he dreamed a terrifying dream.

He saw a skiff dancing across Charleston Harbor, running before an offshore breeze that raised what mariners called white horses on the water. Lydia sat in the skiff's bow, laughing and enjoying herself; her hair flew in the wind like a yellow banner.

He couldn't see the face of the man at the tiller, only his back. But he was not the man, of that he was sure. Though he was athletic, a superb horseman, he'd never learned to swim or sail. His mother called it passing strange, since his father, a wharf owner, made his living from the commerce of the creeks and rivers and oceans.

Unseen bells began to peal—the eight church bells of St. Michael's parish, cast by Messrs. Lester and Pack, London, where he lay dreaming. The bells didn't ring the sequence of notes that called the faithful to Sunday worship. They rang another familiar call, the call to calamity: a fire, an impending hurricane. Great danger.

When he woke in his room on the third floor above Fountain Court, the meaning of the dream came clear. He'd been absent from America a year and a half. The desirable young woman he wanted to marry could be slipping away from him.

Edward Bell, twenty-one, was at that time studying at the Middle Temple. He had resisted his father's wish to send him there, saying, "I have no ambition to practice law in South Carolina."

"Nor do most of the young men from Charleston who enroll at the Inns of Court, but it will be useful. It broadens you, like a grand tour. It makes you a keener student of business contracts. It prepares you to be a leader of society—to hold office if you wish."

"Why not send Adrian? He's firstborn."

"I don't mean to speak unkindly of your brother, but to be truthful, he hasn't the head for it. Adrian's a shrewd young man. Shrewd is not the same as smart."

"But we're in the middle of a war with England."

"Where do you think we learned that we have a right to rebel against the injustices of the king's ministers? From English constitutional law, taught at the Middle Temple. Who stood up to the king in Parliament and defended our right to rebel? Edmund Burke, of the Middle Temple."

"Is this a scheme to keep me out of the militia?"

"Do you want to join the militia, Edward?"

"Not particularly. I'm not an ardent patriot like you."

"You're more of one than your brother. Worry about the militia at such time as the British return to Carolina. It may never happen. They've left us alone three years now." In '76, Col. William Moultrie and his brave men had repulsed an invasion attempt at the palmetto log fort on nearby Sullivan's Island, the fort now bearing Moultrie's name. After that humiliation Gen. Henry Clinton and Adm. Sir Peter Parker sailed away and Great Britain concentrated on fighting in the North.

Edward ran out of objections. Soon thereafter he departed for London and the Inns of Court.

★ ★ ★

On a cold but windless evening in early December, he left his apartment in Essex Court, crossed Fountain Court, and entered Middle Temple Hall. Edward was a tall and lanky young man, not handsome, but possessed of strong features and an engaging smile. There was no fat on him. He'd inherited his height and build from his father, Tom Bell. He was dressed like a sober colonial in a double-breasted kersey greatcoat, a white stock and lace cravat, black leather top boots, and a black felt hat with a flat crown and broad brim. He owned a wig but preferred to keep his brown hair tied back with a black ribbon. He carried a stout walking stick for self-defense at night.

In the corridor he passed a broad open doorway on his right. Students and masters still sat at table in the great hall, a high cathedral of a room walled with plaques bearing the arms of the Templars from whom the Middle Temple took its name. Student friends of Edward's were deep into port and private argument, even as an old lawyer droned on from the dais. Something about torts, in which Edward had no interest. Since coming to London he'd spent most of his time at gambling clubs, cockfights, bearbaitings, and his favorite table at the Carolina Coffeehouse in Birchin Lane, where he hobnobbed with rowdy clerks from the London branch of Crokatt's, a Charleston trading firm.

No one in the Temple's great hall noticed him as he slipped by. A door at the end of the corridor brought him to the water gate. As usual, a boatman stood by, waiting to bear a young gentleman off to the night's adventures. Edward stepped down on a thwart.

"South Bank. I'll show you where."

Half an hour later he elbowed his way to the edge of an oval cockfighting pit raised twenty inches above the floor in the center of a large, bare room. Noisy and smoky, the room opened off a narrow passage fittingly called Cocker's Alley. It was packed with roughly dressed lowlifes and young men in fancy silks and powdered wigs. The pit's carpeted floor was strewn with feathers. Dark stains showed where birds had bled. Cocks ready for their matches crowed periodically, adding to the racket.

Edward spoke to a stout man. "Anyone special here tonight?"

"Corday's here, with his black-breasted red. Won the three-day main at Clerkenwell last week."

"Corday." Edward frowned. He'd had run-ins with that gentleman, chiefly over the American rebellion. Mr. Clive Corday had come down from Oxford to study at Gray's Inn. He was notorious for spending even less time at it than Edward did. He was well placed; a relative sat in the House of Lords. Edward always bet against Corday's birds because he detested the man.

A shout went up as Corday appeared, his feeder right behind him carrying the bird. The black-breasted red weighed almost five pounds, Edward guessed. He was a fierce bird with cropped tail feathers, a comb cut into a half moon, and steel fighting spurs. Corday greeted his admirers boisterously. He was a fleshy young dandy with a round face perpetually red and sweaty. He always dressed with fashionable flamboyance, in this case a coat of Italian silk with vertical red and white stripes, a solid red waistcoat, and striped knee stockings that matched his coat.

Corday was contemptuous of the American colonies and all who lived there. It showed when he spied Edward and favored him with a slow nod, a scornful smile. Edward returned the nod, pulled his purse from his pocket, and pointed at the contender. Corday's face reddened all the more.

"Save my spot, if you please." Edward tipped the stout man tuppence and went off to bet.

Corday's first opponent, a loutish fellow wearing farmer's boots, stepped up to the pit looking hangdog, as though his smaller four-pound bird had already lost. At a signal from the master of the matches, Corday and his opponent pitted their birds close to one another, then quickly retreated to the floor outside the oval. Corday's red crowed defiantly. The birds circled one another, darting their heads forward. Suddenly the red flew at the opponent and began to slash with its beak and spurs. The patrons applauded and yelled profane encouragements.

The birds fought fiercely, leaping off the carpet, slashing and pecking. The red disposed of the smaller cock in ten minutes. It lay dying, its head flopping on its neck, its side torn open and bleeding. Edward had wagered two shillings and lost. Corday glanced at him with a smug smile, then turned to accept congratulations from a crowd of sycophants.

A second challenger carried his bird into the pit. This one lasted almost half an hour before the red disposed of it. The third opponent died in twenty minutes, and the red finished off the fourth and fifth in half that time. Corday's feeder picked up the red while, in the back of the hall, the next contenders crowed raucously. Corday's prize was ten guineas. Having steadfastly bet against him, Edward had lost ten shillings of his father's money.

Corday found Edward in the crowd. "Another bad evening, Mr. Bell?" Corday stuck his thumbs in the pockets of his fine waistcoat. Trickles of sweat had washed powder from his wig onto his temples.

Edward stared him down. "I'll get my money back one day."

"Wagering against my big red? I doubt it. You Americans never know when you're whipped. Well, you soon will be, now that Clinton's at sea."

"What are you talking about?"

"Letter from a cousin in New York. Serves aboard the flagship of Admiral Arbuthnot. Big armada's forming up, to sail within the month. Sir Henry Clinton, nine thousand men—a major campaign in the South.

I don't doubt they'll wall up your city and starve you unwashed rabble into submission."

This was stunning news, though perhaps Edward should have seen it coming. A month ago a letter from his father had reported that the British were disquieted because they'd been unable to win a significant victory in the North. Further, the French now stood with the Americans in the war. No doubt Clinton had smarted ever since the defeat at Fort Moultrie. It made a new attack on Charleston seem inevitable.

Tom Bell's letter had sounded a further note of melancholy. Charleston's revolutionary zeal, so hot five years earlier, was waning as the economically hurtful war dragged on.

Corday took advantage of Edward's stunned silence. "It would surely suit me if you were one of those beaten down by General Clinton, Mr. Bell. You're nothing but an ill-bred parvenu. What's more, you dress atrociously."

"And you're an arrogant ass, Mr. Corday. You dress like a whoremonger."

Corday's hand flew up to deliver a stinging slap. Edward staggered back. Corday grinned and stepped in, ready to land another blow. Edward rammed his stick into Corday's middle, throwing him off-stride.

The crowd gave them room. Patrons applauded and encouraged Corday. Edward dropped the stick, swung up his right fist, and blasted Corday's chin from underneath. With his left fist he hammered Corday's soft belly. Corday slipped to his knees, gagging. Edward seized Corday's collar at the nape, pushed hard, and slammed his forehead on the floor twice.

Corday flopped on his side. His wig fell off, baring his shaved skull. Edward snatched up his stick and bashed Corday with the knobby end. Clawing at the floor, Corday struggled to rise. Edward hit him again and Corday stretched out with a sigh.

All around him Edward heard ominous grumblings from Corday's partisans. He waved his stick at those nearest—"One side, damn you"—and they fell back. He left the building at a fast walk, not eager to become a victim of a mob.

Once into the darkened ways of the South Bank, he sprinted for the water stairs. He lost his hat and didn't go back for it.

Crossing the river, he made a decision. It was time to abandon his studies. The new British campaign could mean great danger for his family, but more persuasive, perhaps, was the dream: the bells ringing the alarm, an unseen rival stealing Lydia. He wanted Lydia Glass with all his young man's blood and fire. He hadn't heard from her since arriving in London; she said she never wrote letters. It was time to go home, before he lost her.

2

Bell's Bridge

The French brig *Petite Julianne* out of Calais brought Edward across the Atlantic. The ship fought January gales and towering green seas that kept him uneasy because he couldn't swim. When they broke through to calmer waters near the lush green coast of Carolina, lookouts spied sails of British men-o'-war to the south.

The brig crossed the Charleston Bar and sailed into the familiar harbor. Winter sunshine brightened the water and warmed the salt-tanged air. Gulls dived to find a meal. The Bell house at Oyster Point at the south end of the peninsula was just visible above earthworks where gangs of black men labored. To starboard Fort Moultrie swarmed with similar activity. Several warships rode at anchor, flying the *Don't Tread on Me* flag designed for the American navy by Tom Bell's friend Christopher Gadsden.

Edward's eyes misted at the sight of America's loveliest city: the white and pastel houses, the waterfront, the beautiful Exchange Building at the foot of Broad Street, where distinguished visitors arrived at the waterside steps and ascended to the grand portico. The spires of St. Philip's and St. Michael's ornamented the skyline. Edward wanted to hear St. Michael's bells again. He'd grown up with them.

His delight became dismay as the brig made her way up the Cooper. Nine commercial wharves jutted into the river, the longest and largest being Gadsden's. For years the wharves had shipped indigo to the textile mills of England, rice to the dining tables of Europe, Carolina pine to the shipyards of Bermuda. All of that, plus turpentine and pitch, corn and beef and peas, and the incoming slave ships, usually made the wharf district a tumultuous place. Today Edward saw only a few small vessels tied up, none at Bell's Bridge.

Originally it was named Trott's Bridge, *bridge* being an old term for wharf. Tom Bell had gone to work there as a young man. He had proved himself to be smart, worthy, and a hard worker, and married Trott's well-educated daughter Eliza. He took over the business when she inherited it.

Tom had no wish to join the idle planter class, but he soon acquired land anyway, unsought. It came about because he loaned money to young men who bought large tracts of land and slaves to work it. He took his debt service in a percentage of their crops, sold the rice and indigo abroad, and thereby amassed more money to lend.

But some of the overly ambitious young gentlemen had neither the brains nor the industry to operate a plantation. From one failed wastrel Tom foreclosed land that became his summer home, Malvern. From another he got a much larger parcel on the Ashley. This he deeded to his son Adrian, five years Edward's senior, on favorable terms. Adrian had done well with the land, creating a profitable plantation, Prosperity Hall, in a matter of a few years.

The Frenchman dropped anchor just off Bell's Bridge, where a man was examining the brig with a spyglass. Edward climbed down to the ship's gig; two small trunks were already stowed. Four oarsmen rowed him toward wooden steps on the wharf. The observer, whom Edward identified as the wharf manager, Esau Willing, sent a black boy racing up the pier to announce the arrival.

The gig tied up, Edward climbed the stairs and greeted the astonished Mr. Willing, a plain, sober man of middle years. Two eight-person canoes used for the busy ferry traffic to the other side of the Cooper were turned over and roped to cleats on the wharf; more commerce curtailed by war.

"Before God," Willing said, thrusting out his hand, which Edward shook, "I wondered what that Frenchman was up to. I thought it might be some British trick. No one expected you, Mr. Edward."

"Least of all my father, I'm sure," Edward said. And there he was, Tom Bell, summoned by the boy and stalking down the pier like vengeance itself. Oarsmen threw Edward's trunks on the pier and pushed off.

Tom Bell was a tall, slender man nearing sixty, with weather-browned skin and a piratical mustache white as his hair. He dressed like a mechanic, in a loose linen shirt and old breeches of blue-and-white striped ticking. He didn't own a peruke and never powdered his hair, simply left it tied, like his son's. For these and other reasons the town's elite had always dismissed Tom Bell as a half-gentleman. The eighteenth century's ideal was the landed proprietor. Someone in trade who didn't amass and hold land enthusiastically was suspect.

"Sir, look who fell out of the sea," Willing exclaimed to his employer.

"The prodigal son." Tom gave Edward a fierce look. "You have abandoned your studies?"

"For the moment, sir. I left London because—"

"We'll discuss your reasons in private." He wheeled about, his tone an unspoken command to follow.

Not too loudly, Mr. Willing said, "Welcome back. I'll have a boy deliver your trunks." Edward thanked him and hurried off, forgetting to make a polite inquiry about Willing's daughter.

In the years since the Fort Moultrie victory Charleston had remained a busy open port. Obviously the Crown's new campaign in the South was closing it down. Sheds that warehoused rice and indigo on Bell's Bridge were empty. The scale house and small kitchen building were padlocked.

Edward followed his father into a dim and cluttered office. Tom Bell sat behind his desk and began to pack his pipe with the fragrant tobacco he flavored with vanilla. He didn't offer his son a chair.

"Now, sir. Explain yourself."

"Yes, sir. Last month I heard news of Clinton's armada. I was worried about you, and mother."

Tom pounced on Edward's hesitation: "Is that all?"

"Lydia. I was worried about her too."

"As well you might be," Tom said with a curious look Edward didn't understand. "Sir Henry Clinton has marched up the coast from Savannah with approximately nine thousand men, including mercenary companies from the German province of Hesse. Admiral Arbuthnot's fleet is anchored off Simmons Island[1] and will soon bottle up the harbor. Commodore Whipple was sent down by Congress with seven ships."

"I saw them inside the bar."

"No match for the enemy squadron. I expect Sir Henry will be on

[1]Present-day Seabrook Island

James Island, within artillery range, in a matter of days. You chose a poor time to return."

"Well, the deed's done, so I hope we needn't wrangle about it."

"You expect me to accept this calmly, Edward? I spent a devil of a lot of money to send you abroad. I am grossly disappointed in your behavior."

"I'm sorry, sir. I'll try to make it up somehow. If not the money, at least the disappointment. May I ask whether you've seen Lydia?"

Again that odd look. "Not lately, no."

"Is mother at Oyster Point?" That was the site of their house, the southern point of the peninsula, named for the middens of oyster shell that bleached white in the sun.

"No, I sent her out to Malvern as soon as we got word of the enemy landing at Savannah. I thought the countryside would be safer. Now I'm not sure. Clinton may cross the Ashley and occupy the Neck, cutting us off by land as well as by sea. Further, there are loyalist partisans operating in the parishes. They are not honorable men."

"I'll bring mother to Charleston anytime you say."

"Thank you. Your brother's already left Prosperity Hall in the care of his slaves. He's staying at his town house."

"I'll go there now, if I may."

"You're more likely to find him at William Holliday's tavern on Queen Street, idling his time away with his friends of similar disposition."

"And Poorly, sir? What about him?"

"At the moment Daniel Poorly is working at Malvern."

"You wrote that he's married."

"Sally, a light-skinned kitchen girl."

"So I own two slaves?"

"Not yet. Remember that under the code, slave marriages have no legal standing. Is that all?"

Awkwardly, Edward extended a hand, as though to touch his father. He hoped Tom might stand, let Edward embrace him. He didn't. Edward's hand fell. "Only this, sir. Whatever else happens, I'm very glad to see you."

After a long, steady look Tom said, "My feeling as well." He spoke gruffly, to hide any trace of sentimentality. "If you choose to walk through the city, you'll hardly recognize it. Much of the damage from the great fire of two years ago has been repaired, but the damage from this war grows more evident every day."

Edward took his leave. Near the head of the pier he passed by three large iron cages designed to hold slaves fresh off the ships. The cages were empty, free of their usual stench. From the top bars of each cage hung pairs of chains and manacles, to restrain any man or woman feeling rebellious after the long passage from Africa. The breeze rang the metal cuffs and chains like chimes.

A few steps beyond, near the hurly-burly of Bay Street, Edward saw a young woman approaching; Mr. Willing's daughter Joanna. She wore a workaday long-sleeved dress, brown wool, a laced-up leather bodice, a small round cap, latched shoes of cowhide. "Edward. What in heaven are you doing in Charleston?"

"Change of plans. I heard about the invasion. I thought my father might need me."

"Indeed he may. They say Clinton's brought artillery, horses, and those dreadful Germans who fight for money."

Edward remembered Joanna as a small, serious girl, exceptionally neat in her personal habits. That was not a trait inherited from her father. Esau Willing kept an untidy office that Joanna continually tried to clean and organize. Her mother came from the German colony up at Orangeburg. He recalled little about the woman except her face and the different spelling of her name, Johanna.

During his absence Joanna had matured into a beautifully proportioned young woman no taller than his shoulder. She had her father's round face, a good bosom, large brown eyes, and lustrous brown hair with strong reddish lights in it. Always neatly arranged, her hair reminded him of a hunter's cap. Her forehead was high and smooth. She smiled easily, and with warmth; she had good teeth.

A constant subtle tension gave her body a slight forward tilt, as though she was anticipating a problem or searching for one that needed her attention. Even when she conversed, he felt that her mind was clicking with a hundred other concerns. Joanna Willing was a person he'd known reasonably well but had no great interest in, especially since she tended to be an annoying scold on one subject.

"Are you looking for Mr. Willing?" he asked.

"No. I'm going out in the harbor with an oyster rake. I found a bed where the oysters are big as dinner plates. Two of those will feed Papa and me nicely."

"My father says the city's greatly changed."

"Not in every respect." She glanced at the cages. A hanging chain and manacle moved in the wind, throwing its shadow on her face.

"You still believe we're wrong to trade in slaves?"

"Absolutely. The British are on the right side of that issue. They're encouraging slaves to run away and join their army."

Her air of rectitude annoyed him. "Joanna, for years part of your father's salary has come from the profits of slave trading on this wharf."

"I am not my father."

"Still, slavery paid for your education at that fine young ladies' academy."

"And education taught me to hate slavery."

"Well, there's independency, eh? I surrender." He smiled. "I'm out of arguments."

"I don't find the subject amusing. Slavery is an abomination before God. It paid for your glorious holiday in England, didn't it?"

"Damn, Joanna, you're—"

"The tide's running. I must hurry. Good day, Edward."

And off she went, her broad hips swinging in a way that might have intrigued him in other circumstances. He shook his head. Not much of a homecoming, this. He hoped he'd experienced the worst of it.

3

Adrian's Thunderbolt

The return of the British had changed his city. Soldiers, vagrants, blacks, bawds, and refugees from the country crowded the dirt streets and the footpaths on either side. Wagons and chaises and couriers on horseback added to the clamor and congestion. Families squatted on empty patches of land with barrows and bundles holding their few possessions. Edward guessed that Charleston's population of twelve or thirteen thousand might have doubled.

North of Boundary Street at Meeting, slaves with shovels and barrows were building a sizable hornwork from tabby, a kind of masonry made of lime mixed with oyster shells. The hornwork was the centerpiece of a line of fortifications running east and west toward the two rivers. He climbed a mound of dirt to observe more black men digging a broad ditch some distance in front of the earthworks and parallel to them. He approached a sweating engineer studying a diagram. "Sir, what's the purpose of the ditch?"

The annoyed man barked at him. "To save your life, sir. We expect Clinton to cross the Ashley and come at us from the Neck. The ditch will be dammed at each end, and tidal seepage will fill it. Behind it we'll have two abatis, another moat, and there"—he pointed downward—"a fraise."

"I'm sorry, I don't know the term."

"A fraise is a barricade of sharp stakes, pointing at the enemy. Obviously you're not an army man. You certainly look old enough." He didn't mean it as a compliment.

Edward walked south again. The soldiers he saw were a hard lot, armed with muskets and fowlers, tomahawks and knives. Blue uniform coats with white-edged buttonholes, the uniform of South Carolina regulars, were scarce. Most of the soldiers wore leggings and long hunting shirts dyed an assortment of bright colors. Whether the men were regulars or militia, Edward couldn't say.

He turned over to King Street a block west of Meeting and found more than one merchant hammering up boards to protect a shop. Packs of wild dogs fought for garbage strewn about. The only laughter came from youngsters romping as though no enemy threatened.

☆ ☆ ☆

Mr. William Holliday's Queen Street taproom, a successor to Dillon's, was a favorite of the young gentry. Here, in the middle of the afternoon, Adrian Bell sat drinking and chatting with two friends.

Adrian resembled his younger brother and was nearly as tall. The strongest differences were large jug-handle ears and a pinched, off-putting face; Adrian's eyes were set too close together. What he lacked in good looks, he made up for with a prosperous appearance and a cultivated air of importance.

Adrian's friends were scions of wealthy plantation owners. The first, Storey Wragg, was a glutton with a face as red as an uncooked mutton chop and a stomach big enough for a woman about to deliver triplets. The other, Archibald Lescock, was a fop who perfumed his wig with cloves and cinnamon and padded his breeches to enhance the shape of his legs. All three young men were in fashion: long, narrow-tailed coats showing elaborate turnback cuffs, standing collars, stocks, fancy hose garters. Lescock's wig was expensive human hair. Adrian's was of less costly goat hair. The miserly Wragg settled for horse mane.

"I thought Gadsden was our resident radical madman, not Henry Laurens," Wragg said between forkfuls from his trencher of pork loin. "I consider Laurens a man of moderation. I can't believe he endorsed the wish of General Lincoln and the Congress to put slaves under arms."

"And free them afterward," Adrian said. "But surely they'd be poor soldiers. Then the battle would be lost, and we could return to being a Crown colony. Not entirely undesirable, in my estimation."

"You think niggers wouldn't fight?" Wragg plucked at a piece of fat dangling from the corner of his mouth. "Don't forget Stono." In 1739 slaves had massacred a dozen whites at Stono Bridge, twenty miles south of the city. Planters on horseback interrupted the slaves' dash to freedom in Florida, killed fourteen immediately, and shot others after questioning them. But some escaped, provoking a manhunt that lasted for weeks. More than forty suspects were rounded up and executed. The memory of this worst and bloodiest slave rebellion had terrified Charlestonians ever since.

"My wife can't forget Stono," Lescock said in a hushed voice. "Her parents told her how awful it was to tremble in their beds every night, fearing they'd be murdered."

Adrian mused aloud. "I wonder what Mr. Laurens would have us do if he takes away our chattels? Slosh around in the rice fields ourselves? Sweat to death in the heat?" The others laughed at the ridiculous idea.

At that moment Adrian saw his brother approaching. "My God. Am I looking at a ghost?"

Edward smiled. "No, I'm back. And not in our father's favor because of it."

"I'm stunned. Stunned," Adrian repeated as he rose and embraced his brother. "These are my friends." He introduced Wragg and Lescock. Edward thought, *Corday's cousins.* Smooth, pale hands; an air of condescension as they in turn looked the new arrival up and down. Edward's clothes bore stains and patches unsuitable to a man of quality.

"You must tell me how this came about," Adrian said. "Storey, Archibald—you'll excuse us?" They left, Adrian called for tankards of ale, and Edward briefly described his decision to break off his studies. When he mentioned Lydia Glass, he noticed a sudden nervousness in his brother's manner. Adrian asked, "Have you been home?"

"Not yet. Father told me you might be here, so I stopped."

"You know mother's at Malvern?"

"Yes."

"Edward, I've something to tell you. Duty compels it."

"Fine, I'm listening." With some of the rich dark ale in him he felt relaxed and happy.

"While you were away, I asked Lydia to marry me. She consented."

Edward slammed the tankard down so hard, other patrons broke off conversations to stare.

Adrian flushed, leaned toward him, spoke in a pleading way. "Look here, it shouldn't be so hard to understand. I've always admired her. What man in Charleston doesn't? You were too busy to notice."

"I don't believe this."

"Why? You may be the romantic in the family, but I'm the steady one. I offer Lydia a better future. I will make a pile of money. I'm also on the right side. I believe the British will win the war."

"Because you're an opportunist," Edward snarled. "I've a right to knock your head off your shoulders, you damned—" He choked back the filthy name.

"Edward, she made the choice."

"I want to hear it from her."

"Yes, you should. She's in town, with her father. Please, Edward. Try not to be too angry."

"What were you expecting, congratulations, or my hearty thanks for stealing Lydia behind my back?" He knocked over the tankard with a sweep of his hand; the contents slopped on the pegged floor. He stood abruptly, overturning his chair.

"Edward—"

"Go to hell, Adrian. You just go to hell."

✹ ✹ ✹

Edward wandered the streets and visited dramshops for most of the afternoon. Twice he almost turned his steps toward Lydia's house but decided he was too angry.

Sunset found him by the State House at the northwest corner of Broad and Meeting. In the crossway grateful citizens had erected a marble statue of William Pitt, honoring the great statesman's defense of the colonists when they protested the Stamp Act. Edward gazed up at St. Michael's steeple and listened to the sweet notes of the eight bells announcing the hour.

The sky was pale as his hopes, the stars dim as his future.

✹ ✹ ✹

The fine single house of the Bell family, stucco on brick, fronted the harbor at Oyster Point, sometimes called White Point. It overlooked a vista of marsh grass, the middens of bleached oyster shells, and the partially constructed fortifications he'd seen when he sailed in. In the hazy dusk the lanterns of Commodore Whipple's warships rode the gentle swells of the evening tide.

The three-story house was rectangular, the narrow end toward the street. A gate on the east side led into a walled garden dominated by a live oak taller than the house. A long piazza with the family entrance in the center faced the garden. Tom and Eliza had built the house at the end of the Seven Years' War, when Bell's Bridge shared Charleston's economic boom, and many merchants and planters "bragged in brick" to announce their newfound affluence.

Candlelight washed the windows of the front room on the ground floor that Tom used for a combination office and library. Edward went in through the garden and the piazza. Pharaoh, the aging black house man, greeted him and said his trunks had already been delivered. He found his father writing in a leather-covered book with a gilded clasp; one of his diaries. Tom Bell had filled several in Edward's lifetime. The room was warm and welcoming with its dark furniture and walls of bookshelves.

The books were there because of Eliza. Shortly after her wedding, Eliza Trott had taken over her young husband's education. Tom had learned only basics at the St. Philip's Free School, which was no longer favored by the gentry because it attracted too many poor children.

Eliza had directed Tom's reading; instilled in him a lifelong passion for learning. Tom supported the Charles Town Library Society and kept a private collection of over two hundred volumes, weighted heavily toward works on dissent. Locke and Rousseau were there, as were *Cato's Speeches, The Independent Whig,* Davila's *History of the Civil Wars in France,* and several works on revolutions in the Roman republics. From these books had come Tom's conviction that the Crown was interfering with Englishmen's rights to self-government and full enjoyment of life, liberty, and property, said property including human beings.

"I saw Adrian," Edward said without preamble. "He informed me of his wedding plans."

Tom laid down his quill, more sympathetic than he'd been that afternoon. "Several times your mother suggested I write you. It wasn't my place. Adrian should have. Your brother often avoids the hard choices. I'm afraid he's a secret Tory."

Edward slumped in a chair, stuck out his legs, picked a bit of dried dung off his boot. His eyes looked sunken, shadowed with strain. After a prolonged silence Tom said, "What will you do?"

"Speak to Lydia about it. Ask for an explanation."

"She was never formally promised to you, Edward."

He stamped the floor. "My own damn fault. I should have seen to it. I was too confident of her feelings."

"What if she's determined to marry Adrian? What will you do then?"

"I don't know. Join the militia. Give myself up for cannon fodder. Doesn't make a hell of a lot of difference, does it?"

Tom sat silent, unable to find a useful answer.

4

Lydia's Proposal

Two days later, lookouts climbed to the steeple of St. Michael's to observe the British advance. Troops were moving northward on the west shore of the Ashley. Edward wrote a note to Lydia, saying he would call in the afternoon on a matter of *utmost urgency*. He sent it to Tradd Street with Pharaoh's boy, another house slave, instructing him not to wait for a reply.

In Charleston the Glass family was older and more distinguished than the Bells, though it hadn't started that way. Lydia's great-grandfather had fled Barbados in 1698, under a cloud of cuckoldry and murder. Whether he was the seducer or the cuckold was never clear, but he'd killed a man.

South Carolina was a logical destination. For years Glass had imported Carolina pinewood to heat kettles that boiled the sugarcane on his plantation. Several wealthy Barbadians he knew had already emigrated to the colony to make a new start, and he followed them.

The Carolina low country had no sugarcane culture, but a culture of slavery was well established. Having sold his Barbadian holdings for capital, the new arrival financed traders who caught Indians in the highlands and marched them to the coast in coffles to be sold. It proved a lucrative business; Great-Grandfather Glass soon expanded into the importation of blacks from Africa.

Glass was one of the Goose Creek men, so called because they settled in that area north of the small city of some four thousand residents. The Goose Creek men were opportunistic and relatively lawless, buying and selling slaves and trading openly with the buccaneers who cruised the coast in the early years of the eighteenth century. Among their customers were Maj. Stede Bonnet, the famous "gentleman pirate," and the mad Edward Teach, Blackbeard, who lit slow matches in his hair and beard to terrify his victims.

A faction loyal to the Lords Proprietors loathed the unsavory dealings of the Goose Creek men and constantly fought with them for control of the colonial legislature. As the pirates were caught and hung, that trade declined. The town's merchants and lawyers assumed greater control in the Commons House of Assembly. The old Barbadians were by then moderately wealthy, and important.

Those advantages aside, the Glass family was a virtual case book of tragedy. Lydia's grandfather saw his wife and two daughters hauled away in dead carts, victims of Barbados fever.[2] His second wife gave him one son, then a case of syphilis, and early death.

Lydia's father, Octavius Catullus Glass IV, had similar misfortunes. Although he traveled to Newport, Rhode Island, "the Carolina hospital," to escape the pestilential summers, he lost two wives before a third lived long enough to bear three sons and a daughter. Only Lydia, born in 1759, survived to adulthood.

When she was ten, Lydia's aging father unwisely rode one of his fast-blooded horses in a Jockey Club race. Though a superb equestrian, that day he couldn't control his mount; he was thrown and paralyzed from the waist down. He retired to his house and never again left it. He saw only his daughter, his physician, his servants, and the lawyers who managed his affairs.

As expenses depleted his money and no more came in, he tried to maintain a position in the outside world by writing letters to the *South Carolina Gazette*. During the terrible smallpox epidemic of 1760, when Dr. Alexander Garden, a young Scot, successfully inoculated over three thousand residents, Glass wrote letters calling vaccination "interference with nature." He wrote letters decrying Dr. Franklin's electrical experiments as "meddlesome tinkering in heaven by an atheist." He wrote letters excoriating the merchants, mechanics, and a few enlightened planters who led the town's patriot faction. He called them "the herd," and "low and ignorant hotheads and incendiaries."

[2] Yellow fever

His letters on slavery were particularly wrathful. He considered "black treachery" a given and urged harsh treatment of slaves, warranted or not, to "deter the vile and criminous intentions of the inferior race." He thought freedmen "a dangerous source of rebellious ideas." Lydia grew up distrusting and fearing anyone with a dark skin.

Lydia lived in a fine three-story Georgian brick house on Tradd Street, a few steps west of Legare. Elias, the stoop-shouldered slave who admitted Edward, carried a candle. The afternoon was gloomy and showery. The flickering light picked out a star-shaped scar on the slave's forehead. He'd been branded for attempting to run away; more of the elder Glass's "deterrence."

Edward shook rain off his broad-brimmed hat and handed it to Elias, who said, "I tell Miss Lydia you be waiting, Mist' Edward."

Edward paced the parlor, looking out to the wet garden. Soon he heard Lydia coming down, and not in a good mood. "Curse your nigger hide, Elias, hold the candle steady. Stop being so careless with fire or I'll send you to the workhouse and you won't stand up straight for a month."

She swept in, blond hair tumbling over her shoulders. No ordinary or proper girl ever let her hair down in that risqué fashion, but Lydia reveled in not being orderly or proper. She was a beautiful, petite creature with delicate features and graceful hands. Small as she was, she'd somehow been blessed with disproportionately large breasts that rose full and ripe under her white sacque gown. Edward had seen those breasts several times when he'd bedded her.

"Darling," she trilled, on tiptoe for his kiss on her cheek. She carried one of her collection of fashion babies, a twelve-inch porcelain doll outfitted in a detailed reproduction of a London gown several years out of date. No fashion babies had come into America since the war began, nor smart clothes of any kind.

"I was ever so surprised to learn that you'd left London."

"I got word of the new British campaign. I felt I belonged here with my family. And you."

She laid the fashion doll on one of the imitation Chippendale tables carved by Mr. Elfe of Broad Street, then settled herself and arranged her skirt. She seemed composed, though surely she knew what he wanted to discuss.

"Adrian told me about your plans," Edward said. "You'll forgive me if I don't offer my good wishes. How could you do it, Lydia? You know I've never wanted anyone but you."

"Wanting isn't loving, Edward."

"Words. A lawyer's quibble."

"No. If you'll only stop pacing like a tomcat, I'll explain." He took a chair.

"I want to marry Adrian because I'll be secure with him. Marrying into the Bell family will be a useful alliance. I'll inherit money of my own, but there's less every day. Father doesn't care much for your father, but he knows Tom Bell is well off."

Edward shook his head. "We had such marvelous times together. I always assumed we'd be married."

With a little shrug she said, "Assumptions are dangerous. You never asked for my hand. Too little too late, isn't that the phrase?" When he turned red, she spoke less sharply. "Dear Edward. Let's not quarrel. You must hear me out." She patted the cushion beside her.

As he sat down, he smelled the faintly scented warmth of her face and throat. When she cupped his right hand in both of hers, his body reacted strongly.

"Yes, I made a decision to marry your brother, but it's you that I love."

"Then how in God's name—" She stopped his lips with her perfumed fingers.

"Let me finish. I've loved you forever, even in your wildest days—all the carousing and gambling—racing horses and consorting with sluts in Roper's Alley. I knew about 'the dissolute Mr. Edward Bell.' So did half the town. I'm sure your behavior was one reason your father sent you to London. It's also why I decided you'd never settle down as a proper husband. But I don't want or need you as a proper husband. I want you as a lover."

Astounded, he sat motionless as she continued. "I recall a letter in the *Gazette* some years ago. Not one of father's screeds, a letter with genuine wit. The writer said Charleston women make very agreeable companions but very expensive wives." She brought her mouth close to his. "You can have the pleasure without the cost. After I marry Adrian, there's no reason you and I can't enjoy an arrangement."

She kissed him with her moist lips and tongue, bringing his left hand up to her right breast, large and soft above the rigid stays under her clothes. She tickled his ear with her index finger.

"You would like that, wouldn't you?"

He jumped up, red faced. "You're asking me to cuckold Adrian? By God, I may be a lowlife in everyone's estimation, but I'm not that low."

"Oh, you're being silly. Prudish."

"He's my *brother*, for Christ's sake." Lydia shot a worried look upward, as though the crippled man hiding in his gloomy lair might hear. "What you suggest is preposterous and wrong."

Her underskirts rustled as she rose. Her own anger seemed to give her height, rob her of softness. "You're refusing me?"

"I would refuse any woman who proposed such a thing."

She rushed at him, little fists battering his shoulders. "I'm not any woman. I'm not." On her toes, she ground her mouth on his, her tongue licking and probing. He felt her hair against his cheek. A kind of delirium briefly weakened his resolve. "I'm not," she repeated in a whisper.

He drew back. "We should end this conversation." In the foyer he called for his hat. Behind him Lydia spoke.

"You'd better not walk out."

He turned back, looked her in the eye. "That's exactly what I intend. I know you're accustomed to getting whatever you want, but this time you'll have to accept failure."

Tears rushed into her eyes. "You don't mean it."

"I do, absolutely."

"You bastard." She snatched up her fashion doll and hurled it. He ducked; the doll broke the window. The porcelain head shattered, pieces falling into the palmettos below. He'd seen this destructive streak in Lydia before.

She ran past him, shoving him aside. She darted down the passage leading to the pantry, bumping into Elias, who had his hat. "Elias, Goddamn you, there's broken glass in the parlor and the garden, clean it up."

She didn't look back. Edward took his hat and let himself out. He wanted to tell Adrian of her perfidy but he didn't dislike his brother enough to do that, ever.

☆   ☆   ☆

Workmen on scaffolds painted St. Michael's steeple black, presuming that would make it a more difficult target for artillery. The British squadron sat off the bar, waiting. Hoping to obstruct their passage, Commodore Whipple sank his ships in the Cooper River across from the Exchange, behind a boom of logs and chains.

Governor John Rutledge was given the virtual authority of a military dictator. Christopher Gadsden, the newly appointed lieutenant governor, told Tom Bell that Carolina militia would not come to Charleston's aid because the British were spreading rumors of a smallpox epidemic.

On March 29 the first British units crossed the Ashley River in shallow-draft boats. They landed at Bee's Ferry and marched down the Neck. Three days later, April 1, they broke ground for a siege line half a mile in front of the Charleston works. The noose was in place around the victim's neck.

5

To Malvern

At supper that evening Tom Bell said, "I want you to bring your mother to the city." There was an unspoken understanding from the past: when circumstances were unusual, or physical hardship called for, Tom Bell looked to his younger son.

"Gladly," Edward said.

"I may have waited too long. A man who came down the Cooper last night told me that partisans led by William Lark sacked and burned Pertwee's store two days ago."

"William Lark?"

"A jackleg Tory. More interested in plunder than principle, I expect. I knocked heads with his father, Ladimer, years ago, when Trott had me driving pine logs from the forest to the wharf."

"Poorly's at Malvern," Edward reminded him.

"Bring him back if you wish. He's yours."

"What about the rest of the Negroes?"

"They may go or stay, as they feel necessary. If they leave, I'll buy others. They'll probably be safer remaining with the house, but I won't coerce them." Edward admired his father for that.

"You'll have to cross the water to Hog Island," Tom continued. "It's the only route left open. I'll have someone row you over before daylight."

"It isn't necessary. I can handle the boat alone. I'd like to say something more about London, sir."

"That's done with. I spoke my piece. If you feel any animosity, turn it on the damned king's men."

Edward started forward to hug his father. This time Tom permitted a robust embrace. When they separated, Edward thought, *Strike me dead. What's that misting his eyes?*

* * *

He armed himself with a ten-inch sheath knife with a deer antler handle and, in black leather holsters, a brace of fine London-bought blunderbuss pistols, each with a spring bayonet under the barrel. He left from Bell's Bridge while the stars still shone. He rowed hard, feeling only mildly queasy about the open water.

The direct journey up the Neck to Malvern was about eleven miles, easily accomplished on horseback. But the British works blocked that route. He rowed to Hog Island and from there followed the shore up to the Wando River and Daniel's Island, where he beached his boat, rested, and ate a hard biscuit. Then he pushed off again.

His arms burned with the pain of steady exertion, but he didn't slacken. He spent the night in his boat in a broad creek on the north side of Daniel's Island. Before dawn, badly bitten by insects while he dozed, he shipped his oars and continued on to the Cooper's western bank. There he found a waterman mending nets on a flimsy pier. He arranged for the man to be at the same spot in twenty-four hours, with a larger boat.

He passed by a familiar crossroads; ashes and black timbers were all that remained of Pertwee's store. He passed several small plantations, then a bigger one with a fenced pasture where a dozen horses grazed. Four were big handsome Chickasaws, the rest marsh tackies, the little horses common in the sea islands and Low Country. What they lacked in beauty they more than made up for in strength and heart.

The horses belonged to Henry Wando, a neighbor but not a friend of Tom and Eliza Bell. Wando was a self-aggrandizing loyalist who lost no opportunity to boast of his affection for the king. The partisans had left his house, barn, and outbuildings untouched.

He trudged on, following a dirt track that wound through dim cloisters of old live oaks, to Malvern. Tom Bell had bought 150 acres for his summer home but took only ten for personal use. The rest he leased to a firm of Amsterdam Jews with an office in Charleston. They grew and sold indigo, a crop initially brought from the Leeward Islands in the 1740s. When Edward emerged from the trees, he rode between fields where slaves were preparing the ground; next month they would sow seeds gathered in last year's harvest.

All the windows of the two-story cypress house were open to catch whatever breeze might stir on this balmy March morning. Near some outbuildings that effectively blocked any glimpse of Malvern's slave cabins, Edward sat on the ground to remove a pebble from his boot. A sound of hammering stopped. Someone hailed him from the carpentry shed.

"Mr. Edward?"

"Poorly." One boot still off, he jumped up, waved. The black man ran to him, tossed down a claw hammer from the shop, gripped Edward's shoulders in his big hands, grinning.

"My friend."

"You're not surprised to see me?" Edward spoke in Gullah, the lilting black patois that allowed slaves, or friends, to talk with a degree of privacy.

"Your papa sent a message to your mother. Everybody knows you're back."

"How are you?"

"Just now this child is lovely, splendid." Poorly was literate, with a fine vocabulary; Eliza had taught him, at Edward's request. He was a handsome Gambian, blue-black, six feet tall and thin as a pole. Sawdust speckled his hair and the sleeves of his white drill blouse. He was the same age as Adrian, five years older than Edward.

While he lived, Poorly's father had been a master carpenter, hired out to others by his white master. He had helped floor the bell tower at St. Michael's. Tom Bell bought young Poorly from the father, to be a body servant and playmate for his two boys. He was called Daniel then. He had frequent spells of sickness; someone in the Bell household started calling him Poorly, and the name stuck.

Young Adrian had taken great pleasure in ordering Poorly about, forcing him to imitate the sounds of animals for hours, or stand on his head until he fell over. Occasionally he whipped Poorly with a willow wand. Out of disgust and sympathy Edward was kinder, and a strong friendship developed. When Adrian matured and launched out on his own, he had other slaves to order about; he didn't object to Poorly remaining with Edward. Sometimes Edward felt the black man was a better brother than his real one.

"You're lovely, and splendid, even with the redcoats knocking at the city gate?"

"Yes, I am a happy man with a beautiful wife."

"I heard you jumped the broom. I'm eager to meet the lucky lady."

"She's in the cookhouse."

As they walked, Edward said, "I'm taking mother back to Charleston tomorrow. Father's orders. You're welcome to come along. Your wife too."

"May do that," Poorly said soberly. "There's king's men in the neighborhood. Burned Pertwee's at the crossroads."

"I saw it. What's in the house in the way of weapons?"

"Two old muskets."

"Give them to men you consider reliable."

"Big Walter, the field driver. His cousin, Sam."

"Make sure they have plenty of powder and ball."

At the cookhouse door Poorly said, "You want to put guns in the hands of slaves? People won't like that."

"I don't give a hang about *people,* only the people who live here." He held the door open. "Where's the charming bride?"

In the hot and smoky interior oval cakes of sweet-potato pone were coming from the oven on broad wooden paddles. At the hearth a black child turned a crank to roast a piglet on a spit. Of the four women working, Poorly's wife was the youngest and by far the prettiest, with rich black hair, slightly tilted brown eyes, and smooth skin the color of coffee infused with milk. Poorly could hardly contain his pride as he said, "Sally, this is Mr. Edward, Miss Eliza's son. This is Sally."

Edward shook Sally's hand, then startled the girl by planting a kiss on her cheek. The other three women and the child looked thunderstruck. "Congratulations to both of you. You're going to have handsome children."

"Thank you, sir," Sally said, flustered. She could be no more than eighteen, but her figure was fine and womanly under her plain cotton dress, once blue but now largely white from endless washing.

Poorly drew his wife to the door, lowered his voice so he couldn't be overheard. "Mister Edward's taking his mother back to town. Thinks we better go with him. I said we would."

Edward excused himself and tramped up the path that isolated the fires in the kitchen from the big house. He went through from the front piazza to a second, broader one facing the river. There he found Eliza Trott Bell sitting in an oak-and-cypress easy chair Poorly had made, reading a book of William Cowper's poems.

"Edward," she exclaimed, in nearly the same tone of voice as everyone else he'd surprise by reappearing. "I knew you were home. I didn't know you were coming to Malvern. Oh, how good you look to these old eyes." Which were not, in fact, all that old; Eliza was fifty-four, slim and sturdy. Her eyes were gray-green, her dark red hair laced with gray. She pressed her cheek to his and held him tightly.

He pulled up a stool and explained the reason for his visit. Eliza said, "Your father really thinks it's dangerous for us to remain here? It's ever so peaceful. I love the river, my garden, the wild deer that visit. I love all the wildlife except the alligators that sleep on our bank. I saw a huge fellow sunning himself this morning. When I was nine, one ate my favorite cat, have I ever told you?"

She had, more than once, but he said no. "There's another visitor we don't want. A Tory partisan named William Lark is marauding in the district."

"Lark." She made a face. "A bad lot, that family. My father knew Ladimer Lark. Called him a rogue and a cheat."

That bolstered Edward's argument for leaving. He described the British siege line under construction in front of the defensive ditch that was already dammed and flooded. "I wouldn't say the situation's good in Charleston, but we won't be alone there. Malvern is too isolated just now."

Eliza sighed. "Then we'll pack and go." She hesitated a moment. "Adrian told you of his engagement?"

"A bit of a blow," Edward admitted with a vain attempt at a smile.

"More than a bit of one, I would imagine." She reached out to caress the back of his hand. "I'll say what I've never said before. I don't care much for Lydia Glass. In fact I wouldn't wish her on either you or Adrian. Let your heart heal, Edward. When it does, find someone better. That won't be difficult."

"I'll try to remember the advice." He suppressed a yawn, brushed his dusty sleeve. "I'm for a bath and a meal, in that order."

"I'll have Chloe heat water. The empty bedroom is yours."

She went inside to give orders to the housemaids. Edward loved his mother with unquestioning love, and he knew she loved him in return. If she was disappointed in the course of his life so far, she never revealed it or criticized.

The day remained warm, with a hint of spring in the wind. He posted Poorly and Big Walter as guards for the first part of the night, the driver watching the dirt track, Poorly the river. "Wake me around one," he said to Poorly. "Sam and I will watch till morning."

In his room on the second floor, on the side of the house away from the river, he loaded his pistols and laid them next to the bed. Then he blew out the candle. Weary and aching from his trek, he was asleep by half past seven.

Not Poorly but a loud noise roused him. He snatched a pistol and ran to the window. He could see nothing of the dirt track in the darkness, but he clearly heard horsemen moving toward the house at a walk. He leaned from the window, his heart thumping. "Walter?"

"Yes, sir. I hear 'em too. They comin'."

Sooner than expected. Edward pulled on his trousers and shirt and rushed past his mother's bedroom, pistols in hand. He prayed she'd stay asleep, safe behind her closed door.

6

The Partisans

A breeze from the river carried sweet, yeasty smells of earth and wet vegetation. A huge full moon revealed the file of horsemen. Edward stepped off the front piazza and walked barefoot to stand beside Big Walter, a bald black man round as a tub. Big Walter's thick fingers held an old smooth-bore musket slanted across his chest. His thumb rested on the S-shaped hammer. Edward whispered, "My father said at least seven raided Pertwee's. I count five. I wonder where the other two—"

The roar of a gun, then another, answered his unfinished question. The echoes went rolling through the night. Behind the outbuildings two men began to shout. Edward guessed the pair had circled wide and fired their weapons to rouse and cow the slaves.

Sweat on Edward's forehead cooled in the breeze. The first horseman crossed a patch of coarse grass and reined up in front of him. His four cohorts hung back within a grove of tall water oaks. Edward couldn't see their faces because of their bicorne hats, but he saw the flash of silver and brass pistol mountings.

"Good evening, sir. You don't know me but I know you. Young Mr. Bell, I believe?"

"You have the advantage of me, sir."

Poorly came dashing around the corner of the house. Edward warned him back with a slashing gesture. The leader of the partisans was hatless but wrapped in a cloak despite the warm night. Edward aimed both pistols at him.

"Turn around and get off this property."

"I think not, sir." The muzzle of a horse pistol peeped from beneath the man's cloak. Two pistols against one; for the moment, a standoff. Edward's stomach hurt.

The leader was a large man of about forty, with a pronounced paunch showing under his cloak. His nose and chin were sharp, his forehead high, his gray-streaked hair tied off behind his head. As he surveyed the situation, moonlight showed one eye wandering toward his nose, then back, a bizarre effect.

He spoke to Edward with the confidence and condescension of a hanging judge. "Malvern plantation is owned by Mr. Thomas Bell, a man known to be an obnoxious traitor. The property is hereby confiscated."

"On whose authority?"

"Mine, sir. William Lark, Esquire, loyal servant of His Majesty King George. Your niggers are being restrained. No harm will come to them so long as you don't offer resistance. My men and I will explore the house, take what goods we want. Some of your wenches, too, perhaps. Then the property will be burned."

"I'll blow you out of the saddle first," Edward promised.

From the corner of his eye Edward detected Big Walter's sudden turn to look behind them. Poorly was staring as well. Edward felt a hard cold ring of iron, a gun muzzle, touch his neck.

"I got him, Captain. 'F he twitches, he's gone."

"One of you disarm him," Lark called over his shoulder. A man jogged out of the shadows of the water oaks. He was passing on Lark's left when the front door opened noisily. Eliza's voice caught them by surprise.

"I heard gunfire."

The man behind Edward jerked his musket from Edward's neck. He spun toward the house. Just as he shouted, "Mother, go back," the partisan shot her.

The ball struck Eliza's chest. A blood flower bloomed on the short bed coat she wore over an ivory chemise. She spilled sideways onto the piazza, her mobcap tumbling off. Edward let out a cry and fired one pistol at Lark.

The ball hit Lark's thigh and left a smoking hole in his trousers. Lark's horse whinnied, rose on hind legs, and pawed the air. Edward didn't jump away in time. A hoof slashed his forehead, nearly knocking him over.

Lark reeled and swayed, trying not to fall out of his saddle. One of his men shot at Edward, missed. Suddenly light flared up; a rider spurred past Lark and hurled a pine torch over Eliza's body and through the open door. Lark shrieked, "Not yet, not yet." He was too late; the torch ignited a wall hanging in the foyer. The man who'd thrown it yanked his mount's head around, charged toward Edward, who shot him in the forehead with his other pistol.

All that in the space of a few heartbeats. Then, chaos.

Maids who slept in the big house ran from a side door, exclaiming and sobbing. Lark's three remaining men separated to outflank the defenders. Big Walter dropped one of them with his musket. Another ducked his head and rode straight at Big Walter. He chopped down with his right hand, burying a tomahawk in Big Walter's skull. The slave went over like a felled tree.

Poorly's musket boomed. The tomahawk man flew sideways, blown off his horse. Edward meantime was running toward the house, clutching two empty pistols. He dropped them, skidded to his mother's side on his knees. The red stain on her bed coat was the size of a plate.

He slipped his arms under her, lifted her against him, heedless of the blood. He began rocking her. "Mother, don't, you can't." He sounded like a terrified child.

Eliza's head lolled. He felt no breath from her open mouth. After a faint tremor her body relaxed and her bowels released. Blood ran off his gashed forehead to mingle with sudden tears.

One of Lark's men was unhorsed. Poorly swung his musket like a club, striking the man from behind, dropping him on his knees, then on his face. Poorly beat him till he stopped moving.

The fire in the house spread to the dining room on one side of the entrance hall, the sitting room on the other. Floors and walls caught and blazed with a roar. Lark had ridden to the periphery of the light, grasping his left thigh. Blood leaked between his fingers.

His eyes caught Edward's, promising another meeting. Edward's eyes, black holes in his wet red face, said he'd welcome it. Lark wheeled his horse and disappeared down the dirt track, his pigtail ribbon gone, his hair spreading out behind him like a peacock's tail.

Heat flayed Edward's face. The fire was consuming the wall of the house behind his mother's body. He lifted Eliza and carried her off the piazza. Her blood smeared him a second time. He put her on the ground gently.

"Poorly, find Sam."

"Is your mama—?"

"She's dead."

So was Sam; Poorly discovered him strangled on the lawn not two yards from where Eliza Trott Bell had sat reading Cowper. Four of Lark's partisans lay dead in the coarse grass, but the instigator was gone into the night, along with his two remaining men.

Sally appeared, disheveled and frantic. She called Poorly's name until she found him in the dancing firelight. The slaves crept from the cabins in frightened pairs and family groups, asking no questions, only staring in a stricken way. As the fire consumed the big house, many of them wept.

The roof fell in, a crashing cascade of burning timbers and flying sparks. By morning the Malvern big house no longer existed, except as a larger version of the black ruins of Pertwee's store.

★ ★ ★

Numb with grief, Edward nevertheless forced himself to think and act. He sent a slave to meet the waterman and tell him to wait as long as necessary. They would need a larger boat. He found an older slave to put in charge of the plantation. At two o'clock, in a tiny burying ground at the end of the lane between the slave cabins, he presided at the last rites for Big Walter and Sam. A slave funeral in daylight was unusual. Customarily they were held at midnight, so as not to rob the master of an hour's work.

Sorrowing black men and women formed a circle around Edward. He thought there were fewer than when the big house burned. With birds warbling cheerily and the sun throwing great shafts of light through the trees, he read Scripture from a Bible belonging to Sam's wife. All of them sang a Gullah hymn. *Dere's a bright side somewhere, gonna keep on till I find it.* The voices in ragged unison had a mournful beauty that stirred Edward's soul. Did heaven exist? He didn't know, but if it did, Sam and Big Walter and his mother would surely be there.

The afternoon remained beautiful and warm. Edward, Poorly, and his new wife set out on the Cooper, bound for Charleston. The boatman put up in a marsh until dark, then rowed downstream on a fast tide. A familiar clean smell of pine rose from Eliza's temporary coffin. Poorly had built it in the carpentry shop.

Edward sat on a thwart, one hand resting on the raw wood. He imagined an advancing line of redcoat infantry. Each man wore William Lark's face. He imagined himself killing them one by one.

Before the events of last night he'd been unsure of his place in the war, or even whether he had one. Now his bleak eyes gazed at the star-lit river and saw a future in which he could no longer be merely a spectator.

7

"Long Live the Congress"

For years afterward people said that when Malvern burned and Eliza Trott Bell died, Edward aged ten years in one night. Any tendency to lightness in his nature disappeared.

Eliza went to her rest on Friday, April 7, in the small graveyard of St. Michael's, where Tom Bell had been a vestryman for eight years. The rector prayed; the sexton tolled the bells. Only the day before, the bells had pealed joyously, with people cheering and celebrating as 750 relief troops, Continentals from North Carolina and Virginia, arrived in a procession of sloops and schooners that slipped down the Cooper while fieldpieces on the Neck banged away, doing no damage because of the range. As family and friends mourned Edward's mother, Charleston enjoyed a few hours of unjustified euphoria.

Mr. Gadsden attended the funeral, as did John Rutledge and members of his governing council. Esau Willing brought his daughter, Joanna. She spoke to Tom Bell with sympathy and tenderness. She was attentive to Edward as well. She laid her gloved hand on his sleeve and said, "I heard you acted bravely at Malvern."

"Not bravely enough, or quickly enough. If I had, she'd be alive."

"Edward, you mustn't blame yourself."

"But you see," he said, "I do."

Lydia stood with Adrian and scarcely glanced in Edward's direction. None of the mourners had decent funeral clothes. Edward's black suit was old and shabby. Good black cloth was loomed in England and no longer available.

Poorly and Sally stood with the house servants, behind the white mourners. Pharaoh's wife, Essie, bowed her head and sobbed softly as the rector concluded his final prayer. Edward had never seen his father so shaken, indeed couldn't remember seeing him cry as he cried when the gravediggers lowered Eliza's coffin.

★   ★   ★

Tom Bell invited a number of men to the house after the burial. On a sideboard he set out rum and his last two bottles of Madeira. Pharaoh served small beer and mugs of hot chocolate or coffee; no tea had been drunk in the house since the troubles over the duty levied by Parliament. Resistance to the tea tax, led by Mr. Gadsden and his Liberty Boys, had been almost as fierce and militant in Charleston as in Boston.

Pharaoh's Essie, who cooked for the household, had baked two huge queen's cakes, rich concoctions of butter and cream and currants that the gentlemen quickly devoured. Conversation and alcohol gradually tempered the mood of the burial. Tongues loosened; voices rose. The chief topic was the city's precarious position.

Most outspoken was Mr. Hughston, a tanner whose loyalty to the patriot cause appeared to be waning. "General Lincoln's strategy will send us all to our graves."

"Or the gallows," another man grumbled. Batteries on the Neck opened up an exchange of fire, distant and desultory; hardly a man took notice, Hughston least of all:

"We cannot defend against a siege of indefinite length. The enemy has an advantage we lack, namely unrestricted ability to resupply ammunition and rations. Lincoln should evacuate the troops while he can still cross the river and get away. Banastre Tarleton's dragoons and infantry are roaming the countryside from here to Moncks Corner. The retreat routes may be cut off at any moment."

"General Washington's in favor of Lincoln withdrawing," Hughston's friend observed.

Christopher Gadsden slapped his hand on the dining room table. "No. The governor's council is responsible for the city's defense and we will not allow Lincoln to abandon us."

Gadsden, a slender man with a receding hairline and dark Irish eyes, was Tom Bell's closest friend among the patriots. He controlled and directed the Liberty Boys—mechanics, artisans—"the herd" so despised by Lydia's father. Loyalists called Gadsden a traitor to his class because he was one of the two or three richest men in America. Henry Laurens, even richer but more conservative, had condemned Gadsden as "a rash, headlong gentleman," and split with him over Gadsden's uncompromising and, to Laurens, "indecent" espousal of revolution.

Adrian drank a considerable amount of Madeira. Seated against the wall opposite his brother at the table, Edward could tell that Adrian was, if not tipsy, then close to it. He slurred his words as he said, "Mr. Gadsden, I beg leave to differ. Whether Lincoln stays or goes, isn't it folly to think that resistance can have a salutary outcome? The British have twelve thousand men surrounding us, perhaps more." Tom Bell glanced at Edward and frowned. "Wouldn't it be better if Governor Rutledge asked Clinton for terms? Food is in short supply. The army is a disorderly rabble."

Tom Bell interrupted. "Adrian, these gentlemen are guests. You forget yourself."

"No, sir. I speak the truth."

Gadsden fixed him with a stern eye. "I am sorry to say it to you, Adrian, but your truth seems to be proclaimed through a Tory trumpet."

"Well, I'm not alone in my feeling that—"

One of Gadsden's adherents broke in. "Could that be the reason Malvern was burned by the irregulars while Prosperity Hall is still standing?"

The speaker was older, a thin and feeble man. It didn't prevent Adrian from rising to confront him. "Sir, in ordinary times that kind of remark would demand satisfaction."

A sudden hush fell over the dining room. A naval gun boomed in the silence. Adrian's face was livid. Edward suspected the reason—the speaker was right about Adrian's plantation.

The thin old man surprised everyone by responding not with anger but laughter. "Adrian my boy, I'm afraid you've just confessed your politics to the world."

Adrian threw a look to his father, hoping for succor. There was none. Tom Bell said, "Gentlemen, I'll see to more refreshments. Please apologize to our guests, Adrian."

"Damme if I will, sir."

Christopher Gadsden said, "We have been friends for many years, Adrian. Now I think our different paths are clearly marked." He saluted Adrian with his cup. "Long live the Congress."

Several others, including Tom Bell, exclaimed, "Hear, hear," and

"Long live the Congress." Edward stepped forward, touched his brother's sleeve.

"Let's walk in the garden. I have a favor to ask."

Under the great live oak Adrian cursed and fumed over Tom Bell's "damned lunatic friends." Edward let him rave until the spleen worked itself out. Then he said, "There's something I need from you if you'll allow me to have it."

"May I know what it is?"

"The French musket that hangs over your mantel. I trust you still have it?"

"The St. Etienne arsenal musket? Yes. Damme if I know why I bought it."

"Because it's beautifully made. A gentleman's gun."

"But I'm not an outdoors man like you. I've only fired it a few times."

"So you'd let it go?"

"I suppose. Why do you need it?"

"To join the militia. Every man must furnish his own weapon."

"Oh, my God, Edward, that's folly. Didn't you hear what I said inside? The battle can't be won. Charleston can't be saved. Don't risk your life for nothing. The men who killed our mother weren't the king's soldiers."

"They were on the king's side."

Adrian strode past the great tree to an ornamental rain basin on a pedestal. "I shouldn't give you the gun. I don't want to be responsible for your death."

"My life is my responsibility. You might consider it a fair exchange for Lydia." He instantly regretted the barb. In the starry darkness he couldn't read his brother's reaction. "I'm sorry, that was low."

"I'm sure you meant it." Adrian's voice had lost its earlier, wine-induced plumminess. There was a chill in it now; a remoteness. "I think I'd better not come back to this house until the issue of surrender is settled. If you want the musket, send Pharaoh's boy."

"Adrian—"

"I have nothing more to say to you. We're quits." Adrian left the garden by the street gate, forgetting his hat inside.

When Edward returned to the dining room, the guests were rising, exchanging handshakes, extending sympathies once again. Edward said to his father, "Adrian's gone."

"Upset?"

"Very much so. He made it clear he's committed to the other side. I don't think he'll pay us another visit anytime soon."

★ ★ ★

Two days later, Sunday, on a favorable tide and strong southeast wind, Adm. Arbuthnot's frigates and ships of the line ran past the booming cannon of Fort Moultrie. One by one the ships dropped anchor in the harbor off James Island, well out of range of Moultrie's guns and those in the city. Arbuthnot's losses were small: some rigging, a topmast, and a few wounded seamen. Edward watched part of the action through a spyglass, from a window at the top of the house.

The elation generated by the relief troops evaporated. Monday, April 10, under a truce flag, emissaries of Clinton and Arbuthnot demanded that Major General Lincoln surrender the city, the alternative being "havoc and devastation." Lincoln politely refused.

Enemy artillery made good on Clinton's threat with a two-hour demonstration bombardment of round shot and incendiaries that set roofs afire, started the bells of St. Michael's and St. Philip's ringing in wild alarm, and drove terrified citizens to any available cellar or place of refuge. Charleston's fire masters directed bucket brigades of slaves from one conflagration to another. The physical damage turned out to be less than the damage to nerves already strained by worry and hunger. Tom Bell told his son that General Lincoln wanted Governor Rutledge to flee across the Cooper before it was too late.

"As I fear it soon will be" was his glum conclusion.

★ ★ ★

On Thursday, April 13, Governor Rutledge finally heeded General Lincoln's warnings and left the city with three other members of the governing council. Lieutenant Governor Gadsden remained in charge of those who stayed.

That same day Edward signed articles of enlistment and became part of the second battalion of Charleston militia, Gen. Isaac Huger commanding. The general himself had moved thirty miles inland with a mixed force of infantry and cavalry, to block any attempt by Clinton to cut the escape routes still left open.

The recruiting officer indicated Edward's French musket. "In addition to that you need a priming pick and brush, flints, a cartridge box, a canteen or wooden bottle."

"I'm acquiring those, sir."

"Have you experience with firearms?"

"I know how to load and fire a fowling piece. I've hunted with my father."

"You must provide your own uniform."

"Someone is sewing it today."

"The pay is a dollar a month, hard coin. When the paymaster can find it." He appreciated his own humor with a great bellowing *har-har*.

Perhaps too eagerly, Edward said he presumed he could join Huger's force in the field after some instruction in loading and firing the musket.

"Why, no, sir," the recruiting officer said. "You won't have to drill before going to the Comings Point fortifications with other new recruits and the niggers we've pressed into service. You'll do your fighting with a wheelbarrow and shovel."

Edward's disgruntled expression prompted a sharp "You're unhappy, sir?"

"No, sir." But he was. No training, no drill—all that was wanted was a strong back. *Devil of a start,* he thought as he walked out.

8

Joanna and the Colonel

To his surprise he reported to a captain he knew. Earle Hughston was the tanner's son, a burly young man with a workingman's lack of pretension. Like many sons in Carolina families Earle Hughston had fallen out with his father over issues of loyalty and duty. Hughston's uniform was standard militia: fringed deerskin hunting shirt and leggings and a bicorne hat decorated with the black cockade of the American armies.

In the breastworks already in place at Comings Point, wooden-wheeled garrison cannon and high-trajectory howitzers annoyed the British on the Ashley's far shore, as well as any small vessels that happened to sail up the channel. Edward fell to with a hundred other men, white and black, extending the breastworks southward past Beaufain Street. Gabion baskets woven of sweet grass were arranged three deep on top of earthen berms. Edward and the others moved barrows of sandy soil to fill the baskets.

Women and children came out to watch, offer encouragement and, occasionally, food and drink. Enemy batteries on the Neck and James Island shelled the city on a random basis, without warning. This inevitably provoked a reply, though because of a dwindling supply of ammunition, Charleston's guns fired less often than those of the besiegers. What Edward found heartening was the calm resolve of the civilian population. People went about their business; sent their daughters to their private academies as usual, searched for food in the public market, evacuated their cows and pigs to the presumed safety of the other side of the Cooper. Unless a shell was whistling down on your own roof, you tended not to be too alarmed by cannon fire. A more common reaction was aggravation. The noise interrupted thought, conversation, and, most annoyingly, sleep.

★   ★   ★

With Hughston's permission Edward limped home after dark rather than spend the night in one of the common tents near the site. The tents were meant for six but presently held ten. Edward's arms and legs and back were a mass of pain. He was fit but not used to long hours of hard labor. Sleep came hard; the pain woke him often.

Because Tom Bell and Hughston the elder knew each other, the captain treated Edward with more civility and cordiality than he did some others under his command. Hughston had a fondness for rum and a seemingly limitless supply for his tin canteen bottle. Every day at midmorning and again at sunset he shared the rum with Edward, relating such news as he happened to have.

On the Neck the British were completing a second siege line parallel to the first, the new one close enough to bring the city within range of howitzers and mortars.

"And we lost a sharp engagement at Moncks Corner. Banastre Tarleton's British Legion attacked General Huger's garrison at three in the morning. When Major Vernier surrendered—he was commanding the late Count Pulaski's hussars—he asked for quarter but Tarleton's dragoons refused it. They sabered him so badly he almost bled to death. Damned bloody butcher, Tarleton. Got away with over eighty remounts for his men. The whole country from Moncks Corner to Haddrell's Point is open to them."

On a sunny, warm morning promising sticky heat later, Edward spied Joanna Willing among town women watching the work. He stepped from the trench where he'd been shoveling, wiped dirt and sweat from his face and bare chest. Smiling, Joanna came straight to him. She presented a large clay monkey jar. "Water, sir?"

"Yes, indeed, and welcome." He uncorked the jug and drank. Slaves working nearby eyed him enviously.

"It's for them as well," she said. Edward gave the jug to the nearest black man. "I had no idea you'd be here."

"It isn't my idea of soldiering. I want to fight."

The black men gulped water and let some splash over their chins and torsos. "Well, I hope you get your wish. The Negroes must go on doing what they're told for the rest of their lives. You may better understand their situation now."

"I fear you're preaching again, Joanna."

"And I will until I go to my grave. You have choices, Edward. They don't, unless it's a choice to give up and end it all in hopes of a better life in heaven."

He studied Esau Willing's daughter, looking so fair in the morning light. Her figure was attractive, her brown eyes warmly appealing. But she put him off with her constant rant about slavery. He took black servitude for granted. It was part of the world in which he'd grown up, and he presumed it always would be, unless the damned British won the war and sanctimoniously abolished it.

"I believe you should think more deeply about the whole matter, Edward. If you inherit Bell's Bridge one day, perhaps you'll tear down those hateful cages. Your father won't. My father can't understand why anyone would wish to."

"You find a great deal wrong with me, don't you?"

"On the contrary. I've always believed you have a mind worth changing. I held that opinion before you sailed off to London, when you were behaving like all the young idlers from wealthy families, wasteful of your time and of yourself. The horse races, the dram shops—"

"Damn, Joanna. How long have you been watching me?"

"Since we were children. Since the first time I saw you at the wharf. I think you were seven. You hid a hopping toad in your father's desk."

"And got soundly thrashed for it. By God"—he shook his head vehemently—"you're a strange woman."

"Too strong for you? Too outspoken?" It was half challenge, half regret. Or did he imagine that?

Captain Hughston shouted from the top of the rampart. "Bell. You've stood on your shovel long enough."

One of the slaves returned the monkey jug with a shy smile. Joanna acknowledged it, nodded to Edward, and walked off to rejoin some other ladies.

He wished he could like her more. Certainly she was comely; perfectly suitable to take to bed. She could be a convenient temporary antidote to Lydia. But as long as she treated him as she did, anything more than casual acquaintance was impossible.

A moment later he scored himself for even entertaining such

thoughts when Charleston was staring at catastrophe in the form of Sir Henry Clinton's army.

✯ ✯ ✯

"But I'm only a private," Edward protested when Earle Hughston invited him to an officer's party at the home of Captain McQueen of the South Carolina 2d. The 2d was a line regiment with a distinguished record going back to the Cherokee Wars of 1759 and 1761. The regiment had fought valiantly at Fort Moultrie and again in last December's failed assault on Savannah. There, Grenadier Sergeant Jasper, who'd saved Moultrie's blue palmetto flag in '76, carried the regiment's red banner to the summit of an enemy redoubt, only to be fatally hit before the regiment was thrown back.

"Don't worry, I'll promote you to lieutenant for the evening," Hughston said. "One hunting shirt fits all ranks."

"I don't understand your generosity."

"It's obvious you're misplaced here. At the party you might make a contact that would afford you a chance to fight. For that you'd tell a lie about your rank, wouldn't you?"

"I would, and a lot more. I'd walk through hell's hot coals barefoot."

"Then it's settled. Corner of Tradd and Orange Streets, half past seven."

✯ ✯ ✯

About thirty officers gathered in the house of their host, Capt. Alexander McQueen. Edward immediately noted varied uniforms: brilliant crimson coats from the 2d Regiment; older coats of brown, the color decreed by Congress at the start of the war; coats of dark blue, the color adopted last year. There were several hunting shirts like his and Hughston's.

Captain McQueen was stiffly cordial when introduced to Edward. "Gentlemen," he announced, "I present a comrade of Captain Hughston's, from his militia company. Lieutenant Edward Bell."

"Relation to Tom Bell?" a bewigged major asked.

"Yes, sir, his son."

The major pressed a bumper of hot spiced wine into Edward's hand. "Drink up, sir, and welcome."

Two black servants kept the guests supplied with beer and wine and gin. Clay pipes filled the downstairs with a thick haze of aromatic smoke. A buffet of meats and cheeses was quickly depleted in the dining room, then replenished. The officers seemed to suffer no shortages.

The party rolled on for an hour amid arguments over strategy and profane condemnations of the enemy, especially the dragoon Tarleton, who seemed to have acquired a Satanic reputation overnight. Edward drank freely without counting the rounds.

At half past eight a new man arrived, greeted with cries of "Francis" and "Hand the colonel a drink."

"You know I take only a little, Alex," the new man said. He was a short, swarthy fellow with lively black eyes, rigidly correct posture, and a neat uniform of white breeches and red jacket. He laid his black leather cap on a table piled high with similar ones. A silver crescent on the cap bore the words *Liberty or Death*.

Edward found himself at the buffet table with the officer. The man seemed friendly, though far less boisterous than his fellows. Emboldened by what he'd drunk, Edward offered his hand. "If I may presume, sir. Edward Bell, Captain Hughston's militia regiment. Lieutenant," he added as a hasty afterthought.

"Lieutenant Colonel Marion, sir. Second Carolina." Edward knew him then—a bachelor soldier with a reputation for courage and superior tactical thinking. Marion's people were Huguenots, Protestant refugees from France; Carolina was thick with them. The Marions had settled in the desolate swamps and forests of the Lower Santee. The colonel was about fifty, Edward judged.

Marion rested his hand on the pommel of his short infantry sword and looked Edward up and down. "Your father owns Bell's Bridge?"

"That's correct, sir."

"An admirable patriot. How are you getting on in the army?"

"At the moment I'm digging and hauling sand on the Ashley fortifications. It seems a poor contribution."

"You'd prefer field duty?"

"I would. I've had no formal training—there's no time for it, I'm told. But I'm a good horseman and a decent shot."

Marion pointed at Edward's brimming cup. "Drinking is not something that contributes to a soldier's effectiveness. The opposite, in fact. If you served with me, you'd be sober as a rock day and night, or you wouldn't serve."

Captain McQueen shouted and clapped for attention. "Gentlemen, gentlemen, the meat of the evening. Toasts to our cause, and the downfall of King George, General Clinton, General Cornwallis—the whole bloody lot. Someone tell the niggers to bar the doors. We want no damned Tory sympathizers interfering."

Like most of the guests McQueen was barely able to stand. Marion seemed appalled by all the lurching and belching and breaking of wind. A servant shot the bolt of the front door. Marion frowned and put his cup of beer aside.

"Lieutenant, you must excuse me. I am not here to drink myself into a stupor." He marched out of the room.

Earle Hughston climbed on a chair to propose the first toast. "Confusion to our enemies. Victory to our cause. Liberty to our land." Nearly as much liquid spilled over chins and uniforms as found its way down the gullets of the drinkers. Edward didn't see Marion anywhere. Had he somehow escaped from the locked house?

When Edward met Captain Hughston next morning, both of them had bloodshot eyes and pounding headaches. "So you talked to the wrong man," Hughston said after Edward told his story.

"Quite. I had a drink in my hand. That finished me. What happened to Marion?"

"Hied himself up to the second floor and leapt out a window. Couldn't stand to be penned up with a crowd of bloody drunkards. Did some harm to his ankle when he landed. May have broken it. Out of action for a while."

And out of Charleston. Marion had been carried to the Cooper on a litter and borne away to recuperate, presumably at his home in the Santee wilderness.

Edward didn't know what to make of the odd little officer. One thing was certain—he'd keep on shoveling dirt rather than serve with someone so puritanical.

9

The Last Days

With the new fortifications built, Hughston's company moved to the northern rampart. The city's defenses were formidable. The thick outer wall of tabby overlooked the flooded ditch, six feet deep, twelve wide, and crossed by small portable bridges. Beyond the ditch lay an abatis and a broad area of open ground. Palisaded communication trenches connected various points of the outer works. Sir Henry Clinton nevertheless had crucial advantages: superior manpower and strategic position.

Edward drew night sentry duty west of the hornwork. From there he could observe the flats of the Neck beyond the American defenses. The flats swarmed with riflemen and artillerists, field pieces and wagons. Clinton's new forward line was finished, cannon in place just 250 yards in front of the ditch. At night a fiery cover of incendiary shells and grapeshot partially protected engineers building a third parallel no more than a hundred yards out. From there the blue-coated Hessian fusiliers, famed for accuracy, would be able to hit the ramparts. It only remained for sappers to drain the ditch, and the enemy would stand at the gates.

Huddled at an embrasure, Edward watched bright campfires and glowing lanterns and thought of Joanna Willing. Her criticism infuriated him, yet he wasn't ready to turn his back on her. She challenged him. He wanted to prove he wasn't an insensitive clod.

One night Major General Lincoln inspected the defense line. Edward was shocked to see how he'd changed. Gone was the genial Father Christmas figure of the early days of the siege. Lincoln's wig was askew. He'd lost weight. The skirts of a shabby greatcoat flapped around his legs as he passed by, ghost-white and grim.

Lincoln's policy of resistance had changed as well. He insisted that the city not be damaged by further attacks. At the end of the third week in April he asked for a parley under a truce flag. He presented his surrender terms, the most important being a guarantee that his troops could leave the city unimpeded and unharmed. Clinton dismissed the demand as presumptuous; bombardment resumed.

Instead of trudging home that morning Edward went to Bell's Bridge, to ask Tom Bell whether he knew of a source of lead. His supply of musket balls was almost gone. He'd become adept at pouring molten lead into a bullet mold, then snipping the sprue off the hardened ball with a cutter. He found his father gathering up papers and account books and baling them with twine.

Edward explained his problem. "Without lead I'll be reduced to firing iron scraps and broken glass. Half the men are doing that already."

"Have you thought of your toy soldiers?"

The painted hussars and dragoons and horse artillery of his childhood? He must have collected a hundred pieces. "But they're gone."

"No, your mother saved them. She kept a great many things you outgrew. I think she would approve of your melting them in the cause of liberty. You'll find her old trunks in the attic."

"Thank you, sir."

"No, sir. Thank your mother. She loved you dearly."

When he left, the batteries were booming again. The air reeked of powder. At the pier head a squad of soldiers ran by, chasing four of the vicious wild dogs that roamed the city. Charleston soldiers had orders to kill the dogs by any means except firing a precious bullet.

When the soldiers passed, there stood Joanna. She greeted him cordially, showed a corked green bottle. "I know it's unpatriotic, but Papa loves his tea, and we happen to have a little left."

"Better not let my father see it."

"You look exhausted, Edward. Is it terribly dangerous on the defense line?"

"No more so than anywhere else." A soothing lie. "I confess I've been thinking a lot about you lately."

"Have you, now? Pleasant thoughts, I hope."

"You've taken me to task pretty severely for"—stuck for a tactful phrase, he pointed to the cages on the wharf—"my opinions on those and related matters."

"Oh, I never mean to antagonize you. I only hope that one day you'll recognize what really exists around you. Have you ever seen the workhouse?"

"Of course. I must have passed it a thousand times." The so-called house of correction was a frame building on Mazyck Street, in the less desirable, western part of Charleston.

"But have you been inside? Seen how they treat those sent there for discipline? Slaves from Prosperity Hall have been punished at the workhouse."

"Adrian's nigras? He won't set foot in the place."

"Of course he won't, nor will many other fine white gentlemen of our slavocracy. The operating principle of the workhouse is this. You pay someone else a fixed price per head to beat and brutalize your chattels. That way your hands are always clean, even if your soul is not."

"Joanna, doesn't this strike you as a peculiar conversation in wartime?"

"Not at all. The war will end."

"Well, our part, certainly. South Carolina is nearly overrun. Our state troops are scattered and fled, and we're barely hanging on here in the city."

She touched his hand. "Faith, Edward. I believe America will prevail, even though the fight is tainted."

"Tainted? How so?"

"In Carolina the idea of freedom includes freedom to own human beings—movable property, that is the pretty phrase, isn't it? Suppose we win, as I believe and pray we will. We'll soon be back to the old system. That's why you should inspect the workhouse. After you do, perhaps we can discuss the subject again."

She squeezed his hand more warmly than necessary and left him bewildered, annoyed, and carrying an erection like a musket barrel. Damn the woman, he thought as he trotted up Bay Street. What was she doing to him?

He ran for cover when a shell exploded a block away, shattering a roof and lifting debris and part of a human body into the blue sky, where they hung for a moment before they fell into a cauldron of smoke and flame.

★　★　★

British reinforcements led by Lord Cornwallis marched into the countryside between the Cooper River and the Atlantic. Tarleton's dragoons rode ahead, seizing and burning boats on the river and closing the last bolt-holes.

On May 6 the redcoats completed their third parallel. Hessian riflemen in blue coats and tall brass caps occupied the line and began to pick off any careless American who raised his head too high. Continued night bombardment covered the work of sappers at the ditch. They soon drained it. American batteries worked themselves to exhaustion returning fire.

Fort Moultrie fell on May 7, assuring that no French or American ship could sail in and relieve the city. A day later drummers signaled for another parley. It lasted until nine the following night. General Lincoln's new surrender terms included a guarantee that citizens and militiamen would have their property respected and protected, and would be given a year to dispose of it if they chose not to live under British rule. Again Clinton threw the terms back in Lincoln's face, accusing him of unwarranted arrogance.

Edward was sitting on the rampart, braced against an onshore gale, at the hour the negotiations foundered. Battery commanders began shouting orders in the darkness. *"Attention. Worm out the piece. Ram down the charge. Prime. Make ready."* He stuffed bits of rag into his ears before the first explosion.

The wind tearing from the ocean carried the clangor of St. Michael's bells. Captain Hughston came up a ladder as St. Philip's joined in. Bellicose and full of rum, Hughston said, "In the name of Christ, why are they ringing the bells? Are they mad? We have nothing to celebrate."

"Captain, I wouldn't stand so near that lantern, you—"

A crackle of musketry ripped the night. A ball blew away Hughston's lower jaw and teeth in a shower of red that speckled Edward's face. The captain pitched off the rampart. By the time Edward climbed down to the body, Hughston was dead.

Two hundred British guns opened a furious bombardment of grape, bombs, and red-hot shot that ignited buildings and killed soldiers and civilians indiscriminately. Edward staggered home through the smoke-laden city, past carts piled with dead. At Broad and Meeting, William Pitt stood forlornly in the crossway, minus his right arm. A British cannonball from James Island had bounced off St. Michael's steeple and hit the statue.

He discovered Pharaoh in the garden, shoveling and tamping down earth in a bed of crape myrtle Eliza had planted next to the piazza. Edward loved the myrtle's burst of purple and crimson blooms every July. He asked Pharaoh what he'd buried.

"House silver an' plate. Master ordered it."

"But you've torn up the ground so much, anyone could find the silver in a minute."

" 'S how he wants it, Mist' Edward. Yonder back of the live oak I got to be lot more careful."

"What are you burying there?"

Tom Bell heard the question as he came out of the house carrying a long iron box. He lifted the lid to show the oilskin-wrapped contents. "Private papers and account books. A delegation of citizens, including your esteemed brother, will call on General Lincoln this afternoon, to plead that he surrender unconditionally. As soon as it happens, those who have no intention of kissing the enemy's fundament will be singled out. Property may be confiscated. I will give the damned British no information about my business, how it's conducted, or what it's worth. The silver and plate are a diversion, meant to be discovered." He handed the box to Pharaoh, who disappeared beyond the live oak's great gnarled trunk.

Edward rubbed his stubbled face with his sleeve. "So you think we're finished?"

Tom Bell's sad, sunken eyes confirmed it before he said, "Only a matter of time now. Hours, perhaps."

"And Adrian's in favor?"

"Aye. No doubt his fiancée is thrilled. Some weeks ago a friend told me Lydia was longing for the British to return and restore order, so there could be a proper social season again."

Edward couldn't find words to voice his disgust.

☆ ☆ ☆

At 9:00 A.M., while Edward drank small beer and chewed one of Essie's last biscuits, Clinton's artillery opened another furious bombardment. Hot shot set fire to more dwellings and commercial buildings. Smoke bannered the soft spring sky for three hours. Then the guns went silent, as if to allow Charlestonians time to contemplate their fate when the attack resumed. Lincoln's adjutant rushed to arrange another parley.

Truce terms were settled by eleven that night. General Lincoln would surrender Charleston at 4:00 P.M. on Friday, May 12. Edward cursed and blasphemed when he heard the news. The object of his wrath wasn't the enemy but himself. He'd failed his mother. He hadn't killed a single redcoat, so far as he knew. His debt remained unpaid.

10

At the Powder Magazine

Major General Lincoln, on horseback, and Brigadier General Moultrie, on foot, went to the hornwork gate to await the conquering army. First came its commanding officers, their staffs and adjutants, and the huge king's flag. The 7th Regiment of foot followed, with their field batteries, then von Linsing's Hessian grenadiers. Drums and fifes and oboes set the cadence with "God Save the King." Once into the city the British moved light field guns up to the ramparts, facing inward.

Surrender of arms by the entire city garrison was not a quick or easy process. Charleston had been defended by 2,600 Continentals and 3,000 militia. On Saturday, Edward and the rest of the 2nd Regiment marched north on King Street with their colors cased. The band played a Turkish air; English marches were forbidden.

Spectators crowded the footpaths on both sides of King. In the balmy sunshine the rutted street breathed up a stench of human waste mingling with the burnt smell from demolished buildings. Edward heard a scattering of applause and one man shouted, "Long live the Congress," but those who'd come to watch were for the most part loyalists. He spied his brother with his friends Lescock and Wragg. If Adrian saw him, he gave no sign.

The militia marched out through the gate to open ground. Watched by armed Hessian jägers and British light infantry, they laid down their muskets and fowlers and cartridge boxes. Edward put the fine French gun on the pile, thinking, *Adrian won't miss it but I will.*

Back in the city he stood in a long queue and signed his parole—his promise not to take up arms against His Majesty's troops again. Afterward, like the rest of the militia, he was free to go home. The Continentals would be confined in barracks in town, or over at Haddrell's Point.

The Bell house was silent, as though in mourning. Essie served a meager supper of bone marrow broth and stale bread. She wore a white camellia pinned to her blouse. Poorly's wife, Sally, wore one as well.

"The camellia is a hardy rebel bloom," Tom Bell explained. "It thrives when trampled. Just as we will."

General Clinton occupied number 27 King Street, the fine Georgian double house, brick with white pillars, built by Miles Brewton, another Charleston man who'd grown wealthy in the slave trade. It was said the new tenant would soon return north. For the moment Maj. Gen. Alexander Leslie commanded in Charleston. Redcoats camped everywhere, like a rash spread on the body of the city.

Monday afternoon, as St. Michael's rang one o'clock, Edward happened to be walking north on Church Street with Poorly. Essie had sent them to forage for food. The Bell household, like many others, was at the point of starvation.

Where Church intersected the first cross street above Queen, Cumberland, they found a chaotic jam of wagons, horses, imperious artillery officers, and two bedraggled platoons of militia surrendering arms. Negroes filed in and out of a masonry building on the south side of Cumberland, the city powder magazine, carrying muskets from the soldiers and kegs from the wagons.

Two young ladies squired by officers in white trousers, smart forest-green coats, and tall fur shakos watched the activity from the southeast corner of the intersection. As Edward and his slave passed by, the taller officer said, "Damme if those Yankees don't look like a pack of lice from a dog's back." His companion and the young ladies laughed heartily. The tall officer snapped a monocle into his eye, preening.

Poorly whispered, "Who are those greencoats?"

"Banastre Tarleton's legion. The commandant himself is in town, no doubt enjoying the spectacle of Charleston prostrate. God curse them all."

He and Poorly avoided an empty wagon pulling away and another arriving. Negroes climbed up via its wheels and began passing kegs to others, who took them inside. One of the artillery captains slapped the face of a black man obviously frightened of handling powder. "Step along, nigger, or I'll find a crocodile for you to ride." The other British officers found that amusing; the colonial militiamen looked sullen or wrathful. Edward and Poorly finally managed to squeeze through the press and strike out for Market Street.

Whether the tragedy was caused by a musket not properly unloaded, then carelessly handled so that it went off inside the magazine, or by some act of a patriot sympathizer, remained forever a mystery. On the point of speaking to Poorly, Edward was deafened by an explosion. He and Poorly spun around as the magazine building flew apart and hurled its contents skyward—muskets twisted into corkscrews, bayonets and ramrods sailing like enchanted swords. Edward goggled at a bare-chested Negro tumbling through the air with a musket rammer impaling his throat, a flying horse's head gushing blood from the severed neck, a militiaman lifted and thrown against a wall, snapping his neck. A half-dozen bayonets flew at the same wall and lodged there like pins in a cushion.

The explosions continued, one keg after another detonating. Towering flames erupted. Some of the militiamen ran like wild animals. Some lay dead or injured. Edward shouted, "There are people hurt." He dashed back toward the corner, Poorly at his heels.

He stayed close to the nearest wall; explosions were less frequent. Vomit churned in his throat when he saw the carnage. Bodies littered the street, some crushed by blocks of masonry. The wounded lay writhing and crying out. Negroes, human cinders, staggered through a wall of flame to drop and die. The stench was unbelievable.

A militiaman in a bloodied hunting shirt lay half hidden beneath a dead horse. The man's mouth moved, a silent plea for help. Edward plunged into the street, hopping across the rubble, hiding his face behind his arms because of the fire's heat. He seized the militiaman's arms, tugged once, again, and with the third effort pulled him free. The soldier was a towhead, more boy than man. Edward threw him over his shoulder.

☆　☆　☆

The taller of the two dragoons had left his safe corner and wandered among the fallen. He had no interest in succoring injured officers from his own army. He preferred to jab a wounded American with his boot, or lean down and whisper something that he found amusing.

The towhead's limp body and dangling arms partly obscured Edward's vision; he was unprepared for an unexpected collision with the dragoon, who booted Edward's leg out from under him. "Damned Yankee clod." Edward fell with his burden. His face hit a slab of masonry; a corner tore his left cheek open.

Smoke choked him. All around he heard the screaming and thrashing of the wounded and dying. He jumped up, blood staining his chin. Edward recognized the British officer as one of those he'd seen earlier. He was slender, with a classically oval face spoiled by a large pointed nose. *Bird's beak,* Edward thought. The officer's eyes were ice-pale, some indeterminate shade between gray and blue. He'd lost his shako. His companion and one of the ladies were bending over the second young woman now lying prostrate in the street.

Edward snatched up a rock, threw it hard. The officer easily dodged, then drew his saber. He lunged forward, one long smooth step. Edward darted aside a moment before the injured militiaman lurched to his feet. Six inches of steel buried itself in the towhead's belly.

His eyes grew huge and round. He grabbed the blade with both hands, vainly tried to pull it out. His palms bled as he dropped to his knees and pitched sideways, dying.

"Venables, Venables," the other dragoon shouted. "Lud's sake, man, Beatrice has swooned, we must find a doctor."

The tall dragoon seemed not to hear. His behavior outraged Edward. He ran at the dragoon. "You fucking butcher."

The dragoon had his saber and swung it in an arc that might have severed Edward's head if he hadn't thrown himself to one side. He fell again. The dragoon smiled with thin lips and those icy eyes and ran his blade through Edward's left thigh.

He wrenched it out, whipped it in the air; droplets of blood flew. "We can do with a few less colonials." The other dragoon cried, "Percy, hurry, Beatrice is gasping for air." The tall man spat on Edward and trotted away.

Edward lay clutching his bleeding leg. Darkness lapped at his mind. The screams went on. Bells rang. A last cache of powder exploded.

"Venables," he mumbled, fixing it in memory. "Bird's beak. Percy. Venables." The darkness closed.

11

Aftermath

Poorly tied off Edward's bleeding leg and improvised a litter from hunting shirts stripped from dead bodies. He dragged Edward home through the streets, helped part of the way by two slaves he didn't know. In Edward's second-floor bedroom the family doctor examined him and pronounced it a lucky wound: no major muscles or blood vessels cut. Edward knew none of this until he woke with a light fever some twenty hours after the explosion.

Each evening thereafter Tom Bell brought news to the bedside.

"Horrible casualties at the magazine. Two hundred, perhaps more. So far the cause is undetermined. The British would like to fix blame on us."

And "Did you hear the commotion downstairs earlier?" Bleary eyed, Edward said no; he slept long hours under the doctor's opiate. "Four vultures in red coats searched the house for valuables. They gave the garden only a cursory look. However, to be safe, the buried silver will rest where it is for a while yet."

And "Two hundred of our finest citizens addressed a memorial to General Clinton and Admiral Arbuthnot." He read part of it from a copy of Peter Timothy's *South Carolina Gazette*. " 'We tender to Your Excellencies our warmest congratulations on the restoration of this capital and province to their rightful connection with the Crown and government of Great Britain.' "

Edward asked whether Adrian had signed. In a scathing tone his father replied, "Do you have any doubt? Old Glass signed, too, and my friend Hughston, who lost his son."

And "They are billeting officers in private homes. We have acquired a Hessian, Captain Marburg. He arrived with a knapsack of books and a tendency to chat at every opportunity. He'll sleep on a cot in my office. He seems a decent sort."

Carolina's soft spring sunshine burst into Edward's room every morning, bringing balmy airs from the sea and birdsong from the garden. Yet to Edward it seemed the bleakest of seasons. The Charleston surrender was the largest capitulation in the brief history of the American army. At Waxhaws on the colony's far northern border, Banastre Tarleton's green dragoons had overtaken a retreating force of Virginians and cavalry under Col. Abraham Buford. When Buford gave up and asked for quarter, Tarleton defied military tradition and refused it. Edward supposed Venables, he of the bird beak, took part in the ensuing massacre. *Tarleton's quarter* became a term of hatred and contempt.

The Hessian came upstairs one evening to pay his respects. Captain Moses Marburg of von Huyn's regiment was a round-faced man, perhaps thirty, with curly carrot-colored hair and eyes like small blue pebbles. Edward drowsily invited him to draw up a chair.

Marburg spoke heavily accented English with considerable fluency; his commandant had insisted his officers learn. "I am a Jew, from the village of Wilnsdorf, in Hesse. I began as a forester, in the service of a duke of some distinction. Others in my family are more scholarly. My older brother is a rabbi. But all of us love books. In the duke's service the pay was decent, the position secure. However, the lady with whom I fell in love was permanently out of reach. The duke's daughter. She was a"—he foundered—"*Nichtjude.*" Then he remembered. "Gentile."

"So you joined the army?"

"Yes, it seemed a good opportunity to cleanse the sorrows of the past and see the world."

"Do you like soldiering?"

"Less than I expected. I do, however, like this country, South Carolina."

"We've had a Hebrew temple in the city since around 1750. Charlestonians are tolerant people."

"Good to hear. What I like most is the warm weather. All my life I've been a cold-blooded fellow. Always shivering, even in August. Here, I'm told, you can cook an egg in the sand in summertime." He gave a little shrug, a shy smile. "I could be happy in Carolina."

Edward agreed with his father. If they had to harbor an enemy soldier, Marburg was probably better than most.

After two weeks Edward was out of bed and taking short steps with a cane. He limped slightly. The long-faced doctor said the condition might be permanent.

Early in June, General Clinton and the bulk of his army prepared to set sail for New York. The general ordered citizens to swear a new loyalty oath. Many with important names—Middleton, Pinckney, Manigault, Hayne—obliged, but some forty patriots would not. They included Tom Bell and his friend Christopher Gadsden.

On June 8 the general and his troops embarked from the Cooper docks, leaving two Hessian regiments and three regiments of foot to garrison the town. Captain Marburg's regiment stayed.

Lord Cornwallis assumed command of the South. Command in Charleston fell to a recent Clinton appointment, Col. Nisbet Balfour. "A dour and arrogant Scot" was Tom Bell's unhappy appraisal, "intent on rooting out traitors. Be assured, he will have his eye on Christopher, and me—anyone who refused to take the oath."

One hot June morning, with flies buzzing and a fat mockingbird surveying the garden from the shrubs where he nested, Edward sat under the great live oak reading the latest *Gazette*. Joanna appeared at the gate. She carried a small sweet-grass basket draped with a napkin. Edward stood up too quickly, without using the cane. He staggered, dizzy. She rushed to him.

"Gracious, are you all right?"

"The leg's weak. I fear it's a permanent souvenir of the powder magazine."

"What a terrible thing to go through."

"More terrible for those who didn't walk away."

"Father thought I ought not visit before this, but I've been concerned."

Belatedly he took notice of her black dress, bonnet, and mittens. "Are you in mourning?"

"Many women are wearing weeds to protest the British presence."

He pointed his cane at an iron bench; they sat. He admired the sweet full curve of her breasts that no amount of black drapery could minimize. She drew the napkin off the basket. "Gooseberry tarts. I made them."

"Where did you find gooseberries?"

"My garden." He had never seen it, though her father said it was elaborate, as many Charleston gardens were. "The cuttings came from England before the war."

"Why the devil are you being so kind to me?" He meant it to be funny, but it came out as a quarrelsome bark.

"Well, sir, it isn't because of your courtly ways."

Reddening, he made his apology. Joanna accepted it with a pretty tilt of her head. She took off her black bonnet. The day was hot, the air still; her face glowed with a light sheen of sweat.

"Is it really so hard to understand why I was concerned, Edward? We're friends. At least I believe so."

The warmth of her eyes and smile relieved his embarrassment. He touched her hand. "We are, positively."

"Thank heaven that issue is resolved. Now tell me, what will you do when you're recovered?"

He gazed toward the harbor, where an osprey sailed on the air currents. "I can't take up arms again. I gave my word when I signed the parole. Besides, there's no army worth the name left in Carolina. The garrisons at Camden and Ninety Six surrendered when they heard that Charleston fell. Relief from the North is the only hope."

They chatted on about circumstances in the city. Neither felt cheerful about the occupation even though the redcoats were reasonably well behaved, with few incidents of looting or abuse of women. When Joanna rose to go, he saw her to the gate and thanked her for the tarts. "What can I possibly do in return?"

Her smile never wavered. "Why, this. If you've time on your hands, visit the workhouse." She slipped through the gate and away before he could react.

"Damme if I will," he grumbled. A week later, tired of idling in the house, he changed his mind. He took his cane and limped slowly to the large wooden building on Mazyck Street above Queen.

A block away he heard the shrill cry of someone in pain. He caught the stench of unwashed bodies and human waste. A coffle of seven blacks emerged from a compound behind the workhouse and trudged east on Magazine Street, guarded by a grubby white man carrying two muskets.

The man in charge of the workhouse greeted him in a small antechamber, where the smell was even more pronounced. The man's wig sat crookedly on his grotesquely oversized head. He was unctuous to a fault.

"Welcome, sir, welcome. Samuel Mouzon, your servant. And your name?"

"Edward Bell, sir."

"Bell, Bell—not a relative of Squire Bell of Prosperity Hall, by chance?" The smack of a whip laid on flesh came from behind a thick oak door.

"His brother."

"How excellent. Prosperity Hall sends us a nigger every few months. Do you own black property?"

"Some. I understand you discipline slaves for so much per head?" The whip hit again; Mouzon paid no attention to the scream. He rubbed his hands and bounced on his toes behind his high desk.

"Yes, sir, absolutely correct. Fees are negotiable."

"And the punishment prevents a repetition of rebellious behavior?"

"We firmly believe so, sir. As do our clients."

The next scream was even more harrowing. Edward pressed on. "You believe that what you do here makes a man more docile rather than more angry?"

"Oh, indeed. The best cure for future lapses is prevention. And we do not deal solely with bucks, sir. We apply the same treatment to wenches who misbehave. Would you care to observe?"

"That's the purpose of my visit."

Mouzon led him to the door. "Forgive the foul odor, we're hellishly crowded. We also house some of the niggers swarming into town to find work. They may be runaways, we simply don't know." Edward had seen gangs of blacks shoveling up garbage and rubble in the streets. He remembered the coffle leaving as he arrived.

Mr. Mouzon opened the creaking door to a large, dim room whose wood floor was scabrously stained by old blood and nameless filth. A thin mulatto, stripped to his trousers, turned to look at the newcomers. A bloodied cowhide, strips of leather braided into a long, supple whip, dangled from his hand.

Edward's eye fixed on the large wood frame behind him. Ropes from an iron wheel ran through pulleys on the crossbeam, then down to loops around the wrists of the woman being punished. The ropes stretched her arms straight over her head. Her skirt had been torn off and lay in a heap at her feet. Edward couldn't see her face.

The only sound in the room was the woman sobbing. A dozen bloody stripes marked her spine and buttocks. "What was her offense?"

"Deliberately spilling hot tea on the dress of her mistress while serving."

"How do you know it was deliberate? Did the wench confess?"

"Wasn't necessary. The daughter of Mr. Octavius Glass has an unfailing eye for the concealed malice of niggers." Excitedly, Mouzon went on, "Notice how we pull her up on tiptoe? Extremely painful. Enhances the punishment dramatically."

Edward was pale. Mouzon signaled the mulatto youth, who delivered a stroke that made the woman jerk forward and shriek. A fresh stripe leaked blood.

"Yes, I have the idea," Edward said, abruptly whirling and striding to the door. Mouzon pursued him.

"When might we anticipate serving you, sir?"

Edward slammed the street door and leaned against it. "Sweet Jesus." Joanna had said the place was a hellhole, and it was. Charleston's prosperity was maintained by the very thing he'd witnessed. He'd always known such cruelties existed, he'd just never involved himself. Poorly, thank God, didn't need that sort of discipline, nor did Tom Bell's house slaves.

Profoundly upset, he limped to Thomas Pike's tavern on Church Street and drank himself into forgetfulness.

12

The Red Monkey

Edward's experience at the workhouse undermined his lifelong tolerance of slavery, though he didn't call on Joanna to tell her. At twenty-one, admitting a mistake, or the possibility of bad judgment, came hard.

The loyalists feted their military friends with nightly banquets and balls that lasted until dawn. The knowledge fueled Edward's need to avenge his mother. He didn't know how; he'd signed his parole. Both parents had taught him that a promise once given was not to be broken.

His wound was nearly healed. Only a slight leftward list remained when he stepped out with that foot. He drifted through the humid summer days feeling useless and worthless, and spent more and more time in dramshops.

☆ ☆ ☆

"Marion's on the Santee, burning boats and watching the fords."

"Colonel Marion of the Second?" Edward said.

"The same. He has no official rank and no more than twenty men. Some are colored. You've never seen such a miserably equipped rabble. All they have is the will to fight."

The speaker was Micah Youngblood, a young man Edward's age with whom he'd fished and hunted in happier times. Micah had been a printer's devil in the employ of Peter Timothy until Col. Nisbet Balfour shut down the *South Carolina Gazette* as part of his campaign to intimidate those still resisting Crown authority. Mr. Wells, the popular bookseller who published a loyalist paper, was thriving unmolested.

"I saw Marion three days ago," Youngblood went on. "He said he had taken his men up to Deep River, in North Carolina, to offer their services to General Gates." Over Washington's objection the hero of Saratoga had been given command of a mixed force of Maryland, Delaware, and Virginia Continentals in the south. "Pompous old Horatio couldn't stand the sight of ragged men bit to pieces by red bugs and ticks. He sent them right back to detached duty in South Carolina. Which Marion prefers anyway."

★ ★ ★

Seven men gathered in the great room of Thomas Singleton's house on Church Street: Tom Bell and Edward; Christopher Gadsden; Storrow, a blacksmith; Levy, an upholsterer; Holderman, a portrait painter; and Danes, a carpenter. August heat lay heavy, as did a general depression of spirit. Balfour's new Board of Police was enforcing its own civil tyranny. If you signed the loyalty oath, you could bring someone up before the Board to settle a debt or contract claim, but if you'd refused to sign, you were denied the privilege. Balfour was sending suspected persons to the provost dungeon under the Exchange, where they shared the company of thugs and whores.

"Christopher," Tom Bell said, "while General Gates rushes to our rescue, where is our esteemed governor, Mr. Rutledge?"

Gadsden waved at an unseen horizon. "Out there, governing as best he can from his rolling carriage. More to the point, where's our host? I'm thirsty. Singleton?"

"Here, coming, with my little surprise," answered a loud voice from the hall. An ungodly screeching jerked every man's head up. Their host marched into the room holding a thin chain. He bowed to his guests. "Gentlemen, you have met my friend Mr. Jolly before. A fine acquisition from Brazil two years ago. In honor of our esteemed city commandant I have renamed him Colonel Balfour."

Colonel Balfour leapt on the table. With one furry paw he knocked a tankard off the edge. *Mein Gott,* Levy cried, his coat soaked, his face dripping ale. Colonel Balfour hopped up and down, showed his teeth, and screeched. Singleton's pet was a reddish-brown capuchin with a white front and face. He wore a perfect little replica of a British officer's red coat, braid and all.

Singleton yanked the chain. "Colonel, compose yourself. You've been very naughty." He pulled grapes from his pocket and fed them to the monkey. To Levy he said, "I'm sorry he soiled your shirt. I'll buy you another."

"Never mind, I want to know why you named a monkey after that damned arrogant Scot."

"Simple enough, Otto. I did it because an ass is much too large to wear a red coat."

*   *   *

Edward and his father walked home through streets whose lamps were lit by the civic lamplighter for a fee established by the Board of Police. Edward mused aloud. "I wonder if Marion would have me as a recruit?"

"You told me you'd never serve with a man like him. A puritan."

"I know I did. Things keep changing. I'm ready to serve with Satan if he's the only general left."

"Be careful when you say that. Break your parole and you could find yourself at the end of a rope."

*   *   *

On August 16, at Camden, Charles Lord Cornwallis and Francis Lord Rawdon, with a force of some two thousand effectives, routed the larger but less seasoned army of Gen. Horatio Gates. The Continentals fled the field in disarray. Baron Johann de Kalb, the brilliant Bavarian soldier, took a fatal wound. Tarleton's legion of infantry and horse chased the fleeing Americans, killing ruthlessly. After Camden no American military presence of any significance existed in South Carolina.

Occupied Charleston celebrated the victory with illuminations, fireworks, and enforced ringing of church bells. For the first time in Edward's life St. Michael's peal sounded discordant. One elderly lady of good reputation was hauled off to the Exchange because she stood in front of her dark windows and told a squad of armed redcoats, "Shoot me if you wish, I will not illuminate for an American defeat."

Next evening Christopher Gadsden came to the house with word of a new outrage. "They intend to sequester the property of suspected rebels. I saw the list. Bell's Bridge is on it, and Malvern."

"If they think they can bluff me into signing their damned oath, they're wrong. They're welcome to Malvern's ashes until we win the war. Bell's Bridge is another matter. Let them try to seize that, and Esau and I will meet them with guns."

"No you won't, Tom. It's exactly the excuse Balfour would need to lock you away." Gadsden's dark eyes gleamed in the candlelight. "There are more important battles."

"But when will we fight them?"

Edward wondered the same thing.

☆　☆　☆

A few nights later another group of patriotic gentlemen gathered at Mr. Pike's Church Street tavern. When Edward arrived, his eyes and ears told him that all the men, including his father, had been drinking for some time. Tom Bell's condition surprised his son; he always drank moderately, if at all. The prospect of having Bell's Bridge wrested away was weighing on him.

The taproom rang with raucous hoots, whistles, applause. Colonel Balfour was capering on a table, alternately baring his tiny teeth and squealing, and refreshing himself with a mug of beer. His amused owner reposed in a chair, chain in hand.

The tavern keeper, Mr. Pike, tried to quiet his guests. "There are British officers in the long room. More will be arriving."

"Introduce them to the colonel," Tom Bell said. Another man said, "What are they doing upstairs, Pike, buggering each other?"

The publican winced. "They have engaged the room for the night, for a ball to celebrate Camden. Ladies of the town have been invited." Sweatily fearful, he lowered his voice. "Women of color."

The uproar died. For the first time Edward heard a harpsichord, hautbois, and flute playing a minuet. Someone said, "Whores, are they?"

"Some are, I suppose. Some may be free persons. I don't ask questions. I'll tell you this, the women are elegantly gowned."

"By God, I must see that." Singleton tugged the chain. "Let us present ourselves, Colonel."

The street door opened suddenly and six boisterous celebrants trooped in. Two of the men wore red coats. The third, in green, was the bird-beaked dragoon, Venables. Edward had learned through quiet inquiries that Maj. Percy Venables was temporarily attached to Balfour's staff.

"Upstairs, ladies," one of the redcoats said. He smacked the bottom of a Negress whose breasts were nearly falling out of her stiffly boned bodice. The second girl was light brown, with a glittering necklace adorning her throat.

Venables was escorting the most beautiful black woman Edward had ever seen. Six feet tall and black as night, she'd painted her face as aristocratic white ladies did: a base of flour or cornstarch with vivid reddish-purple lip color and rouge made from berries. Lampblack accented her lashes. A red diamond beauty spot adorned her left cheek, a red heart her exposed cleavage. Her high cylindrical wig was pure white.

To the plainly dressed men watching silently, the first redcoat said, "Gentlemen, good evening." He saluted them with his bearskin cap, too drunk to recognize the animosity on their faces.

Venables pointed at the monkey. "And who is this little beast?" Edward was startled when his father spoke up.

"Isn't the uniform familiar, sir? The monkey is Colonel Balfour."

One woman giggled; her companion twisted her wrist to silence her. Tom Bell held fast to the back of a chair; he was weaving on his feet. Venables threw off the hand of his beautiful companion.

"You're mocking a king's officer. Are you the owner of that nasty little creature?"

Silence. Tom Bell stared his defiance. Venables caught Tom Bell's chin in one hand.

"I say, sir. Are you the owner?"

Silence again.

"You will answer me." The dragoon's hand flew, a stinging slap.

Edward hurled himself forward, fists up. His friends scrambled to give him room. Venables drew his dress sword. The sharp point touched Edward's throat, stopping him. Venables addressed Tom Bell. "You know this young puppy?"

Edward answered. "I'm his son."

"His son. Well. Pity I didn't finish you at our first encounter." His wrist turned; the point of the sword drew blood. Then he pulled the blade away. "Someone remove that filthy monkey before I gut it on the spot."

Singleton leapt to seize Colonel Balfour and rush him from the room. Venables sheathed his sword. "Ladies, let's away to the supper and dancing. No reason to let this scum spoil it."

He pushed the tall woman to one side and ascended the stairs ahead of her. He turned back long enough to fix Tom Bell and Edward with ugly looks. His companions, somewhat subdued, followed him. The musicians struck up a Scottish reel.

Tom Bell said, "Do you know that man?"

"I do. He's the same whoreson who sabered my leg."

Overhead, booted feet moved in time with the lively music. In the back of the house Colonel Balfour shrieked and gibbered.

"Fortunately, he doesn't know my name," Edward added.

"He will," Tom Bell said. "He will."

13

Arrested

At low tide the pale gray mud flats breathed out their pungent mix of fish and decay that to Edward would always be the smell of a Charleston summer. The sickly season brought its usual tropical rains and pestilence. This year the city's Tory elite, which now included Adrian and Lydia, could not conveniently board a packet for Newport, "the Carolina hospital," there to remain until the weather improved. Tom Bell sadly referred to his older son as one of the "Protection Gentry," a term coined by Edward Rutledge for those who would switch sides as often as necessary for personal convenience and profit.

On three successive evenings Edward noticed his father slipping out of the house for several hours, with no explanation. The fourth morning he discovered two saddles in a storage shed behind the house. Next day they were gone. When he asked who had brought them, then removed them, Tom Bell said, "Friends. It's safer if you don't know any more."

Captain Marburg took pains to remind his hosts that not everything about the occupation was onerous. By regulating prices of what farmers brought into the city, the British gradually increased the food supply. Meat and common victuals reappeared in the stalls of the public market off Meeting Street. Pharaoh and Essie went there between sunrise and noon, with the required written pass from their master, to buy pork, peas, and rice for the larder.

The captive Board of Police supervised everything from distribution of food to the poor to fire control. Householders failing to have sooty chimneys swept once every fortnight were fined. Slaves who had run away from loyalist masters to join the British army were quietly returned, with a charge that harsh punishment be avoided. Whether the charge was widely observed, Edward couldn't say. One day, when he saw Joanna at Bell's Bridge, she said the workhouse was busier than ever. He withheld any mention of his visit.

Traffic in and out of the city remained restricted. Soldiers at the gate searched wagons and carts for concealed saddles, boots, ammunition, or boxes of precious salt that might go to patriot partisans in the countryside. Loyalists had their own partisan brigades. Those of "Captain" Paddy Carr and "Captain" William Lark were burning and pillaging patriot property.

Bell's Bridge and the other wharves saw a modest resumption of trade. Foreign ships arrived with nonessential goods—Belgian lace, French shoe buckles, Spanish wines. The military inspectors passed these to the retail shops without interference. Tom Bell left all dealings with the British to Esau Willing. The matter of sequestration of his property seemed to be in abeyance.

A slave brought Edward a single folded sheet sealed with red wax, bearing the seal of Octavius Catullus Glass. The message was inscribed in Lydia's fine slanting hand.

I am desperate to see you. I beg you to grant my request and not humiliate me with a refusal.

After he read the note he limped out the back door to the cookhouse. He threw the paper into Essie's stove and watched it burn.

☆ ☆ ☆

On a hot Sunday afternoon in mid-August Edward returned from a stroll along Bay Street to find Captain Marburg in the dining room, gazing at a framed engraving that hung above the elegant sideboard with rice leaves carved into its legs. The sideboard was the work of Mr. Elfe of Broad Street, a craftsman widely respected until he signed the loyalty oath, claiming intimidation. "Oh, yes," Tom Bell had been heard to say publicly, "the intimidation of his empty purse."

Marburg's moon face gleamed with perspiration as he admired Mr. Leitch's famous "View of Charles Town." The handsome engraving depicted the city from the harbor, with church steeples and the Exchange prominent on the skyline. A ship with billowing sails filled part of the foreground; a Carolina sky spread over all.

"You are fortunate to live in such a beautiful place, Mr. Edward." Marburg moved to examine the engraving from a different angle. His white linen shirt stuck to his back. Edward was no less uncomfortable.

"I wouldn't say it's beautiful just now."

"I look beyond the war. I imagine what it was and what it will be again. I am thinking I would like to make it my home."

"Well, it is, until your regiment's ordered back to Germany."

"I would like to make it my home even then."

Edward understood Marburg's meaning. Presently the captain said, "You will not tell others of my intent, will you, Mr. Edward?"

"No, I won't."

"You are a gentleman. My friend forever."

★　★　★

The heat persisted. Rowboats brought shrouded bodies from the harbor. Graves were dug in the Strangers' and Transients' Cemetery as dysentery and smallpox decimated the crews of the British ships.

On Sunday night, August 27, the household was wakened shortly before midnight by a commotion at the street gate. Intruders stormed through the garden and hammered on the piazza door. Edward ran downstairs in his nightshirt, a candle in hand. Tom Bell followed; sleep had twisted his thin white hair into spikes. Marburg stumbled out of the front room muttering, "What idiot calls at this hour?"

Shafts of light crisscrossed the ceiling, thrown through the fanlight by bull's-eye lanterns. "Friends of yours, I think," Tom Bell said. "Christopher warned me something like this was coming."

He opened the door. A hot, hissing rain fell on the garden. The lieutenant leading a detail of four soldiers said sharply, "Thomas Bell?"

"I am Bell, sir."

The lieutenant showed a paper. "You are hereby commanded into the king's custody."

"On what charge?"

"Seditious conduct. Organization of conspiratorial gatherings."

"Oh? When and where were those gatherings held, sir? Give me the evidence."

"It is not in my possession, sir. I only have this writ charging you with manifesting the utmost opposition to His Majesty's just and lawful authority. One of my men will accompany you upstairs while you dress."

"And then?"

"You will join some of your friends aboard His Majesty's frigate *Sandwich* anchored in the harbor."

Marburg said, "She is a prison ship."

"Who the devil are you, sir?" said the officer.

"Captain Marburg, sir"—he emphasized the rank—"of Major General von Huyn's garrison detachment."

The lieutenant moderated his tone. "You're quartered here? I respectfully ask you not to interfere. I am carrying out the orders of Colonel Balfour."

"Who else is arrested?" Tom Bell said. "I demand to know."

"Lieutenant Governor Gadsden. Several judges and former privy counselors. I do not have the entire list."

"They're not going to take you out of this house," Edward said.

"Go back to bed," Tom Bell said in a calm voice. "I will survive this. I'm not afraid."

As though it would be possible for Edward to sleep with his gut knotted and sweat running down his chest under his sticky nightshirt. Ten minutes later he and Marburg watched the redcoats march Tom Bell away into the rainy night.

☆ ☆ ☆

Two dozen were arrested and confined aboard *Sandwich*. The prisoners were allowed visitors. Essie packed a basket of stewed chicken parts and bread. From Bell's Bridge, Poorly rowed Edward out to the frigate. It was a dank, airless morning. Green swells in the harbor had an oily glint; they broke occasionally into white horses as a storm rumbled offshore and the wind picked up. Edward gripped the gunwales and tried not to fear the churning water.

Poorly stayed with the rowboat while Edward climbed the rope ladder with his basket. He found his father on deck, taking the air with Gadsden, Levy the upholsterer, and Danes the carpenter. Perhaps there had been secret, conspiratorial meetings of some Liberty Boys after all.

Edward embraced his father. "How are they treating you?"

"Decently. Whatever else you may say about our enemies, most of them are well mannered."

"I'll bring food every day."

"It's welcome. The gruel this morning was full of maggots."

Christopher Gadsden stepped over to them. "Extra food won't be necessary for long. I've been informed that we're to be removed to the British fort at St. Augustine. There are more arrests to come."

★ ★ ★

Sandwich raised sail and left the harbor before Edward could pay a second visit. Two days after the departure a military courier delivered an unexpected note.

Edw. Bell, Esq.
Sir,
I am informed that your father is among the dangerous traitors to be detained by His Majesty's garrison at St. Augustine. In view of the gentleman's insolence, and yours, when last we met, I have despatched an earnest request to the commandant in Florida that he show special attention to Mr. Bell. I wished to convey this information before leaving Charles Town to return to duty with my unit.

> *I have the honour to remain,*
> *Yr. obdt., etc.*
> *P. Venables*
> *Major, British Legion*

14

Joanna's Vow

"I need your help."

Edward spoke the words in the brick-walled garden of Esau Willing's modest house on Elliott Street near East Bay. Intermittent rain had deluged the coast for days. The earth was soggy under his boots; leaves of three small umbrella trees still glistened. Beds of foxglove and snapdragon and their periwinkle borders had lost their blooms.

Joanna wore a threadbare muslin dress. He'd discovered her with dirt on her knuckles and the tip of her nose, happily digging up West Indian lantana and potting them for winter houseplants. He found her disarrayed state curiously appealing.

She laid her trowel aside, rose, and brushed off her skirt. "It's yours for the asking, Edward."

"I must get out of the city without a search. I'm leaving to join the partisans if I can find them. Poorly's going with me. He asked to go, even though Sally's expecting a child in the spring." He described Venables's threat against Tom Bell. "I can't help him, but I can take a few pounds of flesh for him, and my mother. I've hesitated and vacillated too long."

"What can I do?"

"I have to smuggle two pistols and a powder horn past the sentries. A woman would never be searched."

Her eyes sparkled. "Ah. You want me to hide them under my skirts."

"Yes, yes," he stammered.

She clapped her hands and laughed. "Edward Bell, I have never seen you so red faced."

"Well, it's a damned, um, rather delicate subject, speaking of a lady's, um, clothing."

"Haven't you learned by now that I am not a conventional young woman?" He was conscious of their isolation in the walled garden. "I think it's brave of you to go. Your visit to the workhouse can wait."

"I went there, Joanna." Her mouth rounded in a silent O. Quickly he added, "We'll talk about it some other time."

Raindrops began to patter the ground. "As you wish. I'll take you through the gate and pray for you while you're gone." She laid her palm against his cheek. "I want you to come back to Charleston. You see"— she leaned close; her breath was warm as the rainy air—"I've thought and thought about you of late. Reached a decision too. I intend to marry you, Edward Bell."

She threw her left arm around his neck and kissed him, pressing close to let him feel her slim body. Astonished and overwhelmed by the emotions she aroused, he held her tightly.

She drew away, gazed at him, appraising his reaction. He felt warm waves of pleasure and desire. He took her shoulders in his hands and kissed her again. The kiss was like a revelation of possibilities never imagined before.

The sky opened. They embraced in the downpour, not caring.

* * *

He assembled necessary supplies: blankets, his tin canteen, a wooden one for Poorly. Sally sewed two burlap sacks into a rough approximation of saddlebags. It wouldn't do to arouse the suspicion of sentries by carrying real ones. The bags held smaller sacks of parched corn and dried peas.

The late-summer rains continued. Edward chose a stormy morning for departure, hoping thunder and lightning would be added distraction. Poorly kissed and hugged his tearful Sally. Edward drove the family's two-wheeled cart to Elliott Street and there removed his pistols, holsters, and powder horn from the burlap bags. While he and Poorly looked the other way, Joanna hid them, then settled her skirts and picked up the reins. Edward sat beside her on the driver's bench. Poorly dangled his long legs off the rear of the cart.

As they reached the gate the rain stopped. Sunlight slanted through a broken cloud canopy. Edward cursed under his breath—suddenly it was a brilliant morning. Steam rose from the ground.

They pulled up to the sentry box. A young redcoat came out to challenge them. "Your name, sir?"

"Edward Bell. On parole from the Second Militia Battalion."

"Where are you going?"

"My family owns a small property on the Cooper River. We were advised that partisans burned us out. I am traveling up there to assess the damage."

"Your nigger too?"

"Yes."

The soldier rudely gigged Joanna's arm with the barrel of his musket. "And who's this?"

"My sister."

"Not much of a family resemblance. She's pretty." Edward tried to smile; he wanted to break the soldier's jaw.

"What are you carrying in the cart?"

"Two drinking bottles and some food."

The strutting soldier pushed Poorly off his seat, then took an excessive amount of time opening and shaking each canteen. He turned the sacks inside out, found the smaller ones, and emptied the corn and peas on the ground. A vein in Poorly's forehead jumped under his shiny skin. Edward cautioned him with a look.

Finally, almost regretfully, the soldier said, "Pass on."

The cart rolled through the gate, over the drained ditch, and through the torn-up ground of the siege lines. Joanna drove with her right hand and held Edward's hand with her left. She was visibly relieved. His heart still hammered like an Indian drum.

☆ ☆ ☆

After two miles they said good-bye with decorous handshakes. Her eyes spoke a good deal more intimately. He slung the sacks over his shoulder and watched her turn back along the rough road to Charleston. As they started trudging, Poorly said, "Where we find this colonel of yours?"

"God knows. They say he moves fast as lightning. We'll ask people and hope they aren't on the wrong side."

☆ ☆ ☆

"Now, George—that is your name, George?"

"Yessir, George my name all right." The trembling black man could barely speak, which wasn't surprising, since Edward was pressing the muzzle of a pistol under his chin. They stood in the hot shade at the side of a small barn.

"Where's your master, George?"

"Squire Wando be in Charleston, hobnobbing with them lordships an' generals."

"What we want, George, are two good horses, and saddlery."

"Then we want you to forget you ever saw us," Poorly said with a visage so threatening, Edward almost laughed.

"You don't do that, George, this child will be back to haunt you."

George showed the pinkish palms of his hands. "Ain't saying nothing, ever."

"Any firearms on the property?" Edward asked. "Your master must allow you to protect yourself when he's away."

"Got an ol' fowler. Pretty bad rusted up."

"My friend here will have that, and some shot, and thank you." Since Henry Wando was a Tory, Edward had no qualms about stealing from him. The old slave was another matter. "Tell Wando that thieves struck in the middle of the night, while you slept. Or, I can tie you up."

"No, no, sir, Squire Wando trus' me. I be all right."

With the deception agreed upon George helped them select two of the Chickasaw horses from Wando's pastures. "Mighty fine animals," he assured them. "Raised up on the limestone water round Eutaw Springs. You ought take this one, sir"—he rubbed the flank of a sorrel mare—"her name's Brown Eyes. Sweet tempered as an angel, but she run like the devil."

They rode away from Wando's farm on two strong mounts. Edward hoped he wasn't demeaning Joanna by letting the mare's soulful eyes reminded him of hers. He found himself lonely for Willing's daughter, and for the first time he harbored a fear that something might happen to prevent him from seeing her again.

✻　　✻　　✻

They passed the night at the ruins of Malvern and in the morning set out to the northeast, through a divided and devastated land.

The countryside swarmed with British regulars and loyalist militia, as well as irregulars who respected no authority but their own. It was impossible to know whether a cabin or plantation was patriot or Tory, and thus better to avoid them all. They stole food where they could and when they couldn't, they let their bellies growl.

They crossed low sand hills and broad savannahs, skirted marshes and swamps where black gum and cypress grew from the water. Rain fell every day, in one of the wettest Septembers that Edward could recall. Near the Santee they saw a wagon train guarded by redcoats moving on the supply road from Charleston to Camden.

They swung west to avoid Georgetown, known to have a heavy concentration of enemy troops. Turning northeast again, they took the torn-up Post Road that connected Savannah and Boston. Many homeless families camped along it. Few had anything but what they wore and carried.

The land along the Black River, settled mostly by Scotch-Irish Whigs, was a known patriot stronghold. They took a chance and stopped at a small plantation. The master, an Irishman, fed them a meal and surprised them with news of another commander in the field, Col. Thomas Sumter, whose name Edward knew. "Redcoats call him a gamecock 'cause he fights like one."

"Do you know Colonel Francis Marion?" Edward asked.

"Of Pond Bluff on the Santee. I know him by reputation."

"They say he's in the field. We want to find him."

"Heard he was way north. He moves fast."

At a puncheon causeway crossing Black Mingo Creek they came on a family of three with a broken axle on their wagon. The bearded father forlornly pointed at a buxom girl sitting on the edge of the causeway talking to herself. She was, Edward guessed, no more than fourteen. He thought of Hamlet's Ophelia.

"Mind's gone," the father said.

Edward took off his old tricorne and wiped his sweaty forehead. "What happened?"

"Partisans. Before they burned our place, the captain ate supper while six of his sons of bitches took Marietta into the pines. I could hear her scream but I couldn't help her, I was trussed like a hog." At the mention of it his wife cried. The girl hummed and chattered. A suspicion stirred.

"Did the captain identify himself?"

"Oh, yes, he bragged on his name. William Lark."

Edward swung up on Brown Eyes. The mare turned her head to acknowledge his presence; they got along splendidly. The father took hold of the bridle.

"Kill some of the bastards, sir. As many as you can."

"That's our intention," Edward said.

*   *   *

Soon after, they veered west again to avoid a column of horses. From a canebrake where they hid under a peach-colored sunset sky, Edward saw the riders clearly. They wore green coats. He wondered if Venables was with them.

Riding toward Lynches River and the Pee Dee beyond, they discovered a horrific burned area ten miles wide. It stretched on and on toward the northern horizon. At a crossroads a man picked through ashes and blackened timbers. He told them he was pastor of the destroyed Presbyterian chapel. "They said it was a sedition shop."

"Who did this?"

The pastor's haggard face showed un-Christian bitterness. "Major James Wemyss, under orders from Cornwallis. They had the most specific instructions, which they were pleased to recite repeatedly. 'Disarm in the most rigid manner all persons who cannot be depended upon, and punish them with total demolition of their property.' From here up to Cheraw everything's gone. They broke looms people depend on for a livelihood. They burned gristmills and smithies. They shot milk cows and bayoneted sheep."

Edward could offer no solace. "Do you have information about Marion? Where he is?"

"We've heard North Carolina. White Marsh, the southern reaches of the Waccamaw."

Edward thanked him. "May God bless you," the pastor said. "For the moment He has abandoned us." They left him standing in the black rubble.

*   *   *

They crossed the border into Bladen County and approached White Marsh late one afternoon, through a forest so densely grown with pines and oaks, only chinks of sun showed between the trunks. Mosquitoes whined around their ears. The only other sounds were the slow tread of the horses on matted leaves and pine straw, and the whistling and cawing of unseen birds.

"Never heard so many in one place," Poorly said, frowning. "Don't seem quite right."

They passed under the low limb of an immense live oak. Edward heard the familiar click of a musket cocking. A man hidden in the tree above them said, "Hold your places or breathe your last, boys. Your choice."

15

Marion

Edward raised his hands. Poorly did the same. The man in the tree sounded like a Carolinian, so Edward said, "We're searching for Colonel Marion."

The man in the tree whistled, a perfect imitation of a Carolina wren. A second man, wearing a hunting shirt, jumped down from a water oak to Edward's right. Brown Eyes shied, then reared as the lookout advanced with his musket. "You found him."

"We're Charleston men. We want to volunteer."

The first sentry scrambled out of the live oak tree. He was fat, and as grubby and ill clad as his younger counterpart. Edward quieted Brown Eyes with stroking and whispering. The heavy man circled around them warily.

"You better be telling the truth, boys. If you ain't, North Carolina will be your resting place. Samuel, fetch the horses."

☆   ☆   ☆

The sentries led them to an encampment on the edge of reedy wetlands. Edward guessed the camp held sixty or seventy men. Most wore homespun. They sat or lay in lean-tos thatched with palmetto fronds. Details were hard to make out because of fading daylight and thick smoke from smudge fires. The smoke didn't help much; a deerfly bit Edward's cheek.

They found Francis Marion by his campfire, munching a roasted sweet potato. The little officer looked as severe as ever. He wore a short red coat, clean and brushed. His infantry sword hung from a tree branch. He listened to the report of the sentries and dismissed them. To Edward he said, "We've met before."

"At Captain McQueen's in Charleston, sir. My name's Edward Bell."

"I remember." Marion wasn't unfriendly, though he didn't accept Edward's outstretched hand. "We discussed the issue of drinking."

"Yes, sir. We've been hunting for you since we left Charleston almost three weeks ago."

"If you'd come this way tomorrow, you'd have missed us. We're moving on. Have you eaten?"

Poorly said, "Not much in the last few days, Colonel."

"I can offer these." With a knife he speared two sweet potatoes from a pan. He dropped them on a slab of bark. "Let them cool. Tell me why you want to join us."

Edward gave a brief but impassioned account of the loss of his mother, and his father's imprisonment. He described Major Venables's threat against Tom Bell. "More of Tarleton's quarter," Marion said with a chilly smile. "So you broke your parole. If you're caught, you can be hung, though in this command we're all gallows birds."

"It's a risk I gladly accept. My colored man as well."

"All right, but ours isn't an easy service." He paced in front of the fire, limping as badly as Edward did. A consequence of his jump from McQueen's window? "We're poorly equipped. We have sufficient ammunition only when we steal it. You won't be paid. The only liquid in your canteen will be water cut with vinegar. The Roman legions marched and conquered the world drinking nothing else."

"Yes, sir."

"Find a bit of rag or white cloth. Make cockades for your hats. Then we won't shoot the wrong men. I enforce strict discipline though not excessive protocol. Our strategy is simple. We fight and run. We ambush when we can. We do not needlessly kill wounded enemies, and if possible, we always leave what Scipio Africanus called a golden bridge of retreat for our enemies. Better that they live to tell of their defeat than die silent. And, the less brutality to our countrymen, the sooner wounds will heal when we win the war. Any questions?"

Edward and Poorly said no.

"Major Horry." Marion's summons brought a lanky officer with the look of a beleaguered schoolmaster. Horry took them to a lean-to and introduced them to a four-man mess. He drew Edward aside. "One of our best men died of malaria last week. His musket was immediately taken, but I have his saber. Do you want it?"

"Yes, sir, and thank you."

"Tend and tether your horses and spread your blankets. Get some rest. You can have the sword in the morning. We break camp at noon."

☆   ☆   ☆

They moved south from White Marsh, a double file of unkempt farmers, youths, ex-militia, ex-Continentals, and even a few grandpas. Their weapons were equally ill assorted. One old man showed off a sword made from a plantation wood saw. At first Edward felt uncomfortable wearing a dead man's saber, but he soon got over it.

At dusk they camped on the Waccamaw near Kingston. Next day they left the sandy road they'd been following. Two local men guided them through the Little Pee Dee Swamp, a place of greenish light and black water with the knees of ancient cypresses rising from it. The guides knew narrow and treacherous pathways. Green herons watched from branches hung with Spanish moss, as though expecting the swamp to swallow the interlopers. Some said the water harbored deadly snakes, but they saw none.

After several miles they jogged into the sunlight, assuming the worst was behind them. Instead, they came to the broad and sunlit Little Pee Dee, swollen and flowing fast because of the rains. Edward and Poorly had crossed the river on a bridge while traveling north. Here there was no bridge, or even a discernible ford; nothing but a deserted boat landing fallen into ruin on the far shore. The officers ordered weapons tied to saddles to keep them dry.

While the column waited, Marion walked into the water leading his horse. The current caught them. Marion clung to the pommel as the water reached his waist, then his chest. Edward's mouth went dry. For a moment it seemed as though Marion and his horse would be washed downstream, perhaps drowned, but the animal swam strongly, and the colonel hung on. Both emerged dripping on the far bank. Men whistled and cheered.

The first two riders in the column stepped into the stream beside their horses. Poorly looked at Edward. "You all right?"

"I didn't come this far to drown." He expressed more confidence than he felt.

When it was their turn, he walked Brown Eyes into the river. Immediately he felt the strength of the rushing current. When the water reached his waist, panic set in. He swallowed and gasped, hanging onto the saddle as Marion had.

He sank deeper. A broken branch sailed under Brown Eyes and tangled his legs. He began to thrash. He almost let go. Brown Eyes snorted and struggled. His mind seemed to blank out as he held fast, trusting the mare. After a seemingly interminable time, he felt mud under his feet.

He staggered up the bank and clung to the old boat landing a moment. He patted the wet mare and praised her. She whinnied and shook herself, showering him. He laughed, a crazy cackle of relief. His heart slowed.

Poorly had no difficulty; he was a powerful, apparently fearless swimmer, much like his horse. When all the column had made the crossing, Major Horry rode up beside Edward. "You looked green out there. Were you in trouble?"

"No, sir," Edward lied. "It's just that I never learned to swim."

He didn't understand the major's tight smile until Horry said, "Neither did the colonel."

★ ★ ★

They pressed steadily southward. Their crossing of the Pee Dee was accomplished more easily, on flatboats manned by sympathetic locals. At twilight on the fourth day of the march, a party of a dozen scouts met them at Lynches River. Marion and his aides trotted out to confer with them. Edward's belly was empty. He stank of dirt and sweat. He could do little more than slump in the saddle and close his eyes as a red evening haze deepened around them.

Briskly, Marion rode back and addressed his weary company. "Surprising news. Most of you will remember Colonel John Coming Ball who, along with Colonel Wigfall, forced our retreat into North Carolina." The names produced an angry reaction. "They had a thousand men to our sixty. Now I'm informed that Ball is camped at the Red House Tavern on Black Mingo Creek, guarding the Post Road with no more than fifty men. It is my inclination to catch them napping, but you have ridden more than thirty miles today. I want your sense of the issue."

No one spoke immediately. Then a man with long white hair in braids nudged his swaybacked horse from the ranks. "Colonel, sir, this here's my home county. The redcoats drove me out. I say we take 'em."

A ragged cry seconded the idea. Edward joined in. Pleased, Marion doffed his black leather cap to salute them; the silver faceplate, *Liberty or Death,* flashed in the sullen red of the sundown.

"Rest fifteen minutes. Then we ride the final twelve miles. See to your powder and ball."

The company dispersed. Edward slung a leg over Brown Eyes and slid to the ground, excitement easing his weariness. Poorly scraped Wando's rusty fowling piece with his fingernail. "Be some blood let tonight."

Edward pulled his blunderbuss pistols from the saddle holsters. "About time," he said.

16

Blooded

Loose puncheons on the causeway rattled and banged as Marion's men galloped across. On the bank of Black Mingo Creek the colonel signaled a halt. Under the white stars a sentinel's gun exploded in the stillness. Marion spoke softly to the circle of horsemen.

"They know we're here. The tavern stands on the Post Road, just there, to the west. Behind it lies a field, where I expect Coming Ball is bivouacked. Major Horry, dismount twenty men as infantry and take the right flank, around the building. Captain Waites, dismount another twenty and charge the tavern on my order. Remaining cavalry to the left flank. Questions?"

There were none. Major Horry counted off his men, including Edward and Poorly. Two men were chosen to hold the horses. Pistol in one hand, saber in the other, Edward advanced with the rest through broom sedge and dog fennel toward the Red House, where no light showed. He caught faint sounds of movement in the field.

Marion and his riders passed in the rear, trotting toward the other side of the tavern. The slow and stealthy advance continued. The shadow of the building fell over them. On the march from Lynches River, Horry had told them the Mingo tribe believed the creek was haunted by those who had died nearby. Edward shivered. How many new spirits would be released in the next few minutes?

In the field behind the tavern an excited voice was audible. Horry's saber rose, flashing in the starlight. "Charge," he cried. The unseen commander yelled, "Fire." As Edward ran to the battle, he thought of Joanna.

He was beside Poorly in the second rank. A sheet of light seemed to leap from the field, silhouetting the rank in front. Two men fell, hit by ball and buckshot. Spent pellets pattered the ground. One stung Edward's cheek. He planted himself, aimed his pistol, pulled the trigger, hit nothing.

Poorly's old fowler misfired. He swore. Another volley from the field cut down a man on Edward's right. Edward dropped to one knee, shoved the hot pistol into his belt, and jerked out the other. When the next volley came, he used the brief glare to sight on a soldier. His ball threw the soldier to the ground.

"Forward, forward," Horry shouted, saber swinging. Half a dozen men in Edward's group turned and bolted. He and Poorly and others followed the major, dodging and ducking. Behind them gunfire signaled the opening of the frontal assault. The drum of Marion's horses grew louder on the other side of the tavern.

Edward came face-to-face with an enemy soldier struggling to load his Brown Bess. The man took his musket by the barrel and swung it like a club. Edward ducked and the musket swooshed over his head. He sank his saber into the man's middle. The soldier fell in the weeds. A piece of the debt settled.

By now the field was a confusion of clanging swords, exploding firearms, acrid smoke, shouted commands, wails and groans of the injured. The British soldiers were breaking and scattering, overturning tents and cooking tripods. Marion left the far side of the bivouac open; the golden bridge of retreat. The demoralized enemy ran toward Black Mingo Swamp.

Edward stabbed at a fleeing soldier but missed. Off balance, he slipped and fell. The soldier wheeled around, pointed his musket at Edward's head. There was a roar, a flash of fire; the soldier windmilled backward, shot through the forehead. In the blurry perimeter of Edward's vision Poorly appeared, smiling. He presented the smoking fowler for Edward's approval.

"Finally got the damn thing to shoot."

★　★　★

The battle of Black Mingo lasted barely fifteen minutes. Colonel John Coming Ball and his vanquished men left Marion with four prisoners, abandoned baggage and wagons, a supply of muskets and ammunition, and all their horses. Marion took the enemy commander's fine sorrel gelding and on the spot named him Ball. Edward and Poorly each equipped themselves with a Brown Bess musket.

Edward had been in a state of nervous uncertainty during the fight, but he'd acquitted himself honorably; he was blooded in battle. He'd never considered the duty on the Charleston rampart to be anything like combat.

In the morning Marion assembled the company. He didn't chastise or even mention those who had run. Instead he complimented everyone on the victory. "You have endured many days of hard duty in the field. Any man who is near his home and wants to see his family has permission to leave." At midday just twenty of the company remained at the Red House Tavern.

Although the battle was small, it had a profound effect on the British, and on loyalists in the district between the Santee and Pee Dee rivers. It was the genesis of Marion's legend as a crafty, elusive fighter who knew the swamps and pine barrens better than any adversary and who could not be detected before he struck out of the dark, and could not be caught when he galloped away.

Marion withdrew northward, across the sandy scrubland called Blue Savannah, where he'd won a skirmish before Edward and Poorly joined him. Farther north they camped at Amis's Mill on Drowning Creek. There, one of the dispatch riders who carried messages to and from General Gates brought word of a stunning victory. In early October nine hundred mounted Americans had caught Maj. Patrick Ferguson atop Kings Mountain with a thousand provincials and militia. Ferguson had been marching to join up with Cornwallis at Charlotte.

The Americans stormed the summit in the face of brutal fire. A chance shot killed Ferguson. Minutes later a white flag showed. Those not captured died as they ran. General Cornwallis abandoned Charlotte and turned south with Tarleton's dragoons riding ahead, in search of a winter base. The news buoyed spirits in Marion's little band.

Marion regularly sent pairs of scouts across the countryside to hunt for the enemy, whether British or American. Toward the middle of October, from a camp above the Black River, he ordered Edward and Poorly to ride northwest, in response to reports that Cornwallis was marching toward Winnsboro. They were to travel as far as they could in two days, then turn back. Marion would advance to meet them late on the third day.

The first morning passed without incident. The two scouts saw nothing more alarming than half a dozen red-coated vedettes resting horses at a plantation flying a huge Union Jack. The second day was equally uneventful, although a large dust cloud floated on the horizon west of them, toward Wateree Pond. By midafternoon Edward knew they couldn't find the source of the cloud by evening. They would retreat as ordered.

Poorly caught and roasted a wild pig for supper. They reclined on soft ground in a fragrant pine grove, warmed by a popping fatwood fire. Edward gazed into the flames and sang softly. "Drink to me only with thine eyes, and I will pledge with mine." Poorly sucked meat from a rib and cocked an eyebrow.

"Don't think I ever heard you sing before, Mr. Edward."

Edward flushed. "It's a pretty tune. Popular in London."

"That's all there is to it, uh." Poorly didn't pose it as a question but a statement. He was well acquainted with Joanna but didn't know what place she had in Edward's thoughts. Edward didn't inform him.

☆   ☆   ☆

Next morning they set out to the southwest to rejoin Marion. In the sand hills they traversed, they twice crossed the trail of a small group of riders. Edward kept his pistols loaded and primed. The sky was a deep clear blue, the air crisp and bracing after days of soggy humidity. He felt vigorous, alert. Worth something again.

By late in the day his concern for the unseen horsemen eased. He was beginning to think they'd end the mission without danger when Poorly trotted out of sight on the far side of a scrub-covered hill. A moment later he let out a fearsome yell. "Yellow jackets." Edward booted Brown Eyes. He heard the alarmed neighing of Poorly's horse.

He burst over the crest to see Poorly's mount floundering on its side and Poorly himself unhorsed, backing away from a hundred angry yellow jackets rising from a cavity in the hillside. Poorly covered his face with his arms, but it was a feeble defense. The yellow jackets stung and stung, raising welts on Poorly's face even as he shouted and flailed. Edward yanked out a pistol and fired at the nest, thinking it foolish the moment he did it. The shot boomed and echoed across the hills.

Not watching his footing, Poorly retreated down the sandy slope. One leg twisted under him; he tumbled. Edward rode to the bottom, well clear of the angry insects. "Wounds of Jesus," he said when he saw Poorly's right boot turned out at an extreme angle.

He jumped from the saddle, knelt by his slave. Poorly rose on one elbow, grimaced; his face was a mass of swollen stings. The base of the sand hill was already in shadow. Edward was aware of the lonely countryside, the lack of human habitation. He had no maps.

"Can you move your foot?"

"Try," Poorly gasped. The slight effort only produced more pain. "I think she's broke, Mr. Edward. Didn't see those damn bees 'fore I rode into the nest and riled them."

"We can't linger here. You need a doctor. I'll lift you. Don't put weight on that foot."

Poorly's arm hooked around Edward's neck. "Sally's baby grows up, asks me 'f I fought in this here war, this child will say, 'Oh, yes, I fought yellow jackets an' they brought me down.' "

"Be quiet and hang on. Where'd your horse get to?"

Behind them, on the hill crest, someone said, "Right here she is, sir."

There were three of them, scrofulous men on lathered mounts. With all the excitement he hadn't heard them approach. One had a Kentucky pistol aimed at him. Another held the bridle of Poorly's horse. Edward took in their beards and ragged clothes and rendered his gloomy verdict: partisans.

"My slave is hurt. He's in need of attention."

"We'll see what the captain says about that," said the man with the pistol. He craned around in the saddle. "Sir?"

A fourth horseman loomed against the deep blue sky. "Stab me, is that an old acquaintance?" Edward's gut heaved. No mistaking the wandering eye, the paunch, the high forehead, the gray-streaked hair tied with a ribbon.

"Why, yes, indeed, it's Mr. Bell of Malvern Plantation," said William Lark.

17

Poorly's Name

Captain Lark trotted to the bottom of the sand hill and dismounted. With his fists jammed on his hips, he studied Edward and Poorly. The man smelled like a barn. His loose white shirt was gray with dirt. A waistcoat of light-blue satin bore streaks of rust or dried blood. A metal cartridge box painted bright red hung on his belt.

"Slowly, slowly," he advised as Edward got up. Two of Lark's men ran down the hill to back up their captain. Their pistols pointed at Edward.

"Far from home, aren't you, Mr. Bell? Surely not a journey for pleasure, not in these times. Are you one of Sumter's boys? Or is it that pious shit Marion?"

Edward stared, defiantly silent. Lark's eye rolled toward his nose, then back again. Color in his stubbled cheeks hinted at anger, but he kept a stiff smile. "Either way, it's my obligation to reduce the enemy by two. My duty as a military officer."

"Does military duty include permitting your men to rape young women?"

Lark flayed Edward's cheek with the back of his hand. "Curb your tongue. I owe you no explanations. You gave me a wound that was a long time healing." He touched his left leg.

"It wasn't enough to pay you for murdering my mother."

Lark dismissed the accusation with a shrug. "Fortunes of war. You resisted."

Edward shouted at him. "Damn you, are we going to stand here while this man suffers? He's badly hurt."

"I am not blind, laddie. I see his crooked foot."

"Then help him."

Twilight was settling. A breeze blew across the hills. Loose strands of gray hair fluttered around Lark's ears. "Happy to oblige. We'll send him to meet his Heavenly Father posthaste."

Edward lunged. Lark's men rushed to seize him, clubbed him with pistol butts. One man rammed his knee into Edward's crotch; the other man's weapon whacked the back of his head. On his knees, Edward pushed at the ground to keep from keeling over sideways.

Lark opened his red box, removed a paper cartridge and ball marked with a black dot. When he'd loaded the cartridge and used the rammer, he found something else in the box; held it out for inspection. Edward thought it an ordinary ball until he saw two deep knife marks partially quartering the sphere of lead.

"Recognize this, Mr. Bell?"

"Those are outlawed by both armies." Balls partly halved or quartered did inhumane damage if fired at close range. Even worse was a ball with a small nail driven through.

"I answer to no one but myself, sir." Despite the pistol pressed against the back of his head, Edward stood up. "Hold him, hold him," Lark exclaimed. "I see I must make short work of this."

The lookout on the hill waved in an agitated way. Lark didn't notice. Standing astride Poorly's legs, he fired the pistol into Poorly's stomach.

Poorly's spine arched. His outcry tore across the empty hills and sky. Black hands turned red where they pressed against a smoking hole in his shirt. Lark reached into his cartridge box again. "I've reserved another for you," he said to Edward. Then he noticed the alarmed look of one of his men. The man bobbed his head toward the hill, called out:

"Twenty, thirty on horseback, coming fast."

Marion? Hope ran through Edward like a dizzying draft of spirits. He shot his elbows backward into the bellies of his guards. When one fired his pistol, Edward was already running away from it; the shot missed.

He dashed into a palmetto thicket as the second man fired. He dived for the ground and heard the ball buzz by. Lying on his side, ear in the sand, he detected the throbbing rhythm of horses at the gallop.

Captain Lark was furious but had the sense to retreat. Halfway up the slope he screamed at Edward. "Another time, lad, count on that. The war has a long way to run."

Then he was in the saddle and wheeling away. He and his men disappeared below the hill. Edward swept hair out of his eyes and hurried back to Poorly, who lay unmoving.

Five minutes later Francis Marion arrived with thirty riders. Edward shouted to warn them of the nest of yellow jackets but few heard him. Four men were badly stung.

☆ ☆ ☆

When Marion saw Poorly's condition, he ordered camp to be pitched on the other side of the sand hill where Lark had appeared, thus affording Edward a measure of privacy with his dying slave. Edward built a small fire and sat beside Poorly; bathed his forehead with water and vinegar from his canteen. The quartered ball had torn Poorly's vitals. He moaned occasionally. When at last he opened his eyes, he gazed at Edward in a vacant way. "We in Charleston?"

"No, but we'll get you back there soon."

"Don't think so, Mr. Edward. Can you"—his tongue moistened his dry lips—"can you lean down closer?"

Edward obliged. Poorly whispered, "Need to ask a boon. This child's bound for his reward, whatever it may be. Look after Sally, and the baby."

Edward slipped his hand into Poorly's, bloodying his fingers. "Of course I will."

"I know she'll have a boy baby. Change his name. No more Poorly. I earned it being such a sickly child, but I never liked it. Isn't strong. Been thinking how to ask you."

"I promise we'll give him a new name."

"A good one."

A sudden thought. "Why not call him Strong? What's wrong with that?"

"Nothing wrong. I like that fine."

"He'll need a first name."

Poorly coughed hard; more blood soaked his shirt. "Always liked Bible names. Joshua. Amos. Oh, Hamnet too. I like Hamnet real well."

Edward squeezed the red hand. "Done. And something else. I'll set him free. I'll write the paper the moment I'm home. And one for Sally." Poorly's eyes closed. "Did you hear what I said? Your wife and son will be free people."

Voices drifted from Marion's campfires. Someone laughed. A sentry imitated a nightjar's call; another sentry answered.

"Poorly?"

A rising full moon cast brilliant light on Poorly's face. The black hand slipped from Edward's. He turned away, unable to hold back tears.

Some minutes later he crossed the moon-silvered hill, to find Colonel Marion seated beside the largest of several fires. When Marion's men saw Edward's hands, talking ceased. The colonel stood as Edward approached.

"He's gone."

"I'm mightily sorry, Edward. Poorly was a brave soldier. He served our cause well. I know you regarded him highly."

"He was the finest."

"Did he suffer?"

"Yes."

"I have never met William Lark, but I know his reputation for cruelty. Men like that sometimes escape judgment on earth, but they are always judged in heaven."

"I'd like to see the bastard hung, drawn, and quartered."

Marion put a calming hand on Edward's arm. "We'll give Poorly the Christian burial he deserves. I have a Bible. I also travel with a flask of rum for emergencies. It's time I broke my rule and allowed you a drink. Wait here."

He left Edward standing in the moonlight with red hands and haunted eyes. Marion's men sat silent, not knowing what to say.

18

The Year of the Damned Old Fox

Francis Marion's legend grew from that war-torn autumn.

In late October, at Tearcoat Swamp, he attacked Tory militia commanded by Col. Samuel Tynes. The Tories were newly equipped and overly confident, drinking and gaming noisily into the night while Marion's men lurked in the darkness, waiting.

At midnight Marion fired a pistol; Edward and his comrades charged the encampment, shooting and yelling. Again Marion left a path of retreat open; Tynes used it to escape. Marion's men counted eighty fine horses and eighty muskets captured.

After Black Mingo and Tearcoat Swamp volunteers poured in. Marion soon had four hundred men. These he took to the High Hills of the Santee, to harry enemy traffic at Nelson's Ferry on the Congaree. His presence had a profound effect. Teamsters feared to travel from Charleston to the inland forts. The British had to deploy large detachments to guard the supply trains.

Unknown to Marion himself Lord Cornwallis was taking notice of the upstart colonel whose name he'd been unable to remember a month before. Cornwallis ordered Banastre Tarleton's Legion to pursue Marion and end his depredations. On November 7 Tarleton, his dragoons, and two cannon lay in wait at the plantation of the late Gen. Richard Richardson.

Marion advanced to within sight of ruddy clouds reflecting campfires hidden by heavy woods. While he was pondering strategy, the widow Richardson sent her son, a paroled Continental officer, to warn of the superior numbers waiting in ambush.

Marion turned aside, galloped to the head of Jack's Creek, then down along the Pocotaligo River through harvested fields and dense pine forests. Tarleton chased him for seven hours. Then, confronted by a trackless bog near Ox Swamp, he gave up, announcing that he would go after Gen. Thomas Sumter's militia brigade instead. Weeks later an express rider brought Marion word of what Tarleton said after making his decision:

"As for that damned old fox Marion, the devil himself couldn't catch him."

The anecdote might have been amusing if it hadn't been accompanied by an account of Tarleton's retreat. He burned over thirty houses, and corncribs full of precious winter food. At the Richardson plantation he ordered the general's body dug up, punishment for Mrs. Richardson's alarm to Marion. He demanded a lavish dinner and left the general's rotting body beside the desecrated grave while he dined. Before he rode away, his men herded Richardson cattle, pigs, and chickens into a barn, locked it, and burned the animals alive.

"The man who threw the torch was your old friend Venables," Marion told Edward.

☆ ☆ ☆

Revenge became Edward's obsession. It flowed in every vein and tinctured every thought like a poison. He soon learned that his commander had no tolerance for personal vendettas. Marion sent a small detachment to stop the slaughter of cattle at the farm of a prominent Whig. The party included a recent recruit, Lt. Gabriel Marion.

British soldiers surprised and caught the Americans. Someone identified Gabriel as the colonel's nephew. Someone else fetched a musket loaded with buckshot, put it against Gabriel's chest, and fired.

The others managed to escape. Next day a patrol captured a mulatto who admitted he belonged to a Tory master. At the nightly campfire a sergeant walked up to the mulatto, shoved a pistol in his ear, and blew half his head away. Marion could barely control his fury. "Why did you do it?"

"For your nephew, Colonel. For Gabriel."

"Gabriel's gone. Another murder won't bring him back. They may be animals, but we are not. There will be no such action in this company ever again." To Major Horry he said, "Chain that man's wrists. When we move out tomorrow, he walks. No food or water until I say so. This lesson will not be forgotten."

Edward hid his passion for vengeance.

☆ ☆ ☆

In the late autumn they went to ground on Snow's Island, a low ridge of land five miles long and two miles wide, bounded by the Pee Dee, the Lynches, and Clark's Creek, a virtual moat surrounded by swamps and pine forests. It was a haven safer than most.

December brought a change of command in the South. One of Washington's most trusted officers, Gen. Nathaniel Greene, relieved Horatio Gates. Greene, not yet forty, was a Quaker from Warwick, Rhode Island. He took command of three thousand Continentals who faced at least four thousand of the enemy in the Carolinas.

Greene's first letter to Marion praised the colonel's reputation and hoped for an early meeting. Meanwhile, to bolster Marion's command, he dispatched Lt. Col. Henry Lee of Virginia. Light Horse Harry arrived with his men impeccably clad in smart green coats, spotless white breeches, and shiny brass helmets crowned with horsehair plumes.

Lee and Marion sat under a live oak dining on hominy and corn bread. Lee was clean and manicured, his wig properly powdered. Marion's red jacket showed months of hard wear. His boots were scuffed, his neckcloth grimy. As Edward observed the colloquy from a distance, however, it seemed to him that Lee and Marion got on splendidly. Each recognized the other as an accomplished soldier.

A courier arrived on New Year's day 1781 with another express from Greene, promoting Marion to brigadier. A great celebration followed. Rum appeared surreptitiously, obtained from unknown sources in the neighborhood. That day drinking was not punished.

☆ ☆ ☆

Edward rode on into a stormy and eventful year. In January, with barges, canoes, and piraguas spirited to Snow's Island by sympathetic country folk, Lee and Marion launched a waterway attack on Georgetown. It failed, but they captured the British commandant.

After each sortie Marion slipped back to Snow's Island. Lieutenant Colonel John Watson, five hundred loyalists, and a full British regiment moved against the base in March. Marion ordered all supplies burned before his company of seven hundred broke camp. After a sharp engagement at Wiboo Swamp on the Santee, Marion allowed Watson to send two wagons of wounded to Georgetown without harassment.

April took them to Fort Watson at Scott's Lake. The fort had a high, almost impregnable palisade. They overcame it by erecting a forty-foot tower made of swamp lumber. They built it at night, by stealth, and in the morning Edward was one of the marksmen who scrambled up ladders to the protected platform on top. He looked down the muzzle of his Brown Bess into the fort's central compound. Small red figures scurried about in panic. On command he fired, dropping one of them. Conquered from the sky as it were, Fort Watson surrendered.

Edward knew many men in the company, but he had no close friends. He was a private and solemn person, usually spending the evening staring at the fire and brooding about Venables and Lark. Or Joanna. He wanted to see her, see whether he could find a life with her after the war. But that had to wait.

Nathaniel Greene won no stunning victories, yet he exhausted the British with his ferocious fighting when he engaged. After Guilford Court House, Hobkirk's Hill, Eutaw Springs in early September, Greene was in a position to advance toward the coast. A farmer's wife Edward met on patrol said joyfully, "There's a new motto in South Carolina. 'Soon everything will be Greene down to Moncks Corner.' "

Eutaw Springs proved to be the last battle of consequence. Shortly afterward Marion announced that militia under his command would be released to go home after a year's hard service. Edward hired a farmer's boy to carry a letter into Charleston, asking Joanna whether she could leave the city safely, and if so, would she meet him on the first of November at Malvern?

In late October he said good-bye to the general whose fame had spread to all the great cities of the North. Exploits of the "Swamp Fox," true or otherwise, were regularly presented in the papers. Marion might be less important than General Washington, but throughout the North he was more celebrated, colorful, and mysterious, galloping in and out of Carolina's gloomy swamps to strike and confound the enemy.

Edward rode down to the coast on Brown Eyes, a ragged blanket wrapped around himself. At a roadside dramhouse he heard great news from Virginia. Cornwallis and his army had surrendered at Yorktown on October 19; his musicians had ironically mocked the defeat by playing a familiar British air, "The World Turn'd Upside Down."

"And across the York, at Gloucester," said a little button-eyed tailor at the blazing hearth, "that rogue Tarleton gave up with a thousand men. He feared for his life, so he threw himself on the mercies of Count de Rochambeau. The count protected him but would have nothing to do with him personally. My cousin wrote that General Washington invited Lord Cornwallis and his officers to dine but would not invite Tarleton."

Edward's fingers closed around his tankard. "I knew a Major Venables in Tarleton's Legion. Any word of him?"

"Never heard of him, sir. However, the senior officers will sail to New York and after that, I suppose, hie off to England to enumerate a thousand reasons for their defeat." Edward remembered Marion's little homily on life's unfairness and the certainty of ultimate judgment. It didn't help.

He approached Malvern on a golden afternoon that spoke of summer more than autumn. Saddle sore, he dismounted near the weedy rubble lying untouched since the fire. Birds chattered; the river sparkled. The lawn was sere from summer drought. He'd passed slaves working the indigo fields again. He saw no sign of Joanna.

"We'll wait till morning," he said to Brown Eyes, rubbing her flank affectionately. He heard a horse whicker in a palmetto grove near the riverbank. He spied a small, sturdy marsh tacky, and then its rider.

He flung off the stinking blanket, vaulted over black timbers and stonework, and ran down the lawn, full of such strong emotion, he felt like a drunken man. He nearly crashed into her, whipping his arms around her waist, lifting and whirling her, feeling her warmth, her youth and strength.

Her hair flew against his face. She laughed and let herself be whirled again and again. Finally he set her down beside the purling river. He touched her face as though unable to believe its reality. Tears came to her brown eyes while she clung to him. "Oh, Edward. How tired you look. And how wonderful."

He pulled her to him more roughly than he intended, desperate to kiss her, feel affection to counter the dark pus of hatred. She opened her lips and touched his tongue with hers. Before he knew it he'd carried her farther down the bank, scaring a white egret into graceful flight. She reclined on her back while his hand worked at her skirt. Her hands came up to his chest, holding him away.

"Only if you love me, Edward."

"I do. Today and forever. All these months away from you made me know that."

She lowered her hands, smiling.

✷ ✷ ✷

She was astonishingly ardent for a sheltered young woman, yet maintained that she was inexperienced until this very day on the bank of the Cooper. Dressed again, she helped him build a small fire near the ruined house. "There's a great deal of news to relate."

"Tell me. I heard nothing while I was galloping hither and yon with the old fox."

"Early in August, Colonel Isaac Hayne was hung for violating his parole and taking up arms. The British thought his death would send a warning. Instead it roused the wrath of the city like nothing else before."

"My father knew Hayne. He signed his parole only so he could leave Charleston to help his family. There was smallpox at their country home. What else?"

"Mr. Henry Laurens was apprehended on the high seas near Newfoundland in September, en route to the Netherlands. He and"—hesitation—"many of the exiles were sent from Florida to Philadelphia. Laurens sailed from there. He's locked up in the Tower of London accused of high treason. Dr. Benjamin Franklin is waging a vigorous campaign for his exchange."

She tucked a stray lock of hair behind her ear. "Sally's baby boy is fine and healthy, awaiting a name. Do let Poorly know."

"I can't." He told her about the killing, and Poorly's wish that his boy be called Hamnet Strong.

Joanna gazed at the river. "I seem to have nothing but bad news for this reunion." He waited. "In May your brother married Miss Glass at St. Michael's."

Edward felt a stab of hatred but he said, "It's no concern of mine. They'll find themselves on the wrong side again."

"The British show every intention of remaining in Charleston for a while."

"It won't be forever. Anything else?"

"Yes, Edward, and the worst, I fear. Your father—" She stopped. He gripped her hand. Her colorless lips showed he was hurting her. He let go, feeling the lub of his heart in his chest.

"While in the St. Augustine dungeons your father succumbed. Late March, it was. The formal report said it was self-induced starvation." *Or the special attention requested by Venables?* "They buried him in Florida," she said.

Edward's voice was wrathful. "My mother was shot down in this very place because of me. My father died in exile because of me. Sally is widowed and the boy orphaned because of me. Who's next?" Deep-socketed eyes held hers. "You might do better to stay away from me lest something happen to you."

"Stay away?" She kissed him. "Not in a million, million years, my love. We're going to have a long and happy life together."

He stared at the first faint stars, saying nothing.

She tried to be cheerful. "Will you ride back to Charleston with me? There's hardly a guard presence anymore. People come and go freely."

"I'll come in a few days. I have one more task."

☆ ☆ ☆

The small farmhouse faced the Sampit River, a few miles below Georgetown. Sweet woodsmoke threaded from the chimney into blue autumn dusk. After his supper William Lark carried a lantern outside and crossed the yard. It was possible to observe him through a cracked window in the barn.

A rusty hinge squealed as Lark entered. Two horses neighed. It had been hell's own task to sneak in and keep them quiet.

Lark smelled of beer. He petted the muzzle of a big gray, murmured endearments. Edward rose in the empty stall behind Lark, laid his pistol on his left elbow to steady it.

The horses stamped and snorted. Lark turned around. All he could say was "How did you find me?"

"Many people know where you live. I tracked you here a week ago. I've been planning this moment for a long time."

Lark's bravado deserted him; he knew what was coming when he looked into the eyes of the filthy scarecrow with the pistol. A tremor in his hand shook the lantern. Edward said, "Put it down."

Lark obeyed.

"See here, lad. I've never borne you a grudge. We do what we must in wartime."

"No, with you it went beyond that."

"If this is all about your slave, what's the concern? He was just a common nigger."

"He was an uncommonly good man. He was my friend since childhood. There is also the matter of my mother." Edward cocked the pistol. "Do you have any other last words?"

Bloody Bill Lark was reduced to mumbling fright. A dark stain spread at the crotch of his breeches. "I appeal to your decency. I have a family."

"So did my slave."

"My wife, Bridgit, my new little boy, Crittenden—oh, if you saw him, you'd love him—they depend on me."

"They'll have to find someone else," Edward said, and shot him in the stomach.

While the horses reared and kicked the stalls, he pulled his other pistol. Lark was on his knees, weeping and clutching himself. Edward put the second ball in his chest.

He coughed in the powder smoke as he slipped out. A woman rushed from the house, calling, "Bill? *Bill?*" Edward untied Brown Eyes from a willow branch and rode away in the night.

★　★　★

He rode slowly down Meeting Street, looking every bit the ragpicker. He was twenty-three years old and felt ten times that.

A clock in a shop window showed him it was nearly three in the afternoon. At the corner of Broad he waited, gazing upward, but the hour came and went in silence.

He touched Brown Eyes with his heels and approached a knife grinder wheeling his cart beside the footpath. "Doesn't St. Michael's ring the hours anymore?"

"You must have been away, young man. Major Traille of the Royal Artillery took down the bells. Spoils of war. The British lost, but they will make us pay for winning."

19

The List

Although troops of the Crown still controlled Charleston, commanded by the noxious Balfour and Lord Cornwallis's replacement, Gen. Alexander Leslie, the rest of South Carolina belonged to the Americans. Redcoats in the city still tended to swagger, but abuse of civilians declined noticeably. The Board of Police pursued its duties with less zeal and thoroughness. The occupying forces surely would leave after negotiating with Nathaniel Greene, though no one knew when.

Tory sympathizers made themselves less visible. Edward's brother and his new wife stayed close to the white frame house they'd purchased, two and a half stories of Georgian elegance on Legare Street. Edward grudgingly sent a wedding gift, a beautiful swan made of glass on the island of Murano in the Venetian lagoon. He'd bought it from the master of an Italian schooner, one of the first European ships to dock at Bell's Bridge when the hurricane season ended and the December-to-March trading season began. Vessels from England called only to supply the garrison. Charleston was, realistically, an American port.

Lydia wrote a cool note of thanks for the gift, closing, *We would be glad to receive you at your convenience. I am most sorrowful over your father's death, as is my husband. We remain, we sincerely hope, objects of your deep familial affection.*

A little too personal and pointed, that last line, he thought. Or was he inventing hidden meaning to flatter himself? No matter; she was out of his life. She was an old wound that Joanna's love would heal.

Christmas Eve was a blustery warm day. Edward and Esau Willing walked to the end of Bell's Bridge at the close of business. Edward's eyes ached from adding numbers and studying bills of lading. Esau carried biscuits in his pocket. He tossed pieces in the water; soon they had a great cloud of black-headed gulls wheeling and diving and squabbling over the floating morsels.

"I am thrilled that you and Joanna will marry," Esau said.

Edward rubbed his aching left leg. "After the soldiers leave and life's normal again." As if it could be with Lark's blood on his hands and both parents casualties of the savage war. "Meanwhile I'm trying to learn the business. One day I may want rooms on Broad Street for a legal practice, but for now my place is here."

"I wish we had better records. Your father carried off the ledgers before the city surrendered. I have no idea where he took them."

"They're at the house. He buried them in our garden to hide them from the British. I dug up the iron box myself."

"Excellent, that's heartening news." Esau's gray locks tossed in the ocean breeze. "I am sixty-four years old, Edward. I will not want to keep at this work forever."

"Understood. When you decide to leave, we'll remove the cages. And commencing immediately, we'll receive no more black cargoes. When the slave trade resumes, plenty of wharf owners will be eager to take our place."

Esau's face showed an initial negative reaction, but a smile smoothed away his frown. "This is my daughter's work."

"But my decision."

"If it's all the same, let's tear down the cages immediately. I lost that battle with Joanna long ago. She is a strong-willed woman, as you'll discover."

"I already have. It's one of her fine characteristics, if not exactly a restful one."

Both were able to smile at that. Arm-in-arm they walked back to the office to drink a Christmas toddy.

✷ ✷ ✷

On the last day of December the gates of the Tower of London opened and Henry Laurens of Charleston walked out, free to travel to Paris to negotiate a peace treaty in company with Mr. Adams, Mr. Jay, and Dr. Franklin. Half a world away Edward wrote a deed of manu-mission for Sally Strong and her son, Hamnet. Sally was joyful at hav-ing a last name. Edward promised her something else:

"A place in my household, at fair wages, for as long as you want it. When you don't, you may leave. You're a free person, Sally."

"Takes some getting used to," Sally said as Edward dandled her gur-gling beige-colored infant on his knee. "Feels mighty wonderful, though."

✯   ✯   ✯

At Epiphany, Edward's morning was spent attending worship service at St. Michael's, sans bells. The rector informed him that the British would soon ship the bells to New York. He showed Edward a memo-rial from the vestry, addressed to the perpetrator of the theft, and that gentleman's punctilious reply:

> *I can assure you I am not Possessed of any "private property" such as you Describe. I trust you will do me the the justice to be-lieve that, in the matter of the Bells, I have not been actuated by Avarice, but solely by a desire to assert that Prerogative which our Corps has always maintained at Towns or Garrisons con-quered from the Enemy.*
>
> > *I have the honour to be*
> > *Yours faithfully,*
> > *P. Traille*
> > *Commandg. 3d Batt.*
> > *Royal Artill'y.*

In the afternoon Edward presented small wooden boxes of money to all the Negroes at home and at Bell's Bridge. Captain Marburg was off duty, so Edward invited him to Tom Bell's office for a mug of bumbo, a potent punch concocted of rum, sugar, and water.

Though Marburg was a Jew, he had a liberal spirit about the Chris-tian holidays. He described the German custom of bringing a tree into the house and decorating it for Christmas. Edward had never heard of such.

He told Marburg of his decision about the cages, and the reason for it. The Hessian said, "A principled woman, Fraulein Joanna. Where did she come by it?"

"Her mother. German, like you. In Joanna's words, the woman had a conscience of steel. Read the Bible constantly. The Old Testament prophets were her heroes. She died when I was about ten, and frankly I can't even remember the sound of her voice. She was shy with outsiders. I do recall she spoke with an accent."

"Heavy as mine?"

"Heavier."

"And she disliked slavery?"

"She loathed it. She told Joanna it promoted godless behavior because it gave the owner the right to take slave women to bed, no permission needed. It's still true. The masters sire bastards and then treat them as step-asides."

"I do not know that term."

"It means the child of a master who steps aside from responsibility. Never acknowledges his illegitimate son or daughter."

Marburg reflected a moment. "If you and Fraulein Joanna raise children, this strong lady may give them a gift that is sometimes unwelcome and almost always vexing."

"What's that?"

"A conscience," Marburg said.

★　★　★

Governor John Rutledge, soon to retire, called for a special legislative assembly at Jacksonboro, thirty-six miles south of Charleston. The selection of delegates surprised no one: thirty of the sixty-three St. Augustine prisoners were chosen, including Mr. Gadsden and the governor's brother, Edward Rutledge. General Marion and General Sumter were among those representing the military.

A vindictive spirit prevailed in the Jacksonboro assembly. Under a confiscation act that it passed, 239 loyalist estates were taken from their owners. Another forty-seven were amerced at twelve percent of assessed value; these estates belonged to those deemed lesser offenders.

Charleston's *Royal Gazette* published the list of forfeited properties, together with a fiery denunciation of the assembly. *This mock government has enacted ruinous and impolitic measures solely to disburse plunder to its members, buffoons and criminals who dare to sit in judgment of their betters.* Edward wasn't surprised to find Adrian's name on the confiscation list.

Lydia called on him at Bell's Bridge one afternoon in March. Her husband's Tory prosperity was evident in the closed coach with an ostentatious quartet of horses; before the surrender Adrian had run about in a modest chaise. The coach's enameled door panels bore a new crest incorporating golden bells and a Latin motto.

Lydia's arrival caught Edward by surprise. He'd been helping to unload a lighter from a Belgian trader anchored in the harbor, and he smelled like it.

"Edward dearest," Lydia trilled as she swept to the office door ahead of him, a picture of petite beauty. She removed a green silk mask she wore to protect her skin from the bright sun. "You haven't called on us."

"That's right, I have not."

"You haven't even kissed the bride." The sight of her still stirred him. His weakness made him angry.

In the office he nervously shifted papers and an inkhorn on the desk. "Please take my chair. I'm sorry there's only one." He positioned it for her.

She arranged her skirts and settled gracefully. He lit a strong green cigar to cover the awkward moment; the smoke barely masked the stink of his sweat. "Really, my dear," she said, "you must visit our new home. It's grand."

"I've seen it from the outside and I agree."

"Everyone knows you served with the old Swamp Fox last year. Was there great danger?"

"There was some. I survived."

"Adrian heard you freed a slave. That won't enhance your popularity in Charleston."

"I didn't do it for popularity. I don't mean to be rude, Lydia—"

"But you are," she broke in, her blue eyes afire. "Rude, cold—not at all cordial as a brother-in-law should be. I've come on a most important mission."

He guessed its nature. "Something to do with land?"

"Yes, yes, the terrible crime of the Jacksonboro men. Prosperity Hall is to be taken away from Adrian. It's damned unfair," she exclaimed, color in her cheeks. Polite ladies didn't use such language, at least not in the presence of gentlemen.

"You may find it unfair, but it should hardly be a surprise. Adrian belongs to an exclusive club."

"Club? What club?"

"Those who congratulated Clinton and Cornwallis. The memorials addressed to them when the city fell haven't been forgotten or forgiven."

"But can't they be? Can't Prosperity Hall be stricken from the list? That's why I'm here, to plead with you to intervene."

"Why didn't Adrian come personally?"

"He's afraid of you. It's true, Edward. He knows how bravely you fought, facing danger, and Colonel Hayne's fate if you were caught. You've always outshone Adrian in matters of courage." She glided to him, trapping him in a corner. "Don't you know that's one more reason I think about you constantly?" She stood close, her yellow hair teasing his chin. "I do, dearest. I dream of you even when Adrian's in my bed and we're—"

"For God's sake, Lydia. Have you no decency?" He seized her wrist, drove her hand down. "I told you I'd never cuckold Adrian. I meant it."

"I don't believe you." On tiptoe she kissed him ardently. She pushed his hand against her breast. "You know I'm lively in bed, that I'll do anything you ask."

"But now you've set a price for those favors? Removal of Adrian's name from the list?"

"Is it so much to ask? He's your brother."

"He truckled to the enemy."

"Please, Edward. Speak to Gadsden. Have you seen him?"

"Not yet. He traveled straight down to Jacksonboro from Georgetown. Even if I were willing to talk to him, which I'm not, it would do no good. Christopher put more names on the list than anyone else. I expect Adrian's was one of them. My brother turned his coat to save his land and, presumably, to keep you secure and happy at the end of your golden chain."

"You vile bastard." Her hand flew to the open inkhorn; she dashed ink on him, stinging his eyes, splattering his face, staining his shirt and waistcoat. Someone pounded on the door. One of the Negroes who worked on the wharf nervously asked if Mr. Edward was all right.

"I'm fine, Seth, nothing to worry about. Lydia, you must go." He'd forgotten her temper, the familiar bursts of wrath. Thank God she hadn't been within reach of hot coals, or a hand ax.

Strangely, she started to laugh. "What a sight you are. You look like a filthy nigger. It's appropriate, you have the soul of one. You'd probably murder me if you could."

Edward's face wrenched. With his thumb he wiped a spot of ink from her cheek. He smeared it on the bodice of her dress.

"Oh, you've ruined it."

"Adrian will replace it. Next time tell him not to send a woman to do his begging."

Lydia's rage dissolved into tears as she started for the door. "Oh, Edward, Edward. You hurt me so. How I wish to God I didn't love you."

Sunlight flashed in his eyes as she donned her mask and went out. He watched the coach clatter away toward the pierhead. He'd wash out the ink stains easily enough. The stain left in memory by the violent scene would be less easy to erase.

20

War's End

A month later Edward dined with Christopher Gadsden and his wife at Thomas Pike's. Ann Gadsden had followed her husband to Philadelphia when the British shipped him there from St. Augustine. Mrs. Gadsden and the lieutenant governor looked careworn. Edward asked Gadsden what he knew of Tom Bell's death.

"Very little. At Castillo de San Marcos they wanted us to give our paroles. Most did, but I did not. They clapped me into a *cárcel,* a dungeon with a dirt floor and no windows. There I stayed with my candles and my books. I saw no one but guards and was never allowed outside. Only on the ship to Philadelphia did I learn Tom's fate. He also would not give his parole, and was similarly imprisoned. He died in the dungeon, having refused food as a form of protest."

"I doubt they offered him food. I think a certain British officer conspired with the authorities to keep it from him."

"Yes, I heard that said. And now we're bowing and exchanging compliments with 'em as though they hadn't treated us like vermin." His wife took his hand to calm him. "No, Ann. The war's over for some, but not for me."

★ ★ ★

That kind of hatred growled beneath the surface of Charleston life in the spring of 1782. At Jacksonboro, Pocotaligo, and Georgetown, sales of confiscated estates netted a million pounds sterling. When summer came, terms for evacuation were still in limbo. General Leslie had no arrangement for the British to trade with farmers in the countryside, but it was necessary because of the large numbers of loyalists flooding in from all over the state. They came to the port wanting to leave the country on the first available ship.

Leslie dispatched men into the Low Country to forage for food; buy it if they could, steal it if they couldn't. In August, encountering one of these raiding parties at Tar Bluff on the Combahee, Henry Laurens's highly esteemed son, Col. John Laurens, died in what Nathaniel Greene called "a sad and paltry little skirmish."

That same month Leslie received orders to evacuate Charleston as soon as practicable. Greene's army advanced to the west bank of the Ashley while a new governor, John Mathews, negotiated terms of withdrawal. Leslie agreed to leave the city in good order, restore seized property—St. Michael's bells were conveniently overlooked—and return all slaves who hadn't run away to join the British. Mathews in turn pledged no additional confiscatory legislation, and no interference with collection of lawful debts. English merchants would be allowed to remain in Charleston for six months to recoup what was owed them.

"Goddamned lawyers," Gadsden raged to Edward. "Ought to hang them all." Two attorneys, Edward Rutledge and Benjamin Guerard, had assisted Mathews's negotiations. Both men were nominally patriots. "The terms are humbug. They favor the very men who did the least for our cause: planters who only care about exporting fall crops through the merchants and factors we so kindly allow to remain here. There will be bad blood for years."

✳   ✳   ✳

In September a British evacuation fleet sailed into the harbor. In the cool of an early October morning Marburg said to Edward, "We have orders. My regiment leaves on the twenty-seventh. All troops will be gone by December." The captain's round face turned toward the sunlit waves rolling in from the Atlantic. He seemed to gather his nerve before he spoke again. "I wish to stay."

Edward understood why Marburg had asked him to walk along the harbor near the house. This was a matter of utmost privacy, not to say illegality. He said, "You mean desert."

"I am aware of the nature of the deed, Mr. Edward. Also the price if I'm discovered."

"You really want to make Carolina your home?"

"I want to make Charleston my home. I have worshiped at Beth Elohim. The rabbi and the congregation made me welcome."

"In Germany you were a forester, then a soldier. What would you do here?"

"I would like to open a small bookshop, if I can raise the capital. A shop somewhat more American than that of Mr. Wells, who favored the Crown."

Edward lobbed a stick into a bleached oyster bed. He knew what Marburg wanted but waited for him to say it.

"Will you help me? I have no right to endanger you, but I trust no one else."

Edward felt somewhat put upon, but he liked Marburg, who had behaved decently while sharing the house. "Well," he said, thinking aloud, "we'd have to smuggle you out of the city in mufti. Hide you under a blanket in a cart. One of Esau's men can drive you to what's left of Malvern. You'll have to conceal yourself there until all the ships leave. When they come to question me, as they surely will, I can plead ignorance. You simply walked out of the house one night and never came back. I don't think they'll press hard. Their position's untenable."

Marburg's china-blue eyes welled with tears that he dashed away with embarrassment. "Mr. Edward, you are a true friend."

Edward smiled, deprecating the remark. "Get your kit together. We'll pull this off in the next day or so, before either of us changes his mind."

* * *

Marburg's desertion was accomplished without difficulty. Two officers, one English, one Hessian, came to the house. Their interrogation was short and perfunctory. Leaving, the Hessian said, "I never liked the little Jew. I hope a crocodile eats him while he cowers in the swamp. One day we'll rid Germany of all the dirty shit-eating killers of Christ."

* * *

Charleston hummed with preparations for the first evacuation. Embarkation would take place at Gadsden's Wharf; Mr. Gadsen savored the irony of that. The redcoats busily ransacked houses and packed up such plunder as they could steal. A few householders met the raiding squads with weapons, but for the most part owners stood aside in weary acquiescence.

Two days before the first departure, with a hard rain blowing off the ocean, Edward passed Adrian's house on Legare Street. Boards covered the windows. Black men carried trunks from the house to a canvas-topped Conestoga wagon. Lydia stood in the doorway, rain-spattered, bedraggled, and shrill. "Keep that trunk upright, my fine crystal's in there." She boxed the ears of the offending Negro. Edward saw a flash of hatred in his eyes.

He climbed the steps. "I didn't know you were leaving."

"Did you think we'd stay and let your vicious friends trample on us? Or worse?"

"What do you mean?"

"You don't know about Nigel Bezzard, the Liverpool merchant?" Edward said no. A figure loomed in the dark hall; Adrian, minus his wig. His head was a shaven ball of stubble. He carried a decanter of red wine and a goblet. Edward hadn't seen his brother in months. His sunken eyes and stooped posture saddened Edward. Adrian had the look of a whipped dog.

"Nigel Bezzard did business with the wrong people," Adrian said. "Someone put a dirk in his back. They found him in Beddon's Alley at daybreak yesterday."

"The war goes on. I wish it didn't," Edward said. "Where will you go?"

Adrian poured wine for himself. "East Florida. From there"—he shrugged—"it's immaterial, so long as I never see this accursed town again."

"You can petition the legislature to transfer Prosperity Hall to the amerced list. Pay the tax, now or in a year, and the plantation will be yours again."

Adrian sneered. "Pray tell me how I pay the tax without income from land? Even assuming the legislature would permit it? It's a game I can't win. You and your kind have beggared me."

Lydia cried, "We won't have our child born into such circum-stances."

"Your child—?"

"We'll make a new start, prosper somewhere else, you'll see." Her voice was high, strident. Adrian touched her arm.

"Go inside, Lydia. Dry yourself." She flung off his hand and disap-peared. Adrian noticed the four black men huddling by the wagon. "Stop staring. Do your work, you nigger trash."

The black men filed into the house, heads averted. Rain trickled down Edward's cheeks. "I am very sorry for all this, Adrian."

"The hell you are. You revel in it. Well, know this. In the Bible where family names are written, I've struck out yours. I no longer have a brother."

He drank his wine, threw the glass so it broke at Edward's feet. In the boarded-up house Lydia screamed like a termagant. Adrian stumbled and almost fell as he went in to join her.

* * *

On Sunday, October 27, Edward and Joanna stood among hundreds watching a greater number of loyalists, with their slaves and possessions, queuing up to board schooners and frigates moored at Gadsden's Wharf. Forty ships were scheduled to carry off more than three quarters of the occupying army, and more than three thousand refugees who were scattering to Halifax, Florida, Jamaica, St. Lucia, and the Bahamas. Edward and Joanna spied Lydia and Adrian in the crowd, bundled in cloaks too heavy for their destination in the tropics. Edward felt no sense of victory, only dismay.

On Saturday, December 14, the final units left the city, having stripped it of five thousand slaves, huge stocks of dried indigo, and goods from looted homes. The Americans came marching up King Street shortly after 11:00 A.M., led by a young general named Anthony Wayne.

General Leslie had ordered the citizens to stay indoors, conduct no partisan demonstrations, but as the last of the redcoats marched down Boundary Street to Gadsden's Wharf, small flags and bits of bunting appeared at windows on King Street. People of all ages spilled onto the footpaths.

At first they were quiet. Then they began to clap and stamp in rhythm with the fifes and drums serenading Charleston with "Yankee Doodle." Where Edward stood with his arm around Joanna, an old lady in a mobcap leaned from an upper window and waved a handkerchief at the soldiers. "God bless you, gentlemen. Welcome home, gentlemen." It grew to a chant, a roar that drowned the music. *"God bless you, gentlemen. Welcome home, gentlemen."*

Joanna pressed her cheek against Edward's shoulder. "Oh, I do think it's over at last."

"I believe so, yes." He spoke reflectively, without enthusiasm, because he wasn't sure. In the last month two more British merchants had been mysteriously murdered. He thought of his estranged brother, and the Larks, and all the grime and guilt left on him by the war. With time he hoped his dark feelings would pass, but he wasn't sanguine. He hugged Joanna. "Marburg can come back to town, anyway."

The chanting roared over them, waves of joyful noise. It was a day of triumph, but incomplete. St. Michael's steeple, painted white again, rang no bells in celebration.

21

1791

"There he is, Edgar, the President, do you see him? The tall man in the custom house barge? It's the biggest boat, with the American flag."

Edward was vastly more excited than the small boy riding on his shoulder in the midst of the crowd on East Bay. Edgar was six. He'd inherited his father's lanky build, his mother's round face and russet curls. Instead of being duly appreciative of the pomp and ceremony of this first Monday in May, he wriggled until he attracted the attention of the handsome ten-year-old who'd come with them to the foot of Queen Street. Poorly and Sally's son, Hamnet, had light-brown skin and a ready smile; only his black hair and full lips spoke of black parentage.

Edgar pulled out the corners of his mouth, a hideous face. Hamnet laughed and said, "Hush, you, I want to see General Washington."

"And sit still," Edward said with a firm hand on his son's leg. Edward was thirty-three now, beginning to thicken at the waist. Joanna kept a good kitchen.

Band music reached them from the nautical procession crossing the Cooper. Washington was in the midst of a ceremonial tour of the South. His retinue included a second boatload of musicians. Sailboats and rowboats, fifty or more, trailed the President's party. Spectators hung from windows, sat on roof peaks, filled the decks of vessels anchored in the river and tied up at piers. A few daring men and boys had climbed masts to watch from spars and rigging.

As the barge drew into Prioleau's Wharf, Edward read the words blazoned on it above the state seal. LONG LIVE THE PRESIDENT. Twelve navy captains in sky-blue jackets worked the oars, a thirteenth calling the stroke. Washington remained standing in the bow, a commanding man of fifty-nine years. He raised his cocked hat to acknowledge the crowd's ovation.

The wharf itself was closed off by an honor guard from the German Fusilier Company. City and state dignitaries waited at the landing stage. Edward recognized Governor Pinckney, South Carolina's two senators, and the intendant, Vanderhorst.

After the ceremonial welcome the fusiliers fired fifteen rounds in salute. Over the rooftops came the sweet familiar sound of St. Michael's bells. They'd been sold in London to the successor to the original foundry, where two broken bells had been recast. Then the entire peal was bought by a member of Parliament. That enterprising gentleman shipped the bells to Charleston in the autumn of 1783, expecting to receive a fine price from St. Michael's vestry. A subscription was undertaken but after eight years had raised little money. Paid for or not, the bells hung in their rightful place and serenaded the visiting President.

"I want to go home," Edgar announced.

"What, you don't want to follow the parade?"

The boy shook his head. Edward lowered him from an aching shoulder and clasped his hand. "Well, I do, so keep your peace."

Edgar pouted, but he knew better than to argue; his father was a disciplinarian. Hamnet put his arm around the boy's shoulder, said something that brought a giggle and immediate improvement of Edgar's spirits.

The sheriff, carrying the great mace of the city, led the parade to the Exchange at the eastern end of Broad Street. Local and state officials followed, including representatives of the city's thirteen wards. Hired scavengers had removed litter from the line of march, as well as dead dogs, cats, and rats, which typically lay rotting in the public ways. The air didn't smell too badly; cattle- and hogpens near East Bay had been emptied for the occasion.

Washington appeared briefly on the steps of the Exchange. Then, with his hosts and retinue, he set off on foot for his lodgings in the mansion of Judge Thomas Heyward on Church Street. So began Charleston's week of presidential jubilee. Edward's life came to a halt, as did the life of almost every prominent citizen.

Much had changed in Charleston since the war. The new nation had a new government and constitution. Four South Carolinians, men of property dedicated to the concept of a republic guided by aristocrats, had led and won the fight at the constitutional convention for extension of the slave trade until 1808.

By act of the state legislature South Carolina had a new capital, an upstart town on the Congaree in the scrubby hills of the midlands. A contest of names, Washington versus Columbia, had been won by the latter. Some state offices were still duplicated in Charleston, whose prideful citizens pretended that the other capital didn't exist.

The city had incorporated in 1783, officially doing away with older spellings of the name, as if to show that nothing tied it to the mother country except history. Charleston's chief executive, the intendant, governed with his thirteen wardens, white men who paid a substantial amount of tax for the privilege.

The city had grown. Population now stood somewhere above sixteen thousand, more than half black. Attractive homes lined the streets of the lower peninsula, but odious rookeries crowded too many sections, pouring their garbage and night soil into the open, until the earth itself reeked. Above Boundary Street, where the air was fresher, developers were confidently laying out new residential lots.

Fine new buildings abounded. A new State House at Broad and Meeting replaced the earlier one destroyed in a fire. A handsome four-story brick structure housed orphans and abandoned bastards, of which the city had a large supply.

A small and struggling college was educating a few students. There was a Catholic chapel, the city's first. A climate of tolerance still prevailed, except in matters of slave discipline.

In this atmosphere of growth and prosperity Edward conducted a part-time law practice in two rooms on Broad Street. On the wall behind his desk hung a large faux-bronze copy of the new city seal. His membership in the local Chamber of Commerce prompted this demonstration of civic pride. Adam Fleet, a free mulatto carpenter of Hard Work Alley, had carved and painted the seal. Fleet was the artisan to whom young Hamnet was apprenticed.

Moses Marburg had married a black-haired beauty named Sarah Levi. Sarah was the daughter of the local agent of the Amsterdam indigo merchants Edward had dealt with. Marburg had successfully made the transition from soldier to retailer. In 1786, with a loan from Edward, already repaid, he'd opened his small shop on King Street. Over the front door he hung a wooden sign saying simply MARBURG BOOKSELLER. A decoration in somber colors depicted a bearded scholar in a black skullcap seated with his lamp and book. Marburg was not one to hide his faith.

The port of Charleston still shipped tons of rice and indigo to the world, but cotton was a crop of rising importance. Edward had terminated the indigo leases at Malvern and put the land into long-staple sea island cotton. Upland farmers grew the short-staple variety, less hardy and more difficult and expensive to process and loom. It yielded a cloth less luxurious than the other. The upland cotton was produced and shipped, to be sure, but it was a stepchild in the trade.

Not necessarily forever, Edward's new wharf manager said. Simon Buckles, a devout Scots Presbyterian, twice had journeyed down to Georgia to inspect machinery designed by a man named Eli Whitney. If Whitney could perfect a gin to efficiently remove seeds from short-staple cotton, Buckles believed that segment of the market would explode. As it was, Charleston's cotton shipments were huge; over a million and a half pounds this year. A lot of it passed through Bell's Bridge.

The only commodity that did not was the one Edward had banned in 1782. By state law Charleston wharves no longer trafficked in imported slaves. A narrow margin of up-country votes controlled the legislature, and that section of the state opposed slavery. A 1787 law closed down the trade for three years. Friends of Edward's in the business community said the ban might be lifted if matters of profit and loss forced a change. Edward looked at the state's booming cotton crop and suspected that it might come to pass.

Buckles was a bluff, red-bearded man whose wife, Fiona, had given him nine children, all but the last born in Scotland. Simon was an enthusiast and an optimist, his only bad trait being a tendency to lard his speech with so many unfamiliar words from his native land that Edward often lost his temper, demanded a translation and even a special dictionary. It was Buckles and his fellow Scots of the South Carolina Golf Club who had introduced Edward to the curious and frustrating sport at Harleston's Green. Edward played when he could, but he didn't play well. He tended to swish by the feather-stuffed leather ball with the great wooden club head, cursing violently afterward.

Edward and Joanna moved comfortably in respected social circles. They attended balls in the winter social season, and sat through evenings of Mozart and Haydn organized by the St. Cecilia Society. Edward squirmed the whole time, but he did enjoy the traveling theatrical companies that played the new Harmony Hall on upper King Street. He had his own gentlemen's smoking and discussion club, the Fortnightly.

In 1787, with Bell's Bridge thriving, he'd rebuilt Malvern. It offered memories of his youth and a retreat from the epidemics, storms, and soggy heat of the summer. Joanna and Edgar loved the place.

It had taken a long time for Edward and Joanna to conceive a child. Edgar's birth had been hard. No other children blessed their house, so they lavished all their love on one. Joanna's father had gone to his rest in 1783, too soon to see his grandson.

In 1788 a letter from St. Lucia in the West Indies informed Edward that Adrian had died of Barbados fever.

He was but thirty-five, on the threshold of great success with the cultivation of cotton. Here, too, our infant daughter perished five years ago, at age three. Your brother and I would not have been exiled to this pestilential place were it not for you. I trust you do not sleep easy.

Lydia's outburst testified to an unsteady mind. Edward wrote her saying he'd arranged for Prosperity Hall to be transferred to the list of amerced lands.

No great hardship these days, as the strongest animosities of the late war are cooling.

Not hers, obviously.

I await your decision on whether you wish to pay the tax or sell the plantation. The question need not be settled quickly. Many properties remain in the same uncertain state, free of undue pressure for resolution.

He received no answer.

☆ ☆ ☆

The week was a whirl of civic and social activities. On Tuesday, Edward joined a delegation from the Chamber of Commerce to present compliments to the President at Heyward's mansion. That evening he attended a citizens' dinner in the Exchange while Joanna frantically sewed a gown for a ball the next night.

Wednesday, Washington toured the remains of the wartime fortifications, received a delegation from the Sons of Cincinnati and another from the Masonic order to which he belonged. For the ball the Exchange blazed with lanterns and a great transparency of the initials G. W. over the entrance. Edward wore his best suit of indigo-blue velvet. Joanna, whom he thought lovely in her peach-colored dress, had paid to have her hair done up and powdered. A spangled medallion bearing the words *Long Live the President* was pinned to the high pile.

"Isn't he a handsome man?" she whispered as the President moved gracefully among the guests, a striking figure in black velvet, white stockings, silver knee buckles, sword, and yellow gloves. Standing well over six feet, he never escaped notice in a crowd.

"I can't see anyone but you," Edward said. She laughed and teased his chin with her souvenir fan, on which a painted Goddess of Fame crowned Washington with a laurel wreath. The motto read *Magnus in Pace, Magnus in Bello.*

On it went—inspection of the harbor forts; a concert at the Exchange sponsored by the St. Cecilia Society (Edward writhed through more Haydn). Friday brought the capstone, another ball, with a much restricted guest list, at Governor Pinckney's mansion on lower Meeting Street.

The house was a fantasy of colored lanterns, music, sparkling wine, fashionable women, important men. The walled garden had been turned into an outdoor promenade, perfect for the mild spring evening. Here Edward encountered Adrian's friend Lescock, a vision of bright shoe buckles, gold frogging, and a tall peruke showering powder on his shoulders.

Lescock waved a lace handkerchief to catch Edward's eye. "Dear man, how is that Arabian horse you bought?"

Emboldened by wine, Edward said, "Faster than your mare, Archie." The new horse was pastured at Malvern with Brown Eyes, who was enjoying a peaceful old age.

"Is that so? We shall have to put that assertion to the test when the Jockey Club resumes its meetings."

"So long as there's a substantial wager on the outcome, I'm for it. I'll ride Prince Mahmoud myself."

"Brave boy," Lescock purred with a roll of his eyes. Like many in Charleston he still venerated the king and aped the court. Edward excused himself. Lescock fluttered his handkerchief. "I shall call you to account about that wager."

On Saturday, Washington visited the new Orphan House, then climbed to the belfry of St. Michael's for a view of the city and harbor islands from 186 feet in the air. The evening brought a final banquet, sponsored by town merchants. The President attended Sunday services at both St. Philip's and St. Michael's. The pews overflowed; Edward felt as though he was imprisoned in a clothes press.

Then it was over. Early Monday the great man and his party took the road for Savannah. Edward rose in a good mood, though he found himself belching and breaking wind as a consequence of all the rich food and fine wine consumed during the week. He could no longer roister as he had in the old days.

On a brisk walk from home to his law office, he focused on a complicated legal matter he was trying to unsnarl. It involved two sisters and their avaricious husbands. Both sisters claimed the family's original headright acreage in Saxe Gotha Township. Edward was mulling a compromise to propose when he accidentally collided with a woman in a mobcap that shadowed her garishly rouged face. He presumed she was just another of the drabs who solicited in public. "Beg pardon." He tipped his hat and hurried by.

"I know you." Her cry stopped him, swung him around. "Edward Bell."

"I'm afraid I can't reciprocate, madam. I'm sure we haven't met before."

She stepped closer. Along with the scent of cloves she was chewing, he got a whiff of rotten teeth. "Bridgit Lark's my name. I know it was you killed William."

"William . . . ?"

"My husband. I know it was you. He feared you would, because of military action he took against you."

Edward's stupefaction changed to ire. "Military action? Better to use the word *murder*."

"And you repaid it in kind." She spoke so loudly, people on the footpath stared.

Pierced by guilt, Edward replied awkwardly. "You've no proof of that, madam."

"I don't need any. I've taught my son to remember your name and what you did. You'll pay for killing my William, you and your tribe, don't think you won't."

And she was gone, leaving Edward speechless in the sunshine.

22

Tales of Terror

Admiration for all things French consumed the nation. Lafayette was venerated. Marburg sold many copies of *The Rights of Man,* Tom Paine's tract extolling the ideals of the French Revolution. Edward stayed up late reading it and next day asked Joanna to fashion a tricolor cockade. He pinned it to a new Parisian-style hat, tall and tapering, with a round brim. For wear at the wharf she made a pair of white trousers with thin vertical stripes of red and blue. His Fortnightly Club celebrated the anniversary of the fall of the Bastille with a special dinner on July 14.

Not all Charlestonians caught the revolutionary spirit. Archibald Lescock paraded in the apparel of an *elegant,* an antirevolutionist. Edward encountered him at a coffeehouse, resplendent in an emerald silk frock coat with a high turndown collar. He wore enough musk scent for a woman.

Lescock said plans were being made to reopen the racetrack north of the original city wall. He would pit his mare against Edward's stallion at the first opportunity. "What a pleasure it will be to beat a sans-culotte," he said, smirking and tapping Edward's striped trousers with his weighted stick.

Edward decided to prepare for the race, whenever it might occur. He began taking Joanna and Edgar to Malvern on weekends. There he saddled Prince Mahmoud and raced him along the country roads. The white Arabian was a big animal, strong but high-strung. A sudden noise, a flash of lightning, could throw him off stride, even make him balk. When he was fearless, he ran faster than any horse Edward had ever ridden.

★　★　★

A man named Joseph Vesey came to Bell's Bridge to sell cordage to a master whose schooner had lost much of it in a fierce Atlantic blow. Edward knew Vesey slightly. He'd captained slave ships in the seventies and eighties. Now, in his middle years, he was retired in Charleston, where he wholesaled marine goods. He owned a substantial home in one of the new northern boroughs, and several slaves.

When Edward arrived at the busy wharf after two hours at his law office, he noticed a black man of twenty-five or so, with smooth, almost Grecian features, lounging on a bollard reading a book—a bold thing to do in public. The young man wore breeches and a frilled shirt, obviously hand-me-down.

The young man raised his head as Edward approached; gave him a frank stare. There was neither friendliness nor animosity in it, just careful appraisal from large dark eyes. Edward wasn't one to raise an alarm or issue a reprimand, but Negroes didn't look at white men that way if they wanted to avoid the workhouse.

"Who's that colored man outside?" he asked Simon Buckles in the office.

"Cap'n Vesey owns him. I talked to him a little." Big Simon scratched his luxuriant red beard. "Can't say as I took to him. Pert, he is. A sleeky sort."

"Sleeky? Stop that damned Scots cant or I'll come after you with a *chabouk*."

"What's a *chabouk*?"

"Oriental horsewhip. I asked Marburg to find me some suitably obscure words for retaliation. What's the meaning of *sleeky*?"

"Sly."

"Well, kindly say as much. Speak the king's English."

"I dinna have any love for English kings, but I'll try, to keep the chabouk off my arse," Buckles said, grinning.

A few days later, paying a call on Marburg's shop, Edward was surprised to bump into the black man coming out the door. Captain Vesey's slave gave him a blank look, yet Edward had a feeling the man recognized him and had stored the moment away for some future use.

Marburg was busy cleaning his shelves and bins with a feather duster. Edward mentioned the Negro. "I saw him at the Bridge not long ago. What do you know about him?"

"Name's Denmark. He's a bright one. Reads and writes English, French, some Danish, Portuguese, a little Arabic, and speaks Gullah. He comes in to examine my Bibles." Marburg kept a suitably ecumenical supply of religious literature. "Says he'll buy a new one someday. Says he'll buy or earn his freedom too. He told me a lot, he's a talkative sort."

Curious, Edward said, "And?"

"Vesey bought him about twelve years ago, in the Danish Virgin Islands, where the lad was born. Later the captain sold him to a sugar planter on Saint-Domingue.[3] A year later Vesey refunded the boy's price. The buyer complained that the fellow constantly had strange fits when he cut cane in the broiling sun. He laughed when he told me that. I suspect the fits were of his own manufacture, to escape the sugar fields.

"Vesey took him back aboard and carried him on voyages to West Africa. There he picked up languages so fast, Vesey found him highly useful in negotiations at the slave factories. Vesey brought him here when he retired, and changed his name from Telemaque to Denmark. He's friendly enough, but his taste in Scripture is peculiar."

"For instance?"

From the shelf of religious material Marburg drew down an Old Testament. He showed Edward a page from the book of Joshua. "Sixth chapter, twenty-first verse. It's his favorite."

And they utterly destroyed all that was in the city, both man and woman, young and old, and ox, and sheep, and ass, with the edge of the sword.

Scowling, Edward closed the book. "He cited this to you, a white man?"

"He did. Bit unsettling, isn't it?"

"He'll be in trouble with the authorities if he isn't careful."

"I think he's too clever for that."

"Sleeky," Edward said without thinking.

★　★　★

---

[3]Present-day Haiti

In early September the ardor for the French Revolution cooled unexpectedly. Trading ships from the Caribbean brought disturbing news from the island of Saint-Domingue. For decades nearly three quarters of a million slaves had worked the coffee and sugar plantations of the *grands blancs,* the white landowners. Recently, some had run away to the inland mountains and forests. Led by a strange cadre that included disciples of voodoo and educated *affranchisés*—free blacks, the island's third caste—the runaways, or *macrons,* burned outlying plantations and butchered the owners. Within a month ships from southern waters brought a few French refugees. Then boatloads of them arrived. They came with wives, husbands, children, the few possessions left to them—and stories of atrocities.

* * *

The Fortnightly Club rotated its meetings among the homes of twenty-two members. The evenings varied: sometimes a member reviewed a book of the moment, or presented a paper on a learned subject. Occasionally an invited guest spoke. Whatever the program, members could count on three hours of intelligent masculine company, and good Madeira.

Edward's turn as host came in March of 1792. Marburg invited a refugee with whom he'd become acquainted at the shop. Emile Epernay was a cadaverous middle-aged gentleman with a shock of white hair, a white goatee, and a yellowish, haunted face. An air of sadness, even failure, seemed to sit on his shoulders. Marburg introduced him almost apologetically.

"Monsieur Epernay is establishing himself as a dancing master and teacher of French. He comes tonight to tell us of recent events in his homeland."

Epernay had a good command of English. "I was born on Saint-Domingue. I inherited four hundred acres near the northern settlement of Limb. Some of the richest coffee lands on the island.

"I increased the holdings to one thousand acres, building a lucrative trade with Marseilles and the French Channel ports. When the trouble came, inspired by the damned lovers of Madame Guillotine in Paris, all but ten of my one hundred slaves deserted to join the savages who subsequently attacked the plantation. We could not stand against them. We ran to a wood, and from there I watched the whole sum of my life devoured by flames. All over the island fields like mine were torched.

Saint-Domingue became an inferno. Fires were still burning when we took ship."

Epernay, his wife, and three unmarried daughters made their way to the city of Cap Français on the coast. "Even there the horde of godless brutes followed us. They raped and burned beneath a ghastly standard—a pike, upon which was impaled the body of a white infant. A new one every few days." A club member seated near Edward covered his mouth and excused himself.

"When they came to the Cap, we turned them back with our weapons, but at dreadful cost. A thousand fine plantations destroyed. Two thousand white men, women, and children slaughtered, and perhaps five times as many Negroes. Which is hardly enough to pay for the damage they wrought," he said with a vicious expression.

"Had my wife not escaped with her casket of jewels, I could not have paid the outrageous price demanded for passage to Charleston. I was one of the fortunate, but my blessed island is destroyed. Most who run amok there are ignorant and superstitious, but some are educated, hence more dangerous. A former house servant named Toussaint L'Ouverture was taught to read and write by owners whom he subsequently warned in time for them to escape. He is a student of the writings and campaigns of Julius Caesar."

At the end of Epernay's monologue one of the members said, "We are heartily glad you escaped, sir. We welcome you to a new life in America. Thankfully, we do not have to worry about events so far away."

"You think not, monsieur? Count all the black sailors coming and going in this port. Ideas travel swiftly on sailing ships. Be wary, lest you have another Saint-Domingue in Charleston. I urge you to be vigilant. Arm yourselves in your homes. Organize a civil guard. Prepare for insurrection as though it were a certainty. Primitive Africans are not to be trusted. As a race they are barbaric."

Or is it the way they've been sold and subjugated? Edward thought. Joanna had changed him in many ways.

☆　☆　☆

In the beautiful spring of 1792 Edward raced Prince Mahmoud every weekend. One hot Sunday afternoon in May a rattlesnake wriggled into the road ahead of horse and rider. The Arabian reacted, rearing, neighing, throwing Edward out of the saddle.

The steed's slashing fore hoofs cut the snake in half. Edward lay in the dust with his left leg twisted and, as his Charleston physician told him later that day, his right arm broken. After setting, it required a sling, which placed the burden of all of his writing on his law clerk and Simon Buckles.

On the Friday after the accident Simon came into the office without his usual cheerful expression. "I chanced to be over to Rhett's Wharf an hour ago. The brig *Rover,* out of New Providence Island, Nassau, has just put in."

"What of it?"

"The passenger list excited some comment. It was called to my attention that Mrs. Adrian Bell and son have arrived in Charleston."

23

Chameleon

Edward wore a black sling on his right arm. He complained to Joanna that given the sling and his limp, he felt like Job. What else did the Almighty have in store? Boils?

She laughed at his conceit, kissed his forehead, and said he should be ashamed of such dark thoughts. As a family they were secure, well provided for thanks to the Bridge and his small practice. Life was good. As always her affection charmed him out of his funk. He made love to her twice that night after the household went to sleep.

To replace his first clerk, who had married and hied off to Augusta to set up his own office, Edward hired Simon Buckles's second child and oldest son, Argyll. The young man weighed eighteen stone at least, his corpulence all the more evident because the top of his head barely reached Edward's shoulder. He waddled rather than walked. A seamstress made his clothes, because no fashionable tailor would sew such tentlike garments. Like his father, he had a sunny disposition, a quick mind, and a fierce Presbyterian bent for hard work.

"Argyll," Edward said one morning in May, "enough time has passed since my sister-in-law's return. We should clear up the matter of Prosperity Hall. Kindly take this letter to Legare Street. I'd like her to call here." He wasn't looking forward to it. "Arrange a day and time before you return."

Argyll departed, creaking the floorboards mightily.

The appointment was set for Saturday morning. Edward rather expected his sister-in-law to present a picture of impoverished gentility after her exile. He was startled when she appeared pink and healthy, and only slightly heavier than when he'd seen her last. Her clothes suggested that Adrian had indeed made a profitable start in cotton before his untimely death. Her frock was the latest style: cotton, with a narrow vertical stripe of royal blue, enhanced by a sash of matching blue satin and worn with flat slippers. Fewer undergarments made a slimmer silhouette and more clearly revealed the line of her breasts. Her blond hair hung to her shoulders in flowing curls set off by a white gauze turban sporting an ostrich plume. Poor women did not wear the *chemise à l'anglaise* or its expensive accompaniments.

She brought her boy, Simms, to the office. Simms was eight. He resembled his mother with one unfortunate exception. Where Lydia's eyes were round and blue and enticing, Simms's blue eyes bulged slightly, giving the illusion of two small bird's eggs protruding from his face.

He suffered from a wheezy cough. More time outdoors would cure that, Edward thought; the boy was white as a maiden's drawers. Blond curls and fair brows only enhanced his air of hothouse fragility. Edward left him on a stool in the outer office, there to pester Argyll while the adults conferred with the door closed.

Lydia took the visitor's chair. Edward still saw much to admire in her soft and buxom beauty, but now, with Joanna as a comparison, he wondered how he'd ever been in love with her, or come running back to Charleston for fear of losing her.

He again offered condolences on her double loss. Her only response was a flat "Thank you." In her eyes he saw animosity, or thought he did. Perhaps he imagined it because of her letter.

She asked how he'd broken his arm. He explained, concluding, "Damned inconvenient, it's the hand I use most."

They exchanged a few bland pleasantries about the changes in Charleston: the welcome disappearance of war damage, the new wealth showing up in expensive homes and fancy coaches of a rising cotton elite. "Prosperity Hall would be excellent for raising cotton," he said to introduce his subject.

"You forget that I no longer own the property, Edward."

"Not quite true. Do you recall my letter? I believe I informed you that I managed to have Adrian's plantation transferred to the amercement list, rather than offered for sale as confiscated land."

"Oh, yes, I read that. I didn't understand it."

Patiently, he told her about the punitive tax, twelve percent of Prosperity Hall's assessed value, awaiting payment. He opened a large vellum folder, showed a sheet of figures that Argyll had prepared. "This is the significant amount." He turned the sheet around so she could read it. "Can you afford to pay it?"

She studied the paper, then sat back and brushed some invisible speck of dirt or piece of lint off the upper curve of her breast. The act was somehow provocative and stirred Edward in a guilty way. He expected that it was deliberate on her part.

She smiled for the first time. "Yes, I believe I can. Most of my funds remain on deposit in a bank in St. Lucia, but I intended to transfer them. It appears that doing so promptly would be advantageous."

"Yes. The plantation's valuable. With river frontage you're in a prime position to barge cotton down here for shipment. Prices are high at the moment. The mill owners in England have forgotten we were ever enemies. Their demand is voracious."

"You're very generous."

"Lydia, he was my brother. The war pushed us apart, but family ties aren't easily sundered."

A new, husky note came into her voice. "Was it only the war?"

Somehow a green chameleon had found its way into his office and was climbing a cliff of shelved books. In a patch of sunlight the little creature rested on top of a fat, boring volume on notes and bills. It inflated its throat into a vivid pink bubble. The mating season had come.

He noticed light perspiration on Lydia's upper lip. "I don't think it's useful to go over that," he said.

"You no longer have any feeling for me?"

"You're my sister-in-law. I have the highest regard—"

She reached across the desk to trap his left hand. Her fingers were warm and strong. "I'm not talking about that kind of feeling. You take my meaning."

"I do, but we mustn't revisit the past."

"Because you're afraid of the outcome if we do?" Beyond the door the boy Simms coughed loudly enough to frighten the chameleon into hiding. While Edward searched for the right response, his eye raked the desk to see whether there were any lethal objects in view. Trying not to appear deliberate, he tapped his fingertips on the vellum folder, then casually withdrew a pointed letter opener from her side of the desk.

"Lydia, there's no profit for either of us in answering such a question." Her sudden flush suggested anger. "Regarding the amercement and restoration of Prosperity Hall, I'll be pleased to handle all the legal work at no expense to you."

"And then we're quits?"

"Why, no. I hope you might visit our family someday soon."

"You're happy, are you?"

"Very," he said, truthfully.

"Well, of course I have a vague memory of your wife, but I'd love to renew the acquaintance." Absolutely untrue, he thought. "We'll have ample opportunity. If Prosperity Hall passes into my hands again, I'll make Charleston my permanent home. I'll see you often."

Those four words, spoken with a voluptuous little smile, made silent promises: she wouldn't give up on him. She had every confidence that he would succumb eventually. His heart raced.

Lydia rose, came around the desk to clasp his left hand again. "Thank you for your kindness. I'm sorry if circumstances led me to be harsh with you in the past. I will endeavor to remedy that."

All he could say to shorten the moment was "Allow me to show you out."

He stepped in front of her; they were very close. She touched his chin, brought her moist mouth near his, whispered, "Dear man. It could have been so different. It still could be."

Before he could reply, she opened the door and cried, "Poor thing, Mama's here," to her coughing boy. She bade Argyll good morning and left without a backward look.

God, why had she come back to stir old feelings he didn't want? He felt angry, with her and with himself. He remembered the little chameleon lost somewhere on the high shelves. In a way Lydia was a chameleon, unpredictably changeable. There was one difference: a real chameleon was harmless.

24

At Prosperity Hall

Edward had no secrets from his wife, except that concerning the death of William Lark, which he'd never mentioned. Joanna knew about his past infatuation with his sister-in-law, and accepted his word that she had long ago replaced Lydia and claimed all his affection. She wasn't unwilling to ask Lydia and Simms to supper, though not enthusiastic either. A week after the conversation in the office she sent an invitation to Legare Street. Lydia didn't respond.

Two more weeks passed, while Edward assembled papers for Lydia's signature. He sent Argyll into the pouring rain with a request that she pay a second call to Broad Street. The clerk came back to say, "Her boy's at home with servants but she's gone to inspect Prosperity Hall."

Edward sighed. "Bad timing. I suggested she look it over, and obtained the consent of the tax authorities. We'll wait for her return."

Two days later a black youth carrying a pass signed by his owner, Lydia, delivered a letter.

Will you kindly meet me at the plantation late afternoon Friday? I need to consult you on several questions of restoration of the property, and can more readily explain them if you make an inspection. I am residing, respectably & safely, at Biggins's Inn, on the river road between Mont Royal and Prosperity Hall. I am accompanied by a docile nigger who I am confident will not murder me while I sleep!

The language gave him no room to demur. He discussed it with Joanna. She thought making the short trip would be all right, so long as he stayed the night at the inn Lydia mentioned. "In separate quarters, naturally," she said as she hugged him.

Friday found him in his chaise on the Ashley River Road. Using a driving glove, he was able to handle the horse with one hand. The May air was heavy with dampness from recent rains. The sun fell through the pines and live oaks in shafts of pearly light. He passed the splendid avenue of trees leading to the plantation of the Main family, then a mile farther passed the inn. Three miles beyond he came to the lane leading to Prosperity Hall.

He hadn't seen Adrian's plantation since the war and remembered few details. Sad vistas of decay greeted him. Fallow fields thick with briers, volunteer palmettos, and tall weeds flanked the entrance road. Empty slave cabins showed broken walls and collapsed roofs. The main house rose up gray as an old tombstone, all the window glass on both floors broken out. One of its four piazza columns was missing except for a ragged stump. Directly above, the second-floor piazza sagged in a dangerous V.

Lydia's carriage was nowhere in sight. Her supposedly docile colored man lounged on the sagging stoop, amusing himself with a stick and a jackknife. He quickly hid the knife when he saw Edward coming. Lydia would send the man to the workhouse if she knew he was carrying an illegal weapon.

"How do, sir, my name Mountjoy," the man said. "You be Mr. Bell?"

"That's right. She's expecting me, then?"

"Other side of the house."

"The place looks terrible. Is it as bad inside?"

"Yes, sir. Everything wrecked. Two ceilings done fell in. Take a mighty lot of money to put it back right." *But the acreage,* Edward thought—*in cotton the acreage will bring the money.*

"Thank you, Mountjoy. Please watch my horse."

As he walked to the side of the house, his shadow lay long on burnt and weedy grass. Much of it had died, leaving ugly scabs of sandy soil. An eerie stillness made every small sound noticeable.

"Lydia?" he called. Then he saw her, halfway down the sweep of ruined lawn leading to the river. The boat dock seemed in decent repair, but the banks around it were overgrown with reeds. The Ashley's ebb tide ran swiftly. The rain-swollen river resembled a gray-brown banner rippling in the wind.

"Here I am," Lydia called unnecessarily, waving. They walked to one another. She wore the same English frock he'd seen before. She squeezed his good hand and bussed his cheek. "How grand and kind of you to come."

"My duty and my pleasure," he answered, aware of their isolation. Mountjoy would never dare spy on them. "Shall we look into these problems you mentioned? I suppose they have to do with the condition of the place. Let's go inside and inspect—"

"They're more easily seen from a distance." She linked her right arm in his left; the press of her round breast wasn't accidental. "Stroll down to the dock with me, I'll show you from there."

The steamy day was dying. Tiny gnats flitted in patches of golden light. The river's far bank was wild and greenly dense; nothing was built there. Edward had to admit that Adrian had been shrewd to buy such an attractive piece of real estate. The view of the Ashley was grand and uncluttered by any sight of human habitation.

Lydia led him onto the sturdy pier; someone had kept it in repair. A stirring in the reeds to the left drew his attention. A fish or something larger, but hidden. He fanned himself with his tall round hat, now minus the French rosette. He raised it to shield his eyes as he inspected the tumbledown house.

"Is there one problem, or is everything the problem?"

She stepped in front of him, inches from his chest. "The problem's here, Edward. The problem is you and me." Her eyes were blue as a cold January sky. Her breath caressed him like perfumed air. *Goddamn fool, she gulled you.* He'd almost suspected something like this but had dismissed it as an unfounded fear.

Her hand dropped and closed on his manhood. She squeezed gently, teasingly, but there was no teasing in her voice. "We belong together. You know that but you won't admit it to yourself."

"Lydia, I hate deceit. You brought me here under false colors. You will excuse me if I don't prolong this interview." He stepped back, pushing her hand away and cursing himself because he'd hardened.

She blocked his path to the lawn. She threw her arms around his neck, pressured him with her grinding belly as she kissed his face. "Oh, Edward, come to your senses. I love you. All I'm asking is a beautiful future for both of us. Leave your wife."

"Leave—?" He couldn't continue.

"Yes, yes, dearest." She kissed his chin, his throat, then his mouth, her wet tongue finding his. "We can have a fine life together. Think of our land, Prosperity Hall and Malvern, joined. You have the talent to manage it. That's why you became a lawyer, to know how to control land, you told me so before you sailed to England. But that's not the end, dearest. You can go to the legislature, I'll help you. Then you can control more than land, you can control people. You could go to Washington. Southern statesmen rule this country. They will for years."

He interrupted her breathless daydream, broke her hold with his left hand. He'd dropped his hat. It rolled off the dock and sailed downriver on the fast current. His anger was nearly unmanageable.

"Lydia, it's over. It was over long ago. I love Joanna."

"It can't be. She's common."

"I'll hear no more. Stand out of my way. I don't want to be rude with you, but I will be if you continue this."

"You hypocritical bastard. You want me, you know it. You want to fuck me day and night."

"God, you're impossible." He stepped left, to go around her. She countered it. She hit the black sling, setting off a raging pain in his arm.

"You can't stay married to that woman, that dockside nobody."

He raised his fisted left hand. "Shut your foul mouth. Joanna's the best woman I've ever known or ever will."

"And she's the last one." Lydia smashed him in the chest with both hands. He pitched off the end of the dock.

He hit the silted water in panic. The strong current tugged his legs, pushed him away from the shore. He flung out his left hand. Kicking, gagging as water splashed in his mouth, he managed to seize the end of the dock.

"Lydia, for God's sake"—he sputtered, gasping for air—"call your man. Help me. I can't swim."

She smiled sweetly. "I know that, dearest. I've known that for years." She stamped on his left hand, then twice more. He lost his hold, fell backward with a faint cry.

He sank, bobbed up again. The current swept him past tall reeds and out toward the center of the river. Something in the reeds disturbed the water. Tiny round eyes broke the surface, then a long, wrinkled snout. "Oh, Christ. Lydia, help me."

"Help yourself, you unfaithful whoreson," she said, beating her fists on her hips and weeping. Edward's feeble attempt to swim was doomed. The alligator opened its jaws, snapped them shut on his left shoulder and torso, and whipped him underwater.

The alligator lashed him one way, then another. Edward surfaced twice, his throat filling, his body screaming with pain from the great jaws. Before the alligator bore him down the last time, he heard Lydia cry out in a perfect imitation of feminine distress.

"Oh, help. Mountjoy, help me. There's been a terrible accident."

25

Omens

The bells of St. Michael's tolled for Edward's funeral. Three hundred people attended. Sally, Hamnet, ancient Pharaoh, and other slaves from the house and Bell's Bridge clustered in the segregated balcony, weeping more emotionally than the whites in the pews below. General Marion and his wife, Mary Esther, his first cousin, had come down from Pond Bluff, their home on the Santee. Marion was sixty now, a national hero. He hadn't married until his mid-fifties.

Joanna sat with Edgar. Across the aisle and one row back Lydia, heavily veiled, kept her restless popeyed son under control with a gloved hand. Edgar squirmed around to look at his cousin during the rector's praise of the deceased. The boys peered at each other with a vague distrust.

As the service ended, a storm broke: wailing wind and sheets of rain off the sea. If it hadn't been springtime, mourners might have thought it a hurricane. It made the burial in the little churchyard difficult. Only the immediate family was allowed inside the iron fence, but Sally huddled outside, her arm around her son, who was already an inch taller than his mother.

Though Edward's remains had never been found, a grave was dug for him beside that of his mother. Trying to lower the empty casket gently, the black sextons slipped and slid; one let go of his rope. The casket crashed the last two feet to its resting place. Joanna covered her eyes.

After the closing prayer Lydia approached. Her expression was impossible to read because of the veil. She attempted to touch Joanna, who stepped back.

Lydia said, "It was such a terrible accident, tripping and falling that way. I tried desperately to pull him out but the current was too swift. If I'd remembered he couldn't swim, I never would have encouraged a stroll to the dock. I blame myself for what happened. I am so sorry."

Joanna's best impulse was to thank Lydia for her sentiments, which had previously been expressed in a flowery letter. Something in her sister-in-law's manner, an intonation, a glibness, struck her as wrong. It overcame her generosity and prompted a caustic reply.

"If only that would bring him back."

Lydia recoiled, snatched up her son's hand, and marched from the graveyard.

The rain-soaked rector offered words of sympathy Joanna couldn't remember a moment later. There was enmity in Lydia's heart, Joanna believed that. Should she accept her sister-in-law's explanation of the accident? How could she not? To do otherwise was to court misery and suspicion for the rest of her life.

A woman lingered on the public footpath. The sodden state of her cloak and mobcap said she'd been there awhile. Small and coarse and painted with too much rouge, she stared at Joanna and Edgar.

Joanna had never seen her before. The scrutiny was unsettling. Joanna started to speak when the woman picked up her muddy skirts and scurried away up Meeting Street. Surely the attention wasn't accidental, though she had no explanation for it.

"Let's go home, Edgar. I'm cold."

☆   ☆   ☆

Mr. Whitney's ginning machine, patent applied for, revolutionized agriculture in South Carolina and the South. Short-staple cotton became a profitable crop, eagerly planted, processed, and shipped by yeoman farmers in the midlands. These were the same men who had railed against slavery as practiced by the aristocratic planters of the Low Country. The new profitability of their crop changed their attitude and, across the state, created a singularity of opinion about the virtue of, the absolute necessity for, importation of more and more slaves. This in turn profoundly influenced the state's political thinking, and its future.

A year after Edward's funeral there occurred a melancholy foretaste of this future as it affected Charleston. From New York, Marburg imported a dozen copies of a small book, *A Graphick Account of Revolutionary Atrocities in the French Colony of Sante-Domingue, by One Who Witnessed Them. Tr. from the French of M. Georges Boucher.*

He placed a dozen copies in his window and within a few days sold six. He was then called on by a trio of local planters. The spokesman said, "A friend lent me that Frenchman's book in the window. You don't appreciate the possible consequences of having such inflammatory material purveyed here. We respectfully request that you sell no more copies."

"For what reason?" Marburg said affably.

"One might fall into the wrong hands."

"Provoke behavior similar to that which it describes," said a second man.

"Gentlemen, I don't believe books inspire acts of violence and barbarity. Certainly they don't among my patrons."

The visitors exchanged sneering smiles. The spokesman said, "I refer to freedmen. A whole class of resentful niggers, many of whom can read. You may add to that a certain number of slaves who have been taught illegally. We dare not give them ideas when we as white people are outnumbered."

Marburg's expression became pensive, even troubled. "What you ask would choke off a person's right to read whatever he chooses. I must respectfully decline your request."

"Marburg, we insist. We demand you remove those books."

"I still decline." The bell over the door jingled. "Excuse me, gentlemen, I have a customer." The callers left, all glares and grumbles. Marburg heard one say, "Just another money-grubbing Jew," before the door slammed.

Two nights later Marburg and Sarah were wakened by a ferocious crash from the shop. While Sarah calmed the frightened children, Marburg ran downstairs in his nightshirt, his old military sword in hand.

Broken glass lay in the window like a scattering of sapphires. Marburg saw immediately that every book on display had been pulled out, thrown in the gutter, and set afire. They smoldered in a heap, throwing off more smoke than flame.

He ran to the door, stormed into the street, shouted, "Cowards!" to the moonlit night. Only a mongrel's bark answered.

Sarah came to the door. Marburg said, "Go back inside, stay warm." Shivering in his nightclothes, he waited for the watch to arrive as the books turned to ash.

The Years Between
1793–1822

From 1793 until the collapse of the worldwide cotton market in 1819, Charleston enjoyed prosperity such as it had not seen before and never would again. Lydia Bell was determined to share it. She would not let widowhood drive her into poverty or diminish her social standing. She taught herself what she needed to know to manage Prosperity Hall.

To do this she spent long, exhausting evenings and Sundays with her overseer at Prosperity Hall, Josef Lessard, who came from the French Santee district, where many Saint-Domingue refugees had settled. She forced herself to be Lessard's diligent pupil. Growing up, she'd been a lazy, indifferent student, gaining no more than a rudimentary knowledge of mathematics. Now she pored over ledgers with the overseer, struggling to add and subtract figures from the pages, and, most importantly, learn how to attach meaning to them.

The effort rewarded her. As she gained confidence and took control of the plantation, crops of cotton and rice brought in large sums. She kept the money in the Crescent Bank founded by Morris Marburg, son of the Hessian soldier. Lydia scorned Jews as a group but set that aside because, in a relatively short time, Morris had established himself as a shrewd steward of depositors' funds. He hadn't abandoned the family bookstore or his father's principles. His clerks continued to resist pressure to keep literature critical of slavery off the shelves.

With newfound wealth Lydia bought more land and slaves. Other planters agreed privately that Mrs. Bell, who had once seemed no more than a pretty ornament, like so many Charleston women, somehow had acquired a head for business very nearly the equal of a man's. They of course didn't repeat the remark to their docile, unaccomplished wives.

To take full advantage of the cotton market South Carolina needed a larger labor force. State law had stopped the importation of slaves in 1787. In 1803 Lydia traveled to Columbia with a Low Country delegation, joining yeoman farmers from up-country to demand reopening of the trade.

By a narrow margin the legislature voted in favor. After December 1803 fresh cargoes from West Africa began to arrive. During the next four and a half years, until the constitutionally mandated abolition of the trade in 1808, nearly fifty thousand men, women, and children were imported and sold on Charleston's vendue blocks. Lydia steadily bought more of this movable property, as it was called, though her fear of dark skins remained undiminished. Lessard dealt with all but the house servants.

Lydia raised her son, Simms, as a landed aristocrat, one of those privileged young men destined to control not only personal wealth but also the machinery of state politics. Forever popeyed, young Simms nevertheless emerged as a slender, graceful youth of manly appearance and polished manners. From his earliest days he heard his mother preach that slavery was necessary and good. South Carolina's economy depended on it, as did personal security. The system maintained order and reduced chances of a bloody revolt in a society dominated by a black majority.

Charleston's population in 1800 numbered roughly nine thousand whites and eleven thousand Africans. New laws and regulations recognized the danger in this imbalance. Negroes were forbidden from assembling in groups of more than seven, except at funerals or with a white person observing them. Public dancing and displays of merriment were prohibited. A slave or freedman could not carry a stick or cane unless he was feeble or blind. After drums beat a tattoo at nine in the evening, any black person still abroad was subject to arrest, a fine, and a flogging. An enlarged City Guard drilled with muskets and bayonets to intimidate anyone tempted to break the rules.

One of the city's newer freedmen was Capt. Joseph Vesey's man Denmark. In 1799 he'd picked a winning number in the East Bay Lottery. Using $600 of the $1,500 prize, he bought his freedom. He then set up

a household and carpentry business on Bull Street, where he studied the
Bible and quietly preached rebellion.

☆   ☆   ☆

Simms Bell attended Yale College, where he met a lanky, hazel-eyed
South Carolinian, John Calhoun, from the Ninety Six district in the
northwest part of the state up along the Savannah River. Calhoun was
two years ahead of Simms. He came of a pioneering family that had seen
some of its members massacred by marauding Cherokees forty years
earlier. He'd grown up a farmer's son, educated by itinerant schoolmas-
ters, then at Reverend Moses Waddel's well-regarded Carmel Academy
in Appling, Georgia.

Calhoun made no secret of disliking Charleston and its effete
planters who never soiled their hands; he worked family land himself.
He informed Simms that the epidemics and hurricanes that periodically
decimated Charleston were "a curse for her intemperance and de-
baucheries."

Simms was in awe of John Calhoun, whose austere appearance and
personality set him apart. At six two, with brown hair standing up stiff
as a brush and eyes deeply sunken in a craggy face, he had the look of
a primitive. There was nothing primitive about his mind or ambition.
What he would be in the future, other than a lawyer, was not yet clear,
but Simms expected that Mr. Calhoun would amount to something in
their home state, if not the nation. He was already a dedicated
Democratic-Republican, intolerant of the Federalist vision of a strong,
expanding central government.

Simms didn't share Calhoun's political ambition or his puritanical attitude. Simms became a regular patron of New Haven's dramshops and
brothels, assuring his mother by letter that of course he was too busy
with studies to indulge in such behavior. After graduation he planned to
go home and devote himself to the family lands whose profits he meant
to increase, with a corresponding rise in his own comfort and importance.

☆   ☆   ☆

The backdrop for all of this was the new nation, expanding and
changing dramatically.

The Federalists who had shaped and secured the Constitution saw
their power threatened by the Democratic-Republican party. Its candidates in the election of 1800, Mr. Jefferson and Mr. Burr, ascended to

the presidency and vice presidency after a tie in the electoral college threw the vote into the House. Philadelphia was no longer the seat of government; Jefferson and Burr took up their duties in Washington.

Napoleon bestrode Europe. War between France and England prompted British interference with neutral shipping that might aid the French. The issue of harassment of American ships and impressment of American seamen grew from an irritant to a potential cause of conflict, at a time when the young nation felt a burgeoning national power and pride. The American navy had humiliated the Barbary pirates in the Mediterranean and forced an end to extortion of tribute.

In 1811 members of the Eleventh Congress took their seats. A group known as War Hawks advocated hostilities with Britain. One of the War Hawks was Simms's old classmate, John Calhoun.

★ ★ ★

Lydia ignored the threatened crisis, wrongly assuming it would ignore her and her city. She appeared to have cleansed her conscience of any guilt connected with Edward's death. It was seldom in her thoughts and never in a troubling way.

Distorted scenes from the river dock did appear occasionally in her dreams. More than once she saw Edward trapped in the alligator's jaws, his eyes horrific fires of accusation. She no longer admitted any love for Edward, only hatred. His stiff-necked righteousness had robbed her of what she'd wanted most in all the world, Edward himself.

Then a curious incident changed everything.

Lydia was fifty-two in 1811. The year brought her two great satisfactions. The first was the natural death of Edward's widow, Joanna. Lydia attended the funeral, thought herself coolly treated, but took pleasure in the passing of a rival she'd failed to defeat.

Even more gratifying was her son's announcement that after the sickly season, he planned to wed Miss Bethel Vanderhorst, a pretty, bland young woman from an impeccable family. Lydia approved of the alliance, indeed had urged Simms to pursue it. She knew she could dominate the simpleminded girl and thereby continue to guide her son.

She traveled to New York to shop for wedding finery. She'd made the journey before. She liked the variety of merchandise available in the grubby, noisy city, though she loathed the rude Yankees, who hadn't the sense to hide their rapacious commercialism behind a smile and a pleasantry, as Charleston people did. In a roundabout way she liked

New York for its contrast with her home. Charleston's climate and gracious ways were all the more pleasing after exposure to the crudeness of the North.

Because of the international situation sea travel presented dangers beyond the usual ones of weather. Lydia chose to sail to and from New York anyway. It was that or endure a long trip squeezed in a stagecoach, bumping and banging over wretched roads among low-class strangers who smelled bad. After ten days spent in New York's finest emporiums, she sailed south on the sidewheel steamer *Decatur,* named after the hero of the 1804 battle of Tripoli.

On the third day of the voyage the ship plowed through a heavy green sea. Lightning crackled above the yards. Gale winds howled; waves crashed over the bow. Despite that Lydia managed a nap in the late afternoon. When she woke, the ship's violent rolling and pitching had stopped.

She left her tiny cabin eagerly. One of the ship's six passengers, a Methodist pastor, had suffered attacks of seasickness; the smell in the cabin gangway was vile. She went up into the stormy twilight wearing a fine traveling dress of black pongee with a straight Greco-Roman skirt. Cost in New York, $110. However mean the circumstances in which she found herself, Lydia always wanted to represent the very best of Southern society.

According to the captain they should now be off the coast of North Carolina. It was impossible to see land; a fog had settled. *Decatur* moved ahead dead slow, clanging its bell.

She peered across the port rail, then abruptly rubbed her eyes. In the gray-green murk she saw a shape hovering several feet above the waves. It floated slowly toward the ship. A moment later she identified it.

"Edward?"

Water streamed from his chin, elbows, the hem of his coat. Weeds festooned his hair. Bits of scum speckled his face like marks of some foul disease. As he drifted closer, she saw that his eyes were white, without irises. His face was twisted into malevolence, as though the features once so attractive to her had melted like candle wax, then hardened.

She screamed and fainted.

She was discovered on the wet deck a few minutes later and rushed to her cabin. She awoke sweating and trembling. Edward was *alive.* That is, some part of him was alive, mysteriously and malignantly, and had come back to haunt and possibly harm her.

She couldn't have feared him more if he'd been black.

* * *

Lydia reached Charleston safely but soon went into a decline. Years of suppressed guilt gave way to a persistent dread of discovery and punishment. It painted permanent gray semicircles under her eyes. She woke in the night, raving and thrashing. She ate normally but lost weight. Simms summoned the learned Dr. Hippocrates Sapp to Prosperity Hall.

Dr. Sapp appeared with the physician's traditional long black coat and gold-headed cane. He questioned Lydia at length, privately. Afterward he told Simms that his mother was quite obviously disturbed but he was baffled as to the cause. Nor would she reveal it. Sapp wrote an order for a calmative containing opium. Lydia learned to gulp it by the spoonful, several times a day.

* * *

In 1812 the militant congressional junto carried the day. The United States declared war against Britain.

The navy won stunning victories off Nova Scotia, Brazil, the Madeira Islands, then in Lake Erie in 1813. Charleston remained far from the actual fighting but prepared nonetheless, building fortifications on the Neck similar to those in the Revolution. Fifteen artillery pieces guarded White Point, which people began to refer to as the Battery.

* * *

During this time Lydia alternated between periods of peaceful lucidity and frenetic anxiety. She became increasingly hostile toward the household slaves, regularly accusing them of plotting to poison her food or set the house on fire while she slept. When a pearl earring disappeared from her jewel box, she blamed a fourteen-year-old girl named Aphrodite. Despite the girl's tearful denial Lydia ordered her earlobes slit with a sharp knife. She calmly read a newspaper in another room while the girl screamed.

Days later Aphrodite ran away. She was never caught. Her replacement found the earring in a dark corner of Lydia's wardrobe.

By default, the management of the family's affairs had fallen to Simms, now settled with the phlegmatic and obedient Bethel in a small house of his own not far from Malvern. There, a daughter, Ouida, was born in 1813, and a son, Gibbes, four years later.

* * *

The war dramatically improved the fortunes of another Charlestonian, William Lark's son, Crittenden. Crittenden's late mother had taught him to hate Edward Bell's family. From his father he'd inherited a lack of scruples; he was not remotely acquainted with anything resembling morality.

He organized a syndicate to build and outfit a 140-ton privateer, *Saucy Lady*, at a yard on the Wando River. He controlled only a small number of shares in the syndicate, yet he was its motor and ultimately made all the decisions. This was because he was an abrasive, domineering partner and because he sailed with his vessel as supercargo, the only investor brave enough, or greedy enough, to do so.

Saucy Lady eluded British blockade ships, captured an enemy frigate off the Atlantic coast, then two smaller Spanish merchantmen. Prize courts made Crittenden Lark a wealthy man before his twenty-fifth birthday.

* * *

Edward's son, Edgar, meanwhile, had continued to live in the house of his grandfather. Edgar read law at the prestigious firm of Henry De-Saussure. Calhoun had done it before him, then gone off to finish his legal training in Connecticut.

Like his father, Edgar took up law for its practical value in the business of Bell's Bridge, a business that demanded his full attention in the years of the cotton boom. He did establish a law office in partnership with Argyll Buckles. Simon's son handled virtually all the cases brought to Buckles & Bell.

Edgar Bell was a plain, quiet, conservative man, with strong opinions on the affairs of his city, state, and country. In 1813 he married Cassandra Mayfield, daughter of Llewellyn Mayfield, a retired schoolmaster from Moncks Corner.

Mayfield was a large, amiable man with a talent for making unprofitable investments. He was a founding shareholder of the Santee Canal Company, which financed a water link between the Santee River and the head of the Cooper, for easier transportation of cotton and rice to the coast. Though busy for a time, the canal never became the overwhelming success Mayfield and his colleagues envisioned.

Mayfield ably fulfilled the role of doting grandfather after the arrival of his daughter's children, Hampton in 1814 and a sister, Alexandra, one year later. Subsequently Cassandra delivered two stillborn daughters. She and Edgar decided that God meant them to have only two children, but that was enough for them, and for Mayfield. He constantly overextended himself buying books, toys, and sweets for infants too young to appreciate them.

✷ ✷ ✷

In 1814 enemy ships bombarded Fort McHenry in Baltimore Harbor but failed to reduce and capture it. Out of this came verses for a new patriotic song, "The Star-Spangled Banner."

The British marched on Washington, savaging and burning the capital. Yet they couldn't find a victory; the Americans were too fierce and determined.

That same year, at the Horseshoe Bend of Alabama's Tallapoosa River, Gen. Andrew Jackson of Tennessee, sometimes called Old Hickory, sometimes Old Sharp Knife, defeated the Cherokee and the feared Red Stick warriors of the Creek nation in a spectacular battle. When this became known in Charleston, a few graybeards recalled a skinny hot-tempered boy from the Waxhaws, Andy by name, who had come down to the city in 1783 to claim a small inheritance. Fascinated by the rattle and snap of dice in Charleston's gambling dens, he lost it all.

Jackson gambled again in 1815, vanquishing British regulars at New Orleans two weeks after the Treaty of Ghent was signed; news of the peace had not yet reached America. Jackson's reputation was made. When he visited Washington, he was hailed as enthusiastically as any Roman Caesar. He would loom large in the country's future, and that of John Calhoun, and South Carolina.

✷ ✷ ✷

Of these events Lydia was only marginally aware. Simms continued to question his mother about the source of her nervous condition. She refused to name it, but another incident in the summer of 1816 offered a clue.

Simms and Bethel invited Lydia to one of the city-sponsored concerts in the public garden at White Point. They left three-year-old Ouida with her Negro nurse at Simms's new town house on Legare Street. The house was an older one that the Bells had enlarged and redecorated. Its finest feature was a pair of intricate gates to the side garden. The unknown craftsman had created a pattern of swords and spears in wrought iron. Simms, never wildly imaginative, christened the house Sword Gate.

Charleston's full burden of summer heat and humidity had not yet arrived. The evening air on the Battery was mild and pleasant. The only thing unpleasant for Lydia and, to a lesser degree, Simms, was the proximity of Tom Bell's house. Relations between the two sides of the family were cool; social meetings were few and always strained.

The concert crowd was largely elite, representative of old families, and those of newly rich planters. One of the latter, an unidentified gentleman who bore a slight resemblance to Tom Bell's younger son, caught Lydia's attention. From the first note of the first selection, the rousing "Hail, Columbia," she ignored the performance, her son, and Bethel, fixing her eyes on the stranger. Her expression grew strained. Nervous excitement made her blink and breathe rapidly.

Simms asked if she felt ill; his mother had enjoyed several months of relatively normal behavior. Her hand clamped on his sleeve. She whispered, "He's here. Don't look."

"Who's here, Mother?" Simms said as the chamber orchestra began a piece by Mozart. Those on nearby benches cast disapproving looks at the talkers. Lydia lunged to her feet.

"His ghost."

"Please sit down. There's no such thing."

"Yes, he's here, he's here." Lydia threw off her son's hand. "He won't let me alone. He won't rest until our family's destroyed." Tears streamed from her eyes.

Unnerved, Bethel issued one of her rare fiats. "Simms, we must go. This is humiliating."

Simms put his arm around his mother. Lydia began to struggle. Heads turned. The musicians stopped randomly, creating a cacophony of strings and woodwinds. Red faced, Simms said, "Ladies and gentlemen, forgive the interruption. My mother is indisposed."

He led her away. She continued to struggle, but he was stronger. Leaving the garden, she threw looks over her shoulder at the baffled nonentity whose appearance had triggered the outburst. She kept whispering. "He'll see us all ruined. Ruined or dead."

In bed on Legare Street after a heavy dose of her calmative, Lydia refused to answer questions about her imagined tormentor, or name him.

* * *

Edgar's son, Hampton, grew up a frail boy who showed signs of remaining that way. His sister, Alexandra, was large at birth. Cassandra fretted over the possibility that her daughter would be an inordinately tall woman, very inconvenient for romance. A dear friend had stayed a spinster due to extreme height and a paltry dowry.

The four years from 1815 to 1819 were the summit of Charleston's prosperity. People invested and expanded, built and bought, with reckless enthusiasm. In 1818 Edgar emulated Crittenden Lark and put money into a scheme to launch two oceangoing cargo ships. When the price of cotton plunged a year later, he faced heavy interest debt on the first ship, which sat unfinished on the ways of the Pritchard & Shrewsbury yard. At the same time, with trade declining, Edgar's income from the wharf was sharply down.

He had been approached more than once about selling Malvern. He and Cassandra and the children seldom visited the river house. Looking after it complicated his life, but he felt he owed it to the memory of his forebears to hold on to it. By 1820 his financial position required a rethinking of family loyalty.

An attorney known for sharp dealing came to him with an offer from a Mr. Stiles Blevins, merchant, of Georgetown. Edgar had never heard of Blevins, but his money was safely in escrow, so after consultation with Cassandra, Edgar signed the settlement papers and transferred the deed. Six months later Blevins sold Malvern to Simms Bell.

Edgar was furious. He confronted Simms at a performance of the reopened Charleston Theater at Savage's Green, on Broad Street west of Meeting. For years people of color, free and slave, had been permitted to buy seats in the third tier. In 1818 that was stopped.

Edgar accused Simms of using deception to acquire Malvern. Simms was all charm and good humor.

"Of course I had to resort to a subterfuge, cousin. My dear mother wanted the place, but I knew you wouldn't sell it to us directly."

Edgar would have knocked him down and challenged him to a duel at Washington Race Course if he'd been that sort of man. He had a conservative's dislike of duels and those who resorted to them. Dueling broke the law and set a bad example for the lower classes. Turning his back on Simms, Edgar collected Cassandra from their first-tier box and missed the last two acts of *Richard III*.

Edgar and his late mother had always suspected that Lydia Bell had a hand in Edward's death, or at least knew more about it than she would admit. Since there was no evidence to support the suspicions, the mystery remained unsolved, a source of frustration and private pain.

✫ ✫ ✫

Inevitably, slavery became a national issue. In 1819 Congress confronted the expansion of slavery, specifically in the Louisiana Territory purchased from France in 1803. It was more than a question of a state's right to choose its system of labor—it affected the fragile balance of power in the country.

Maine and Missouri wanted to enter the Union of twenty-two states, half of them free, half slave. Maine would join as the former, Missouri the latter. Debate in Washington was fierce and partisan. An 1820 compromise admitted both states and, with the exception of Missouri, prohibited slavery above an east-west line running along the northern border of the Arkansas territory. Ex-President Jefferson, himself a slave owner, heard a warning in the divisive clash of North and South. He called it "a firebell in the night."

☆　☆　☆

From 1800 to 1820 Charleston had not escaped its familiar civic woes: another catastrophic fire in 1812; a devastating hurricane a year later. Epidemics of smallpox and malaria came as regularly as the seasons. Through it all the better sections of the city had grown more opulent and attractive, while the run-down areas became filthier and more crowded.

By 1820 nearly sixty percent of Charleston's population was Negro, three thousand of them free. The lightest of these made up the so-called brown elite, a minority of proud, prosperous people of color who felt they had more in common with whites than with their darker brethren. Most looked down on other Negroes. Some owned slaves.

The wife of Morris Marburg came from the brown elite. So did the cabinetmaker Hamnet Strong, Poorly's son; he married a woman named Mary Ward, whose skin was scarcely darker than old ivory. Their children were correspondingly light. Edgar's son and daughter were friends and playmates of Henry and Marcelle Strong.

Whether black or brown the city's colored population still intimidated whites. More laws were drafted to restrict the rights and behavior of slaves and freedmen. Edward had freed Sally and Hamnet by signing a simple statement. Now manumission required a special, individual dispensation from the state legislature.

In the early summer of 1822 Charleston saw its oldest nightmare realized. On June 14, a Friday, a mulatto slave named George heard of a plot to murder every white man, woman, and child, then burn the city. George's owner informed the intendant, James Hamilton.

In the next two days rumors of the impending revolt ran through the white community like a grass fire. If the rumors were true, the slaves had secret caches of weapons and would rise up to kill and burn when darkness fell on Sunday night.

Alexandra Bell, already called Alex, was seven years old on that night of terror.

BOOK TWO
CITY ON FIRE
1822–1842

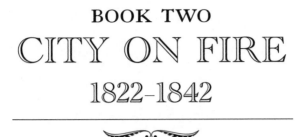

Everywhere I looked I saw mountains of cotton. . . . Conversation everywhere was on the price of cotton lands or cotton itself. . . . I believe that in the three days I was in Charleston I must have heard the word "cotton" pronounced more than three thousand times.

> A visitor to Charleston,
> circa 1827

The laws of the United States must be executed. . . . Those who told you that you might peaceably prevent their execution deceived you. . . . Their object is disunion. But do not be deceived by names. Disunion by armed force is treason. *Are you really ready to incur its guilt?*

> President Andrew Jackson
> Nullification Proclamation
> December 1832

This is the question—and the only question: whether it is not the sacred duty of the nation to abolish the system of slavery now, and to recognize the people of color as brethren and countrymen who have been unjustly treated and covered with unmerited shame.

> William Lloyd Garrison,
> 1832

26

Rebellion

Sunset painted White Point a deep red. The pathways of the broad, sandy promenade were deserted, unusual for a summer evening. Out of sight on Church Street, horses galloped, coming fast. Five curious children squeezed against the garden gate of the Bell house, watching for them.

Drayton, the black gardener, called out, "You best come away from there." The children ignored him. Two of them were white—Alex and her brother, Hampton. At seven Alex was already an inch above four feet, taller than the rest. She was slender as a reed, with a long waist and large blue-gray eyes. Ten-year-old Maudie, Drayton's daughter, served Alex as a personal maid, though Alex preferred to call her a friend instead of a slave. Like Alex she was barefoot.

Both Henry Strong and Ham were eight. Ham was sallow, and slender like his sister. Loose limbed, with round shoulders, he already had the look of a little old man. Henry was a handsome, stocky boy with smooth beige skin and curly black hair. Henry's sister, Marcelle, was four. Henry loved Marcelle but resented her following him everywhere. Marcelle's threadbare doll, her eternal companion, rested on her shoulder. The doll's china face was white.

Half a dozen armed men galloped out of Church Street and across South Battery past the house. As the dust cloud settled and the mounted patrol disappeared up King Street, footsteps on the piazza announced the arrival of someone with more authority than Drayton. Edgar Bell's normally pale face glowed pink from the June sun. Coming up behind the children, he clapped for attention.

"Henry, Marcelle, time to run along home. Maudie, take Alex inside. Don't put on your nightclothes or get in bed. The same for you, Hampton. We'll stay downstairs tonight. You children can make pallets on the floor. We must remain alert. There are rumors of unrest."

Henry said, "We heard them, Mr. Bell. Pa says Gullah Jack's been all over town, stirring up the colored."

Alex tugged the exposed tail of Henry's much-laundered gray shirt. "Who's Gullah Jack?"

"Conjure man. People are scared of him. They say he can't be killed. I say that's stupid, anyone can be killed."

"Jack's a born troublemaker," Edgar said. "The worst kind of colored man." He tapped the shoulders of his children. They backed away from the gate, Ham obediently, Alex with an annoyed toss of her long blond hair. Edgar prodded her. "Inside, missy."

Henry said good-night. Leaving, he managed to brush Alex's hand with his. As he opened the gate, she blew him a kiss. Maudie giggled. Edgar wheeled around to see the cause of the merriment. Alex smiled sweetly, curtseyed to him, and ran inside.

In the hall by the large Henry Benbridge portrait of Joanna, Cassandra directed Alex to the downstairs front, Tom Bell's old office. Alex puzzled over the unusual precautions. Were Charleston's Negroes really preparing to do something bad? She had trouble believing it. The Negroes she knew best, those in the household, were quiet, polite—her friends. She adored Maudie. The only black person who scared her was a sullen houseboy, fourteen or so, owned by Great-Aunt Lydia. He always looked mad enough to bite the head off a nail. Oddly, his name was Virtue.

Alex, Ham, and Maudie settled down on blankets. The red light leached from the sky; the tall windows turned black. Alex beat Ham at three games of checkers. After the last one Ham shouted, "Oh, damn you anyway." Cassandra smacked his hand and ordered them to lie down.

Itchy and hot without a bath, Alex still managed to doze. Maudie snuggled against Alex's bare feet, snoring softly. Sometime later Alex woke to see her father rush from the room with a pistol. Another mounted patrol thundered by. She heard distant shouting. Cassandra knelt, kissed Alex's forehead, and murmured soothing words. Alex fell back to sleep.

A terrific clang, and her mother's shriek, jolted her upright again. Ham jumped up, ran to the dark hall, whispered, "Someone's in the house." He raised his fists.

Titus, the black butler, appeared from the back of the house. "Ain't nothing wrong, Mist' Ham. Just my wife, stirrin' around when she shouldn't. Dropped a chamber pot, clumsy woman. We's very sorry, Miz Bell." Cassandra managed a forgiving smile.

Alex slept soundly until daylight woke her. Through slitted eyes she saw Ham sitting up with his Latin grammar. She couldn't see her mother, who was behind her, but she saw Papa, his legs stretched out, his boots dusty, the pistol on the rug beside his chair. His heavy dark beard showed; it always did in the morning, before he used his razor.

Cassandra said, "We sat up all night, Edgar. Nothing happened." She sounded cranky.

"You should be thankful. Now you understand the purpose of the slave code you're always criticizing. It may be onerous, but it's necessary."

Drowsy, Alex wondered what the slave code was, and why it was necessary.

"I suspect the trouble isn't over yet," Edgar added.

He was wrong; there was no public disorder, nor had there been any during the night. A hundred and forty Charleston blacks were quickly rounded up and thrown in the workhouse, however. Whips and truncheons soon loosened tongues about the aborted uprising.

The headquarters was said to be Reverend Morris Brown's African Methodist Episcopal Church in the outlying district of Hampstead. Jack Pritchard, the bandy-legged Angolan known as Gullah Jack, was a recruiter. The workhouse interrogators heard one name more than others—Denmark Vesey, a communicant of Brown's AME church and a teacher in Bible classes. One informant said he feared Vesey more than he feared God.

The following Saturday, in a raging tropical storm, authorities broke into a Bull Street house and seized Denmark Vesey. The freedman's hatred had grown until he refused to bow or step aside for whites on public footpaths, as was expected. Year after year he'd traveled the Low Country, secretly promoting his plot—his vision from Joshua: *And they utterly destroyed all that was in the city.*

Or so it was alleged by the white court convened on the second floor of the workhouse to try Denmark Vesey and his fellow conspirators. They were convicted with virtually no evidence but the self-serving accusations of others. On July 5 five of them were removed to a desolate area of brush and tidal inlets known as Blake's Marsh and hung. Vesey was taken to Ashley Street where it straggled out of town at the city's northern limits, for a similar end. The executions were hasty, the burial sites of the six kept secret.

Alex learned most of this from Henry Strong. He took her to see the oak where Vesey died. "You ever say a word to your pa, he'll whip me to pieces," Henry said. The wide-eyed girl clung to his arm. The intimacy drew fierce looks from a farmer in a wagon passing by.

"I won't, Henry, I swear to the Lord Jesus I won't," Alex said.

"You're crying. What the devil's wrong?"

"I know they say Mr. Vesey was a bad man, but I feel sorry for him. And I never saw a place like this before. A place where they killed someone."

"Don't worry, you'll see plenty more before this settles down."

"Do you think Vesey's gone to heaven?"

"No. He was a sinner. Anyway, I don't expect niggers can go to heaven, just like they can't go a lot of places in Charleston."

☆ ☆ ☆

Later executions were less secretive. The *Courier* and the *City Gazette* advertised that twenty-two conspirators would be hung en masse on July 26, Friday, at the Lines, an area outside the city where defensive earthworks once stood. Grandfather Mayfield was visiting the Bells. He wanted to take Alex and Ham to see the condemned men. "Not an edifying experience, I grant you, but educational," he said at the breakfast table. The children picked at their food, heads down. Maudie ate on a stool in the corner.

Cassandra said, "I think it's cruel. I don't want them to go."

"Permit me to decide," Edgar said.

"As you decide everything important in this house. What does a mere woman know?" She put down her linen napkin and left the room.

Mayfield wiped a smear of egg from his chin. "Get much of that from my daughter, do you?"

"Enough to make it annoying, frankly," Edgar said. Alex felt bad. Papa must think that being female was less desirable, less important, than being a man.

Mayfield said, "What I'm suggesting will be a good lesson for them. They'll see how the Negroes must be treated if we are to have peace." Mayfield owned no slaves but never questioned the propriety of the system.

Edgar said, "Children, would you be upset if you went with your grandfather to see such a thing?"

"No, sir," Ham cried loudly, to show his bravery. Alex covered her ears and made a face.

"Alex?" Edgar said.

"No, sir." Her cheeks felt feverish; she was sure Papa saw through her lie. Two hours later Grandfather Mayfield and the children stood in a huge crowd on Meeting Street. Maudie had asked to stay behind; Alex gave her permission.

In the middle of the street the City Guard escorted a long line of horse-drawn carts, each one carrying a prisoner with his hands tied behind him. Most looked frail and helpless. Almost all were badly bruised. Alex tugged Ham's sleeve.

"What are those boxes they're sitting on?"

"Their coffins."

A few white people cursed or jeered the condemned men, but mostly it was a solemn crowd. Alex saw few Negro spectators. Then suddenly, across Meeting, she spied Aunt Lydia's houseboy. Virtue stood out because scowling whites had drawn back to call attention to him, and the black rag tied around his sleeve.

"That's trouble," Grandfather Mayfield said when he saw the armband. "No nigger's permitted to mourn Vesey or his gang. It won't be long before—"

The sentence ended there. Armed men of the City Guard quickly surrounded Virtue. He flung off the first hand that touched him. The butts of muskets beat him to the ground. A knife flashed, cutting the armband and gashing his shoulder.

"For that he'll get thirty-nine stripes in the workhouse," Mayfield said. "Surely the boy knew the penalty before he flouted the law."

Alex yearned to go home but feared her grandfather would think it cowardly if she asked. They joined the procession of carriages and pedestrians following the carts. At the Lines drummers beat a slow rhythm while the first three blacks fearfully climbed the steps of a new scaffold.

Ropes dangling from a projecting beam dropped over their heads. One by one the men were booted off the edge of the scaffold. A sigh ran through the crowd. Alex's eyes watered.

Mayfield muttered, "Something's wrong." Ham gasped, pointed.

"They're not dead, Grandpa."

Alex wanted to scream and run. The three black men seemed to dance in the air, naked feet just inches from the ground. An officer of the City Guard stepped forward, put his pistol against a bare stomach, fired. The victim stopped his mad dance. His head lolled; blood ran from his belly and sopped his trousers. The officer signaled his men to shoot the others.

Grandfather Mayfield's voice was strangely subdued. "Children, I am so sorry. I was not prepared for this. We are leaving."

Trying not to weep, Alex clung to his big hand. Two more shots crashed as they fled.

At home she ran to her room. For the rest of the day she refused to come out or speak to anyone, even Maudie. Grandfather Mayfield was not welcome in Edgar Bell's house for months.

☆   ☆   ☆

Thirty-five black men died in the summer of 1822. Denmark Vesey's rebellion, the rebellion that never was, permanently scarred Charleston, the state of South Carolina, and all the South. It scarred Alex. Something new and horrible had spoiled the beautiful city she loved.

27

. . . . *And After*

Beauty was Alex's first, best memory of her childhood: the beauty of the sun-struck harbor, the white sails of ships bound for exotic ports. Even the pine dust that fell in the spring, coating every surface with a fine lime-colored powder, had a fairylike charm.

She loved the sight of men casting shrimp nets from sturdy piraguas or spearing flatfish by lantern light. She loved the mockingbirds perched on the pittosporum, guarding their nests and trilling their song; the great blue herons standing still as statuary; white egrets stepping high through marsh reeds in search of a meal; gulls diving to snatch one from the water.

She loved the steamy shade of summer; the rattle of rain on palmetto fronds. She loved the pealing bells of St. Michael's—she grew up listening to them sweetly ring the hours, or wildly ring fire alarms. Great Michael, the eighth and largest, tolled by himself to announce the fire's end. Evenings, the bells rang to warn Negroes to leave the streets in one hour. When they rang again, it signaled the City Guard to patrol for violators of the curfew. The evening bells were no more than pretty serenades until Alex discovered their purpose.

In the wake of the Vesey affair the AME church was torn down, its pastor driven from the city. New regulations further restricted the behavior of blacks. Respected men, including Alex's father, petitioned city council for a larger, stronger arsenal—a citadel, they called it—to arm an enlarged defense force. She overheard Titus whisper to his wife about a terrible new machine of punishment at the workhouse, the treadmill.

She hated having to fear black people. Evidently most adults in Charleston did. Out of this realization came questions. She took them to her friend Henry; Maudie accompanied her.

The Strongs had a two-story frame house and carpentry shop on John Street, above Boundary, near the city line. In that section of town freedmen and whites of the commercial class lived together in relative harmony. Alex found her friend astride a shaving horse in the sandy yard of the shop.

Henry plied his two-handled draw knife skillfully, shaving and shaping a square wooden rod held in a clamp in front of him. Henry's knife peeled off thin slivers to round the wood. Alex pointed to it. "What's that for?"

"Pegs, for joints in a serpentine sideboard Pa's building for a customer."

Maudie wandered inside to visit Mr. Strong. Alex inhaled the lovely wood smell of the chip-strewn yard. "You'll make a fine carpenter when you're grown up, Henry."

"Not sure I want that, but it's all right for now."

"Can I ask you some things? Vesey made me think of them." Henry bobbed his head, giving permission. "Why do we have slaves at all?"

"Because white folks want to make money but they don't want to do the hard work. Too hot most of the time."

"Are there slaves all over the world?"

"Only certain countries." The answer, the rich bass voice, came from Hamnet Strong, a larger, brawnier version of his son. Maudie had followed him outside.

"The American system is more cruel than most," Hamnet said. "Families are broken up, children sold away from parents without a second thought." Hamnet inspected the work. "That's good, Henry."

"Thank you, Pa."

Alex gnawed her lip. "I heard about something at the workhouse called a treadmill. Do you know what it is?"

Hamnet's normally placid face twisted into sourness. "By hearsay. It's a work-saving device. It can also punish twelve slaves at one time. That's all I'm going to tell you. Come inside, Mary's brewing tea. Henry, you may rest five minutes and join us."

★　★　★

Either the slave troubles had always been there, and she'd never noticed, or they'd gotten worse, hence were more freely discussed.

A stranger, a man a few years younger than Edgar, visited their house. He was what the town called a dandy. He wore polished Hessian boots, a waistcoat embroidered with tiny flowers, voluminous Cossack trousers tied near the ankles with black ribbons. Edgar received him in the side garden on a Sunday afternoon in September. The air was fresh after a cleansing rain that morning.

The visitor, Crittenden Lark, had flashing brown eyes and a smile so broad and white, it reminded Alex of Maudie's china doll. Edgar invited Lark to be seated on an iron bench. Alex eavesdropped from the back of the garden, where Drayton was pruning the brilliant gold and orange lantana, the West Indian perennial he loved. He'd given Alex a saw-toothed knife to prune a nearby row of crape myrtle that had bloomed pink and watermelon-red in July.

Lark spoke rapidly, as if to prevent interruption or disagreement. "Our families don't have the most cordial of relationships, Mr. Bell. We all know why. But you are a man of standing in Charleston, and the moment calls for putting aside old grievances. We must unite to deal with the growing nigger threat. I've come at the request of my good friend, your cousin Mr. Simms Bell, to invite you to join a new citizens' protective association. It's a private group seeking more forceful regulation of the slave population by all available means."

"Do you include extralegal means?"

"Construe it as you will, sir."

"Then I'm afraid I must decline."

The young dandy's smile froze. "That position could be harmful to your business."

"I'll stand the risk."

"Are you suggesting you're not in favor of regulating slaves?"

Alex pushed a strand of blond hair off her sweaty forehead. She glanced at Drayton. His head was bowed; his blue-black cheek shone in a random ray of sun. He never looked up.

"I suggest nothing of the kind," Edgar said. "I am simply in favor of enforcing existing codes. I must bid you good day, Mr. Lark, I'm extremely busy."

Crittenden Lark jammed his hat on his head and marched to the street gate. His murderous expression made Alex shiver.

★ ★ ★

Another thing Alex hated was obeying rules. There were so many, chief among them dos and don'ts handed down twenty times a day at Miss Ladylou Fancher's Academy for Young Ladies. Edgar and Cassandra enrolled Alex in the school for the first time that autumn.

Miss Ladylou Fancher weighed at least 250 pounds. She wore too much scent and never appeared without a ferronière, a fashionable white satin headband with a large pearl located in the middle of her forehead. Miss Fancher taught fundamentals of grammar, French, needlework, and music. When she disciplined her pupils, she peered at them through a long-handled quizzing glass.

Alex soon became a favorite target because of her resistance to practicing the harpsichord. In preparation for Miss Fancher's lessons Papa had bought a fine single-manual spinet, walnut, made in London. The spinet collected dust in a back corner of the downstairs hall. Alex was supposed to practice an hour a day, but she had to be pushed. She hated the pieces Miss Fancher forced on her—dull music by Corelli and Pescatore and other dead, deservedly forgotten composers.

Not that she disliked music. Soon after the Vesey trouble Maudie took her to Drayton's small brick slave house next to the stable at the rear of the property. There she proudly showed Alex a curious instrument made of a large calabash, one side cut off so as to be level with a long wooden neck attached to it. Over the opening of the calabash stretched a tanned skin, like a drumhead. Three strings ran from pegs at the top of the neck, down across the skin to the bottom of the gourd. Alex could only ask, "What is it?"

"A banja. Papa brought it from Barbados. You should hear him play."

"Well, I'd like to, if you'll ever give me the opportunity," Alex said, lapsing into the huffiness she heard all the time from the older girls at Miss Fancher's.

"I'll ask him," Maudie promised. At week's end Drayton invited Alex to the cottage in the evening. He picked up the banja, began to pluck the strings and hum. The infectious plink-plunk made her smile. In the music she heard the rhythm of bare feet in a merry dance.

"Oh, Drayton, that's wonderful," she exclaimed. "I wish I had a banja."

"I think they sell them ready made up North. Mr. President Jefferson in Virginia, he knows the banja." Drayton began a new tune. Just then Edgar was returning from Bell's Bridge, having stabled his horse. At the open window where a muslin curtain had been tied back for air, he paused to listen. Drayton and the children never noticed.

As Alex slipped into bed, Cassandra knocked softly. She asked Maudie to leave, then sat on the edge of the bed.

"I didn't hear you practice this afternoon"—Alex pulled the coverlet over her face—"and yet your father observed you lolling about with Drayton and Maudie, listening to him play that silly gourd with strings."

"His banja."

"Yes, I know its name. Your father says it's a slave instrument, from Africa. I will not have my daughter listening to that kind of music."

"But, Mama—"

"That's the last I want to hear of Drayton's banja or your interest in it."

She gave Alex a cool, reserved kiss on the cheek. "Sometimes I do wonder what kind of child I'm raising. Your father thinks you may have inherited some of your grandfather Edward's wild blood. You're not like other girls your age. You must learn to be, else you'll be miserable, a social outcast, all your life. I only say that because I love you."

Cassandra hugged her daughter and glided to the door. Before she called Maudie back, she shook her finger. "No more banja."

Which of course only propelled Alex to greater interest and, eventually, lessons from Drayton in secret.

★   ★   ★

The final thing Alex devoutly hated, though she never dared repeat it to anyone but Henry, was a girl at Miss Fancher's. Two years older than Alex, the girl was overbearing. She mingled her scorn with a condescending pity all the more galling because it was plainly insincere. Alex would have bloodied Ouida's nose or kicked her shins but for the fact that it would bring punishment at home. Ouida was the daughter of Uncle Simms and Aunt Bethel, the granddaughter of Great-Aunt Lydia. She was Alex's first cousin. There was no avoiding her.

28

Cousin Ouida

Ouida Bell was a Christmas baby. As she grew, she came to resent the birthday of Jesus. It took precedence over hers; robbed her of attention and gifts.

Ouida was a plump and pretty child whose round face resembled that of Maudie's doll. The prettiness concealed more than a few animosities. The person she hated most was her younger cousin Alex. The reasons were so numerous, it sometimes dizzied her head.

Alex's eyes were a vivid hydrangea-blue. Ouida's were blue, but pale. In the wrong light they were almost colorless.

Alex was smarter than Ouida, although Mama said that counted for nothing when it was time to marry, indeed could work against a girl.

Alex wasn't nearly as well off or well dressed as Ouida, Mama assured her. Yet Ouida's little brother, Gibbes, two years younger than Alex, mooned over her like a lovesick swain.

Alex was more popular at Miss Fancher's. Whenever the headmistress stepped out for a bit, Alex shamelessly unbuckled her hideous high-lows, lifted her skirts to show her pantalets, and danced barefoot like the lowest of street boys. The other girls clustered around, clapped, and tried to imitate her while Ouida hung back, ignored.

Alex loved to work in her garden, dirtying herself like a field hand. She seemed to do everything a girl shouldn't, while Ouida behaved as well-bred young ladies of Charleston were taught. Even so, Ouida couldn't escape the feeling that she, not Alex, was the inferior.

Ouida didn't give a fig for things her father talked about at home: the "banditry" of Massachusetts shoe manufacturers from whom he bought slave shoes by the barrel, or a despised Kentucky politician named Clay who was promoting an import tariff, whatever that was. Simms was always praising the accomplishments of his Yale classmate, John Calhoun, secretary of war under President Monroe and now mentioned as a possible running mate for Gen. Andy Jackson. Ouida heard these things, and more, and promptly forgot them.

Ouida's deportment was appropriate to every occasion. At a family levee at Sword Gate the night before the St. Cecilia Ball, during the madness of Race Week, she overheard a male guest say, "Have you seen Beau Pratt's new girl Phoebe? Quite a leg on her." Hearing the word *leg* uttered in mixed company, Ouida fell on a fragile taboret and broke it as she went into the required swoon. Bethel revived her with an ammonia-scented handkerchief. The offending gentleman sent a bouquet and a note apologizing for his "lewd and unseemly language."

At Prosperity Hall, Ouida learned to accept the presence of mulatto babies who appeared suddenly, as though dropped from the clouds. One time she mentioned such a new arrival to her mother. Bethel, sipping Madeira, replied with appropriate bitterness, "You will learn someday that a plantation wife is the chief slave in her husband's harem. Never tell anyone I told you."

★　★　★

Despite Virtue's rebellious nature he was promoted to footman before his sixteenth birthday. Lydia objected. "You should sell that troublemaker," she told Simms.

"Mother, he's stronger than any other man in the house. He can be very useful if he takes a mind to it."

"Have you looked into his eyes? He's dangerous."

"He took his punishment for the black armband without protest. His spine's a mass of scars from it. He's been obedient ever since."

"Just wait. Niggers are secretive. They harbor grudges for years, then they turn on you. You are too gentle with them."

Simms didn't prolong an argument he couldn't win. He kissed Lydia's powdered forehead and said, "I promise to keep an eye on him, don't you fret."

"But I do, because you're so weak." He stepped back, flushing.

"Where's that shiftless wench with my medicine? I always have my afternoon medicine at three. It's five minutes past."

Simms welcomed the excuse to leave the room in pursuit of the medicine and the errant slave.

* * *

Lydia dealt harshly with all the house blacks but reserved special attention for Virtue. When one of his looks offended her—she called it a glare—she ordered him to the pantry, to stand on one leg for an hour, holding his other foot. A Charleston acquaintance had told her it was an excruciating punishment.

A few weeks later Virtue removed a crystal goblet from the dinner table carelessly, dropping and shattering it. When dinner ended at half past three, Lydia had him repeat the hour of punishment, with an improvement she'd discovered. A rope went around Virtue's neck; the other end was tied to the foot he held. Any relaxation or lowering of the foot tightened the noose. Lydia smiled at his expression of pain and fury.

* * *

In the summer of 1824, before the presidential election, Simms traveled up to Pendleton, near Greenville. John Calhoun had invited him to have dinner and spend the night with the Calhoun family at their new home, Clergy Hall.

Calhoun's honored guest was Thomas Cooper, president of South Carolina College at Columbia. "A man who clearly understands what the North's up to," Simms said to his wife before he left. "Cooper questions the value of our so-called union, because Clay and his crowd want tariffs that will sacrifice the South to Northern interests. We can't abide it."

The day after Simms's departure brought a white sky, oppressive humidity, and distant thunder. Ouida, now eleven, found herself abandoned in the great plantation house. Mama lay abed with a feminine complaint and was not to be disturbed. Gibbes had gone off riding with a slave boy. Ouida went in search of her grandmother. She felt no great affection for the old woman but catered to her because it was expected. Despite eccentricities and a violent temper Lydia was an important figure in the family.

Lydia's quarters consisted of a combination bedroom and sitting room on the second floor. A large inner closet overflowed with her dresses, some of them twenty years old. Ouida had no more than a vague understanding of old age. She thought her grandmother about fifty; actually she was sixty-five.

She tapped softly at the hall door. No answer. She was about to repeat the knock when she heard Lydia pleading with someone in a loud voice, in a way that alarmed Ouida.

She opened the door, crept into the gloomy bedchamber. Heavy velvet drapes showed only a sliver of gray between. Lydia's shrill voice issued from the dark closet. "Go away, go away."

Ouida called, "Grandmother? Do you need help?"

Lydia kept ranting: "Don't torment me, Edward."

Edward? Who was that? Could it be the relative who had drowned in the Ashley River years ago?

"I never meant to harm you. I was angry, because I loved you and you refused me. Why do you stand there accusing me? Why don't you speak? I'll go mad if you don't leave me alone."

Ouida didn't want to face Lydia during one of her spells, so she turned to steal out. Her toe caught the edge of the carpet. She fell against the door, slamming it. "Who's there?"

Lydia rushed from the closet. Her appearance terrified Ouida. Her gray hair was a tangle. She wore a chemise that served as her summer night dress, and knee-length white stockings, without slippers. Over the chemise was a striped banyan, an informal morning coat with flared skirts; the front bore many spots and stains. Patches of Lydia's face powder were cracked by lines from tears or sweat.

"You wicked girl. How long have you been spying? What did you hear?"

"Nothing, Grandma, I didn't hear any—"

Lydia's hand flew; the slap sounded like a shot.

She seized Ouida's shoulders, shook her. Ouida nearly gagged at the smell of the old woman's breath.

"That's right, you heard nothing. You saw nothing. You weren't here. Tell me that." *Slap.* "Tell me."

Gasping and tearful, Ouida said, "I wasn't here. I saw and heard nothing."

"Swear to that, God strike you dead if you lie."

"I swear, Grandma. Please don't hurt me any mo—"

Slap. "Pay attention. If you ever whisper a word of this to your mother or father, or anyone, I'll do to you what I do to a nigger who misbehaves. I'll punish you."

"I won't tell. I'm so sorry, I thought you were in danger. I thought someone was in there with—"

"No one was in there. You imagined it." A roll of thunder rattled windows. She flung the door open, pushed Ouida into the hall. Weeping into her hands, Ouida ran to her room. She locked the door and threw herself on the bed.

She didn't see her grandmother until breakfast next morning. She hardly dared look at her. The old woman chatted and laughed with Bethel, who'd come down in a quilted robe. Lydia glanced at Ouida every now and then, her eyes like tiny stones, devoid of emotion or even recognition.

Gradually, the pain of the awful scene receded. Ouida pushed the memory down deep inside her. There it festered, refusing to die.

Her poor grandmother saw things that didn't exist. She was "nervously distraught"—Ouida's mother used that term to describe women who had hysterics, a condition mysteriously related to childbearing. Perhaps the medicine Lydia took affected her badly. Still, she couldn't seriously harm anyone. Ouida convinced herself of that in desperate defense of her peace of mind.

☆　☆　☆

In 1825 the Marquis de Lafayette, hero of the Revolution, visited Charleston on his triumphant tour of the nation for which he'd fought. The city honored him with banquets and balls, military parades and fireworks. Presented to the marquis, Ouida knew she should be impressed but she found him just a melon-faced little old man.

John Quincy Adams was the new president. Failing to gain a majority in the electoral college, he'd been elected by a vote in the House of Representatives. John Calhoun had won the vice presidency with a clear majority; South Carolina continued to have a strong voice in national affairs. As they said in Charleston, Mr. Calhoun was a big toad in the Washington puddle.

That autumn Lydia told Simms she'd overheard Virtue calling her a filthy name. Although the young slave denied it, Lydia insisted Simms punish him by cropping his ear. "And give him no spirits beforehand to make it easy." Virtue disappeared from the household for a month. Simms announced plans to sell him.

The holidays intervened. Ouida was maturing; Bethel said she deserved a party to celebrate her thirteenth birthday. They would hold it at Sword Gate, decorate lavishly, hire musicians, prepare luxurious buffets of food and drink, in short, give a party that reflected not only Ouida's approaching womanhood but also the family's wealth and social eminence.

"Invite cousin Alex and her family," Ouida begged her mother.

"I thought you disliked Alex. You say so often enough."

"I only say it when I'm feeling cross." Bethel understood; the word *cross* referred to symptoms of a certain unpleasant, and unmentionable, feminine burden Ouida had begun to experience. "I do so want her to come, Mama."

Eight-year-old Gibbes noisily seconded the idea. Bethel agreed, though without enthusiasm. Ouida hugged her. "Oh, thank you, Mama." Ouida's intention was to buy and wear the most lavish dress her parents would allow, thereby showing Alex she was dowdy by comparison. When Cassandra accepted the party invitation on behalf of herself, Edgar, and the children, Ouida was elated.

Christmas was a season dreaded in Charleston and the Low Country. Masters were more lenient then; slaves had more leisure, thus more time to succumb to evil impulses. While the world celebrated the birth of the Prince of Peace, whites were on guard against poison, arson, murder.

Virtue had returned to his duties in early December. His left ear was gone, leaving a gnarly black rim of scar tissue around the canal opening. Simms insisted he hide it with a white scarf. It was imperative that he not upset guests at the party, which fell on Friday, two days before Christmas.

29

Bloody Friday

Sword Gate shone like a lighthouse in the warm December dark. House slaves had set out scores of candles. Bethel wanted a grand display, and for once Simms had overridden Lydia's warnings about mixing slaves and fire.

The splendor of the lights awed Alex as she and her family arrived. Edgar handed the phaeton's reins to a black youth at the hitching block. "Everyone behave," Cassandra said as they entered through the side garden. "No matter how you feel about them, they're relatives."

Alex thought her family handsomely dressed for the occasion. Papa looked elegant in his black frock coat, white vest, white tie, and full-length black inexpressibles[4] held down by loops under his shoes. Mama's bell-shaped skirt with its stiffened hem nicely showed off her red slippers. She and Alex had done their hair with sausage curls. Alex's dress was royal blue velvet with two overlapping shoulder capes. She wished she could show it off to Henry. Of course there wasn't any way he could come to the party, unless he held carriage horses at the curb.

There was a huge crowd in the house; Alex pictured the walls bulging and cracking if too many more came in. Aromas of food and drink, pine boughs and perfume, mingled in a tobacco haze. Cheerful

[4]A euphemism for trousers, another word banned in polite society.

conversation competed with a string quartet on the piazza, where couples danced in the mild evening air.

Simms, Bethel, and Lydia received their guests in the front hall, beside a tall pine tree sparkling with wax lights, gilt cord, and glass ornaments. Uncle Simms wore traditional satin knee breeches. Alex thought he looked like something from an old picture book. Lydia's eyes kept darting to the burning candles.

"So pleased to see you all," Bethel said. "It doesn't happen often enough. Ham, you look ever so handsome." Ham grimaced. Dressed like his father, he was miserable in his tight collar.

Bethel fanned herself. "Isn't it a crush? Half of Charleston's here."

Simms laughed. "Bethel can't stop writing invitations. You children will find special refreshments at the rear of the piazza. Eggnog, chocolates, ice cream—things young people enjoy. Ouida and Gibbes are eager to see you. And please do look around, we have a new suite of furniture in Sheraton style." Brag, brag. As if Alex cared. She'd rather sit on a rock with Henry than on a Sheraton, whatever that was.

Cassandra was polite, asking, "Did you import the furniture from London?"

Simms said, "Oh, of course. I wouldn't have it from any other place." Alex wanted to stamp on his shoe and say, *What's wrong with Mr. Strong's furniture? It's beautiful.*

Other arrivals were waiting; Edgar and his family moved on. Servants glided through the crowd taking orders for flips, gin slings, brandy toddies, French champagne, claret, and syllabub. Alex loved syllabub, a combination of brandy, white wine, sugar, and whipped cream. Occasionally she was allowed a sip, but Cassandra had forbidden it tonight, for the sake of appearances.

The dining-room table and double-tiered sideboards held more food than Alex had ever seen in one place: suckling pig, two turkeys, a beef roast, veal croquettes, corn pie, onions in cream, and of course Charleston oysters, fried, steamed, and curried. Miss Ladylou Fancher, her head adorned with a gaudy turban, was devouring a plateful of fried oysters with a zeal that prohibited conversation. Alex didn't want to speak to her anyway.

By the dessert sideboard she encountered Virtue slicing a pale yellow cheese cake with a silver knife. He wore a white silk scarf tied around his head. He glowered at Alex; she retreated.

Ouida tapped her shoulder. "Dear cousin, there you are." She embraced Alex, kissed both cheeks. Ouida wore a stunning dress of red velvet with large padded sleeves and swags of gilt passementerie accenting her budding bosom and broad hips. Fashionable ladies piled their hair high on the back of the head, but Ouida had gone to extreme with the very tallest of such arrangements, called *à la giraffe*.

"That's a dear little dress, Alex, is it new?"

"Oh, no, it's a year old."

"Well, the way you're shooting up, poor thing, you'll soon outgrow it." Ouida would be thirteen in two days; Alex, ten, was taller and, as Ouida hinted, ungainly. She forced herself to compliment Ouida's red dress.

"Mama had it made at Miss Teller's on King Street. The fabric's from Paris. I feel so fortunate. You know what they say in England."

"I guess I don't," Alex said, noticing Gibbes peering at her from behind his sister's skirts. He reminded her of a mournful puppy.

"They say nothing from America can be fashionable or worthwhile. Have you read *The Spy*?"

"Yes. Mr. Cooper's books are exciting."

"Mama refuses to let me read him. I'm stuck on *Kenilworth*. So boring. I think that's terrible, don't you?"

Before Alex could decide, Gibbes stepped forward and bowed. "Will you dance with me, Alex? I've had lessons. I know how to do the cotillion and the waltz."

"I don't. Besides, you're too short for me." She fled, feeling plain and out of place all at once. She wished she weren't *shooting up,* as Ouida called it. No doubt people snickered behind their hands and said she was growing *à la giraffe*.

She lingered near her father while he and Simms chatted. Edgar was describing a new gas lighting system in Baltimore. Simms didn't share his enthusiasm: "Sounds like another Yankee scheme to pick our pockets and intrude on our way of life."

The party grew loud. Guests discussed recipes, the playhouses, favorable and unfavorable characteristics of their pastors, and, inevitably, cotton prices. Gentlemen chewed cigars and spit into brass pots called cuspidors; these recent innovations kept floors cleaner but endangered the clothing of ladies standing too near.

Alex watched Crittenden Lark pass by her father and cut him dead. Mr. Lark was a peacock—pink silk coat, ruffled shirt, black breeches, and white stockings. He cornered Mr. Petigru, a feisty little lawyer and good friend of Edgar's. Lark was soon shaking his finger in Petigru's face.

The quartet on the piazza finished "Home Sweet Home," a popular tune from a London opera. Aware of Gibbes trailing her, Alex wriggled through the crowd to escape him. She greeted Morris Marburg and his wife. Papa said Simms despised Jews, but Mr. Marburg was a banker, and Papa also said you befriended every banker you met.

Finding Ham, she whispered, "When can we go home?" Ham shrugged, rolled his eyes, and yanked his collar again.

Alex took his hand. "Come along, let's have some chocolates." They started for the piazza, only to be stopped by Ouida's outcry:

"You stepped on my dress. You tore it."

Alex's cousin confronted Virtue at the dessert sideboard. He was gazing down at the ruinous rip, clasping and unclasping his white-gloved hands. "Wasn't me, Miss Ouida. Must been one of the gen'men."

Lydia thrust between them. "Don't you contradict my granddaughter." There was a sudden hush in the room.

A blood vessel in Virtue's forehead rose. "I tell you I did'n do nothing."

Aunt Lydia wheeled around. "Simms?"

"Here, Mother."

"He's calling Ouida a liar."

Forcefully, Virtue said, "No, I ain't."

"Remove him, Simms. Punish him."

Virtue's expression turned ugly. "He better not. You people done enough to me." He tore off the white scarf. His left ear was missing. The sight of lumpy scar tissue made Alex queasy.

Lydia said, "Is that a threat? Losing your ear apparently taught you nothing. This time we'll cut off your foot and make you worthless. You're not much better than that now." She turned her back, dismissing him.

Virtue seized her around the waist. A communal gasp ran around the room. With his right hand Virtue snatched the knife from the cheesecake plate. A man exclaimed, "Oh, my God, don't hurt her." Virtue reached over Lydia's shoulder and slashed her throat twice.

A great fan of arterial blood spewed from the wounds, raining on the heart-pine floor and the feet of the nearest guests. Virtue pushed Lydia away. She fell against Ouida, dragging the two of them down in a heap. Ouida wailed and writhed, trapped underneath. Lydia's heart kept pumping, reddening Ouida's face and throat and flailing hands.

Two older housemen rushed Virtue. He cut an arc in the air with the red knife, driving them back. Blood flew off the blade, speckling the wall and a woman's white turban. She fainted into the arms of her escort. Other ladies had fallen in similar fashion.

Crouching, Virtue swung the knife in a little circle to deter other attackers. Guests crowded in from the hall as Virtue backed toward a tall window. Simms ran at him. Virtue leapt at the window, flung his arms over his head. In a rain of glass he dropped into a narrow passage between houses. "Catch him, he's escaping," Simms shouted. Still pinned beneath her grandmother's twitching body, Ouida screamed like a mad thing.

Simms crawled through the frame of sawtooth glass and dropped from sight as Virtue had. Cassandra ran to Alex and Ham. "Are you children all right?" Ham said yes. Alex could only swallow and nod. Cassandra hugged them. "Oh, this is horrible, frightful. What provoked it?"

Several other men followed Simms through the broken window. It turned out to be a futile pursuit. According to reports Edgar brought home later, Virtue ran to the street, fatally stabbing the boy at the hitching block. He stole a buggy and raced away in the night. He was never caught. Many believed he slipped aboard a ship manned by black sailors who hid him until the vessel crossed the Charleston Bar at the next high tide.

Alex had nightmares about the tragedy. She asked the same question Cassandra had. *"What provoked it?"*

★ ★ ★

The weeks following Lydia's funeral brought forth different answers. At Prosperity Hall, where Simms's family wore black and Ouida moved in a strange state of withdrawal, the answer required no thought. What provoked it was Virtue's bestial nature—the nature of all Negroes.

Cassandra's answer was not so glib. Alex heard it as she and her mother stood gazing at the Benbridge portrait of Joanna.

"What provoked it? Why, what we've done to the blacks. Treating them as chattels. Tormenting and demeaning them without remorse or the slightest thought of remedy. Your grandmother knew."

Cassandra's soft, sad words struck into Alex's heart and mind like a white iron on flesh. *Please God,* she prayed, *I hope you hear me. I will never treat anyone so cruelly. I'll never be like those who do. I'll hate them and be their enemy forever.*

30

A Warning

In 1829 the business community hummed with talk of the "rail road" to be constructed next year. Its coming was prompted by continuing depression in cotton prices, the expansion of settlement away from the coast, and a general decline in Charleston commerce.

Two years earlier Edgar and other civic leaders had traveled to the capital to lobby for a bold remedy. The legislature responded by chartering the South Carolina Canal and Railroad Company to create a rail or water link between the Ashley and Savannah rivers. Most Carolina waterways were too shallow for anything larger than rafts or poleboats, while the broad Savannah carried cargo on sizable barges. Backers of the scheme expected a canal or railway to divert a significant and profitable amount of freight and passenger traffic from the port of Savannah. Edgar shared the vision and bought shares in the new company.

The canal idea soon faltered, left in the shadow of England's innovative experiments with iron and wooden rails. Planners of the SCC & R considered systems using horsepower, sail power, or steam power. Edgar said a decision would soon be made in favor of steam, and a contract let for construction of a "loco-motive" with a required speed of eight to ten miles an hour.

New men led the nation: President Andrew Jackson and Vice President John Calhoun. Locally, Crittenden Lark had easily defeated his opponent for a seat in Congress.

Soon after the election Henry Strong surprised Alex by taking a menial job at the Charleston Theater at Savage's Green, Broad and New Streets. The theater dated to 1793. An early manager, Alexander Placide, was fondly remembered in the city. A rope walker who entertained the French court before he emigrated, Placide had presented plays and other entertainments—acrobats, bird call artists, Indians doing war dances—at his own smaller theater before taking over the larger venue. There, he brought celebrated actors to Charleston: Henry Wallack, Junius Brutus Booth, the arrogant Englishman, Kean, who made too many hostile remarks about America during his engagement and was driven off Placide's stage by a rain of eggs and rotten vegetables.

Placide died in the summer of 1812. His wife and five children, all performers, tried to keep the house going but failed. After that it operated with a change of managers every season or so. Each said he couldn't make money because Charleston wasn't a good theater town. Audiences were unsophisticated and fickle, often preferring an exhibition of wax figures, or a panorama of the battle of Lake Erie, or Morton's Live Whale and Magic Show, to something by Shakespeare or Sheridan.

Which is exactly how Alex felt. She and Ham had been dragged to a box at the Charleston only three times, once to see a diverting spectacle called *Aladdin, or The Wonderful Lamp,* and then to suffer through *Romeo and Juliet* and *Macbeth.* Ham liked the swordplay and bloodletting, but Alex found the language strange and the plays boring.

She asked Henry why he'd taken such a job. They talked in Gullah, as they usually did when by themselves.

"Pa made two beautiful lobby doors for them. He heard they wanted to hire a boy and I went to see about it, without telling him. I did it because I can't get in the theater otherwise. 'People of color not be admitted to any part of the house.' Says so on every handbill."

"You're mad about being kept out and you want to show them up? That's the reason?"

"Not the only one. Mama sees theater when she visits her relatives. Her aunt, Miss Rose Ward, she's a ladies' maid in New York, she takes Mama to a Negro playhouse called Brown's. Mama says it's wonderful, magical, watching people pretend to be other people. On her last trip she heard about a young Negro from America, Ira Aldridge, who's getting famous in London where they don't care about color."

"Yes, but how do you watch the plays if they won't admit Negroes?"

"They let me stand behind the prompt table."

"How does your father feel about it?"

"He had a pretty long face when I told him, but he wants me to do whatever I want to do. Pa wouldn't make me a slave against my will, is how he put it."

"Your father's a noble man."

Henry nodded. "Wouldn't you like to see the theater? When the company leaves to play three weeks in Savannah, I can show you around."

Late in January 1829 the moment arrived. The Charleston Theater was a handsome stone building modeled after playhouses in London. Henry met Alex at the artists' entrance. She wore a black armband that day. Grandfather Mayfield had gone to his reward, if any, two days before Christmas.

As they peeked into dressing rooms used by the artists, Alex said, "What exactly do you do here?"

"Sweep. Paint. Help build scenery. Burnish the footlight reflectors. Sometimes they let me call the half and quarter hour. Last week Mrs. Leigh Waring from the company, she's Mr. Placide's daughter, she complimented my voice."

Alex could understand. Henry's voice had matured; grown deep and beautiful. Its tone reminded her of the tolling of Great Michael.

"I might be an actor," he added.

"Oh, could you? I mean, is it possible for . . . ?" She didn't finish. He knew what she meant.

"For a colored man? Not in this town. I'd have to go to New York. Or England, like Mr. Aldridge."

Upset by the thought, Alex said, "What about that law they passed after Denmark Vesey? Any free person of color who leaves South Carolina and returns can be arrested. Made a slave again."

"Heard about it. Guess if I go, I can't come back."

"Oh, Henry, no. What would I do?"

"Find a good white man to marry and give you babies."

Alex feigned shock at his language. Henry had surely changed. But so had she; the shape of her front was testimony.

She touched his sleeve. "You know I couldn't find anyone who'd be as good a friend as you."

"Who says your husband has to be your friend?"

"I do. Don't change the subject. You and I are soul mates."

"What's that?"

"People who care about each other. I read it in one of Mama's novels."

"Well, if you think we're soul mates, maybe both of us should leave."

They walked through the scene room to the stage. Beyond the apron lay the pit, dark as a chasm, with three tiers of boxes above, and then the gallery. "Holds twelve hundred people," Henry said.

The talk of leaving Charleston depressed her. "Mr. Thomas Grimké's sister Sarah left, you know."

"She the woman who changed churches?"

"Yes, she became a Quaker, up in Philadelphia. Mr. Grimké told Papa that his sister left because of slavery. His other sister, Angelina, may be next. She's already going to the Quaker meeting here. People like Uncle Simms and Ouida sneer and scorn her for it. But, Henry, if a person hates slavery—"

"I surely do."

"—must the person go somewhere else?"

"Don't see any other way, 'less you want to try Vesey's way and get hung."

Alex shivered, clasped his hand. "Let's go outside. This place is too gloomy."

☆   ☆   ☆

Alex's relationship with her cousins hadn't improved. Gibbes continued to chase her. Each time they met, he sidled up and tried to whisper flattery or tell a joke in a lame effort to be entertaining. Alex always rebuffed him, to the point of being insulting. It didn't seem to stop him, so she avoided him whenever possible.

She had less chance of avoiding Ouida, who was finishing her studies at Miss Fancher's. Ouida would receive no further education, nor would Alex. All that remained for Miss Fancher's young ladies was marriage and motherhood, or the one profession open to women, teaching. Alex resented that.

Puberty had brought Ouida from her childhood cocoon but failed to turn her into a beautiful butterfly. She was, Alex thought with a definite tincture of dislike, a drab moth who hid the drabness with rouge, powder, and pretty clothes. Ouida had weak eyes; tended to squint. She needed thick spectacles but she was vain and wouldn't wear them. This produced collisions with furniture and, sometimes, people. If Ouida bumped into a slave and hurt herself, she punished the slave. She was known for mistreating the Negroes at Sword Gate and Prosperity Hall. Lydia had taught her well.

Though just sixteen, Ouida appeared to have a gentleman interested in her. "Oh pooh," she protested when questioned. "Dr. Hayward's twenty-nine. Old as Methuselah."

"But he calls on you regularly, doesn't he?" a classmate asked.

"No. He calls at our house, because Mama gets the vapors, and he's her doctor."

Alex had met Dr. Xeno Hayward at a Christmas levee. A stout man, he had a lovely warm smile and an easygoing manner. She wondered what he saw in Ouida. Beyond her wealth and position, of course. Perhaps that was all he needed to see, Charleston being Charleston. There was just no accounting for choices in love.

Alex's assumption was speculative; nearing fourteen, she had no experience with the subject. Because of her height, her dislike of coquetry, and the quirky way she thought about things, perhaps she never would.

☆   ☆   ☆

In a rosy spring twilight Alex and Henry strolled in White Point garden, observing barges anchored near a harbor shoal where army engineers were starting construction of a fort. Alex had brought her new banjo, as white people called the instrument. She wanted to show it off to Henry. His father had helped make it, over Cassandra's continuing objections.

The banjo's round body, or ring, came from a wooden cheese box. Hamnet had sculpted the underside of the neck with his screw-crank lathe, then finished the piece and attached it using hand tools. Old Drayton, who was losing his eyesight, somehow found a tanned coonskin for the head. Humoring his daughter, Edgar brought home strings made of sheep's gut. It wasn't a beautiful or expensive instrument, but it produced a ringing tone. Drayton had taught Alex to play it with an upstroke of thumb and forefinger. She learned the guitar downstroke on her own.

The garden was nearly deserted; long shadows lay on the rose-tinted paths. Henry looked around cautiously, then flopped on a cast-iron bench. "Play me something." Alex happily obliged.

> "Possum up a gum tree,
> Tink dat none can folla.
> Him damn mistaken,
> Raccoon's in de holla."

He interrupted. "You allowed to say *damn*?"

"I guess I am if I do, Henry." She sang the rest of the song, culminating in the coon's downfall, removal from the tree by a clever black man who caught hold of his tail.

Henry grinned and applauded. On South Battery a seller of gooseberries and strawberries with a basket on his head wearily chanted his offerings. Alex retuned two of the four strings, played and sang again.

> "Little Henry Strong,
> At a tender age
> Hankers to be acting
> On the public stage."

He blinked. "Where'd that come from?"

"Me. I made it up."

"You make up songs?"

"Yes. I don't play them for anyone."

"You played one for me."

"I can trust you not to make fun."

"Why'd I make fun?" He leaned back, brawny arms draped over the bench. "Tune's nice. I don't much like the 'little' part." He pumped himself up with a deep breath and showed a muscle. Alex laughed and touched his bare arm, just as a handsomely dressed stranger walked by. The gentleman dug in his heels, poked Alex's arm with the ferrule of his cane.

"You're Attorney Bell's daughter. What are you doing in the public garden with him?"

"Henry is a free person of color, sir. He's my friend."

"He's a nigger. Mixing is against the laws of God and nature. Stop your folly or you'll come to grief. There are people in Charleston who will see to it. As for you"—he jabbed Henry—"it will soon be curfew."

Henry jutted his chin. "But it ain't yet. Sir."

The stranger pointed the cane at Alex. "Your father handled a breach-of-contract suit for me. He'll never handle another." He wheeled and walked off. Alex and Henry exchanged looks.

She told Edgar of the experience, and of the stranger's belligerence. He hugged her, murmured that it didn't matter, Henry was a fine young man. Alex wondered if he was secretly disappointed, or worried about her indiscretion. If so he kept it to himself.

31

Visitor from the Midlands

A meeting of the Fortnightly Club brought some of Edgar's like-minded friends to the Battery. These included Mr. Petigru and Mr. Grimké, fellow attorneys; banker Marburg; the stout and stentorian Judge Beaufurt Porcher, retired from the bench but still handing down opinions; Mr. Poinsett, who had given Cassandra an exotic Christmas plant with brilliant red leaves, discovered while he served as America's first minister to Mexico. It was a balmy spring evening, so the members gathered on the piazza. Despite the presence of biting midges,[5] windows were raised to catch a breeze in the house. Alex and Ham lingered downstairs to listen, at his insistence.

"You don't want to be a dumbbell, do you? You want to know what's going on, don't you?" Alex said no, and yes, but she really wanted to run off and practice the banjo. Edgar had forbidden it while he entertained.

Judge Porcher presented the evening program, a review and commentary on something called the *South Carolina Exposition and Protest*, printed in Columbia and endorsed by the legislature last December. "An ably reasoned document, gentlemen, though pernicious in one respect. Its author puts forth his arguments but withholds his name.

[5]Today we call these unpopular creatures no-see-ums. The term, supposedly of Indian origin, entered the language in the mid-1840s.

Washington swirls with rumors that Jackson suspects his own vice president, Mr. Calhoun of Fort Hill and Pendleton. Doubts of Calhoun's loyalty to the union have thus arisen, together with suspicions that he is protecting his good name because of well-known presidential ambitions. Such dissembling sadly soils the record of a man who for so long was the union's steadfast promoter and defender."

A lantern on a small table lit the judge's perspiring face. "Calhoun now interposes himself between state and federal governments. He continues to stand against internal improvements, characterizing them as schemes to benefit Northern industry at the expense of Southern agriculture. The so-called tariff of abominations is of course a particular target. On major issues Mr. Calhoun is less and less a national man, more and more a man of narrowing provincialism, not to say isolation." The judge's vocal volume steadily increased, until Alex imagined that people could hear him in Broad Street.

"Inspired by the *Exposition and Protest,* which does not in itself advocate antigovernment violence, those less moderate are thumping strange new tubs and tooting dangerous new horns. I hear a cry of 'disunion,' a term lately coined by Mr. Turnbull. I hear, in reference to federal laws deemed unfair to South Carolina, a call for 'nullification' of those laws, by the very author of that term, our esteemed governor, Mr. Hamilton. Many moderate men abhor these clamors, while hotter heads utter them as threats. I speak not of crazed nobodies, but of respected, educated men, including the governor, and the fiery Mr. Rhett, whose *Mercury* newspaper has the ear of the public."

Sunk in his chair, Thomas Grimké muttered unhappily, "He's my cousin."

"You may add our own Congressman Lark," Edgar said. "God alone knows why the electorate chose that self-serving coxcomb for Congress." Ayes and hear-hears sounded in the soft darkness. The judge seconded Edgar's comment and continued.

"The *Exposition and Protest* pushes us all that much farther down the road to a national schism. Men of sense and propriety must stand up and declare themselves in opposition, lest our beloved state go too far and lead us to the unthinkable. Those who threaten disunion do not understand the potentially sanguinary consequences of that which they so blithely promote. But that is another topic. I entertain your questions and responses."

The guests applauded. Crouched on the floor by the window, Alex asked Ham the meaning of *schism*. "A split, a division. What it means to the judge is trouble. Terrible trouble."

* * *

On a bright and breezy April day Miss Fancher suffered a toothache and sent her pupils home at noon. An hour later a runner for Buckles & Bell brought a summons from Edgar. Would Alex come to the office and bring Maudie? Alex tossed aside her trowel, stomped out of the garden, and went to make herself presentable.

She and Maudie reached the office within the hour. At seventeen Maudie had ripened into a gorgeous young woman. Alex envied her figure. Wherever Maudie went, she attracted attention from men of both races. She was now a house servant, because Alex had insisted she no longer needed or wanted a personal slave. The two of them remained best friends.

They found Edgar and the cheerfully obese Argyll Buckles with two visitors. Edgar presented a tall, lean man with russet chin whiskers. "Mr. Anson Riddle, of Columbia, and his son Richard." Riddle and son sprang from their chairs. The young man's hat tumbled off his lap. He grabbed for it, but it rolled across the floor and fell against a cuspidor.

"And this is my daughter, Alexandra, and Maudie, one of our house girls."

Richard Riddle mumbled, "How do you do?" Alex had never seen such an unpromising youth. As tall as his father, he was a weed that had grown too fast. His dull brown coatee fit badly; two inches of linen hung out at the cuffs. He had a prominent Adam's apple and a horrid skin problem. His eyes were his only attractive feature; large and brown, speckled with gold, they reminded her of a cat's.

"Mr. Riddle owns a freight company," Edgar explained. "His Conestoga wagons haul cotton for several planters in the midlands. He is searching for a factor to represent the group, and Bell's Bridge is under consideration. While we discuss the matter, would you and Maudie entertain Richard? Maudie will chaperone them," he assured Mr. Riddle. "Please return by half past four, Alex." Alex felt put upon. The floor creaked under Argyll Buckles as he showed them the door.

"What would you like to do, Mr. Riddle?" Alex said in the anteroom. "I can show you the town. Or we could go for a sail, out to the new fort."

"Either would be fine." Alex rolled her eyes. Had she said they could stand on their heads for an hour, he'd probably find that fine too.

"A sail, then. The boat's at Bell's Bridge. Follow me." She marched out.

Maudie caught up, whispering. "Not room for three in the skiff."

"I'm sure you'll find someone to talk to while we're gone." Maudie grinned and covered her mouth. A certain young stevedore with skin like black ivory had taken notice of Maudie recently.

Bell's Bridge swarmed with men loading cotton bales onto a Liverpool steamer. A slave helped Alex down the slippery stairs to the little blue-bottomed skiff, then the visitor. "Have you sailed before?" Alex asked.

"I'm afraid not."

"Then please sit there and follow orders."

She gauged the tide and the offshore wind, then hoisted her skirts to step over Richard. She cast off the bowline, clambered back to the stern, and cast off there. As the tide bore them away from the stairs, she called thanks to the black man and raised the sail. She handed the boom line to Richard. "Keep that taut and cleat it when I tell you."

"Cleat it?"

"That's a cleat, there, on the gunwale." She stifled a comment about the lumpy mess he made of tying the line.

The sail snapped, caught the wind, and filled. They sped into the channel. Alex pushed her flying hair out of her eyes and kicked off her shoes. Richard looked startled. "I suggest you put your hat under the thwart unless you want it to cross the Atlantic," she said. He didn't understand *thwart*. "What you're sitting on."

"Oh."

Alex was a good sailor. She maneuvered the skiff between larger vessels coming and going. Soon they were skimming across the harbor, making for three barges anchored at the site of the new fort. The day was so fair and invigorating, the water so gloriously bright with silver sparkles, Alex's mood soon improved.

"They've been planning the fort for two years, but they've only just gotten started."

"Does it have a name?"

"It'll be called Sumter, after the general."

"Why does Charleston need another fort?"

"To defend the harbor, I suppose."

"Against who?"

"I'm sure I don't know. Papa's friend Judge Porcher says politicians never explain, they just spend money. If they're forced to explain, it's mostly lies. May I ask your age, Mr. Riddle?"

"Seventeen. Won't you call me Richard?"

"All right, Richard."

"Is it impertinent to ask how old you are?"

"Fifteen."

He struggled for a compliment. "Really. You're very . . . tall."

"Yes, and I don't like it. Put your head down, we're coming about."
She did it so quickly, she nearly brained him with the boom.

She brought them close to the barges. Two surveyors stood ankle
deep on the shoal, using a theodolite on a tripod. Negro workmen transferred granite blocks from the barge to the start of a foundation wall.
Three white men, noncommissioned army artificers, bossed the work
gang. Richard listened carefully to Alex's comments about the work but
made none of his own. When she thought it time to leave, they sailed
back in silence. His poor blotchy skin oozed and glistened in the sunshine. She felt sorry for him. Boys and girls had to suffer that while maturing, though girls had other burdens as well. Fortunately Alex was
sturdy, never forced to halt her activities and rush to bed with cramps
once a month.

After tying up she put on her shoes and searched for Maudie, whom
she found behind a rampart of cotton bales, chatting and laughing with
her handsome malingering stevedore. On the way to the law office
Maudie remained a respectful two steps behind Alex and the visitor.

Near the alley leading to the office the young man cleared his throat.
"Let me thank you for that interesting trip. I enjoyed your company. I
wish"—it took him a moment to bring out the rest—"I do wish I could
call on you."

"Well, I don't live in the midlands, and I don't expect to visit, so I
guess you can't."

He smiled in a shy way. "You surely don't talk like ordinary girls,
Miss Bell."

"Because I'm not like ordinary girls. I can introduce you to plenty of
those."

"No, thank you. I'd rather have your company."

"If you were around me a lot, you probably wouldn't like me. I have
only one male friend, and he's a Negro."

"Reckon he knows a good thing, whatever the color."

For once she didn't know how to reply. She stepped into the alley
ahead of him, experiencing a curious mix of annoyance and pleasure.

They found Riddle, Edgar, and Argyll Buckles concluding their discussion. Edgar promised a written proposal in a few days. After Richard

enthusiastically described the sail to his father, Alex said good-bye to the visitors. When Richard shook her hand, he gave her a piercing look with those luminous, flecked eyes. It made her spine tingle oddly.

As she and Maudie trooped homeward along East Bay, Maudie said, "Looked to me like you didn't care for that boy too much."

"Funny thing is, right at the end, I did. Well, he's gone." She tossed her head, her unpinned hair flying. "There are other fish in the sea."

"That's true, but I recollect you never go fishing. Fact is, you hate fishing."

"You're too smart for your own good, Maudie."

Maudie laughed and they walked on.

The midland cotton planters rejected Edgar's proposed fees as too costly. Anson Riddle and son disappeared from the lives of the Bells. In a few weeks Alex forgot her visitor.

32

Lark and Angelina

The Bell family's box pew at St. Michael's was third from the front on the left side of the aisle as you faced the altar. Here the family had worshiped since Tom Bell's time.

Somehow the parvenu Crittenden Lark managed to buy a pew across the aisle and one row back. On a Sunday of clouds and drizzle the congressman appeared in his finery—high collar, canary vest, garishly checked fawn trousers, violet-blue coat—with his wife, Sophie, and his son by a previous marriage, Folsey, who was a friend of Gibbes Bell.

Sophie was Lark's second wife. His first, deceased, had been a von Schreck, of good social standing. That couldn't be said of the former Sophie See, a voluptuous creature whom Lark obviously had not married for her brains or pedigree. Sophie's father raised pigs near Orangeburg. When Sophie snared Lark, she put her low origins behind her and pretended to be well born. She still had not convinced the Charleston elite, who joked about it, but never in Crittenden Lark's presence, fearing his temper. Whenever the Larks attended church, Alex fancied she felt a burning on her neck, as though the heat of their animosity was a physical thing.

After the service Edgar and his family slipped out a side door to the churchyard, where they bowed their heads over Joanna's grave and the empty casket beneath Edward's stone. Edgar knelt on the wet grass, tearful.

The family left by the churchyard's beautiful iron gates, each with a great funeral urn worked into the design. On the street Alex saw Congressman Lark standing on the step of his black landau, waiting for someone. "I have something to say to you, Edgar," Lark called.

Cassandra squeezed Alex's hand. Edgar confronted Lark calmly. On the carriage step Lark had an advantage of height. "I understand from a friend that you lately referred to me as a coxcomb."

Edgar didn't resort to lies or evasion. He gazed at Lark steadily. "And so?"

"If I hear of it again, I'll forget my congressional oath to uphold the law and demand satisfaction. Nothing would make me happier. The Lark family has a long memory. Keep it in mind next time you're inclined to babble."

He flung himself into the landau, where Alex glimpsed the venomous faces of Mrs. Lark and Folsey. The congressman rapped the carriage roof, the team lunged forward, and the wheels threw off a fan of brown water from a puddle. Cassandra exclaimed and leapt back, soaked and muddied from waist to forehead. Alex's father looked mad enough to kill. Almost as mad as the congressman.

★　★　★

"Papa, what's the tariff?"

Edgar looked up from the ledger, his face carved into planes of light and shadow by the hanging lantern. He'd gone to Bell's Bridge to examine the books first thing that morning; Cassandra said shipments had fallen dangerously low. When St. Michael's rang two o'clock, Cassandra dispatched Alex with a dinner sack of cold chicken, cold roasted sweet potatoes, an orange, and Edgar's favorite, benne-seed cookies. Alex hated to see her father sitting in the gloomy little office with the burlap curtain drawn over the only window. He looked haggard.

Edgar laid down his quill and folded his inky hands. "Why do you ask?"

"I hear about it all the time. It's in the air like the gnats in July. Miss Fancher talks about it, though she can't explain it. I don't understand why everyone's on fire about it."

He thought a moment. "A tariff is a special tax imposed when imported goods arrive in this country. It adds to the price of the import. If I'm a New York factory owner manufacturing the same goods, I can sell mine more cheaply. A high import duty protects my market and my profits. But if no one makes those goods here, and we in South Carolina need them, we pay a higher price because of the import duty. Calhoun believes the game is rigged in favor of Northern businessmen. It's a complicated question."

"But must I think about it?"

He rubbed a thumb over his face, leaving an ink smudge. "Not at your age. The politicians are happy to do it. Some of their ideas may be useful. Some may prove dangerous. The concept of nullifying an unpopular law, for instance. Mr. Calhoun is the foremost exponent, though he prefers to call it a state veto. He contends it's a peaceful way to settle sectional issues such as the tariff. Hotheads like our governor take it to dangerous extremes. Their position is, no tariff or no union."

He saw her attention stray to a tiny spider motionless on a corner of his desk. He rattled the sack. "Have another cookie and we'll discuss this another time."

"No, that's all right, I understand," she exclaimed, though she didn't. She kissed and hugged him and ran out with the cookie.

*   *   *

Images of Virtue and Lydia troubled her dreams. Even at home slavery seemed ever present, like some invisible taint in the air.

She told Henry. He suggested she talk with someone outside her family. Edgar openly opposed radical action to protect the institution, but he kept slaves, and that was true of most of his liberal friends such as Judge Porcher. Thus the only person Alex could think of was Thomas Grimké's sister Angelina.

She addressed a note to Miss Grimké, whom she'd seen about town but never met. She carried the note to the Grimké town house on Church Street herself. A sense of disloyalty plagued her. She knew she was taking a rash step, but conscience compelled it.

A week passed before she received a reply to the note. Cleverly, it was delivered to Miss Fancher's. Classmates shrieked that Alex had a beau. "Oh, one or two," she said in a flip way. Her heart beat fast, but it had nothing to do with romance.

Miss Grimké would be pleased to visit with her. She suggested a time and place.

*   *   *

The Quaker meetinghouse on King Street at Queen was as plain as the people who worshiped there. Miss Grimké answered when Alex knocked at the piazza door. "Welcome, Miss Bell. Come sit, be comfortable, and share your concerns. We needn't speak in the formal, Biblical way of the Quakers." Alex was grateful and immediately at ease.

She guessed Angelina Grimké to be about twenty-five. Delicately built, she nevertheless gave an impression of strength. Dark curls framed a face few would call pretty, but Alex found it so, perhaps because Miss Grimké's blue eyes conveyed great warmth. She wore Quaker garb: a simple gray dress without ornament; a white lawn fichu draped over her shoulders and pinned at her bosom. She led Alex to a semicircle of hard chairs. They sat with one chair between, the better to see each other.

Alex began by mentioning her family. Miss Grimké said, "I am acquainted with your parents. People of fine reputation. My brother, Thomas, regards your father highly. Let us speed to the point. Your missive hinted at disquiet in your soul."

"It's the slaves. I see what's done to them. How they're forced to live, with no one caring, or even protesting. My father's a good, decent man, but he will never treat Negroes as equals. He says they're inferior."

"My dear brother believes that. His only remedy is recolonization in Africa. He belongs to a society that promotes it. I find it no answer at all, merely a lesser injustice. In some respects women, too, are enslaved. When my sister, Sarah, was a girl, she loved learning. She longed to emulate our brother, Thomas, and train for the law. When she spoke of it, she was ridiculed. What she desired was not possible for a woman. Not allowed. Women are prisoners of men's rules and men's laws."

"How did you come to such views in Charleston, Miss Grimké?"

"By taking a long, slow, often painful journey. Sarah took it first, quite by chance. Our father fell ill. She went with him to Philadelphia to consult a certain physician. Nothing could be done for him, and he grew weak. Sarah tended him for several months at the New Jersey shore, until he succumbed. By then Sarah had seen differences between Charleston and the North, and they tore her soul. She joined the Society of Friends. Her life changed. When she returned to visit, she quietly began my own conversion."

"You were a member of the established church?"

"Which left many of my questions unanswered, or failed to address them altogether. Simple questions. Why, for example, was a poor slave not given netting in mosquito season, so that he might sleep comfortably, as his master did? In hope of enlightenment I converted to the Presbyterian faith. I taught a Bible class. One of my pupils was a child of a superintendent at the workhouse. I went there to grade her papers. I saw the sinful cruelties of the place. Men and women laboring like beasts on the treadmill."

"I have heard of that machine."

"I hope your eyes will never be afflicted with the sight, but it's well that you know of it." With a shiver of dread Alex laced her hands in her lap.

Miss Grimké's gaze fixed on some distant point. "In the small building behind the workhouse the treadmill grinds corn. The treadmill is a large vertical wooden drum with steps. Six Negroes tread it at one time. Six more Negroes wait on a bench. Every half minute a bell rings. The man or woman on the left of the wheel steps off, the others shift position, and a new person steps on at the right. Those waiting on the bench likewise shift to the left with each change. Thus no one rests during the entire eight hours of their punishment. The edges of the steps knock their legs and only the most agile can avoid eventual injury as they get on and off. If they lag or falter, a black driver with a cowhide whips them. The treadmill is an instrument of the devil."

Alex couldn't speak. She dabbed her brow with a white kerchief. Even Miss Grimké seemed agitated as she resumed.

"I found my Presbyterian pastor, Reverend McDowell, a wise and enlightened man who loathed slavery as I do. He was powerless to do anything about it within the framework of the local church. Two years ago, dissatisfied again, I felt a call to become a Quaker. It is a faith that promotes equality and justice. It is the only sect permitting women to be ministers. I have never regretted my decision, not even when members of my own family questioned my sanity."

She reached across the empty chair to press Alex's hand. "This you must know above all. No matter how visible and flagrant the sins of slavery, one person can do nothing. Reverend McDowell concluded as much, and I concur. That is why I shall do what sister Sarah did and escape."

"Leave Charleston?"

"Both for my own well-being and to bear witness. There is a wonderful book by a Quaker gentleman who lived more than a half century ago in New Jersey. John Woolman was his name. One line he wrote seared itself into my mind. John Woolman said, 'Conduct is more convincing than language.' That is why I am going."

"You really believe there's no help for the slaves?"

"Not in this city or this state. I say it with a heavy heart. Charleston is my home, and many of its people are dear to me despite everything."

"Then what am I to do, Miss Grimké? I have the same doubts as you. What am I to do?" Uncontrollably, she burst into tears.

Angelina Grimké slid to the empty chair and comforted her. "I'm sorry if I upset you. Your question can only be answered in the lonely depths of conscience, and I would not wish that painful examination on any living soul, unless it is freely undertaken."

Alex gulped and wiped her eyes. She heard a clock ticking somewhere. The familiar sound calmed her. She apologized for crying. Miss Grimké dismissed it. Alex stood.

"I have taken too much time." The truth was, she was so upset by what she'd heard, she could stand no more.

Miss Grimké helped her to the door. "I believe you have a good heart, Alexandra. It will lead you to answers for your questions. Come again if your struggle inclines you to do so. I will not remove to the North for some time yet."

"Yes, thank you, I will." Alex had no intention of returning. She'd approached Miss Grimké in hopes of damping fires of doubt. Instead, she'd been thrown into a pit where they burned hotter.

She stumbled to the street, blinded by sunlight and unbidden tears. What if someone saw her coming from the meetinghouse? Well, what could she do about it? Something in her almost wished it would happen.

She went to bed before sunset. Cassandra came in to touch her forehead and ask if she were ill. Alex said no, though she feared she had a disease without a cure. She lay awake listening to a nightjar in the garden, and to Angelina Grimké's voice. *Conduct is more convincing than language.*

Passage of time lessened the shock of her experience. She was able to recall what Miss Grimké had said without reacting emotionally. She went by herself to Marburg's shop, taking a bit of her hoarded Christmas money. She asked the clerk whom she knew to order a copy of John Woolman's book, making him promise to tell no one.

33

The Larks Entertain

Because of close ties with Vice President Calhoun, Crittenden Lark won reelection in 1830 without opposition. To celebrate he invited two hundred friends and political allies to a banquet at the Planter's Hotel on Church Street. Several favor seekers had donated to Lark's campaign even though he incurred no expenses. Part of the money went into a private investment; he used the rest to provide his guests with a menu of pheasant and capon, oysters and French champagne.

On the November evening of the affair a late-season storm struck from the Atlantic, overturning carriages, uprooting trees, making rivers in the streets, and alerting city fire wardens to possible danger. Inside Mr. Calder's hotel, however, all was bright light and conviviality as soon as the guests dismissed their rain-soaked slaves, who had escorted them from carriages with umbrellas.

Sophie Lark had carefully chosen her gown and adorned herself for the occasion. Her hair was braided, the braids brought around to her temples and up to the peak of her forehead. Roses and lily of the valley bound with pearls enhanced the coiffure. Her husband's fine black coat, double breasted and worn open, complemented an ivory waistcoat embroidered with tiny waterfowl. His hair, curled by an iron, aped the latest London style; narrow side whiskers tapered to points near his chin.

Smoke and lively conversation filled the parlor, where guests mingled before the meal. Simms Bell enjoyed a cigar among a group of acquaintances. Simms had been invited because his politics compensated for his hated last name. "Tom Grimké's sister has gone, did you know?" he said to the group.

"Hurrah," a gentleman responded. "That's two nigger-loving harpies the town's rid of."

"Tom's a steady fellow," someone else said. "Great benefactor of charities."

Simms shook his head. "He isn't a loyal Palmetto man anymore. He's thrown in with Joel Poinsett and Hugh Legaré and my cousin and that crowd."

"Unionists," someone sneered.

"Wash out your mouth," Simms said, generating laughter.

★ ★ ★

Across the room Sophie cornered an elderly woman, Iola von Schreck, a distant relative of Lark's first wife. "Iola, I must tell you about the most amazing discovery. At an estate sale up in Florence a dealer in used goods found a Bible that evidently belonged to my family at one time. It shows that my mother is a direct descendant of Governor Johnson."

"Sir Nathaniel Johnson?"

"No, his son Robert, the royal governor." Rather wistfully she added, "I expect he belonged to St. Cecilia, don't you?"

The old lady saw where this was heading; Sophie and her husband weren't members of the elite musical society, though Sophie desperately wished to be. Iola von Schreck pursed her lips. "No, my dear, Governor Johnson arrived in, let me see, 1717, but the Society was not founded until 1762."

Deflated only momentarily, Sophie exclaimed, "In any case I'd love to show you the Bible. Would you call on me some afternoon?"

"Perhaps in a few weeks. I'm dreadfully busy."

The old lady escaped. Sophie Lark's manufactured genealogies and hand-drawn family trees were part of Charleston folklore. No doubt the pages of the Bible from Florence bore all sorts of erasures and clumsy forgeries. Sophie was forever striving to join the upper ranks of society, with no success.

Sailing on, Iola overheard an exchange about Governor Hamilton. "Will he be here?" "He was invited but official business detained him in Columbia."

She greeted Bethel Bell's daughter, Ouida, attended by Dr. Hayward.

Iola wasn't sure Ouida recognized her. Gossip said Ouida's eyesight was hardly better than a mole's. She was maturing rapidly, as the hovering presence of the doctor testified.

Iola continued on; a moment later Ouida stepped in the path of a waiter with a silver tray of champagne flutes. Only his agility with the tray prevented an accident. Ouida berated him for clumsiness. Dr. Hayward took her arm, whispered until she calmed down, though not happily.

Strange young woman, Iola thought with a backward glance at the commotion. But one had to consider the stock, particularly Ouida's murdered grandmother. If Dr. Hayward thought Ouida would make a good wife, he might do well to reconsider.

*　*　*

A man said, "Have you called on the secretary of war and the infamous Peggy, Congressman?"

"I have not." Lark tossed off the last of his fine Monongahela; half the gentlemen in the group were drinking the expensive whiskey. "Floride Calhoun refused to pay a courtesy call. Why should I?"

The Eaton contretemps sprang from the marriage of the former senator from Tennessee, John Eaton, now secretary of war, and the morally suspect Peggy O'Neil Timberlake, a tavern keeper's daughter rumored to have lived with Eaton before marrying him. Many in Washington refused to accept or associate with Peggy, which Jackson considered disloyal; Eaton was a favorite of his. The rebuff of Mrs. Eaton by Calhoun and his heiress wife had further strained the Vice President's relations with Jackson.

A new arrival thrust his hand out so Lark had to shake it. "Soames Bray, sir. Is it true that you were present when Mr. Calhoun publicly defied the President?"

"I was, and I'll testify that it was a thrilling moment." For months Lark had dined out on the famous April banquet at Brown's Indian Queen Hotel in Washington, a gathering of pols and notables celebrating Jefferson's birthday.

"What exactly did he say?"

"After our own Senator Hayne gave the evening's address, clearly and skillfully endorsing the principle of nullification, the special toasts began. King Andrew the First rose and raised his glass. Staring straight at the Vice President, he said, 'Our federal union—it must be preserved.' " Lark's listeners groaned.

"Calhoun wasn't daunted. He's not called the Cast Iron Man for nothing. Never flinching, never hesitating, he threw Jackson's look right back." Lark raised his empty whiskey glass. " 'The Union—next to our liberty most dear. May we all remember that it can only be preserved by respecting the rights of the states and distributing equally the benefits and burdens of the Union.' "

The gentlemen dutifully applauded. Lark smirked. "Then Matty Van Buren leapt in, toasting mutual forbearance and reciprocal concessions, but it was too late, the line was drawn. God bless our champion, the Vice President."

"The lines are drawn, all right," said a man joining the group. His tone was harsh, vaguely threatening. McDuffie of Edgefield was a lawyer and congressional colleague of Lark's, a stern-faced Celt with black hair and sky-blue eyes. "The state is split. The Democratic party is split. Up in Greenville last week, they burned Calhoun in effigy."

Cries of "Oh, my God," and "Unthinkable" followed. McDuffie silenced them with a gesture and a frosty smile. "We got some of our own back. A young fellow who stands foursquare for nullification located one of the instigators of the demonstration, called him out, and ended his rabble-rousing with a bullet."

"Good God. Permanently?" Simms Bell said.

"I am happy to say you're correct." Elsewhere in the hotel a sudden bursting of glass stopped conversations in the parlor. A representative of the hotel rushed in. "No cause for alarm, merely a window broken by the storm." Which Crittenden Lark could hear howling now that the room had quieted. Another storm was howling across the whole state, McDuffie's news confirmed that.

"Tell me, George," Lark said to him, "do you think we must brace for more violence?"

"I do. Jackson won't relent on the tariff, nor will we. I predict that you'll see mobs in the streets of Charleston very soon. I welcome the confrontation. Either we'll have no tariff or we'll have disunion. But it's well to be cautious." He tapped the bosom of his frock coat. "I go armed everywhere." The other gentlemen exchanged looks; McDuffie was a duelist of note.

Doors at one side of the room flew open. A colored footman in black livery and white hose said, "Ladies an' gentlemen, dinner's served." The noise level rose as guests sought their partners and moved to the dining room. Lark found his wife and linked arms. Sophie looked forlorn.

"I asked Iola von Schreck to inspect my Bible, but she put me off."

His public smile still fixed in place, Lark whispered, "For God's sake, when will you stop these social didos? You got the Bible from a junk shop and the inscriptions you added are patently amateurish. Why don't you enjoy the present instead of constantly trying to fabricate the past? It's a wonderful party, a wonderful evening."

Blinking away tears, Sophie said, "Yes, I suppose it is."

For the congressman it was. In George McDuffie's comments about impending violence Crittenden Lark saw a glimmer of an idea. A way to harm Edgar Bell and his family without personally soiling his hands.

34

The Day of the "Best Friend"

That autumn the SCC & R's first engine arrived from New York on the packet *Niagara.* Mr. Allen, chief engineer of the line, supervised its assembly. Mr. Miller, who had designed it, named it the *Best Friend of Charleston,* plainly hoping it would be just that for the sake of the business community. Mr. Tupper, the line's president, issued invitations to 120 prominent people for a Christmas-day excursion on the seven miles of track completed thus far.

Edgar was incensed that the line stopped at the outskirts. "A pack of pompous nitwits including Simms oppose coming farther. They claim it will poison the air and ruin the city's charm. What the devil's the point of bringing cargo to Charleston if you have to transfer it to wagons to reach the docks?"

Alex's father said this on Christmas Eve, when well fortified with rum punch. As he finished, his cheeks grew mottled. Cassandra urged him not to excite himself. His eyes closed, as though he were about to swoon. His napkin at his lips, he raised his hand to signal that he was all right.

Alex worried; she'd witnessed similar spells before. Did Papa have heart trouble? Cassandra said of course he didn't, he simply worked too hard and involved himself too deeply in affairs of his city.

* * *

Excited by the prospect of riding behind what people called "the iron horse," Alex slept poorly that night. Late on Christmas morning the family drove out to the Lines where the track began. A five-piece German band played. Banners flew. Soldiers hauled a small brass fieldpiece up near the engine. Several hundred spectators were already lining both sides of the track.

The *Best Friend* itself was a railed platform on four large iron wheels painted bright red and tied together by connecting rods. The bottle-shaped boiler sat upright on the platform, steam curling from its neck. Coupled behind the engine was a small flatcar holding firewood, then seven larger cars, open, with wooden benches and canopies, all in green. Cassandra remarked that the color scheme certainly fit the holiday.

In the crowd Alex recognized Judge and Mrs. Porcher, the Petigrus with their children, the Crittenden Larks. Folsey Lark set off firecrackers to frighten and annoy the onlookers. The congressman and his wife paid no attention.

Simms Bell and his family greeted Edgar's family politely but without warmth. Ouida looked pretty in a new frock with a muff; flushed and excited too. Dr. Xeno Hayward was in attendance. Alex wondered cynically whether Ouida's mother anticipated an attack of the vapors this bright Saturday.

She saw Gibbes ogling her. At thirteen her cousin was already tall, and handsomer than his pop-eyed father. She promptly turned her back.

She fidgeted through boring speeches by the city intendant, the governor's representative, Congressman Lark, an official of the West Point Foundry of New York, and, lastly, Mr. Tupper. He announced bombastically that during tests, the *Best Friend* had achieved speeds above twenty miles an hour. "More than twice the speed required by our contract!" Cheering followed, and the loud bang of the fieldpiece fired by the soldiers.

"Now, ladies and gentlemen, let me introduce the engineer for this historic journey, Mr. Nicholas Darrell." A bearded gentleman stepped forward to bow. "Mr. Darrell, will you and fireman Chisolm kindly take your places?" The white engineer and the black stoker climbed the wheels to the engine platform. "Will the invited guests please board for the first trip by the first steam locomotive completely manufactured in America for regular passenger and freight service?"

Ham accidentally trampled on Alex's foot in his haste to get a seat on the outside. She stuck her tongue out and squeezed between her father and mother. Two strangers boarded the car, then Judge Porcher and his wife. The judge slipped a metal flask inside his coat.

"Let the journey begin," Tupper cried from the front carriage. The fieldpiece banged again. The *Best Friend* started with a terrific jerk that nearly threw Tupper off. Ladies shrieked and fanned themselves.

Mr. Darrell manipulated mysterious levers on the platform. Chisolm threw wood into the firebox at the base of the boiler. Alex felt rushing air. Cassandra covered her ears and made a face. The locomotive gathered speed, leaving the trackside crowds behind.

The ride was rough, but the sensation of flying through the pines and past the shanties and over the salt creeks was quite incredible. Green woods and gray marshes sped by like a canvas museum panorama cranked at top speed. Not every passenger enjoyed it as much as Alex; a stout woman opened her reticule and threw up in it.

Perhaps encouraged by the contents of his flask, Judge Porcher leapt to his feet. "Traveling at the speed of wind, we leave the world behind. Time and space are annihilated." Amaryllis Porcher tugged his coat, urging him to sit lest he be thrown into a creek or ditch. Smoke and sparks flew from the top of the boiler. One burned a tiny hole in the judge's sleeve; he was oblivious. "Our magnificent steed eats fire and breathes steam. What an age of marvels. What a glorious day for the nation and the great and sovereign state of South Carolina."

Another lurch of the car nearly disposed of him. Mrs. Porcher pulled him down by his coattails. He sat mumbling superlatives no one could hear because of the noise.

They approached a level crossing where a farmer in a buggy awaited the *Best Friend*. The smoking, snorting engine set the horse to pawing the air. The horse broke out of its traces and ran away down the road, leaving the farmer shaking his fists.

The journey ended too soon for Alex. Engineer Darrell brought the *Best Friend* to a stop near a junction of the roads to Dorchester and Columbia. President Tupper announced a rest stop. "At the conclusion Mr. Darrell will employ reverse gear to return us to our starting point. Please stroll and make yourselves comfortable until invited to reboard."

Some of the more bilious passengers stepped down at once. Alex felt fine, invigorated and stimulated by the remarkable experience. Ham ran off somewhere. Cassandra sat on a stump, chatting with the Petigrus. Edgar visited with some of the shareholders, leaving Alex to wander.

She walked to a grove where the air was fragrant with the scent of pines, the ground a soft mat of dried needles and leaves. It was cool; typical winter weather for Carolina. A noise behind her made her turn.

"Gibbes."

He leaned against a pine, his arms folded. Though two years younger, he was already nearly as tall as Alex.

"Hello, sweet girl."

The familiarity offended her. "Gibbes, are you following me?"

"Can't deny that. Always try to get next to ladies I fancy."

"Oh, are there many of those?"

"More'n you might think."

Something in his eyes made her wary. She'd ventured deeper into the grove than she realized. Voices of the passengers were a distant buzz, off beyond the shafts of winter light falling through the trees.

"Excuse me," she said, moving to one side to go around him. He sidestepped. She moved again; again he blocked her.

"What are you trying to do, Gibbes?"

"Be friendly. Every time I come close, you show your heels. That's no way to treat blood kin."

"Will you never learn? I don't care to visit with you. Now, let me by." She started forward. He seized her wrist; looked her up and down as though inspecting a prize animal. Then he released her.

"You're a piece of work, you are. Do you treat all the boys this bad? That colored boy you hang with?"

Alex's stomach flipflopped. "I'm sure I don't know what you mean."

"Come on. Mr. Lacy Olcott, friend of ours, he saw you and that carpenter's boy at White Point last year. Plenty of people heard about it later. Took your family's reputation down a few pegs, I don't mind telling you." He stuck his head forward like a turtle coming from its shell. "Give me a kiss. Why not? You probably kiss Henry Strong's nigger lips."

"Gibbes, if you don't stop this, in just about one more second I'm going to kick you from here to breakfast."

It made him laugh. "One kiss."

"Stop it. You're not old enough to fool with girls. You don't know a thing about them."

"I guess I do too. I've been with one."

"What?"

"I've been with one of our house wenches at the Hall. More'n once."

"That's revolting."

"Don't be so sure. You might like it." He grabbed her hand and pulled it against his trousers. "Does that feel like a boy?"

Alex slapped him with all the power of her right arm. He touched his cheek where the print of her fingers showed. "You dirty snotty bitch."

He grabbed for her with both hands. She darted aside, leaned down, scooped up dirt and pine needles, and threw them. He rubbed his eyes, cursing her with the vilest language she'd ever heard. She slapped him a second time.

"Gibbes Bell, shut up. If you ever, ever, lay hands on me again, I'll tell everybody how you made me touch you, and exactly where. I'll say it so often and so loud, no one will doubt me. Then we'll see if *your* reputation doesn't slip a few pegs."

Gibbes slid his coat sleeve across his mouth, staining the fabric with a little streak of blood. Heaven above—he was still smiling.

"Reckon you would do that. You suppose that's why I like you—because you won't have me? I'll get my way one of these days, don't think I won't."

The *Best Friend*'s bell rang; a man called for passengers to reboard. Alex ran past Gibbes, skirts held high.

The reverse journey was an ordeal. She kept her head down. If she looked up, there he was, smirking at her from his carriage. *I'll get my way one of these days.*

Just how long would he torment her? She couldn't imagine what went on inside his head, but she knew she had reason to fear him.

35

Temptation

In June 1831 a fireman accidentally closed the *Best Friend*'s safety valve and the boiler exploded; escaping steam scalded engineer Darrell badly. While Edgar worried about his investment, a second engine, *West Point,* was rushed from New York and repairs begun on the damaged *Best Friend*, rechristened *Phoenix*. The rails of the Charleston & Hamburg line crept toward Summerville and Branchville.

Alex's fear of Gibbes was unfounded. After the encounter in the pine grove he didn't bother her. Their paths never crossed.

Edgar's friends talked passionately of Nullifiers and Unionists, Edgar standing staunchly with the latter. The Nullies, as he scornfully called them, hoped to win a two-thirds majority in the legislature next year, two thirds being necessary for calling a special convention to write a nullification law.

Support for nullification was by no means solid throughout the state, but Charleston was a stronghold. On July 4 more than a hundred Nullifiers marched to the Circular Congregational Church on Meeting Street to hear a fiery noontime address by Senator Hayne. At the same hour Edgar joined another, smaller march to the Scots Presbyterian Church, where William Drayton spoke. Drayton raised the specter of a divided Union if the Nullifiers prevailed.

In the evening each faction held a banquet, with more oratory. Edgar reeled home full of wine, zeal, and praise for President Jackson. In a letter read at the banquet Jackson equated nullification with secession and vowed to resist it with all the powers of his office. Cassandra said it sounded like war talk.

In mid-July the family took a steamer to Newport, where they rented rooms at a harbor-side hotel for several weeks. Alex missed Maudie and Henry. She hated to be away from familiar people and surroundings. She didn't mind Charleston's summer heat, in fact found it comforting somehow.

Edgar's holiday was spoiled by a letter from Judge Porcher. He enclosed a piece written from Fort Hill and published in the *Pendleton Messenger*; in it Calhoun clearly stated his support of nullification as a conservative and constitutional means of redressing grievances.

Some argue that he came forward because of conscience, the judge said. *Others claim he revealed his convictions because he has realized he will never gather enough support to be elected president. Whatever the motivation for the "Fort Hill Letter," Mr. Calhoun is finished forever.*

"And South Carolina's prestige and influence reduced thereby," Edgar complained.

That same month the nation reeled from reports of a bloody slave uprising in Southampton County, Virginia. Under the leadership of a supposedly well-treated slave named Nat Turner, seventy Negroes massacred nearly sixty whites in a single night. Although the revolt was swiftly put down, panic swept the eastern seaboard and lower South.

On the trip home in September they passed through New Haven, leaving Ham to begin his studies at Yale. They continued by coach to New York, where they boarded a steamer: Cassandra said she had no wish to travel through Virginia, either to risk slaughter in another uprising, or to see the heads of the Nat Turner gang displayed on poles at the roadside.

★ ★ ★

At the Charleston Theater members of the stock company gave Henry play texts, and pointers on understanding and interpreting them. During the winter he and Alex confined their meetings to safe places: the house on South Battery, the friendly kitchen of the Strongs, the theater when it was closed and there were no actors and stage mechanics tripping over one another.

In the Bells' garden one afternoon Alex sat with Maudie, snapping the ends off green beans and pulling the strings. She smiled as she related an amusing remark of Henry's from the day before. Maudie clucked. "You sweet on that boy?"

"Nonsense, what gave you such an idea?"

"Way you talk about him. Henry this, Henry that. Way you smile when you say his name. Nothing so strange about it. Henry's mighty good-looking. Plenty of white men favor colored girls, why not the other way round?"

"It may be all right for white men to cross the line, Maudie, though most do it in secret. It wouldn't be right for a woman."

"Love don't go where it's told. Never has, never will."

"I am not *in love* with Henry Strong." She hit her knee so emphatically that her basin of beans tipped and scattered the contents. "Oh, damn."

Maudie set her own basin aside and went to her knees to pick the beans from the coarse grass. Alex dropped down next to her. "Henry and I are friends, that's all," she said, though her cheeks had acquired color, and she didn't look Maudie in the eye.

✷ ✷ ✷

Alex spent her days reading, sewing, making up little banjo tunes, and fighting off feelings of drifting. She read John Woolman's book twice. His thoughts on the keeping of slaves sharpened her doubts about the system.

A plain brown parcel arrived from Philadelphia: a copy of an antislavery paper called *The Liberator*, published by a Boston printer named Garrison. An accompanying note from Angelina Grimké said, *He does the Lord's work.* Alex found herself in guilty agreement with Garrison's purpose but shocked by his stormy rhetoric. She asked her father for an opinion of it.

"Inflammatory. If slavery must be ended one day, hostility like this won't do it. It only antagonizes the South and entrenches the system more solidly."

In the summer of 1832 the Bells packed trunks and portmanteaus for a second escape to the high cliffs and bracing breezes of Aquidneck Island. Henry's birthday fell three days before their departure. He'd mentioned a Shakespearean play whose tragic protagonist was a Moor, a black man. Alex knew he couldn't afford a personal copy. All his wages went home, because he lived there and ate at Hamnet's table. She bought a copy of *Othello* from Marburg's.

She wrapped the gift in gold paper and carried it to the theater one airless afternoon when the sky was yellow and the air ripe with humidity. People moved languidly. Women protected themselves with parasols. Street dogs found shade and lay panting. Her calico dress clung to her and she breathed almost as hard as her father during one of his spells.

Henry answered her knock at the artists' entrance. The theater was shuttered in the hot months, so Henry worked as day watchman, guarding against intruders and killing the inevitable rats.

"Come in, too hot out there."

"Hotter than hell's ovens," Alex agreed. High up, a grime-coated window filtered yellow light to the dark interior. The theater was no cooler than the street, though perhaps not quite so sticky. Alex offered the present. "For your birthday. How old are you now?"

He laughed and lapsed into Gullah. "The sun done baked out your brains. You know."

"Eighteen?"

"Tomorrow."

He pulled off the fancy paper, turned the slim leather-bound book so the light from the window caught the spine. His brown face broke into that smile Alex adored. "Oh, Lord. The Moor play."

"I knew you wanted it."

" 'Cause I could act that part. Thank you, thank you." He darted forward, kissed her cheek.

It was a chaste kiss, but he'd never been so bold before, in fact seldom touched her now that they were grown. She supposed he felt the same mysterious stirrings that she did—the sense of a new, exciting, but forbidden experience awaiting you if only you dared say yes to it, as Gibbes claimed he had.

Alex wasn't naïve about relations between the sexes. Though such things were never mentioned in the family, she'd watched street animals for years. She and Maudie had discussed the mechanics of the act. Yet she was afraid of it. Except in marriage, it was sinful.

"Little cooler in the auditorium. I opened windows behind the boxes." He led the way. "Sure will miss you when you're way up there with all those Yankees."

"I'll miss you too. I always miss you when we're not together."

"Soul mates."

She laughed and fanned herself with her handkerchief.

He found a pair of gilt chairs left from some production and placed them close together on the stage. He brought a candle from the prop room, fixed it to a saucer with melted wax, set the lighted taper between them. She sat motionless while he turned pages, growing excited.

"If I had some pomatum, and some charcoal dust, I could mix up a greasepaint and blacken up so I'd look like the Moor. We could read parts. The scene where he murders his wife in her bed with a pillow."

"Would you really need the blacking?"

"Makes it more real. Othello, the general, he's dark, it says so. Bad man calls him a big black ram." Henry gave her a swift, unreadable look. "Desdemona, she's a white lady."

"Yes, you told me."

"Othello's tricked so he thinks Desdemona's not faithful and he kills her. It's so sad, he really cares for her." Without looking at the text he spoke slowly, his voice resonant. " 'Then you must speak of one that loved not wisely, but too well.' "

Her legs and breasts felt hot. "If you want to read a scene, I will."

They sat two feet apart, the candle flickering between them. It was as though some elemental force gathered in both of them, then leapt between them. Henry dropped the book, took one long stride to her chair. She was already standing. He swept his arms around her.

His eyes seemed to ask permission. She let her eyes close because she didn't know how to grant it, or whether she dared. She hung limp in his arms, waiting.

His sudden embrace crushed her breasts against his shirt. He kissed her. The salty tang of his lips, the strange masculine scent of him, dizzied her, as though she'd drunk too much claret. The kiss grew more fervent. Her hands flew around him to clasp his broad leather belt and pull him closer.

Something shocked them back to reality. They broke the embrace, each stepping away. Their faces reflected a curious confusion of fright and joy. Henry whispered, "Oh, I'm sorry. We can't do this."

"No, no, we mustn't," she said, although she wanted him to tear her clothes.

"Anyone found out, they'd hang me."

"I wouldn't let them."

He shouted. "Goddammit, you got nothing to say about it, I'm a nigger."

The cry echoed in the auditorium. He shook himself in a way that reminded her of a spaniel after a bath. "You better go home."

Meekly, she said, "I will. I hope your birthday's fine."

"Thank you." He picked up the play. "Thank you for this."

"We'll see each other when summer's over."

"Guess we will." He didn't sound confident.

They gazed at one another and Alex felt the dizziness again, the sense of sliding toward an abyss. He was right, it would be catastrophic if they were caught. After Newport she'd pull away from him.

"Alex, don't stand there, get the hell home 'fore somebody sees us."

She fled through the dark. At the artists' door she threw herself into the fierce yellow daylight and slumped against the building. They'd come so close. What if he'd taken her?

It must never happen. She could love him forever, but never that way.

36

Dangerous Times

Alex told no one of the shattering experience at the theater. In Rhode Island she sat on a windy Atlantic beach with her banjo and began a new song, slow and melancholy.

> "I know a man who loves
> Not wisely, but too well,
> And what his love portends,
> My heart cannot foretell."

She wrote it down on music paper, though when she sang it to herself, she changed the lyric to *I love a man who loves.* Usually she had no trouble finishing a song, but she couldn't take this one beyond the first quatrain.

For all his hostility to Calhoun and proponents of nullification, Edgar was a man of his time and place. He was now forty-seven and, following the pattern of generations before him, becoming more reactionary than he had been at twenty-five. He was angered by the mounting attacks on his city and state from Northern politicians, preachers, pamphleteers, and the press. One evening in late August, after a heavy dinner washed down with ale cocktails, he fell into conversation with a burly ginger-haired man on the veranda of Newport's Harbor Vista Hotel. Cassandra and the children had gone off to watch fireworks.

The gentleman, dressed in sober black despite the heat, introduced himself as Reverend Justus Drew of Boston. "Of the Unitarian faith," he said pleasantly, laying aside his book, Washington Irving's *Conquest of Granada*. Lanterns on sailboats in the harbor gleamed in the dusk. "Your speech would suggest you hail from the South, sir."

"Charleston. We enjoy vacationing here, away from the heat and summer maladies. My name is Edgar Bell."

They shook hands.

A stocky young man of about twenty arrived with two young ladies. Drew introduced his son, William, who strongly resembled him. "We're going for ice cream, see you in the morning." Off they went, the girls giggling, the young man squeezing their waists. Edgar sighed; he felt his age.

"May I ask a question about last summer's slave uprising in Virginia?" Reverend Drew asked.

"Nat Turner? Certainly."

"How did it affect South Carolina?"

"It terrified and inflamed the whole state. For weeks after my family and I returned from Newport, we heard rumors of impending uprisings in various counties. The legislature funded a special hundred-man cavalry unit to patrol Charleston. The uprising stiffened resolve to resist those who inspired Turner's crimes."

"I understood his inspiration was Holy Scripture. The Book of Revelation. His disciples called him the Prophet."

Edgar remembered reports of Turner's fearsome visions—black and white angels locked in a death struggle; fields afire, streams running with blood. "Prophet from hell," he said. "I'm sure Turner was influenced by the kind of Northerners who claim to know how we Southerners should live our lives. They export their propaganda to incite the ignorant. In Columbia, our capital, citizens are offering a thousand dollars for apprehension of anyone distributing such literature. I'm speaking of work by misguided missionaries like Garrison."

Drew lowered his massive head, squinted at Edgar. "A friend of mine, sir. Surely writing and speaking the truth can't do mischief."

"You think not? Gangs of black runaways are living in our Low Country marshes right now. They prey on isolated farms. An overseer was strangled the week I left home. On July 4 some ladies and gentlemen picnicking at the site of Fort Sumter were poisoned by their cook. Two died. Garrison and his kind will bring anarchy and ruin if they persist."

"Mr. Garrison won't be swayed by your objections, Mr. Bell. He's determined to be heard. So are thousands like him."

"I'd say they all deserve a good horsewhipping."

"The kind you administer to your poor niggers?"

"I find that remark offensive, Reverend."

"It's you slavocrats who are offensive. To the nation, and to the Almighty." Along the veranda conversations broke off as people overheard the quarrel. "Are you a slave owner?"

"I am, but—"

"Do you keep black concubines? I understand it's common for owners to lie with them to breed more slaves now that the trade is outlawed."

Edgar rose from his teak chair. "That is even more offensive." He poked Drew's shoulder. "I respect your calling but I will not suffer insults."

Drew revealed himself as huge, a head taller than Edgar when he unfolded himself from his chair. "There's a limit to Christian forbearance, Mr. Bell. Don't lay hands on me again."

"I will if I choose."

"The devil." The reverend pushed Edgar hard enough to jam him against the rail. Someone down the veranda stood up, exclaimed, "Gentlemen, if you please." Edgar knocked Drew's arm aside. His bloodsuffused face contorted. He sagged forward against Drew, almost carrying them both to the floor. Red and white star clusters exploded over the harbor.

★　★　★

When Cassandra, Alex, and Ham returned an hour later, they found Edgar in bed with a Newport doctor attending. Alex clutched her mother's hand as they stared at Edgar's waxy face.

"He fainted, Mrs. Bell," the doctor said. "It is a symptom not to be taken lightly. I gather there was a discussion of sectional issues on the porch. Words exchanged."

"I know nothing of that. Who brought him upstairs?"

"A Unitarian minister. He's left the premises. I advise you to let your husband rest for a day or two. Then you should return him to Carolina speedily, so his own physician can examine him. Despite his robust appearance his heart may be fragile. A person in that state should not become unduly excited."

They left Newport three days later. Edgar said he felt fine, though his pallor and labored breathing denied it. Alex worried. Fortunately there were no repetitions of the disturbing incident during the winter.

✭ ✭ ✭

Edgar wrapped the white cloth around his coat sleeve, knotted it. White showed up well in the dark. In the midst of a melee Unionist friends could be identified.

The nullification crowd wore blue rosettes in their lapels, blue cockades on their hats. Charleston nullifiers included town-dwelling planters such as Simms, and younger gentry, including Gibbes, already expelled from the state college at Columbia for brawling.

It was Monday night, October 8, 1832, the first of two days of voting for state legislators. For weeks the city had been plagued by confrontations, fights, and near riots as the factions campaigned for their candidates. Governor Hamilton and Edgar's friend Petigru, political foes, had acted together to prevent a major bloodletting in King Street after rival meetings let out at Seyle's Hall and the Circus Tavern at the same hour. Bricks thrown in the dark bloodied the governor's head and that of William Drayton. Petigru and others drew the Unionists away east on Hasell Street.

"After I leave, put Titus on watch," Edgar said to Cassandra.

"Titus is far too old. He couldn't fend off an attack from a puppy."

"Then lock the doors."

"I will when Alex returns."

"What? Where the devil is she?"

"She ran to John Street with a tin of fish chowder. Henry Strong's mother has been ill with influenza. She's recovering. Alex wanted to visit."

"And you allowed it?"

"Edgar, your daughter is seventeen. Strong willed."

"Muleheaded. Something's changed her lately. She's quiet, less forthcoming. Is it a boy?"

"I don't know of one."

"Well, roaming the streets is unsafe. The nullies are waylaying derelicts and holding them in houses where they'll be given whiskey all night and sent to vote tomorrow. They're terrified of a defeat upstate. They even stoop to voting dead men whose names are copied from headstones."

"If the streets are dangerous, why are you going out?"

"To prevent more chicanery."

"Alex will be fine, she's hardy," Cassandra assured him, though her glance expressed anxiety. "Please don't excite yourself. The doctor—"

"Hang the doctor. If something happens to her, it's on your head."

He stalked out. On the steps he was caught by a last ray of daylight; Cassandra saw the choler in his face. She blamed herself.

★ ★ ★

Alex said good-bye to Mrs. Strong in her sickroom, and to Henry's sister washing dishes in the kitchen. Henry sat on the chopping block, whittling. Alex glanced at him and went out.

In the shop Hamnet was busy with his latest handiwork, a mahogany clothes press with casters and a beautiful scrolled pediment. "For your relative, Mrs. Simms Bell."

"They get all their furniture from London," Alex said. "Uncle Simms told me so."

Amused, Hamnet said, "Maybe that's the story they peddle in town. I've made their pieces for years. Charge 'em about a third of what an import costs and I still make a profit. But I practically have to swear a blood oath to keep the business a secret. To see how I'm coming with a piece, Mrs. Simms Bell and her stuck-up daughter creep around here like spies. Some folks are passing strange."

He escorted her outside. A luminous azure sky spread over them, speckled with stars. The air smelled of the ocean. With the coming of autumn it had turned cooler.

"Kind of you to come visit. Mary's a whole lot better."

"I was so glad to see that, Mr. Strong."

"Soup will go down just fine, her appetite's back. You best hurry home. There's a lot of trouble in town, the election and all."

"I saw men idling on Meeting Street, but nothing worse. My father was out on patrol last night. I suppose he will be again."

"How's he feeling?"

"Not as well as he should." A distant sound like a gunshot startled them. "I'll tell him you asked." She shook the carpenter's big hand. As she arranged her ivory shawl, she heard footsteps behind her. Henry appeared, still awkwardly silent.

His nearness produced more of those strange, excited feelings Alex remembered from the theater. The sonorous peal of St. Michael's bells reached them. Hamnet Strong frowned.

"Too early for curfew warning. Could be a fire."

"My father saw two last night," Alex said.

"Henry, I want you to keep Alex company on the way home. Still plenty of time before curfew. Stay a ways behind her, you don't want to be stopped for walking with a white girl."

"Really, Mr. Strong, I don't need—"

"Best you let him go along, never can tell what you'll run into, night like this." Reluctantly she thanked Hamnet and left through the gate to John Street.

Deepening shadows seemed all the darker because of the luminous sky. A few steps brought her to Meeting, where she saw St. Michael's white steeple in the distance, painted a lovely dark blue by the evening light. Down by the city market lanterns flashed. All at once she was grateful for Henry's steady step a half block behind.

37

Dangerous Streets

Few people were abroad north of Boundary Street, but to the south lanterns and brandished torches spoke of a large, possibly volatile crowd. Henry called softly, "Best we go another way. Let's ease over to Anson Street."

Despite Hamnet's caution about walking separately, he took her hand. She shivered pleasurably. When he broke into a trot she kept pace. The rising moon limned his forehead and strong chin.

They jogged from Anson over to Church. Odors of garbage and fish and human ordure swirled around them. No one bothered them on the desolate streets. All the hullabaloo seemed to be in the direction of Meeting and King. Above the roof peaks the sky had a hazy copper cast.

St. Michael's bells pealed again. They listened. "Another fire," Henry decided. "Sounds big this time."

☆　☆　☆

On Liberty Street west of King a rickety two-story house was burning. Edgar and two friends were among the first to reach it. They'd been mingling with the crowd in Meeting Street, trying to spot nullies rounding up illegal voters. Apart from glares and occasional shouted obscenities prompted by their white armbands, they weren't molested, perhaps because all three were well known: Edgar; gray-eyed James Petigru, attorney of St. Michael's Alley; and Morris Marburg, the rosy-faced banker. He carried a truncheon.

Edgar was the conservative and retiring one. Petigru, who mesmerized juries with his theatrics and a yellow silk handkerchief he waved about during his arguments, was the most liberal and outspoken. Where Petigru preferred simplicity, seldom throwing legalistic Latin at his listeners, Marburg liked to display his erudition by lacing his speech with Latin and German.

In front of the burning house a man lay facedown on the paving stones. A black pool spread under his nose and mouth. Edgar crouched beside him.

"Dead."

"Drunken sod fell out the second-story window," a man near the front door said. He called into the house, "Hurry up, 'less you want to roast alive." Lit by flames devouring the interior, several vagrants in various stages of inebriation stumbled to safety.

"Found one of their whiskey houses, I think," Marburg said.

St. Michael's bells clanged and clanged. The crowd grew. Edgar and his friends drew back from the heat of the blaze. A fire warden came running from St. Philip Street. "Clear away, clear away." Behind him members of a volunteer company pulled a pumper and a two-wheeled hose cart. Other men brought ladders and hooks. Edgar heard a cry familiar to every Charlestonian who'd lived through a fire: "Throw down your buckets. We need your buckets in the street."

Fortunately it was a calm evening, with no wind to drive the fire across rooftops and spread it. Men positioned themselves at the treadles of the pumper while others unreeled hose. A Charleston fireman took risks—a careless client of Edgar's had lost three fingers when a treadle caught and crushed his hand.

"We can't save her, lads. Use the hooks," the fire warden ordered. Firemen flung two lines to the roof peak; iron hooks caught, dug in. Half a dozen men on each line braced themselves and heaved. A hole in the roof opened; flames shot out. As soon as the roof was off, the walls would be pulled down. Then the pumper and bucket brigade could do their work. Edgar watched intently, failing to notice a man in a dirty black coat and floppy wool hat. The man's left eye resembled milky glass. A bent pin held a grimy blue rosette to his lapel. He worked his way through the crowd, his good eye fixed on Edgar.

★　★　★

At the intersection of Church and Market, Alex paused. Light came from a burning building several blocks west. Behind her, hidden by darkness, Henry said, "Go on across."

In the middle of the intersection her shawl dropped off her shoulders. She turned back for it, right in the path of three men striding from the direction of East Bay. They were young dandies, wearing tall hats with blue cockades. All three were drunk as sinners on Saturday night.

She snatched up the shawl but before she could run, one of the three sprang at her, snared her wrist. "Boys, what's this?" Alex smelled rum.

"Looks like a bit of Unionist cunny, Herbert," one of his companions said. "Look at the shawl." Oh, Lord—she'd completely forgotten the colors of the factions when she put on the ivory shawl.

Herbert sniffed. "Not much titty on her, but she'll do. Where do we take her?"

Alex lunged backward, hair flying in her face. She couldn't get free. Herbert yanked her arm, sending fierce pain up to her shoulder. Henry walked out of the dark. In the glare of the distant fire his skin looked like oiled brass.

"Gentlemen, I ask you kindly. Please let my mistress go."

"You're her property, are you, boy?" said the third one, a beaky chap with a silver-headed cane. "Let's see your pass."

Alex said, "Why does he need a pass? He's with me."

"So you'd best let her go," Henry said.

The beaky one sneered. "Say, here's a brave nigger. Suppose we cut off his balls. He won't be so brave then."

Henry whistled at Alex. *"The one who's holding you, kick him. Between his legs."*

"What are you saying, you damn baboon?" Herbert yelled. He didn't understand Gullah. Alex sank her teeth into Herbert's wrist. "Christ on the cross," he screamed, letting go.

She lifted her skirts, brought her left knee into his groin as hard as she could. He fell and she stomped him in the same place.

The beaky boy raised his cane and ran at Henry. Henry stuck out his foot and tripped him. The boy's feet flew up behind him; he seemed to swim in the air until he fell, landing with a horrendous crack: the sound of a jaw breaking.

Henry ripped the cane from his assailant's hand as the other dandies rushed him. Henry swung the cane like a club, hitting the temple of the nearest attacker. A second blow laid him on his back.

Alex peered down Market Street. The fight had attracted attention; men were moving toward them. "Bell's Bridge," she exclaimed.

"I know the way. Follow me."

Half a block east they darted into a narrow passage. She stumbled over a cat that spat and clawed her ankle. Henry booted the cat away, threw his leg over a board fence. She fell twice before she scaled the fence on the third try. The effort ripped her skirt and drove splinters into her hand.

They dashed through a courtyard strewn with refuse, then more alleys, emerging behind a vendue block, empty and strangely forbidding in the moonlight. The passage beyond it led to the broad avenue along the Cooper.

"Is there a watchman?" Henry said.

"He inspects about once an hour. The rest of the time he sits in a grogshop." The enormity of what Henry had done was sinking in.

☆ ☆ ☆

The front wall of the house had been hooked down into glowing rubble. A stream of water poured from the hose clamped on top of the pumper. Six men worked the treadles, three on a side. The foreman set the rhythm, chanting, "Up, down, fire out, up, down, fire out."

It was Marburg who spied the man with the milky eye sliding up next to Edgar. He reached past Edgar to jab the ruffian with his truncheon. "Stand away, you lout." The man's hand flew from under his filthy coat. Marburg pushed Edgar, too late. The tip of the knife tore Edgar's coat and cut his arm.

Jim Petigru reached for the assailant's neck. The knife flickered; a thin bracelet of blood appeared on Petigru's wrist. Marburg brought the truncheon down on the man's forearm. The knife dropped. The man turned and shoved through bystanders while Marburg shouted, "Hold that fellow." No one did. The night was mad with noise: St. Michael's bells, the pumper foreman's chant, the burning house hissing and crackling as water poured on it.

Petigru said, "Shall we chase him, Morris?"

"No, let him go. Edgar's hurt."

Edgar clutched Marburg's burly arm, blood leaking through the rip in his coat. He didn't want to faint. That was what he wanted most, not to faint.

☆ ☆ ☆

They scanned Bell's Bridge from the other side of East Bay, making sure the watchman was away. Alex left Henry at the small office, ran through the maze of stacked cargo to the slippery stairs where the skiff was tied. A nail under the top step held a key. She hurried back to the office, opened the padlock and undid the chain.

Inside, she shot the bolt, slid the flannel curtain back. The moon gave them light. They were both sweating. "They almost had us. All because I picked the wrong shawl."

"Where is it?"

Her mouth formed an O. "I don't know. I must have left it. Doesn't matter. We're safe, you saved us." She rested her cheek against his chest, listening to his heartbeat. Henry put his arm around her.

She realized their compromising position; raised her face to his. The moon reflected in his eyes. Through her skirt and petticoats she felt his maleness. "Still need to get you home," he said.

Over a rushing in her ears she heard herself saying words she couldn't have imagined an hour ago. "Not yet." She slid her arms around his neck and kissed him.

"Oh, God, Alex, we shouldn't—"

"Be still. Lie down on the floor. I want this. I've never wanted anything as much. It's new to me, we'll have to go slowly."

Silent a moment, he answered her with a long, sibilant sigh. Then, "We will." He pulled her down beside him.

★ ★ ★

When it was over, they lay twined around each other, half dressed, heedless of the hard boards under them. He brushed at hair on her damp forehead. "That was sweet. Sweetest thing ever happened to me. I love you, Miss Alex Bell. I love you so much. Been scared to say it before. Never thought I would."

"Don't talk," she whispered, kissing his chin. A delicious lassitude enfolded her. After the first sharp discomfort she'd slipped into a rhythm, found sensation of a kind she'd never experienced, or even imagined. At the end her whole body had shuddered with pleasure. So had his.

"Got to talk. What we did here is a crime."

"No, Henry. Never."

"In Charleston it is. What'll happen to us?"

"Nothing," she said, though she was far from sure. "We'll go on as we are."

"Can't go on like that. Everything's changed. First time in my life, holding you, I wish I was a white man."

38

Consequences

In Charleston the Honorable Crittenden Lark declared his intention not to stand for reelection. His four years in Washington had been uncomfortable and unsatisfying. He despised the moralizing Yankees who patronized Southerners and continually sniped at them over slavery. He knew they looked down on him personally for his lack of education.

He'd lost favor with the Vice President by befriending the vivacious Peggy Eaton. When he whispered a lewd suggestion to her at one of her levees, she showed him her back. That was the last he saw of her.

Anticipating a crisis when nullification became law, he couched his resignation in patriotic terms. "I take my stand with Carolina." In truth he wanted out of Washington because he couldn't make as much money illegally as he'd anticipated. Crittenden Lark's guiding principle was to make more money, no matter how much he already had.

Lark lived in a spacious house on George Street, in what had once been the suburb of Ansonborough. On Wednesday after the statewide balloting he tottered home at 9:00 A.M. His linen was in disarray; he smelled like a whiskey vat. He found Sophie at the dining-room table with her genealogical materials: leather-bound books, pencils, pens, an inkhorn, a large parchment sheet bearing a family tree marred by strike-outs and alterations. Sophie dressed fastidiously every day, as though expecting some social leader to pay a call. None ever did.

Bending, he kissed her brow. She fanned herself rapidly, her perennial gesture to show disapproval of his drinking. "I didn't fall asleep till nearly three. I was beside myself when you didn't come home." As he did not many a night.

"Dearest"—he belched—"I stayed to watch them count votes." Actually he'd been tupping a sixteen-year-old whore in her crib in Roper's Alley.

Sophie fluttered her pale hands over her work. "I've had the most marvelous idea. Suppose Grandfather See went to London when he was a young man."

"Your grandfather raised pigs, like your father."

"But suppose. What if he'd enrolled at the Inns of Court like so many Carolina boys from good families." She opened a book. "This list says Mr. Edward Rutledge entered the Middle Temple in 1767. Mr. Rutledge, who went to the Continental Congress and signed the Declaration. What if he and Grandfather shared rooms and became fast friends?"

"Jesus," Lark moaned, pressing his throbbing head. "Would you care to tell me how you'd prove the existence of such a friendship?"

"Don't you know someone who could write a letter?"

"A letter?" he repeated, dumbfounded.

"A selection of letters would be better. Written by grandfather to his friend, reminiscing about good times together in London."

"You are proposing to hire some forger to create documents that look sixty years old? Suppose you could. How in God's name would you explain their magical removal from the Rutledge family to your hands?" Tears welled in her eyes. "Do you think this sort of idiocy will do a whit of good, Sophie? Our status in Charleston was permanently established when I married into a family mired in pig shit."

"Oh, God, you can be so vile."

"Truthful. The only thing that buys an ounce of respectability in this town is money." He slapped the back of his right hand into the palm of his left. "*Money.* Christ. I wish you could feel this headache you caused."

He turned to go. Sophie sniffled and wiped her nose. "I forgot something. A message came for you yesterday."

"Who from?"

"I surely don't know, I didn't presume to read it. Bess kept it in the kitchen."

The cook produced the wrinkled paper from a drawer. Lark spread it between his thumbs, read the crooked handwriting:

FAILED

He crushed the paper in his fist. He kicked the stove door open and threw the paper into the flames, leaving the cook to close the stove after he stomped out.

He mastered his rage by reminding himself that it accomplished nothing. He would make another attempt at Edgar Bell at the appropriate time. He would make a hundred attempts, a thousand, until one succeeded.

★　★　★

Like figures in a painting the four sat in amber light flooding Edgar's library and office on South Battery. Hamnet Strong sat beside his son, opposite Edgar and Judge Porcher.

Edgar wore no coat. Cassandra had cut off the left sleeve of his shirt at the shoulder. A sling protected his bandaged wound. The knife-wielding attacker hadn't been caught, nor could anyone identify him.

It was Wednesday after the election. The Charleston Unionists had made a stronger showing than expected. A coalition of professional men and East Bay merchants had brought them within a hundred votes of victory in the city districts.

Henry's expression was not defiant, but neither did it express humility or remorse. He clasped his hands between his knees as Judge Porcher spoke to him.

"In reference to your defense of Alexandra we greatly admire your intent, though we regret the results. You say you recognized none of your assailants?"

"No, Your Honor."

"Nor did she?"

"That's correct, Your Honor."

"You brought Alexandra directly home after you escaped them?"

"We hid for a while before we came here."

"I trust you realize your predicament," Judge Porcher said. "If those men identify you, there may well be a reprisal." Hamnet laid his hand on his son's knee. "If it can't be accomplished by legal means, they'll find another way. For that reason I have made a proposal to Edgar."

"What is it, Judge?" Hamnet said.

"My brother Orlando owns a rice plantation near Beaufort. Henry will go there and spend the next year working for him. He will not be a slave, though for his own protection he will have the status of one. He will draw no wages, but he will be well cared for. Orlando is a good master. After one year a return to Charleston can be considered."

Hamnet was pleased. "He can come into the shop then. As my apprentice."

"I believe it's a prudent plan," Edgar said to Henry. "You were brave to defend Alexandra, but that bravery, unfortunately, carries a high price."

"Because I'm a nigger."

"Please eschew that vulgar word in my presence," Judge Porcher said. "You are a free person of color."

"Hell of a lot of difference it seems to make." Hamnet glared at his son. Henry went on, "Your Honor, I have a job, at the Charleston Theater."

"They'll be notified," Hamnet said. "You took ill suddenly."

"When would I have to go to Beaufort?"

"As soon as Mr. Strong can arrange it," the judge said. "You should travel at night. You'll be given an appropriate pass."

"I'd like to say good-bye to Miss Bell."

Edgar immediately said, "No, that isn't wise. She will be told." He'd prevailed on Cassandra to take Alex out for tea with a friend. She'd been given no hint of the meeting.

Henry reacted badly to Edgar's refusal. He scowled at his hands, gathered his thoughts, then said, "I don't think I want—"

"Enough," Hamnet Strong said, holding Henry's knee. "Thank you, Mr. Bell. Thank you, Judge. We will leave now."

"The back way, please," Edgar said.

Henry slipped out of Charleston on Friday night. That same evening Edgar informed Alex. She broke down, wailing and storming. "He saved me and this is how you treat him?" Edgar couldn't deal with it. He called Cassandra and turned his distraught daughter over to her.

*　*　*

Gibbes Bell and his crony, Archibald Lescock III, galloped their fine horses through sun and shade on a dirt road near Prosperity Hall. They stopped to water the animals at a crossroads store. Lescock put a heavy linen handkerchief to his beaky nose, blew, then used the linen to wipe sweat on his cheeks. He'd been telling his friend about the fight in town on Monday.

Gibbes cupped water from the trough, poured it over his forehead. "You didn't recognize the girl?"

"I thought I might have seen her somewhere but I wasn't sure. It was dark. Her hair was blowing in her face. The nigger I'll remember till eternity. He can hide in some hole, but not forever. When I catch him, I'll kill the black son of a bitch."

Gibbes smiled approval. "Shall we ride on? Mother's waiting dinner."

★　★　★

Candidates favoring nullification carried the state by eight thousand votes. They took nearly three fourths of the seats in the new Senate, four fifths in the House. Two weeks after the election they convened a special session of the legislature to call a Nullification Convention in Columbia on November 24. The convention passed an ordinance declaring the tariffs of 1828 and 1832 null and void; it would be unlawful to collect Federal duties in South Carolina after February 1 next.

The ordinance also established a loyalty oath. At the pleasure of the legislators, state officeholders would be required to swear to enforce nullification. The calculated result would be resignation of Unionist officials who could not in conscience take the oath. Thus the state government would be purged of potential enemies.

Before the convention adjourned, Senator Hayne was nominated to succeed Hamilton as governor. Hayne resigned his seat in Washington, pledging to "maintain the sovereignty of South Carolina or perish in its ruins." Calhoun, all pretense of cooperation with Jackson gone, resigned the vice presidency and was named to succeed Hayne in the U.S. Senate.

Jackson did not sit idly by. In December he issued his own nullification proclamation, declaring South Carolina's actions treasonous and stating that interference with Federal law would be met by force. He sent Gen. Winfield Scott, a hero of the War of 1812, to take command in the state. Federal revenue cutters appeared on the coast. Detachments of Federal troops arrived to reinforce Fort Moultrie and Castle Pinckney in the harbor. In the city civilians began to arm for war.

39

Winter of Misfortune

"Columbia?" Cassandra said. "Now?" Sleet ticked against the dining-room windows. New Year's had brought bleak weather.

"Joel Poinsett needs a confidential document taken to our friends upstate," Edgar said. "He won't trust it to the mails, and other matters occupy him here." Poinsett chaired a Unionist committee of correspondence, set up on the model of similar committees in the Revolution, to respond to the nullification threat.

Edgar went on, "Jackson objects to moving Federal troops from the forts to the city in case of trouble. He's sensitive to charges that he's a military tyrant. He'd prefer to have civilians form a posse comitatus, but Poinsett's opposed. If we did it, and we were captured, we wouldn't be treated as military prisoners. So on one hand Joel must refuse the President and at the same time appeal to him for a supply of grenades and small rockets. He saw them used effectively in street fighting in Mexico."

Cassandra sighed. "Street fighting. Dear heaven." She sneezed. Alex looked up from her plate of rice and slaw, okra and fresh-baked corn dodgers. She'd heard her mother sneeze several times in the past few hours. Cassandra bathed three times a week, which most of the gentry insisted was harmful, especially in cold weather.

"How many men have you recruited?" Cassandra asked.

"In the state, six or seven thousand. It's less than a third of the number mobilizing on the other side." Governor Hayne had been granted authority to draft males between eighteen and forty-five, Unionists included. He wanted an additional force of 2,500 "mounted minutemen" capable of riding to any point in the state within seventy-two hours.

"Promise me you won't go into the streets and fight. Think of your responsibilities."

In his usual unpretentious way Edgar said, "At this moment my responsibilities are to South Carolina and our country. I'll do what I must." He sipped coffee, peered at Alex. "Why so quiet, miss?"

"It all seems terribly confused and sad, Papa."

"There's no confusion in the North. Did you read your brother's letter? National sentiment consigns the Nullies to contempt and infamy. Even some Southern legislatures are voicing objection." He took her hand. "Are you sure you're well? I hardly hear ten words a day from you."

Fortunately Alex didn't have to invent excuses; Cassandra's loud sneeze allowed her to say, "It's Mama we should worry about."

"Just so. Before I leave, I'll ask Dr. Baltus to visit. I want no harm to befall anyone in this family."

☆   ☆   ☆

Alex regarded Dr. Nigel Baltus, and most physicians, with suspicion tinged with dread. Whereas Xeno Hayward had studied two years at the state Medical College established in 1824, Baltus was of the old school, having learned medicine as an apprentice to Hippocrates Sapp. Dr. Baltus examined Cassandra, put her to bed, then spoke to Edgar and Alex downstairs.

"I fear pneumonia. It's essential that we act aggressively to rid her system of poisons. The nigger girl has instructions to sweat her tonight. I've prescribed calomel and an emetic for tomorrow morning. After that I'll apply leeches to bleed her. We may need to take as much as a half pint per day."

Alex said, "That's so harsh. Does any of it do any good?"

"Young lady, these treatments were endorsed by Dr. Benjamin Rush of Pennsylvania. No doctor in America was more highly regarded. Even though he was a Yankee."

The feeble levity failed. Alex said, "I remember a girl at Miss Fancher's who was treated with calomel. Her teeth and gums rotted."

Edgar frowned at her. Baltus said, "Oh, are you a medical expert, then? Do you have a more efficacious routine to suggest?"

His abusive tone sent Alex from the table fighting tears. She'd cried a lot lately. She despised her weakness yet couldn't help it. Everything around her seemed to be crumbling.

Edgar knocked at her door as wintry twilight settled. On his shoulder hung a broad holster belt of black leather, with the English blunderbuss pistols his father had carried in the Revolution.

"I must leave at first light. Look after your mother while I'm away."

"Of course I will, Papa."

"And look after yourself. I hate to see you so unhappy. Are you still suffering with memories of last November?"

"Oh, no, that's past." It wasn't a lie; he had been referring to the street brawl. She was suffering because of Henry's exile. She dared confide in no one, not even Maudie.

★   ★   ★

Five days later the weather moderated. The clear skies and mild temperatures that could make a Charleston winter so pleasant returned. Alex decided on a sail, hoping it might banish her gloom.

She visited Cassandra first. The darkened sickroom smelled of sweat and a full chamber pot. Cassandra was asleep, drawing slow, labored breaths. Alex grieved to see her mother so feeble. The doctor's purging and bleeding—he'd substituted his surgical knife for leeches—appeared to be doing no good. She vowed never to surrender herself to such barbarism. She kissed Cassandra's damp forehead and stole out.

On Broad Street she passed one of the military units drilling in anticipation of February 1, "the Fatal First," as people called it. The Charleston Silver Greys were a volunteer company of Nullifiers over fifty. Few had muskets or rifles; many used walking sticks to prop themselves up. Blue cockades decorated their hats, palmetto buttons their shabby militia blouses.

She sailed into the harbor past Castle Pinckney, avoiding the wake of a side-wheeler outward bound across the bar. The cargo ship flew the Stars and Stripes upside down, a defiance of Washington widely seen in the city.

On Sullivan's Island she beached the skiff and walked the deserted strand. Sitting in the pale sunshine, she listened to the ocean's soothing rush and thought of Henry.

After their lovemaking she'd worried about her personal situation, which was a rarity for her. Henry had had no condom of sheep or pig intestine to protect them—they cost a dollar—and Cassandra believed pessaries unhealthful, so Alex had resorted to a douche with alum. For a week she lost sleep, until her monthly cycle began.

She longed to hold Henry again, or just hear news of him. Mary Strong had taught her son to write an elegant hand, but Alex knew he wouldn't send a letter, out of some tenuous fear of linking the two of them.

She pulled off her shoes and waded in the cold surf. Black-headed gulls swooped around her, hoping to be fed. She raised a hand to greet them. They flew off.

She wished she could be so free, escape so easily from the burdens of emotion and conscience. She thought of running away with Henry to find a new life far from the workhouse and ranting politicians and doctors who tormented patients with cruel and useless treatments. Charleston seemed benighted; surely somewhere the sun rose on a better, brighter day.

When she returned home, she stood awhile before the portrait of Joanna. Slow footsteps came down the stairs. "Mama, should you be up?"

Cassandra wore slippers and a quilted robe over her flannel gown. She was pale and perilously thin.

"The bed linen needed changing. I'll go back up shortly." She stroked her daughter's hair. "You do so like that picture."

"Yes. She was a brave woman, wasn't she?"

"Your father says so."

"How does a person find bravery?"

"Why, I suppose by delving deep into themselves when courage is called for."

"I worry that I'm not brave. That I'll fail some crucial test someday."

"Dear Alex. You've been a creature of worry ever since you were little. You worry over everything but yourself. That's another way you're different. Most young women worry about their wardrobes, their figures, their beaux, their marriage prospects—"

"I can't help what I am, Mama."

"No, and I love you for caring about others. I'm feeling a trifle weak, would you help me upstairs?"

✶ ✶ ✶

Edgar returned after ten days. "The situation's tense," he told the family, "although Hayne and his crowd are desperate to avoid acts of provocation. They realize that if they seize goods or jail customs collectors, sympathy will go immediately to the President."

In a message to Congress on January 16, Jackson presented his program for dealing with nullification. It outlined measures for avoiding armed confrontation while ensuring compliance with federal law, but even so, it quickly became known as the Force Bill. Calhoun rose in the Senate to fulminate against it. Governor Hayne said that if the bill passed, he would recall the Nullification Convention and recommend secession. Jackson let it be known that should that happen, he would try Calhoun for treason and "hang him as high as Haman."

Legislatures throughout the South condemned South Carolina. The Force Bill became law. Then, as the Fatal First approached, Congress enacted a compromise tariff bill transferring many protected goods to the exempt list and lowering rates gradually over the next nine years. Edgar rode to Columbia again, this time in Judge Porcher's coach.

The Unionists watched from a convenient hotel as Hayne reconvened a slate of delegates inclined to be conciliatory. Conservative Nullifiers repealed the November ordinance that had precipitated the crisis, though in a last, meaningless defiance, they also voted to nullify the Force Bill.

"A victory for the republic," Judge Porcher declared. "Old Hickory has shown us the future. The majority rules."

"While the South becomes an isolated minority," someone grumbled. "Surely this same little drama, these threats of secession, and war, will be repeated in the future. The antislavery crowd won't let up. If anything, Jackson's victory encourages them. The next confrontation may not end with a fizzle but a cannonade."

"Not in my lifetime, I pray God." As the judge changed position in his chair, his face screwed up in pain. He pointed to his gouty left leg. "Edgar, I must rest here in Columbia a few days. You're welcome to my coach."

"Thank you, no, I'll find a horse at a stable."

On his homeward ride Carolina's capricious weather dropped the temperature thirty degrees in an afternoon. Black clouds filled the sky. Gale winds tortured trees and every living thing, including Edgar and his hired mare. A downpour caught them ten miles below the Congaree River. Edgar decided he'd better find a place to shelter for the night.

He cantered onto a wood bridge over a shallow stream. Rain falling on the bridge froze instantly. The mare slid sideways, neighing. Her withers broke the rail; a fore hoof slipped over the edge. As the mare bucked and scrambled to stay on the bridge, she threw Edgar sideways into space.

A slave hurrying home at nightfall found the mare standing head down at the edge of the stream. Edgar lay half submerged in a crust of ice, his neck broken.

40

Anger

Edgar's pistols were safe and dry in his saddlebag. The sheriff of the parish returned them to Charleston with his body. Alex begged to have them. Cassandra agreed, though she couldn't understand why her daughter would want souvenirs of a tragedy. Nor could Alex, grief stricken, explain it adequately.

The funeral was delayed a week until Ham sailed home. He'd been in Charleston less than twenty-four hours when he drew Alex aside to say he wouldn't be returning to Yale. He'd already visited Edgar's friend Petigru, who had agreed to let him read law in St. Michael's Alley.

Alex tried to argue him out of it. Ham was firm. "I can't go back. Look at Mama's condition. She's so weak, she can barely raise her head. You and I are the only ones left to run things, care for her."

"I want no part of Bell's Bridge, Ham. I won't spend my life operating a business that employs slaves."

"Nor will I. We'll find someone. I'll attend to it."

He discharged Dr. Baltus and asked Xeno Hayward to take Cassandra as a patient. "I know your affection for our cousin Ouida, and the lack of friendliness between the branches of our family. This is a matter of higher import. A matter of my mother's life."

It took no further persuasion. Hayward stopped the calomel and the bleeding and put Cassandra on a regimen of fresh air and ample rest. "She survived pneumonia no thanks to my colleague," he told Ham and

Alex. "His so-called treatment severely damaged her constitution. I don't know whether she'll ever be as robust or active she was before."

At the mortuary where Edgar lay, Simms, Bethel, Ouida and Gibbes presented their condolences. Ouida stumbled about without glasses as usual. Only Dr. Hayward's arm saved her from a bad fall.

Gibbes cornered Alex and folded his white-gloved hands around hers. He mouthed platitudes, as though the incident in the pine grove hadn't happened. Now sixteen, Gibbes was undeniably handsome. He knew it and carried himself with a smug air. The two-year difference in ages was minimized by his height and maturity.

As the family departed, Simms piously declared, "Political differences are trivialities in the eyes of the Lord." Alex wanted to scream that her father hadn't died in the service of trivialities. She struggled for calm and murmured something unintelligible.

Mourners packed the pews of St. Michael's for the service. All of Edgar's Unionist friends and their families attended, along with the city intendant and members of council. Governor Hayne appeared in his state carriage, bringing Senator Calhoun's letter of sympathy to the family of "my worthy adversary."

Maudie, Titus, and the other house slaves looked down from the gallery. The Strongs sat there without Henry. Scattered around them were some two dozen black men, many with wives. Whether freedmen or slaves they had all worked at Bell's Bridge at one time. The number of Negroes paying respects to Edgar showed Alex that he'd been a decent master.

One front pew at the church sat empty. It belonged to the Larks. A beautifully inscribed card with a black border had arrived the day before.

Hon. Crittenden Lark & family extend their most heartfelt sympathies at this time of loss, & sincerely regret prior commitments will not permit their presence at Mr. Bell's last rites.

The message infuriated Alex. Lark had the gall to pretend friendship. She burned the card without showing it to her mother.

The coffin went into the ground. The bells of St. Michael's tolled. Alex didn't cry. She'd cried at the mortuary, alone, lying with her arms over her father's bier. She wouldn't cry again.

Ham threw the first handful of dirt on the coffin. With a soft moan Cassandra slipped from his supportive grasp and collapsed on the winter-browned grass. Ham and Dr. Hayward carried her limp body to the carriage.

Rage overcame Alex. She blamed the radical Nullifiers for Edgar's death. She blamed Calhoun, Robert Rhett, Hayne and Hamilton, the whole rotten lot. She blamed every person in South Carolina who tolerated black bondage and imperiled their immortal souls for the sake of profit.

She blamed herself.

She blamed Charleston.

☆   ☆   ☆

On a sunny Tuesday in the spring of the following year, 1834, Morris Marburg of the Crescent Bank sat at his great oak desk facing a large ground-floor window that overlooked busy Broad Street, the town's legal and financial heart. A row of oval miniatures decorated the desk: portraits of his lovely coffee-colored wife, Naomi, his daughters, Helena, Sophia, Margaretta, and Gerda, and the baby, Marion, nine, already chosen by his father to be the bank's next president.

At forty-one Marburg was an important citizen of the city he loved, albeit with reservations. His wide-ranging interests had furnished the office with a large globe, a wall map of the expanding nation, marble busts of Washington and Jefferson, Plato and Voltaire. Marburg was a devout Jew but a confirmed deist. He believed in a rational universe of natural laws whose existence verified the presence and power of a supreme being. He believed in reason as the path to resolution of mankind's problems. He grieved that so many in Carolina had forgotten that, or chose to ignore it.

Working in front of the window, Marburg sometimes waved to acquaintances or strangers passing by. He believed that visibility of the president promoted confidence in the bank's solidity and helped lure new depositors.

At the moment he wasn't waving at anyone but studying income statements of the 136-mile Charleston & Hamburg railway. The figures didn't satisfy him. The bank needed to sell its shares before the line collapsed.

A familiar carriage rolled up outside. Out stepped Simms Bell, a picture of prosperity in an English-cut knee-length coat, double-breasted white waistcoat and matching cravat, striped trousers, and tall beaver hat. Shortly, pop-eyed Simms occupied the visitor's chair.

"How can the Crescent Bank serve you today, my friend?"

Simms drew off his white gloves. "I drove in from Prosperity Hall to buy a book for Bethel's birthday. That new English thing. Butler-Somebody."

"Bulwer-Lytton. *The Last Days of Pompeii*. Naomi's engrossed in it."

"I went to your bookshop, hadn't been there in a while." Simms Bell read nothing but account books, Marburg knew that much. "It's a well-appointed store."

"Mr. Watkiss is an excellent manager."

"Effeminate, but seems to know his trade." Marburg said nothing. "I came to speak to you about a particular work offered for sale. It displeased me."

"Alas, we can't please every customer with every book. But the right of every opinion to be aired, even the frivolous or mischievous, is essential. Thomas Cooper of the state college argued that cogently in his treatise on free expression. He maintains, correctly, I believe, that circulation of ideas is usually suppressed to protect the interests of those in authority."

It was said in a friendly way, but phrase by phrase it reddened Simms's face and bulged his eyes. "I expect the good doctor will soon change his mind, given the flood of filth flowing into South Carolina." Simms shoved a thin paper-covered volume across the desk. Marburg read the title. "*A Disquisition on Servile Labor*. Reverend Justus Drew. I'm not familiar with the author, or this work."

"He's another of those damned Boston clergymen who want us dancing to their tune."

"You mean he favors abolition of slavery."

"He promotes the destruction of our way of life. I ask you to stop selling this kind of material."

Marburg's thick reddish brows knitted together. "At one time certain people tried to burn my father out over a similar issue. He resisted. I must do the same. I'm sorry, I can't honor your request."

Simms bridled. "Then beware. Decent Christian citizens will unite against you. Senator Calhoun says unity is the only defense against the South's enemies. Frankly, I anticipated your reaction. I intend to ask the city council to enact a law making it a felony to pass this sort of material through the Charleston mails."

Tempers were rising; Marburg seethed. "I should think the Federal government might have something to say on that."

Simms jammed his tall hat on his head. "I give you notice. I am closing my account at this bank."

"So be it, Simms. I regret it, but the bank will survive."

Simms stormed out. The banker sighed. Outside voices, contrary opinions, increasingly threatened those who owned vast lands and large numbers of slaves. Specters of Vesey, Nat Turner, and financial ruin haunted their dreams. Resistance was the tenor of the times.

★　★　★

A month later, early May, there occurred one of those misfortunes of timing that change lives. At the outset it seemed anything but a misfortune.

Barefoot, Alex was at work in the garden. A few years earlier the annual bombardment of seedpods from neighborhood magnolia trees— grenades, she called them—had planted a volunteer by the wall separating the garden from a new residence under construction next door. The tree was now five feet high. Alex had decided it should remain, a pleasant addition to the flower beds, stone sculptures, and the indestructible live oak that dominated the garden with its shade.

She used shears to prune half a dozen low branches, no more than thin green stalks, so the tree would grow. On a nearby bench Cassandra watched placidly. Despite Dr. Hayward's treatment she hadn't recovered her strength. She deferred to Ham and Alex in household matters and slept a great deal. Alex knew people called her an invalid, which was not far wrong. She wasn't the strong, vibrant woman Alex remembered so fondly from childhood.

A little bell on the street gate jingled while the saws and hammers were temporarily silent next door. "Marcelle," Alex cried, jumping up. Henry's sister, still pudgy from childbearing, stepped into the garden clutching the hand of her two-year-old boy. His father, known only as Roger, was one of many Negro seamen who crewed on cargo ships that plied the coast. He'd come ashore once, then again seven months later when Marcelle was nearing her term. Seeing the result of their dalliance, he slipped away and vanished.

Hamnet and his wife were bitterly disappointed in their daughter when she bore a bastard at fourteen. They nevertheless welcomed the child into the family. Marcelle called him Roger. She always pronounced the name with a certain wistfulness.

Today her face glowed. "Alex—oh, wait. Roger, you stop. Pull up your pants, you can't pee in Miss Alex's garden." Roger desisted. "Wanted to tell you right away, Alex. That judge, he said Henry could come back. Pa took the pony cart to Beaufort yesterday. They should be here late tomorrow."

Alex fairly danced. "Oh, how wonderful. I'll go see him right away. It's been more than a year."

"Best you be a little careful 'f it's daylight."

"Marcelle, your brother's my friend. More than a friend." She weighted her words so Marcelle would be sure to understand. "I care about him very much."

"Oh, Lord. I wondered if it might be that way. Never said a word to Henry or anybody. Told myself a fine educated white lady like you would have more sense. Lord, Lord."

She shook her head, despairing.

41

What Ouida Saw

Pretty as she was, and wealthy as she was, Ouida had few beaux. Young men who escorted her to a ball or concert seldom returned for more. She was too imperious, too quick to blame others for whatever unpleasantness befell her. Her detractors, and there were many, whispered that because she had witnessed her grandmother's horrible murder, she wasn't quite right in the head.

None of this bothered Dr. Xeno Hayward. He'd been attracted to Ouida's pink prettiness the first time he met her. Nor was he put off by her unfortunate personality traits. He thought of them as similar to disease symptoms. Over time they might respond to proper treatment: attention, concern, persuasion. His thoughtful, steady disposition included a large measure of patience.

He nagged Ouida gently about wearing her glasses, for her own safety. She refused to do it in public, but after a year of his urgings she relented at home. She sometimes wore them when she and Xeno were alone. Simms was grateful for the modest victory. "I'm not paying half of what I did to repair broken furniture before you two met."

Ouida challenged the young doctor in many respects. He particularly wanted to moderate her hatred of coloreds. She constantly hectored her father to send this or that offender to the workhouse for what more lenient masters would consider a trivial offense: placing a sugar bowl incorrectly; responding to a command too slowly.

Gibbes had described Lydia's death to Xeno: the blood all over his sister's face and clothes, her hysteria. The young doctor could understand why Ouida's spirit was scarred. He wanted to heal it if he could.

He was honest enough to admit to himself that he wasn't motivated solely by idealism. Before an untimely death at forty-seven Xeno's father had operated a flour mill in Greenville. Two older sisters had died in infancy, leaving Xeno an only child, in circumstances that were comfortable but far from opulent. His mother was confined to a home that cared for old people who no longer recognized surroundings or loved ones. He paid the fees.

Thus, early in the courtship, he concluded that marrying Ouida would free him of financial worry and allow him to pursue his career, perhaps even study abroad one day. From this mix of desire and practicality came a determination to stick with Ouida when others, far more eligible, fled. It was ironic and a bit odd; usually it was the girl who gave the mitten to a suitor.

Xeno was nervous when he proposed to Ouida. He had no sense of what her reaction might be. To his amazement she squealed like a happy child and kissed him frantically while tears flowed from her pale blue eyes. Tears of gratitude? he wondered in an uncharitable moment. He spoke to Simms and quickly gained his consent.

Only one person spoiled the prospect of alliance with the Simms Bell family, Ouida's brother, Gibbes, whom Xeno wholeheartedly disliked. Gibbes was vain, selfish, crude, heedless of the feelings of others. He held all the traditional opinions of the planter class: No Negro could be trusted. Northern abolitionists were disciples of Satan bent on destroying the South. Xeno had little interest in politics, apart from considering the Carolina Unionists courageous men and the Nullifiers dangerous ideologues, but he treated both, and all in between, as human beings who routinely fell ill and needed his services.

He particularly disliked Gibbes because he used women carnally. Paid for it; bragged on it. Gibbes genuinely admired only one woman, his first cousin, Alexandra. He made the surprising admission in February of 1834, soon after Xeno proposed.

Gibbes invited Xeno to the Planter's Hotel for cognac and cigars. Xeno's praise of Ouida led Gibbes to the subject of Alex. "I just adore that bitch. She hates me. But the faster she runs, the harder I want to chase her. Funny kettle of fish, eh, Mr. Doctor?"

"Kettle of lovelorn fish, I'd say," Xeno replied, smiling.

Gibbes lolled in his armchair, puffing a Jamaican cigar. "Reckon you're right. Don't you dare tell anyone. I hear of it, I'll call you out, brother-in-law or no brother-in-law."

The scoundrel meant it. Xeno countered with another smile. "Depend on my silence. I certainly wouldn't want to ruin your reputation as a Don Juan."

Gibbes dropped his half-smoked cigar in the brandy snifter. "Isn't just a fairy tale, you know. At a party the other night one of those bump readers pawed my head and told everybody I have a roving disposition. I do, but then I come right back to my cousin. Goddamn, it makes me mad."

★ ★ ★

The Bells planned the wedding for summer, before hurricane season. Xeno had little part in it. Ouida and Bethel took charge, Ouida showing more enthusiasm than Xeno had ever seen her demonstrate.

Xeno lived in a cottage on a small lot on Beaufain Street, near the Ashley. A side door led to a bedroom converted to his surgery. Ouida hated the house, and the unfashionable neighborhood. Mrs. Ouida Glass Bell Hayward couldn't possibly live there permanently. They would remodel, expand the cottage, but stay no longer than two years. She was emphatic.

He observed that remodeling cost money. He summarized his modest fees: sixty cents for an office consultation, a dollar for a house call, subject to reduction if they fed his horse. Ouida assured him Simms would help.

Equally unsuitable was the old Jersey wagon he drove. The first owner had ripped out the rear seat and Xeno had never replaced it. He stabled horse and wagon in an open shed behind the cottage. Weather had faded and blistered the wagon's bilious yellow side panels. "I'll ride in that thing no more than a year," Ouida said. "Jersey wagons haul passengers to depots and piers. People of our station don't own them." Xeno felt sure another appeal to Simms was pending.

Ouida's spendthrift nature was most apparent in her insistence that they dispose of all of his old furniture, excepting his medical table and cabinets. They would replace it with new bespoke pieces. They went to Hamnet Strong, whom Ouida considered "one of the few half-civilized niggers in Charleston."

As spring warmed the air, she and Xeno visited the carpenter shop once a week. Each time she had new ideas. Instead of one brass-bound, lead-lined cellarette, three.

"Three?" Xeno exclaimed. "Why on earth . . . ?"

"To cool different kinds of wine, silly. We don't want to mix them."

Xeno stifled an objection. Mr. Strong averted his eyes while making a note with his pencil. "Removable tub or a drain cock? The drain cock costs more."

"That's what we'll have," Ouida said. Her eyes sparkled.

So it went. Did Miss Simms wish bellflower inlays? Of course she did—imported African ivory. She wanted no ordinary mahogany for pieces visitors would see; she insisted on the rosy-hued, hard-grained Honduran variety, because it was found in all the best houses. A local mill did nothing but cut and finish it for veneers.

"Shall we discuss the new bedstead?" Hamnet asked.

"What time is it, Xeno?"

"Half past three."

"We'll defer that until next time. Governor Hayne's in town. Mama's giving a tea for his wife. I must be home for it."

"Certainly." Hamnet laid his notes aside and ushered the visitors across the parlor of his small and tidy house. He stepped aside to let them go first down the beautiful spiral stair he'd built.

Ouida heard the carpenter's wife and daughter somewhere in the rear of the house, then the daughter's brat, bawling. Childbirth terrified Ouida. "It is a cross all women bear," Bethel had taught her. "Exquisite agony, and no better the second time than the first."

They walked out through the ground-floor shop fragrant with the smell of newly sawed lumber. In the courtyard Xeno untied the horse and helped her into the Jersey wagon. He drove out past Hamnet's pony cart and waved good-bye as Hamnet's broad-shouldered son sauntered outside.

Xeno turned left onto John Street, intending to take a pleasant drive along the wharves before returning Ouida to Sword Gate. A block behind them someone shouted, "Alex."

Xeno reined in the horse. He and Ouida turned to look. "Who is that?" she said. "I can't see clearly."

"I believe it's your cousin."

Alex was running from the direction of Meeting Street, her hair flying. At the courtyard entrance Hamnet's son waved to her.

"Is that the carpenter's boy?"

"Yes, the one who's been away."

"Alex can't be buying furniture on her own accord. My glasses." She found them in her reticule, nearly dropped them from excitement. She put them on just as Alex reached the house.

She and Henry Strong fairly leapt into each other's arms. He lifted her in the air and whirled her. She whispered something in his ear. He put her down, rushed her into the courtyard. It all happened quickly. Xeno felt sure he and Ouida hadn't been identified, shaded as they were by the wagon canopy.

"Xeno, why is my cousin throwing herself on that nigger?"

"I'm sure I don't know. They must be friends."

"That was far more than a friendly greeting. Why, do you suppose?"

"I have no idea, and I don't expect I'll find out."

I will, Ouida thought. *Oh, yes, indeed.* She slipped her arm through his. "Drive on, we mustn't be late for tea. Don't tell a soul what we saw. It might cause trouble for cousin Alex."

42

Henry and Alex

Xeno kept his vow of silence, but Ouida had no intention of doing so. She spoke to Gibbes at Malvern. He exploded. "Jesus Christ, what'n hell's going on?"

"I wish you would find out, brother dear."

He scratched himself. A little redhead at Madam Boo's had given him crab lice. Three times a day he dabbed on juice of aloes in grain alcohol; hurt like fire. He'd revisited the slut to repay her—broken both her ankles with a hickory bat before Madam Boo threw him out, screaming profanely. She didn't dare order her house thug to hurt him. The Bells had friends who could close her establishment.

He noticed Ouida watching his hand; stopped scratching. He tilted back in his chair, rested bare heels on the rail of the piazza overlooking the river. "I'll scope him out. That boy can't fool with white women."

"If Henry Strong spies you, he'll recognize you."

"Hell, that's right. He's been to Sword Gate delivering furniture."

"Good of you to recall," Ouida said with an acerbic smile. She loved her intemperate brother but didn't consider him a model of intelligence.

"Tell you what. I'll set a couple of chums to the task. If we find out he's messing with Alex, that nigger will lose his privates."

"Gibbes." Ouida feigned shock. It was exactly the kind of response she wanted.

A black man poled by in a piragua piled high with chicken crates. He waved to them. Ouida and Gibbes stared. "Alex is just the sort to cross the line and experiment with colored boys," she mused. "If word got out, the scandal would ruin her in Charleston, forever."

What a pleasant thought.

* * *

Alex knew she'd erred in running impetuously to the Strong house. Soon after she arrived, Hamnet Strong said, "Your cousin was just here, ordering furniture with Dr. Hayward."

Alex caught her breath. "Was he driving an old wagon?"

"He was."

"I saw them down the street."

But did they see me throw myself on Henry? She prayed they hadn't. There was no point in agonizing over it, but it taught a lesson. When Hamnet went inside, she sat with Henry on the sunlit steps of the shop. "I can't come here again."

"Where can we meet?"

"Not Bell's Bridge either. I'll think of something."

"I've plenty to tell you. I went crazy down in Beaufort. They didn't mistreat me. Mr. Orlando Porcher pulled me out of the fields after two weeks, put me in the house in a fancy vest and stockings so I could use his library. I had a garret to myself. Hotter than sin, but I could hide my books. Read by candlelight. Anything to keep from thinking of you."

He saw his mother observing them from an upstairs window, slid sideways to put more space between them. "I'll find a meeting place," Alex promised.

"Just be mighty careful."

They shared a handclasp at the courtyard entrance. A rag-and-bottle man passed, pulling his handcart and calling out his offers to buy. He never gave them a glance.

"Henry, I love you."

"I don't dare say it aloud. Hardly dare say it to myself. You go now." He spun on his heel and ran inside.

* * *

Alex's late father had called James L. Petigru the strongest Unionist in Charleston, perhaps in the whole state. The respected attorney was forty-five, a tall man with leonine hair turning gray. Petigru's unpopular opinions never seemed to harm his standing in the community. He was the solicitor for St. Michael's, a lifetime appointment. He served on boards of charitable institutions. The finest families welcomed him to their homes. On Sunday afternoons, while Simms Bell was riding horseback in the country and Crittenden Lark snoring in a hammock, Petigru and one of his slaves planted flowers and pulled weeds in St. Michael's churchyard.

He had been born James Petigrew; he reverted to the Huguenot spelling after a quarrel with his father. As a young man he taught at a Beaufort academy for a while, then read law. He practiced in a sand-colored two-story building in St. Michael's Alley, where he kept half a dozen clerks busy. One was Ham Bell.

Petigru had been raised to have sympathy for oppressed people. He frequently defended indigents and, occasionally, slaves. That encouraged Ham to climb the stair to Petigru's second-floor office, close the door, and pour out as much of Alex's story as he dared.

Coatless, Petigru sat on a library ladder with a book open on his knee. When Ham finished, Petigru said, "Your sister and her friend are in a dangerous position."

"Alex knows that, sir. I'm the only person in whom she's confided."

"Inevitably, if they choose to remain close, they must leave Charleston. Until then I'll allow them to meet across the street occasionally. When people conduct clandestine business in the open, they are hardly ever suspected. However, they must show no signs of intimacy. Henry Strong must act respectfully, as a hired man would." Petigru smiled. "I'll have to tell my wife, Amelia, that I'm playing cupid. I won't say for whom."

"Bless you, sir," Ham said.

All Charleston knew that Petigru cherished his garden directly opposite the office. Two marble pillars flanked the entrance to the lot. A single huge magnolia towered over azaleas and camellias. Petigru often walked in the garden, hands behind his back, talking to himself as he planned an argument.

Alex and Henry met in the garden ten days after their reunion. She arranged it with a note sent to John Street. Henry reported to St. Michael's Alley that morning, and Petigru set him to weeding and pruning. Alex arrived at noon, with a cut glass decanter of ratafia for the office. She didn't care for the potent liqueur concocted of wine and brandy, fruit and almonds, but Ham liked it. He was providing drinks for the other clerks after hours, to celebrate his birthday.

She sat on a garden bench, shaded by the magnolia. "Tell me more about what you did in Beaufort."

The tattered brim of Henry's straw hat hid his face. "Mostly I suffered. Wasn't for those books, I'd be crazy by now." He tore weeds from the sandy soil. A redheaded lizard ran from under a bush, inspected Henry's busy hands, and ran off again.

"I read all of Shakespeare's plays. Every one. Missed the Charleston Theater something fierce. I decided for good and all that I'm going to be an actor. Play Othello someday."

"That means you'll have to go North."

"I will."

"I'll go with you."

He raised his head. Sweat glistened on his cheeks. "No."

"Why do you say that? You know how I feel."

"I feel the same way."

"Then marry me. I'm nineteen, Henry. Old enough to make up my mind."

"No," he said again. "I'd never let you marry a colored man, even one light as I am."

"What you're like on the outside doesn't matter. I read a poem by Samuel Coleridge, the English poet. I memorized it because it's what I feel." Henry knelt with his hands resting on his thighs. He waited.

> *"I have heard of reasons manifold*
> *Why love must needs be blind,*
> *But this the best of all I hold—*
> *His eyes are in his mind."*

Henry pulled off his hat; wiped his shiny forehead as a horseman rode by in the street.

> *"What outward form and feature are*
> *He guesseth but in part,*
> *But that within is good and fair,*
> *He seeth with the heart."*

"Don't," Henry whispered. "For God's sake, Alex, what does some English poet know about things in America? Marrying me would blight your life. I'd never put that on you."

"You think conditions won't change? Get better for your people?"

"I do not. In Beaufort I saw how Mr. Porcher, kind as he was, couldn't live without his niggers. He wouldn't last an hour in a flooded rice field with the sun frying his skull. Only way he can keep his fine life is to keep slaves. And fight anybody who says he can't."

"Then where's the end of it? How will the cycle ever be broken?"

"Down there in Beaufort I read something I wasn't 'sposed to see. A slave who'd been taught reading and writing in secret gave it to me. *Walker's Appeal to the Colored Citizens of the World*, it's called. Never saw or heard of it in Charleston. Probably they'd hang a man for having a copy. David Walker's a Negro. Ran away from North Carolina, settled in Boston. Sells clothing there. A seaman bought a coat from him. Walker took his pamphlet apart and sewed pages into the coat lining, so all the pages would get to South Carolina. Walker says there's just one way for colored people to free themselves. By rising up and killing their masters."

"Like Denmark Vesey, and Nat Turner? Do you believe that?"

Henry jammed his trowel in the ground. "I get mad enough to believe it."

"This is a devil of a conversation for a reunion."

"Can't help it. I won't let you throw your life away and live in some shanty in New York, despised and spat on because of your husband. I love you too much. Now get out of here, I have to weed this whole place before it's dark. I'll catch hell at home. I didn't tell Pa where I'd be all day."

"Does he know about us?"

"Some. He doesn't like it too much."

"When shall I come here again?"

"Better not. Not for a while. Too hard for me. Too hard for both of us." He tipped his straw hat in a respectful way. "Good afternoon, ma'am."

★ ★ ★

"I seen him," beaky Archie Lescock III said. "Right there in Petigru's weed patch. I followed him in the morning, then kept watch. I rode by and saw him talking to Miss Alex Bell bold as you please. One thing for sure. He's the nigger I tangled with in the street."

"You think the woman that night was my cousin?"

"Never saw her real clear, but I suspicion it was."

Gibbes tilted forward in his chair; the legs banged on the piazza. "That dirty bitch. Free love, niggers—what else?" The thought of Alex lying with anyone but him enraged him. He shook a finger at his friend. "That boy's done for, Archie."

43

Adrift

Ouida married Xeno Hayward at St. Michael's in late June. Alex declined the invitation for herself and her mother. She didn't want to face Gibbes again, and Cassandra showed no interest. Ham refused to attend alone. Alex presumed cousin Ouida would stumble to the altar without her glasses.

On the afternoon of the ceremony Alex sat under the great live oak, vainly trying to resolve the melody for an antislavery anthem, thus far wordless. St. Michael's bells rang to celebrate the marriage. She listened with a sad expression. Imagination conjured a ballroom lit with scores of candles where she danced with Henry, handsome in a tailcoat and white tie. Was there a place on earth where it would be possible?

Following the wedding Dr. and Mrs. Hayward sailed for Portugal and an extended European honeymoon.

☆ ☆ ☆

Weeks passed between meetings in Petigru's garden. Henry grew noticeably thin. He seldom smiled. Alex asked him only once about the shop. He flared. "I hate it. Pa knows I hate it. Marcelle's upset him, too, there's another bastard on the way and she won't say whose it is. I can't take it forever."

"We'll go to New York."

He wouldn't answer.

Lescock beamed.

"Need to figure out how to do it," Gibbes went on. "Got to be careful, so he gets what's coming but we keep our hands clean. Might take a week. Might take a year."

"Worth waiting for, Gibbes."

"Yes indeed."

* * *

Despite the drumfire of abolitionist rhetoric out of the North, cotton boomed again and, with it, commerce on the Cooper River piers. Ham found a young German, Otto Abendschein, to manage Bell's Bridge. Otto was an enthusiast. "By this time next year upland cotton will reach twenty cents a pound. Everybody will be rich as Rothschild. Isn't this a great time to be living?" Ham was noncommittal.

Alex worried about her brother. He had no close friends and no visible interest in women. He seemed content to bury himself in the law office, though he did accept Simms's invitation to hear Senator Calhoun at Prosperity Hall. Petigru refused the invitation.

It was October, nearing the end of the congressional recess. Calhoun was en route from Fort Hill to Charleston to catch a northbound steamer. About fifty people, three-quarters men, gathered in the plantation's great room. Ham wasn't surprised to find feckless Gibbes absent.

Calhoun was still magisterial, though Ham thought he detected a weariness and a bitter attitude. The senator addressed the sedate and respectful audience for an hour. It was his kind of audience; he was known for avoiding noisy political rallies, barbecues, and the like.

"As the years pass, I become ever more convinced that our system of labor represents a positive good. It provides a secure, untroubled life for a race physically and temperamentally suited to agriculture in a warm climate. It separates the races in a manner that reduces friction. It frees us from harmful conflict between capital and labor. Yet we remain under attack. The number of abolitionist petitions reaching the Congress increases annually. All are utterly devoid of legal foundation. The Fifth Amendment clearly stands as an insuperable barrier: no person may be deprived of property without due process. We deal with the petitions by tabling them, but that only seems to encourage more. The agitators are teaching a whole generation to hate one section of our country. We must resist them at all hazards."

Simms raised his hand. "Even if it should mean eventual disunion, Senator? Or armed conflict?"

"At all hazards," Calhoun repeated, his eyes hot with conviction. Ham struggled to compose himself.

Calhoun answered more questions. Autumn shadows grew long. After Calhoun thanked his listeners, house girls came in with silver trays of wine and punch. Simms stepped forward to offer a toast.

"I give you John C. Calhoun, champion of liberty. May any man who opposes him have a scolding wife, disobedient children, small crops, and a mule to ride on that constantly throws him."

Laughter broke the evening's mood of sobriety. Calhoun's phrase rang in Ham's mind. *At all hazards.* The damned fool.

"May I have another?" he said to one of the servants. He drank two more after that. He took the road to Charleston full of Madeira and gloom.

* * *

The winter dragged. Cassandra's listlessness upset Alex and the entire household, but there seemed to be no remedy. Edgar's death had stolen away more than a husband and father.

Twice each week, Tuesdays and Thursdays, Alex hitched up the carriage and made the rounds of homes of acquaintances, there collecting discarded clothing. Sometimes she knocked on the doors of strangers. She avoided Sword Gate and the Lark residence.

She drove her acquisitions to the three-story brick poorhouse built on public lands at the corner of Queen and Mazyck Streets. The building housed more than a hundred paupers. They were put out to work daily if they were able, kept in the medical wards if not. Alex's routine helped alleviate her sense of idleness, though she had to steel herself for every visit. Underground cells housed the deranged poor, men and women who wailed and cursed and cried out incoherently from tiny barred windows at ground level. It burdened Alex with a sense of the wide disparity between those who lived handsomely in Charleston, and those trapped in its lowest reaches.

* * *

Alex visited Naomi Marburg once a week for tea. She loved the spacious Greek Revival house with white Doric columns in the old suburb of Ansonborough. A mezuzah on the doorjamb testified to the faith of the householders.

The interior was a fascinating mix of cultures: in the kitchen, savory German cooking—beef brisket, potato pancakes, red cabbage; in the parlor, an exotic Orientalism—a Turkish carpet, an elaborately bound set of the Talmud, a brass menorah, a silver cup for Sabbath wine on display. Naomi favored heavy lace curtains that diffused sunlight and kept the parlor cool.

The banker's wife was still proudly allied with the brown elite from which she came. Over tea and tiny sandwiches she and Alex discussed copies of *The Emancipator* and *The Liberator* that reached the Marburgs in unlabeled parcels from the North. Morris and Naomi shared Alex's loathing of slavery—the nation's "slow poison" as George Mason of Virginia had called it—but Marburg would not display the papers in the King Street bookstore or allow them to be kept under the counter. He and his manager, William Watkiss, argued about it regularly.

While Naomi dashed off to quell spats between the older girls, or punish Marion for some mischief, Alex read reports of the American Anti-Slavery Society recently organized in Philadelphia to unite societies from that city, Boston, and New York. She learned of a schism within the national group. Some members wanted gradualism, careful preparation for emancipation at some unspecified time in the future. On the other side were men like Garrison, firebrands of immediatism, a term coined by a British Quaker. Both sides had given up resettlement in Africa as a practical solution.

The papers made Alex feel more alienated, out of place in the city she'd once loved without reservation. She saw Charleston as a self-protective enclave ruled by the fearful, the ignorant, and the greedy.

✫ ✫ ✫

Marburg's bookshop manager invited a young writer of short stories and sketches, William Gilmore Simms, to give a reading from his historical romance, *The Yemassee,* as yet unpublished. Alex and Ham attended, along with the Marburgs, two of their older girls, a pair of journalists, gouty Judge Porcher and his wife, and a dozen strangers.

A *Closed* notice hung on the shop door. The author sat in a rocker and read for ninety minutes. At the end Amaryllis Porcher rose to lead the applause. She declared that Simms would rival Fenimore Cooper when the world saw his work.

Watkiss served apple dumplings he'd baked himself. He was a strange, oddly likable young man with prematurely white hair, hands tiny as a child's and constantly aflutter. He was no more than five feet tall; a bachelor. Mr. Simms, not yet thirty, rocked in his rocker, munched a dumpling, and held forth:

"I love the South. I stand by her. Yet the way of life of the planter is intellectually sterile. All they want to do is hunt, ride, lounge, and sleep. Bring up a literary topic, they run off as though you carried plague. Charleston doesn't give a damn—beg pardon, ladies—for literature or art. What's the answer? Stay and suffer, I suppose. I'll not flee to New York or any of those other smoky, dismal places where publishers congregate."

There we differ, Alex thought. *If I can ever persuade Henry, we'll go.*

☆ ☆ ☆

Even the beauty of that spring, 1835, couldn't restore her spirits. Cassandra sat in the garden for hours, gazing into space, responding lethargically when addressed. Dr. Hayward, back from his wedding trip, could find nothing wrong with her except extreme fatigue, brought on, he felt sure, by her withdrawal from life.

Alex received a brown paper packet from Philadelphia. It contained several foolscap sheets written in a fine hand. Angelina Grimké's explanatory note said the pages were a draft of a composition that "God showed me I must write, during one long, sleepless night this winter." She called it *An Appeal to the Christian Women of the Southern States.*

> *These are only sketches for certain paragraphs of the whole,*
> *which I hope to publish as a pamphlet, through the American*
> *Anti-Slavery Society. God revealed to me that Southern people*
> *who would not read a Northern abolitionist might be more likely*
> *to read one of their own. I address women because addressing*
> *men will only reach men, while addressing women may reach all.*

Alex read the pages and immediately saw the rightness of Angelina's arguments. She also saw the inherent perils. Angelina urged women owning slaves to set them free or, barring that, educate them. Should the law forbid it, Angelina was unequivocal. *If a law commands me to sin, I will break it.*

Excitement gave her a sleepless night like Angelina's. In the morning she rushed the pages to Naomi Marburg. They carried them to William Watkiss, whose voice slid up to familiar shrillness as it did whenever a crisis arose or some written work stirred him:

"This we must stock. This we must disseminate. How can we not? She is a voice native to Charleston."

Naomi said, "Certainly there would be repercussions. Such a pamphlet like hers will enrage a majority of the community."

Watkiss waved his tiny hands. "Let it, let it. The righteous must confront the ungodly."

"We need my husband's consent," Naomi reminded him.

Alex sat with Naomi in the Marburg parlor while Morris read the pages with the aid of a magnifier. It was a hot evening, windows open on the garden. No air stirred; another sweltering, temper-fraying Charleston summer in the making.

"Incendiary stuff," Marburg concluded. "I would never put it in the store if it didn't bear the Grimké name."

Alex clapped her hands. "You mean you will?"

"Against all good sense, yes. I will write to the Society, request that they ship us a quantity by steamer mail at such time as the pamphlet's published. We will then brace for the inevitable."

44

Fanning the Flames

On July 29, Wednesday, the steam packet *Columbia* docked with cargo and mail from New York. Custom House men discovered a pouch sent by the American Anti-Slavery Society to Marburg's Books, King Street. The inspector attached a note to the pouch, calling it to the attention of Postmaster Alfred Huger, a conscientious official and a Unionist.

At the Post Office in the Exchange Building, Huger unsealed the pouch and dumped the contents on a sorting table. Bundles of tracts; two hundred copies or more. *An Appeal to the Christian Women of the Southern States.* Huger saw the name Angelina Grimké and scowled.

Huger quickly composed a letter to Andrew Jackson's postmaster general in Washington, another to his friend the postmaster in New York. How should he deal with such literature arriving through the mails? A majority in Charleston would not tolerate circulation of material dealing with "the question on which this community is too sensitive to admit of any compromise—emancipation of the Southern slave."

A messenger rushed the letters to a packet leaving that night. Huger then sent a note to the Crescent Bank informing Morris Marburg that he would keep the "incendiary publications" locked up until receiving advice from Washington on how to resolve the conflict between civic order and the postmaster's sworn duty. Marburg arrived within the hour, demanding release of his shipment.

"Sir, I can't honor that request," Huger said. "I cannot circulate material clearly meant to establish anarchy and misrule."

They argued. Huger held firm. Marburg stormed out, confronting a crowd on the Exchange steps. He saw respectable men such as Simms Bell and Congressman Lark mixed with dram shop riffraff. Damn the customs men for talking freely. Marburg shouldered past, ignoring threats and foul language.

Inside, Huger was gray with worry. "Fetch me the shotgun in my office." A clerk ran. With the weapon in the crook of his arm Huger stepped outside, greeted by more jeers and cursing. A respected Protestant cleric spoke from the step just below.

"We demand surrender of the incendiary publications, Postmaster."

"No, Reverend, not until and unless Washington sends instructions to that effect."

"That could take days."

A ruffian shouted, "Damn if we'll wait. You don't give 'em up, we'll take 'em."

Huger showed the crowd both shotgun barrels. "Then I will defend them, and you will suffer. Don't force that."

Simms and others counseled restraint. The crowd dispersed, though not happily. As darkness fell, the exhausted Huger locked the Post Office and went home.

Sometime before dawn windows were broken, the building entered, the offending pouch pulled from its shelf. Nothing else was touched. That same night a dozen men slipped through the moonlit street leading to Marburg's residence.

☆   ☆   ☆

At two the next day Ham came home from St. Michael's Alley for dinner. He flung down a copy of the *Southern Patriot*. "Your friend Miss Grimké's pamphlets were removed from the Post Office last night. The consensus of our good citizens is that it was wrong for the pamphlets to be taken clandestinely, because Huger should have surrendered them on demand, in broad daylight. Furthermore, around midnight the Marburg house was mobbed. Windows were broken, burning rags tossed in. Morris fired shots until the men ran."

"Oh, it's my fault," Alex exclaimed. "I took Angelina's first draft to Naomi. I must go to them."

"That isn't wise. The Marburgs are unhurt. Morris hired men to stand guard on his property. There's to be some kind of rally tonight, to destroy the pamphlets. The situation's very nearly out of hand. You should stay off the streets."

Ham was more forceful than she'd ever heard him. She thought of defying him, then reluctantly did as he said.

☆ ☆ ☆

Fueled with refuse and broken furniture, the bonfire on the civic parade ground reddened low-hanging clouds. A riotous crowd of several hundred had gathered. Men raised poles carrying cloth and straw effigies bearing crude signs. WM L GARRISON. ABOLISHINIST FANATIK. GRIMKÉ WHORE. The female effigy had yarn hair, a stuffed bosom, a skirt. Men set the effigies afire. Bitter smoke ascended. The clouds turned scarlet.

In the shadow of a building Henry looked on. Hamnet had argued against his venturing into the streets alone. Henry's curiosity won out. He was careful to stick to dark thoroughfares, alleys, now this heavily shadowed area well back from the center of the demonstration. He felt he could outrun anyone who spotted him.

Men capered around the fire, war-whooping like Indians. They threw rocks at the burning effigies. A squad of city guardsmen watched passively. Volunteer firemen stood by in case sparks carried. A few Negroes huddled at the far edge of the parade ground. Curfew had rung; no one seemed to care.

Men pitched bundles into the fire, inciting the crowd to clap and cheer. A small white-haired man ran up, dived between two rioters, tried to retrieve some of the tracts. Men surrounded him, knocked him down. They stamped on his spine, pounded his head with fists and rocks. They left him prone, white hair bloodied all across the back of his head.

Henry's face was stony. No black man who hoped to pursue a decent life belonged in Charleston. Alex was right, they should steal away, together or separately, meet in New York, then spend a few sweet days or weeks together before he abandoned her. He knew he had to do that, for her sake. He'd go to her tomorrow, tell her he was ready to leave.

Something touched him between the shoulders.

"Hello, nigger."

Henry twisted to the left; glimpsed a beaky nose. Another man slapped the back of his head. "Don't turn around 'less you're told." There were at least four of them.

The beaky man said, "You come along quiet now, Mr. Henry Strong. You refuse, this little old Kentucky pistol"—he dug it into Henry's back—"liable to blow a hole clean through you. Crowd like this wouldn't give a damn. Most likely they'd celebrate."

"What do you want with me?"

"Why, just a little talk is all, Mr. Henry Strong. A little conversation about you and white women, someplace where we won't be disturbed."

A third man said, "Turn real slow. No, the other way. Cross your hands on your shoulders so we see 'em."

Henry's heart pounded. His mouth felt like dust. He marched into the dark with the four white men following. The female effigy disintegrated in sparks and flying bits of cloth. *Alex,* he thought, *never forget I loved you.*

☆ ☆ ☆

Alex's bedroom smelled of smoke when she woke next day. The servants fairly tiptoed, saying nothing. Maudie averted her eyes when Alex came downstairs. Ham had already left the house. She ignored his warning, slipped out the back way.

Merchants on East Bay had shuttered their shops. Some had nailed boards over the windows. Men reeled from side alleys, drunk despite the early hour. One caught her arm, whispered lewd words in her ear. She kicked his shin, wrenched free, ran on.

At Bell's Bridge only one dilapidated packet boat, *Savannah Miss,* was tied up. Four black seamen played cards under an awning. A mate smoked his pipe and whittled. All of them stared as she knocked at the office door.

Otto Abendschein blinked his way into the sun carrying a Hawken rifle. "Not a good day to be out, Miss Alex. Bad men on the street again."

"Any trouble here?"

"Fortunately, no. At breakfast at Jones's Hotel I heard that a special committee is meeting to assess the situation. Feeling is high. The authorities fear riots and lynchings. Best you go back home."

"Soon, Otto, I promise. Take care."

Moving toward King Street, she encountered more drunken men. One carried a rope tied into a noose. The few Negroes she saw were moving quickly, furtively, as though afraid to be noticed.

Marburg's shop window had been smashed. Black scorch marks showed around the edge. Books had been slashed or ripped apart. A funeral wreath hung on the door.

She ran across to a jewelry shop. The owner's pistol lay on a shelf behind the display counter.

"Mr. Rosen, what happened at Marburg's?"

"Poor Mr. Watkiss, they say he tried to rescue some of the abolition literature from the mob. They killed him."

Alex held the counter to steady herself. She heard distant shots; barely managed to offer thanks to the nervous jeweler. She ran out and turned south.

At Broad Street a pack of white boys chased two smaller colored boys westward, throwing rocks and shouting epithets. Alex hurried east to the Crescent Bank. Glass crackled under her shoes; a green canvas was spiked to the window of Morris Marburg's office. Obviously it had been broken. Two iron pipes jammed across the door frame prevented entrance. A sign said CLOSED UNTIL FURTHER NOTICE.

★ ★ ★

At four o'clock the streets drowsed in afternoon heat. Birds sought shade, their songs muted. Alex worked in the garden, constantly swatting at gnats and mosquitoes. Since her experience that morning she'd eaten nothing and worked frantically, trimming and chopping the pink and watermelon-red crape myrtle as she did every July. Finished with that, she'd tried to shape a row of yaupon. After butchering two of the small green hollies she gave up. She sat on a bench, listlessly studying her hands.

Old Drayton, her friend and mentor, was removing the finish from the joggling board on the piazza. His sanding paper rasped. Usually garrulous, he worked silently. Maudie was in the house, scrubbing floors that didn't need it.

Two horsemen appeared outside the gate. One stayed in the saddle. The other handed over his reins, dismounted, jingled the bell. Alex raised her head, pushed back straggling hair. My God, what did he want?

Gibbes was smartly dressed as always. She was filthy, her cheeks dirt streaked, her hands blistered. She walked to the gate.

"How do, Alex. May I come in? I won't be long. The gentleman yonder's my good friend Archie Lescock Third." The beaky horseman tipped his beaver hat. Alex recognized him from the street fight. Did he recognize her?

She opened the gate. Gibbes walked to a patch of shade.

"I regret that I bring you some sad tidings."

"If it's about William Watkiss, I've heard."

"Why, yes, that's tragic. But it concerns a colored man I believe you know. Mr. Hamnet Strong's boy."

Her legs started to shake. "What of him?"

"Some wild fellows must have got hold of him last night. What he was doing out past curfew I surely don't know. This morning his body floated to the foot of Gadsden's old wharf."

"Oh, God, no."

"Whoever did it was mighty cruel. They mutilated him so he was, ah, no longer manly. Decency forbids me from saying any more."

"Where did you hear this?"

"Saloon bar of the Planter's, not an hour ago."

Pain blinded her. She feared she'd throw up. *Don't, that's weakness, it's what he'd like to see.*

A sudden rush of suspicion then. Somehow he'd found out. Who told him? Who put him on the scent? Ouida?

"Gibbes, please leave before I call you a damned murderer."

"Why, cousin, whatever do you—?"

"You did it, didn't you? You and your friends. That man out there—was he with you?"

"I'm sure I don't know what—"

"You killed Henry Strong because of me. You came here to boast."

Calmly, Gibbes said, "I'm really afraid I must plead innocent to the charge, which is purely the most fantastical thing I've ever heard. Don't forget, cousin, Henry Strong was a free person of color. Many consider those people a disruptive and dangerous element. Furthermore, I heard that Henry Strong took liberties with white girls." Gibbes's face was sorrowful, almost maudlin.

"Plain to see you're distraught," he went on. "Very understandable. I'll take my leave. I only wanted to break the news gently. Seems I failed. My sincere regrets."

He grasped her right hand, kissed the grimy knuckles. Alex jerked away.

"God forgive you, Gibbes. I never will."

"That so?" His eye slid down her front. "It's my earnest hope that you'll change your mind someday. Good afternoon."

He set his hat on his head, tapped it, walked briskly to the street. He took his reins from his friend and mounted. Alex clutched the gate. She shook so hard, she feared she'd fall. After the horsemen passed from sight she heard laughter in the afternoon stillness.

45

Decision

Tropical rain fell on Henry's burial. The Brown Fellowship Society, to which the Strongs belonged, had paid for the casket. Morris Marburg contributed the headstone. A hundred mourners, white and colored, huddled under umbrellas while the colored pastor preached and prayed at the grave. Marcelle's first child fussed and had to be led away.

Rain dripped from Alex's black straw bonnet. Wind from the harbor blew against her face. She took no comfort from the pastor's assurances of heaven for Henry. Bitterness ran in her like a poisoned river.

★ ★ ★

For a week conditions in Charleston teetered toward anarchy. A much larger shipment of antislavery tracts arrived. Huger found individual copies addressed to every religious leader in the city, including the rabbi of Beth Elohim. He confiscated the shipment, but word of its arrival spread. Angry men took to the streets again.

Blacks were chased and beaten. Masters sent slaves to the workhouse without provocation. The frightened authorities surrendered control of Charleston to an unruly town meeting. The meeting appointed an extralegal committee of five, led by Robert Hayne; the committee adopted a resolution calling for Northern states to outlaw abolitionist societies, another demanding that Congress forbid delivery of any mail Southern legislatures deemed "inflammatory and seditious, calculated to create an idea that possession of slave property is in any way wrongful or immoral."

Postmaster General Kendall in Washington replied to Huger's letter. While a local postmaster had no authority to interfere with the mails, "extenuating circumstances" justified violation of that rule. Kendall's statement reduced tensions. The authorities took charge again, although armed "committees of vigilance" met incoming packets and accompanied mailbags to the Post Office.

Only one relative of William Watkiss could be found, an aunt in North Carolina too infirm to travel. Less than a dozen people gathered for his interment in a cemetery plot paid for by the Marburgs. The sun shone brilliantly. Alex thought that if a merciful God existed, He had turned His face away from her city.

★ ★ ★

On summer days a ray of light from a window at the stair landing illuminated Joanna's portrait at a certain hour. Alex stood in the light one morning, gazing at the picture and gathering courage. She'd brushed her hair, scrubbed her face, put on a clean dress and shoes.

Alex tapped at her mother's door. Cassandra was awake, though still in bed; she seldom came down before noon. Popular novels like Mrs. Sedgwick's *The Linwoods* and Mr. Paulding's *Westward Ho!* crowded a marble table at the bedside. Alex bought books for her mother, but she'd learned not to ask if Cassandra had enjoyed them. Open windows brought in the smell of mud flats off the Battery.

Drowsily Cassandra said, "Good morning, dear. How nice you look."

"Thank you, Mama. I've come because I have something important to tell you."

Cassandra pointed to the Hepplewhite chair Hamnet Strong had imitated beautifully. Alex drew it to the bed, arranged her skirt. Her mother's face was gaunt, colorless as parchment. Dark blue veins ridged the backs of her hands.

"I'm twenty years old now, Mama. I must do something with my life. That's impossible here."

"You mean in this house?"

"Charleston. I've already discussed my decision with Ham. He doesn't approve, but he knows he can't change my mind."

"And what is this decision?"

"I'm leaving. I want to live in a civilized city. Philadelphia, or New York, or Boston."

Cassandra compressed her colorless lips, her only reaction. "Why, child?"

"Principally because of what happened to Henry."

"Yes, a terrible tragedy. Such a fine boy."

"Henry was my best friend. He had ambition. He wanted to become an actor, and he was willing to leave South Carolina forever to do it. I'm sure white men killed him. I can't prove it, but I think they did it because we were friends. Because someone saw us together and . . . speculated."

"Speculated that it was more than friendship? Was it?"

"I told you, we were friends. I won't stay in a place where they'll murder and mutilate someone because of friendship."

"Alex, Charleston's your home. You know nothing about those Northern cities. They're huge. Overrun with foreigners, and lowlifes."

"Could Yankee lowlifes be worse than the men who killed Henry?"

Frustrated, Cassandra snapped at her. "How will you pay for a steamer ticket? Have you saved money?"

"Since I've never had to work, how could I? Another lack in the lives of young ladies of Charleston."

"I hear such bitterness in your voice."

"Truth, Mama. A commodity not valued locally. Ham will advance the price of the ticket. I'll repay him as soon as I can."

Cassandra collected herself for a new attack. "Then tell me how you'll survive in the North."

"I'm not without education, thanks to you and Papa. I can teach music. I can be a governess. I'll find my way."

Cassandra studied her daughter's determined expression. "You have always done that. You're like your grandmother Joanna in that respect."

Alex clasped her mother's bony hands. "Only one thing worries me. Your health. Ham's promised to take complete charge, together with Dr. Hayward."

"Oh, I'll be fine. I plan to live a good many years. I'm touched that you'd worry, but that's what you've done since you were little." She slipped into a reverie. "You were a scrawny baby, have I ever told you?"

"No," Alex said, though she had, often.

"I nursed you for nearly a year. Every time, your little hands would reach for me, touch me, as though you worried that the milk would run out. If you're determined to leave, only promise me you'll worry about yourself, no one else, until you're safely settled."

"I will."

"And promise to write faithfully. I'll worry constantly if you don't."

Alex hugged her. "I promise. You rest now. I love you, Mama."

"I love you. I think I would like to sleep a while."

As Alex left, Cassandra's eyes closed. She turned her head and buried her cheek in her pillow, crying silently.

✭ ✭ ✭

In between August downpours Alex went to St. Michael's Alley to confer with her brother. She had to wait while James Petigru went over a brief with Ham. Petigru greeted Alex warmly as he returned to his office at the end of a row of desks where clerks labored. Whale-oil lamps relieved the gloom of the dark-paneled office only a little.

Ham had been moved to a small room of his own. His apprenticeship was finished and he was preparing to take the bar. "I've come about a legal matter," Alex told him. "I thought it best to discuss it here. After I leave, I would like you to give Maudie her freedom."

"You know how difficult that's become. The legislature—"

"Must approve it. I know. But we have friends. Judge Porcher, Mr. Petigru—surely they can help. We have money, if it's necessary to bribe someone."

Ham took off his gold-wire spectacles. He looked more like an anchorite every day. He stooped continually, even when he sat. "If that's your earnest wish, I'll get it done somehow."

"Bless you."

"Are you sure of your own mind, Alex? Do you really propose to work against the system that prevails here?"

"Yes. I've already written Angelina."

"You want to be like the Grimkés—an old abolitionist hen? It isn't a popular calling. Even in the North such women are roughly treated."

"Any more roughly than Henry? I doubt it."

"You loved him, didn't you?"

"More than I'll ever love any man."

"I've heard time has a way of tempering that kind of certainty."

"Not mine. I'll confess something I've never said to another human being. I wanted to marry Henry." Ham glanced at the open door, as though fearing listeners. "He wouldn't hear of it. He knew the price I'd pay. I said I'd pay it gladly. He still refused. That's how decent and con-

siderate he was. I believe Gibbes had a hand in his death, at least insti-
gated it, because I'd have nothing to do with him."

"That's a dangerous thought. I find nothing to admire about our
cousin, but you know as well as I do that Simms Bell and his family are
very well connected. Virtually untouchable."

"I have no intention of trying to harm him."

"Your solution is to leave."

"Yes."

"If you go, only a handful will ever welcome you back."

"Those are the only ones I'll miss."

"This is your home. Can you really turn your back on it?"

"Mama asked the same question. Charleston's become a cruel place.
Underneath all the beauty there's a darkness. God will punish this city
someday."

"Lord, you're sounding like a Yankee already." He sighed. "I will be
so lonely without you. When will you go?"

"As soon as possible."

Saying it, she suddenly felt unburdened; free.

46

Leave-Taking

Alex bought passage to Philadelphia on *Atlantic Meteor* of the Red Ball Line. The ship anchored in the harbor on the last day of September.

She scarcely slept that night. She was up at half past five, brewing coffee. Her trunk in the hall held her Bible, what few good clothes she owned, and Edward's pistols wrapped in thick flannel. Her canvas banjo case leaned against the trunk.

She spent a half hour with Cassandra, saying good-bye. She hugged the house slaves one by one, gave them each ten dollars, then told Ham she was ready. They drove to Bell's Bridge in the open carriage. Puddles and a pewter sky lingered from yesterday's rain. Here and there gaps in the clouds opened, bleeding orange light for brief periods. Ham said little, concentrating on the heavy vehicle and foot traffic.

At Bell's Bridge a barouche blocked the head of the pier. An elderly slave in an old brown suit and tall hat sat on the box, pensively examining his hands. Ouida's stiffened skirt nearly filled the backseat. She wore a velvet day coat, bright green, with a wide linen collar and bow knots down the front. Tiny embroidered roses dotted her silk bonnet. Yellow kid gloves matched the roses. Compared to her cousin's plumage Alex was a drab sparrow in her plainly cut white dress, Quaker mantle of gray silk, and black taffeta bonnet.

She felt sure Ouida hadn't driven to the pier with any good intent.

She did her best to think of a pleasantry while Ham reined the carriage alongside the much larger one.

"Good morning, Ouida," Alex said "May I offer congratulations to you and your husband? Dr. Hayward told mother the good news."

"He had no right to do that. Childbearing is a private matter, only discussed inside the family, never in public."

"My apologies, then. I only wanted to say I'm happy for you." She wasn't, really, and Ouida knew it. "Ham will need to write me when the baby's born."

"Whether he does or doesn't is of no interest to me. I came here to deliver a parting message. Given your plan to join your Negro-worshiping friends who want to destroy our way of life, we no longer acknowledge a family connection."

"If that's your message, I don't care to hear any more."

"Oh, but I insist. Charleston is well rid of a person like you. I advise you not to show your face here again."

"Ham, drive on."

Upset by the exchange, he reacted slowly. Alex snatched the whip from its socket, laid it across the horse's croup. The horse lunged, nearly throwing them both off the seat. The carriage careened down the pier. Dock workers scattered.

Ham drove his boot sole against the brake rod and leaned back to haul on the reins. The carriage rocked to a stop. He looked over his shoulder.

"They've gone. I'm sorry, sister. What Ouida said was unconscionable."

"But not surprising. For a minute I expected her to spit in my face." It was her turn to pat and comfort him. "Never mind. She only convinced me that I'm doing what's right."

Otto Abendschein unloaded her trunk. She carried the banjo case by the shoulder strap. Ham helped her down the steps to the waiting rowboat, nervously stepped in after her. Otto unshipped the oars; a Negro cast off the painter and Otto rowed them into a light chop, toward the anchored steamer.

The bearded captain welcomed her as she came up the gangway roped to the hull. A mate led her to a small cabin; Otto and Ham carried her trunk. Otto shook her hand, wished her well, and left.

She and Ham embraced. He went down the gangway and almost fell in the water trying to step in the bobbing rowboat. Alex watched until he and Otto reached Bell's Bridge.

Atlantic Meteor raised her anchor chain an hour later. Paddlewheels revolving in the ornately painted boxes, the packet turned into the harbor channel. The captain had given his few passengers the run of the vessel. She walked to the bow, holding her bonnet so the wind wouldn't snatch it.

The familiar skyline slipped away: the handsome Exchange; scaffolding on St. Philip's, where workmen were rebuilding the steeple that had burned in another devastating fire last February. St. Michael's bells rang the hour. She loved her native city, but what it stood for had turned that love to something very close to loathing.

The packet crossed the bar on the high tide. To starboard Fort Sumter's uneven masonry walls raised the question of whether it would ever be finished. To port, on the gray-green ribbon of Sullivan's Island, Fort Moultrie had filled with drifted sand. Two cows grazed inside, one standing on the parapet. Ahead, small white horses showed on the sea. To counter her feeling of loss Alex tried to envision life in the North. She was sailing into a better day, she must remember that.

Clouds opened above the eastern horizon. Misty amber sunshine streamed through, lighting patches of the ocean. She savored the salt wind. Yes, surely, there'd be a better and brighter day to banish any lingering regrets.

A better day . . .

"Oh," she said softly. The anthem she'd vainly tried to write for so long filled her thoughts. Now she knew how its melody resolved. Now she knew its message.

47

1840

The Cincinnati coach carried Alex through white fields lying under dark December skies. She would never learn to like snow or the bitter Northern winters. In all her childhood she remembered only one overnight snowfall; it melted by noon the next day.

Alex hadn't seen Charleston since the day she sailed away. Letters from Ham kept her apprised of their mother's condition. Although Cassandra's health hadn't worsened, neither had it improved. She lived, in Ham's phrase, apart from the world. At Christmas, Alex and Ham and their mother would exchange gifts and greetings by mail, as usual.

Dayton's broad unpaved streets were largely deserted when they arrived at half past four. It was Alex's first trip to Ohio, but after three years of travel in the Northeast, new places were less daunting. She knew the kind of hostility she might face.

The coach bumped from Main Street onto First, then into a fenced yard where the driver handed down her carpetbag. Alex always kept her banjo case at her side. Other passengers greeted those meeting them. No one was waiting for her.

The winter dark induced a pang of loneliness. She longed for her comfortable rooms in Washington, where she'd settled after a year in Philadelphia. She supported herself by giving lessons in grammar, basic French, and piano. Her pupils were female, from prosperous homes; she never suggested they learn to play the banjo. She didn't live luxuriously, but neither did she starve. When she traveled to speak for antislavery societies, her expenses were paid.

Although five years had passed since Henry's death, she still mourned him. She discouraged those occasional young men who might have qualified as beaux. At twenty-five she considered herself a spinster. Rather surprisingly, her friend and mentor, Angelina Grimké, had married. Angelina's husband, Theodore Dwight Weld, was a seminary graduate and the author of *American Slavery as It Is,* a widely read collection of graphic accounts of abuses under the system.

Two years ago Alex had met Weld in Boston. He introduced her to bald and bespectacled William Lloyd Garrison, editor and publisher of *The Liberator.* Garrison resembled a prim schoolmaster more than the fiery apostle of emancipation. Ham said Southerners thought him kin to the devil, and would hang him without a trial if he ever dared step into South Carolina. In the North, Alex had discovered to her sorrow, hatred of the abolitionists was nearly as virulent in some quarters.

Specks of snow whirled around her as she pulled her cloak tighter and retied her black bonnet. Bulky crinolines that stiffened a skirt were coming into fashion, but she still preferred a simple, straight dress of Quaker cut. Symbolism apart, it was more practical for travel.

She searched for some sign of her host. Wind rattled a broadsheet tacked to the board fence.

PROCLAIM LIBERTY!!

The Managers of the Dayton Auxiliary of

THE AMERICAN ANTI-SLAVERY SOCIETY

Invite, without Regard to Party or Sect, ANY & ALL

Ready to Stand on LIBERTY'S SIDE in the GREAT STRUGGLE

now upon us, to attend a Glorious

FREEDOM RALLY!

Thrill to the testimony of

- Fiery Immediatist -

The Rev. WM. DREW of Boston.

- Erudite Escaped SLAVE -

NICODEMUS BROWN.

- "Songstress of Freedom" -

Miss ALEXANDRA BELL of Charleston.

Listed last, Alex would be first to speak. She wasn't upset by an obscene word defacing the bottom of the poster; she'd seen them in plenty.

A fat man in a tall hat rushed out of the dark, breathless. "Miss Bell? I am Cletus Westerham of the committee. I am so sorry to be late. My carriage horse went lame. Have you waited long?"

"Only a short time."

"Your hotel's just there, in the next block. Let's see you settled, so you can rest a bit. The program's at seven. Would you care for supper beforehand?"

"No, thank you," she said as they crossed the frozen mud of the street. "Eating before a talk steals energy. Sarah Grimké taught me that."

"The others on our committee will greet you at the hall. Of course we're all eager to hear your message. Like the Grimkés you come from the very heart of the slave culture. I have but one request."

"Yes?"

"In your remarks, would you be so kind as to avoid the, ah, woman question? We find it antagonizes many influential men who might otherwise support us with contributions."

"Mr. Westerham, I appreciate the invitation to address your meeting, but I must speak what's in my heart. How can we care about the freedom of Negroes and ignore the bondage of women?"

Westerham sighed. "Oh, dear. Well, as you must."

Alex wasn't angry; she heard the request frequently. Angelina and Sarah had introduced the issue of women's rights into the movement on their initial tour of Massachusetts in 1837. Sarah had declared, "By speaking out, we are only assuming the rights and duties of all moral beings. The Lord opened the way for us to address mixed audiences."

In Boston the sisters had been the first to appear before an all-male state legislature. Yet even there, where Paul Revere and Sam and John Adams had set the torch of liberty afire, the notion that universal emancipation should include women outraged conservatives, especially many of those in the clergy. Garrison, on the other hand, enthusiastically filled his weekly with praise of the idea.

Alex signed the registry at the Swaynie House, then asked Westerham, "Do you expect disturbances at the meeting?"

"I would be untruthful if I said no. Our work is not popular with large segments of the population. We're only sixty miles from the Ohio River, and the Kentucky slave masters. I hope that doesn't alarm you."

"Oh, no," she said, not entirely honestly.

* * *

The New Light Meeting House on Main Street south of Fourth was packed. Satin banners hung from the rafters depicted the Liberty Bell and exhorted the audience to PROCLAIM LIBERTY THROUGHOUT THE LAND.

Peeking from a holding room next to the stage, Alex decided the audience looked respectable, though at the back of the hall she noticed several rough-looking men. In the third row, on the aisle, a man wearing a shabby black suit glowered at the stage. The man's pinched, liverish face gave her pause. She'd encountered fanatics before.

As always, she fretted about the coming performance. Was she suitably dressed? Was her banjo in tune? Her voice adequate? In the wings Westerham introduced her to committee members and the others on the program: Nicodemus Brown, a runaway from an Alabama cotton plantation, and Reverend William Drew, a thickset man of about thirty with a blunt jaw and abundant dark hair worn long. Reverend Drew had a deep, resonant voice and beautiful teeth he showed off to advantage whenever he smiled, which was often. He was shorter than Alex by several inches. She seldom met a man who wasn't.

"Bell, Bell—that's familiar," he said as he shook her hand. "In Newport some years ago my late father met a gentleman from Charleston by that name."

"If you're referring to Edgar Bell, it could have been my father, also deceased. Our family vacationed in Newport."

"Edgar Bell. I believe that's it." His smile charmed her. He didn't have the lugubrious air of many clerics, nor did he wear black or fusty brown. His frock coat was forest green with black velvet lapels. Pale gray trousers matched his vest. His black tie, more scarf than cravat, was full and flowing, as Byronic as his hair.

"I remember the occasion because I met your father briefly," he continued. "I was on holiday between college and my first year at seminary. My father enjoyed his conversation with Mr. Bell, although I understand they quarreled rather sharply at the end. Father was a Unitarian preacher, as am I. That is, I was until I stepped down from my pulpit last year. Here's a thought. Perhaps we could take a little supper together after the program." When Alex hesitated, he said, "Oh, have no fear, I'm a widower. My wife, Filomena, passed away three years ago."

Alex offered her sympathies and was about to refuse the invitation when Westerham plucked her sleeve. "We are ready to begin."

The other men on the committee took seats reserved on front

benches. Westerham stepped onstage to applause and a few catcalls from the rear. William Drew leaned close, his breath redolent of clove. "Some roughnecks out there."

"It doesn't bother me. I've handled them before."

"I thought you looked like a stalwart," Drew said, flashing that marvelous smile.

"Ladies and gentlemen," Westerham announced, "it is my honor and privilege to present our first speaker, the nationally famous composer and balladeer, Miss Alexandra Bell of Charleston, South Carolina."

48

Freedom Song

Alex strode from the wings with her banjo. Her blond hair, worn to her waist, shimmered with reflections of the footlight lamps. Her height and her confident carriage gave her an air of authority. She bowed to acknowledge the applause, consciously wooing the audience with her eyes and her smile. From the back of the hall came the bleat of a tin horn.

"Friends of freedom," she began, "your welcome warms me this wintry evening. I stand before you as a Southerner, exiled from the land of my birth by the sound of the lash and the piteous cry of the slave." Alex spoke from memory. She'd written her speech before the first appearance she ever made, in a tiny hamlet in upstate New York. The speech had been changed and rearranged, added to and subtracted from, many times since.

"I stand before you as a repentant daughter of a family of slaveholders. I stand before you as a woman, and a moral being, feeling that I owe it to the suffering slave and the deluded master, the oppressed wife and the tyrannical husband"—the liverish man in the third row scowled—"to do all that I can to overturn a complicated system of crimes built on the prostrate bodies and broken hearts of my brothers and sisters of both races. But let me speak to you in a different way."

The tin horn blared again. She ignored it and slipped the embroidered strap over her head. Her new, fretless banjo was a beautiful instrument of lustrous gun-stock maple, from the Baltimore workrooms of William Boucher. All five strings had tuning pegs, four at the top of the neck and the fifth lower down. On the solid back of the rim, in contrasting marquetry, the maker had inlaid a North Star of freedom.

She tested the strings, adjusted a peg. "This song, set to a familiar patriotic air, comes from a Massachusetts antislavery hymnal." She struck a chord.

> "My country, 'tis of thee,
> Stronghold of slavery,
> Of thee I sing . . ."

She sang all six stanzas, her passion compensating for her untrained voice. Once more the roughneck tooted his horn. Another jingled sleigh bells. One of the committee members rose and cried, "Shame." Others hissed until the rowdies quieted.

Alex sang a second hymn, then put the banjo aside and launched into an account of her awakening in Charleston. She spoke of the workhouse and the treadmill; Lydia's abusive ways and her harassment of Virtue that had led to her murder. She avoided names, but her descriptions were no less vivid.

She spoke of her friendship with Henry, intolerable to certain Charleston whites. "Parties unknown murdered and horribly mutilated my friend. He was not a slave but a free man whose only crime was his color. They threw his poor tortured body into Charleston Harbor." An audible reaction ran through the hall.

"It was then I realized I couldn't stand by and see such cruelty and intolerance defended and perpetuated. I knew I must leave the South, raise my voice, do my part to bring the wonderful day of jubilee."

She took up the banjo again, tested the strings, and sang "A Better, Brighter Morning."

> "Oh, the old ways, they are dying,
> And the night is pushed away
> By a shining red horizon,
> 'Tis the dawning of the day.
> So take up the righteous hammer,
> Let the evil shackles fall,
> As the blessed beams of freedom
> Spread their beauty o'er all."

A few listeners began to clap with the beat, then more. Everyone knew the anthem; thousands of copies had been sold. She heard strangers whistling the tune wherever she went. She tapped her foot as she sang.

> "From valley green, mountain high,
> Hear the soulful, joyful cry.
> Meek and mighty, black and white,
> Praise the coming of the light.
> A better, brighter morning
> Is the glory that I see.
> Such a better, brighter morning
> On the day—all—men—are
> Free."

People rose to applaud, including a few courageous women. The horns and sleigh bells almost seemed part of the ovation. Alex bowed and returned the banjo to the chair, noting the furious face of the liverish man.

She stepped to the edge of the stage; clasped her hands. "Another form of bondage exists in our country and it, too, must be addressed. I speak of the bondage of women unjustly kept from a full life by chains of the law, and chains of custom, fully as strong as the iron shackles of slaves, for all that they are invisible. We must—"

The liverish man jumped up. "Hold on, woman. Your nigger cant is bad enough, but we won't tolerate heresy."

"Heresy, sir?" Alex began. Someone shouted for the man to sit down; he paid no attention.

"Yes, heresy. You and your scarlet sisters preach the devil's gospel. My wife listened to one of your kind and she left me."

"Sir, I'm deeply sorry for your loss, but—"

He outshouted her. "Are you godless? Don't you read the Bible? You should obey St. Paul's charge to the Corinthians—'Let your women keep silence in the churches, for it is not permitted unto them to speak.' "

"Sir, conscience demands that I offer my message wherever and whenever I feel compelled. I'll be happy to debate the issue privately if you just let me continue."

He pointed an accusing finger. " 'And if they will learn anything, let them ask their husbands at home, for it is a shame for women to speak.' "

Alex appealed to the crowd. "Can we not persuade this gentleman to be courteous enough to give me a hearing?"

"No hearing for a she-devil who destroys families." The man's hand dived in his pocket; a rock flew, gashing Alex's forehead.

She reeled back. Blood dripped in her eyes and onto her dress. She staggered, lost her balance. She sat down on the stage with an unceremonious thump, humiliated.

The man threw a second rock that landed harmlessly behind her. Westerham and Reverend Drew rushed from the wings. Drew leapt off the stage, dragged the attacker into the aisle, and punched him twice. The man collapsed. Drew stepped on his neck. "Someone get this trash out of here."

Two committeemen rushed to remove the offender. Alex struggled to her feet, pressed her handkerchief to her bleeding forehead. Nicodemus Brown, the ex-slave, steadied her while Westerham dithered: "Oh, I am so sorry. The man is a deacon in his church but a known troublemaker."

"We'd better help this lady 'stead of talking," Brown said.

Drew climbed back onstage, his Byronic hair mussed. One of the committee members said, "You sure enough fixed his clock for him, Reverend."

"Men who abuse women deserve no less. Christian forbearance has its limits." He picked up the banjo and followed Brown and Alex to the holding room, where Alex slumped into a chair. While someone ran for a doctor, a committee member found a pint of whiskey. She took a sip gratefully.

The doctor arrived, examined her forehead, said it needed stitches. "My office is three blocks from here."

Reverend Drew said, "I have a carriage outside. Mr. Brown, please address the meeting while we take care of the lady. Mr. Westerham, put this instrument in its case and guard it, she'll want it returned to the hotel undamaged. Miss Bell, can you stand?"

"Yes, of course."

"Then lean on me. I have your cloak."

The ride through the December dark was mostly a blur. The doctor's wife came into the surgery to assist. The doctor gave Alex a wooden rod to bite while he sutured the gash. It hurt hellishly, but she didn't make a sound. Presently the doctor stood back, wiped his hands on his apron.

"There. Minnie, the mirror, please."

When Alex saw the stitches, she groaned. "I look like a rag doll sewn back together." She noticed that someone had cleaned the blood off her hands. She didn't remember. "What is your fee, Doctor?

"Nothing, young lady. We should pay you. Dayton has treated you abominably."

Reverend Drew drove her to the hotel. Her cloak hid her bloody dress. In the lobby he asked how she was feeling.

"Fine, but I'd very much like a glass of wine, if I may be bold enough to say that to a pastor."

"Of course you may. Are you hungry?"

"Famished."

"Then let me renew my offer of supper. I hear the hotel has a decent dining room."

Alex hesitated. He wasn't the handsomest man she'd ever met, but he had soulful brown eyes, a certain dash, and obvious courage. She felt she owed him something for his gallantry.

"I would like that, Reverend. First I must change my dress."

He bowed. "I'll happily await your return. I have some observations about what transpired this evening."

Curious to know what he meant, she went upstairs. She hoped Henry would forgive her disloyalty, wherever he was.

49

The Come-Outer

A sleepy waiter showed them to a table lit by candles. After they were seated Alex said, "I feel sorry for Mr. Brown, left to carry the rest of the program."

"Don't concern yourself. I've heard him speak. He can enthrall a crowd for hours and never flag."

"You certainly quieted that heckler. I'm grateful."

"Rowed him up Salt River, as the saying goes. I consider it a privilege, and I have no congregation to criticize me. Indeed, it's what some of them would expect of a come-outer." *So he's one of those,* Alex thought, startled. Drew snapped his napkin to unfold it. On the little finger of his right hand a heavy gold signet gleamed.

The waiter presented menus. After discussing choices Drew ordered squab, roasted potatoes and succotash, and a bottle of claret. "None of that Ohio frontier whiskey they lace with molasses and red pepper. I drank some in my wild youth. I was sick for days."

She laughed. He asked whether she missed Charleston. "Terribly," she said. "My brother and my mother still live there."

"Would you go back?"

"In an emergency. Never to live."

"Your history and your music are a rare combination, Miss Bell. You're a unique witness for the cause. I must say I love 'A Better, Brighter Morning.' As soon as you wrote it, you must have known the whole country would sing it."

"Not the South, certainly. I really had no idea it would become so popular elsewhere."

"Brings you a lot of money, I don't doubt."

"Yes, but I never intended that. I've always loved making up songs. I sang it the first time I appeared in New York City, at the Broadway Tabernacle. When the song caught on, a publisher came to me and we negotiated an agreement. I live on a small portion of the proceeds and donate the rest to antislavery groups."

"White people don't usually play the banjo. It's considered a Negro instrument."

"A slave in Charleston taught me to play and I never thought twice about it. The banjo came to these shores with the people we brought here in chains. It's an American instrument."

The waiter set plates on the white tablecloth. No other diners remained; most of the candles in the room had been snuffed. The isolation comforted Alex, as did the claret, and Drew's presence.

They talked in an animated way about issues related to their common cause: the future of the troublesome Republic of Texas, whose white citizens wanted admission to the Union as a slave state; the possible outcome of the court case of the Africans who had rebelled and seized the slave ship *Amistad*—they were fighting to avoid extradition to Cuba and eventual execution in Spain. Inevitably, they discussed the dangers of their work, symbolized most vividly by the death of Elijah Lovejoy, a Presbyterian pastor, in Alton, Illinois, four years earlier. A proslavery mob had shut down Lovejoy's abolitionist paper by murdering him and burning his presses.

"Have you encountered violence?" Drew asked.

"Not to any serious degree. I've been cursed and booed. In Albany someone threw a rotten cabbage. Fortunately it hit the podium, not me. I'm not naïve, Reverend. I know that our work can be dangerous. I was warned about it when I first volunteered. I accepted the risk."

Through it all Drew's casual confession that he was a come-outer plagued her with curiosity. Come-outers were religious radicals whose disillusionment with their own churches led them to crusade independently. She wanted to know more. She began by asking how he'd become involved in abolitionism.

"Well, it didn't happen early, even though I was raised by parents who looked down on the Southern slave masters. I had no intention of becoming a preacher like my father until his brother, my uncle Nicholas, took me on a trip to Montgomery, Alabama, one summer. I was eighteen. Still at Harvard."

"Why Alabama?"

"His wife, Aunt Bea, comes from there. Uncle Nick did business with her two brothers, owners of large cotton plantations. The arrangement assured Uncle Nick a steady supply of cotton for his spinning mill in Quincy. Uncle Nick is a hearty, happy man, completely in charge of his wife and family. To this day he seems carefree, unlike my father, who always bore the burdens of the world. I idolized Uncle Nick and Aunt Bea for a long time."

He touched his napkin to his lips; the gold signet blazed in the candlelight. "In Montgomery my eyes were opened. I began to grasp the connection between my uncle's prosperity and the bent backs of Negroes. I saw one of Aunt Bea's brothers inflict a horrible punishment on a fifteen-year-old slave. The boy was cat-hauled."

"I've not heard of that. What is it?"

Drew's cheerful demeanor was gone; he seemed to stare beyond her, to some dark place. He described the slave boy spread-eagled and prone, wrists and ankles tied to stakes. He described the black slave driver pulling on padded gauntlets and opening a croker sack in which a tomcat had been kept for an hour.

"The driver grabbed the tom's front paws and dragged him spitting mad out of the sack. Then he raked the writhing cat's hind legs over the boy's back ten times. The screams were indescribable. I still hear them in my dreams." He drained his wineglass in one gulp.

"After the trip I no longer admired my uncle. And that summer I became my father's true son. Eventually a soldier in his cause."

"But you've left your pastorate," she said.

"Surely in part because of the loss of my wife at too young an age. Filomena had a fragile heart even as a girl. I was alone suddenly, and brooding. I felt that my church, liberal though it is, went forward too slowly in the fight against slavery. Too many of my parishioners were mired in gradualism. When I heard that Abby Kelley had left her Friends meeting in Boston and struck out on her own, something in me responded. Are you familiar with the Scriptural source of the term *come-outer*?"

Alex shook her head.

"Book of Revelation, chapter eighteen. 'And I heard another voice from heaven saying, Come out of her, my people, that ye not be partakers of her sins.'"

"So now you stand up and disturb worship services?"

"I ask questions of the pastor and the congregation that they don't

want to hear," he said. "How, for instance, they can show compassion and tolerance for Southerners who keep concubines and at the same time rant against the sin of brothels in their own city. Unpopular questions. It isn't exactly a safe pursuit. I've been rowed up Salt River myself, by good Christians, several Sunday mornings. I've been jailed for disturbing the peace three times."

"And you're a confirmed immediatist."

"The idea that slavery can be dismantled in some vague, gradual way is not only sinful, it's impractical. Ludicrous. The time for abolition was last year. Last month. Yesterday." He thumped his fist on the table; the silver danced.

"Are you an immediatist, Miss Bell?"

"I'm not sure. Often I believe so. At other times I'm doubtful. I wonder whether demanding an instant solution only makes achieving the goal more difficult."

"We certainly make it more difficult by introducing extraneous issues."

His quiet remark stung her. "Ah. Is that what you meant when you said you had thoughts about what happened this evening?"

"Yes. Much as I understand your passion for the woman question, and admire your devotion to your married sisters, I believe it's harmful. Advocacy of too many ancillary issues has isolated William Lloyd Garrison, until many in the movement want nothing to do with him. Secondary issues are divisive. They slow our progress."

"But tell me, Reverend—how can you separate issues of freedom? A woman in bondage to her husband is little different from a Negro enslaved by a white master."

"That may be so, but tonight you saw clearly that injecting the issue dilutes the primary message. Not incidentally, it also increases the danger to yourself."

"I have no fear or hesitation on that score. In any case I should think it's my affair." She spoke more sharply than she intended.

He replied in kind. "I'm sorry, you're mistaken."

"So you and I really don't stand together, do we?"

"No. I believe the cause mustn't be damaged, which is what you are doing. Slavery is America's greatest sin. No others compare. Slavery must be purged, washed away, very likely in the blood of our own citizens."

"Then I see no way to resolve this argument. Let me thank you for the fine dinner and excuse myself." Under her anger lay disappointment.

She'd enjoyed his company, and as a practical matter he was right. The woman issue created a schism in churches and antislavery societies. Yet she found him too extreme and dogmatic. She should have expected it of a come-outer.

The fatigued waiter shuffled to the table to say the dining room was closing. Drew paid the bill with a generous tip, then escorted her to the foot of the lobby stairs. "I'm sorry if I upset you, Miss Bell."

"We do disagree, Reverend. But I'll always be in your debt for what you did this evening."

"Could we continue our discussion at another time and place?"

"Oh, I don't think so. I never know where I'll be from month to month."

"May I have your address, then? We could exchange ideas in writing."

"No, I think not."

"Because we disagree?"

Without hesitating she said, "Yes." It wasn't the only reason. Further intercourse would be disloyal to Henry. She held out her hand. "Good evening."

She saw disappointment on his face as she turned away. She felt him watching while she ascended the stairs. In her room she lay awake for an hour, recalling details of their exchange and regretting its bad outcome.

50

Lark's Fate

In 1841 former congressman Crittenden Lark was fifty-two and show-ing it. Reckless living had enlarged his nose and his belly. To look more youthful he'd adopted the fashionable tonsure of the old Roman em-perors: hair combed over the forehead and curled into ringlets on top. A brown paste applied regularly hid his gray hair.

The Larks still were not considered part of Charleston's elite. They remained solid members of the city's commercial class. They occupied a handsome residence converted from two adjoining Federal houses, and kept a summer cottage on the Ashley. Lark had successfully invested the money amassed in his privateering days. He had little need to work as that term was commonly understood, but he lived with dissatisfaction. "Enough money" was a concept foreign to him.

Over the years he'd quietly bought tracts of cotton land northwest of Charleston, where the Low Country rose gradually toward the sandy midlands. He'd profited handsomely during years of peak prices. More recently he'd picked up two thousand acres in the Mississippi delta, and joined a syndicate organizing to move into Texas.

Sophie Lark no longer had any interest in the physical side of mar-riage. On rare occasions when he attempted to enjoy her favors she made her distaste evident. He supposed she felt the same way about all men. He left her alone most of the time and found his pleasure elsewhere, chiefly with nubile young Negresses from the household. Whores cost money; slaves cost nothing.

Both of the Lark children were unmarried. Snoo, whose mother was Sophie, was beautiful and stunningly proportioned. She attracted young men Lark considered predators in pursuit of her money. He bullied her into rejecting them. Snoo's older half-brother, Folsey, ran with a wild crowd that included Gibbes Bell. At nineteen he'd gotten a white girl in trouble. The girl's father demanded two hundred dollars and "perpetual care" for his grandchild. Lark preferred to deal with such threats through third parties. He hired two Bay Street toughs to waylay and beat the man until he could barely crawl. Father, daughter, and Folsey's unborn brat left the city and were not heard of again.

Despite these vicissitudes Crittenden Lark considered his life one of personal accomplishment. He had no desire for social position, as Sophie did. Only one page in his mental account book plagued him. It showed the payment owed by the Bells for the murder of William Lark.

Several times Crittenden had thought of moving against Hampton Bell. The right opportunity never presented itself. Ham Bell's sister was another irritant, a strident voice railing against the South. Her name appeared regularly in the national press and millions sang her antislavery ballads, though not locally. Alex and her brother were never out of Crittenden Lark's thoughts for long.

*　*　*

After complicated legal maneuvers and a nine-hour defense oration by seventy-five-year-old John Quincy Adams, the *Amistad* rebels won their victory in the Supreme Court. Chief Justice Story freed them. Abolitionists raised money for their return voyage to West Africa in 1841. Charleston gentlemen, including Lark, went into a rage when they read that a star speaker at one of the New York fund-raisers was "that damned woman," Alexandra Bell.

A few months later inspection of some potentially lucrative cotton acreage in Georgia took Crittenden Lark away for a week. When he returned, his friend Simms Bell invited him to the saloon bar of the Planter's Hotel and there informed him that Sophie Lark had been seen at an inn near Orangeburg, accompanied by a planter named Randolph Routledge III.

"They stayed the night. I'm told it isn't the first time," Simms concluded dolefully.

So it wasn't every man who repulsed Sophie. Lark cursed her for deceiving and humiliating him.

That same evening, with a thunderstorm flinging hail on the roof, Lark stalked into his dining room, where Sophie sat with her genealogic materials. Before she could speak, he grabbed her by the hair and yanked her head up.

"Time for the truth, you bitch. How long has it been going on?"

"I don't know what you—"

He yanked again. Lightning glazed the windows; raindrops glittered. He seized her throat and choked. "You'd better tell me before I hurt you seriously."

"A year," she gasped. "I've known him for a year."

"Where did you meet him?"

"At a church bazaar, when I went up to Orangeburg to see about repairs at Pa's farm. His mother introduced us. Let me go."

"Not until you tell me why you did it."

"Because he's a gentleman. Because he has what you'll never have," Sophie cried. "A proper pedigree. I'm going to marry him. I'm going to be respected."

"The hell," Lark screamed, just as loudly. He released her so he could bunch his fist and break her jaw. Desperately afraid, she was quicker. She sank her teeth into his hand.

Lark howled and lunged at her, but she evaded him. She threw pens, the inkhorn, two leather-bound books. While he retreated, she picked up her chair and broke it over his head. He reeled into a corner and leaned there groggily. She ran.

He shouted obscenities at terrified slaves when they looked in. Thunder shook the house as he ran up the curving staircase. Sophie wasn't in her bedroom. He questioned a frightened house girl.

"She wen' out with a little trunk she carried her'sef. Must been packed a'ready." Furious, he punished the messenger by throwing her bodily down the stairs.

He went to bed unattended. Snoo had traipsed off to visit a former school chum in Moncks Corner. Folsey was, as usual, out with his worthless companions. Next morning Lark didn't shave or dress. At noon, still in his evening robe embroidered with tiny golden peacocks, he sat over a cold cup of coffee, hatching revenge plots. A manservant tiptoed in to announce Simms Bell.

"Bad news," Simms said. "Your wife's fled to the house of Routledge's mother in Orangeburg. Eli Prickett presented himself at my door an hour ago with that information."

"Why the devil's Prickett telling you anything?"

"Because he's acting as Routledge's second. Routledge has challenged you under Rule Ten of the code."

The color left Lark's face. He'd never fought a duel, though he owned a pair of beautiful pistols for that purpose. Most gentlemen did. Sophie had bought them for him in Washington, after he slurred the reputation of another congressman who didn't vote as Lark thought he should.

Thank God for seconds. Their primary obligation was to effect a reconciliation. "Tell Prickett I apologize. Doesn't the code say an apology forestalls a duel?"

"Not when Rule Ten is invoked. Under that rule an insult to a lady who is under a gentleman's protection is considered a greater offense than if the insult is given directly to the gentleman. Is it true that you did bodily harm to Sophie?"

"I Goddamn well tried. She Goddamn well deserved it. Look what the slut did to me." He showed his bandaged hand.

"Because you resorted to force, there's no possibility of a reconciliation. Eli Prickett made that clear."

Crittenden Lark's ruling passion had always been self-preservation, which some called cowardice. As far back as 1812 when he sailed as supercargo on his own privateer, he exercised the owner's prerogative and hid belowdecks at times of danger. No one, including his hired captain, dared chide him, or even speak of it. Lark's instinct for survival dictated his careful, roundabout way of dealing with those who wronged or opposed him. He said to Simms, "I won't fight."

"Do you want to be posted? Force Routledge to distribute a circular telling everyone you refused? You know the papers always print such material. It would ruin you forever."

A fierce pain tortured Lark's belly. Simms was right. Despite clerics and editors ranting against it and municipal ordinances that prohibited its employment, the 1777 Code Duello from Ireland was venerated and frequently invoked. In 1838 the state's own governor had penned a revised version for South Carolina gentry.

"Oh, God, all right," Lark said. "Will you act as my second?"

"That's why Prickett came to me. He presumed I might."

They discussed details. As the challenged party Lark had the right to choose weapons and the location. Obviously they would fight with pistols; men no longer settled affairs of honor with swords. Routledge would set the terms of the actual engagement.

Folsey Lark somewhat reluctantly agreed to join Simms as a second. Simms informed Eli Prickett that the contesting parties would meet at seven o'clock in the morning on the first Monday in March. The site Lark chose was a five-acre plot on the Ashley River, a mile north of his summer home. He'd bought it with the thought of developing it for two or three similar cottages. Deeply shadowed by water oaks, volunteer pines, and thick stands of wild palmetto between, the heart of the property was hidden from traffic on the river road.

On the appointed day Simms, Folsey, and Lark set out in Lark's carriage at half past five. Folsey held a brass-chased wooden box on his knee: the big .70-caliber smoothbore flintlock pistols with hair triggers, until this day never fired in anger.

They arrived to find a light fog drifting over the dueling ground. The chill of Carolina winter still reddened the face and stiffened the joints. Lark continually flexed his fingers as he stepped from the carriage. Last night he'd received an insulting note from Sophie. She intended to marry Routledge after he disposed of Lark, which she deemed a certainty.

The fog muted colors of the deserted woodland. The opponents stood a good distance apart while Simms and Folsey let Routledge's seconds inspect the weapons. Then Simms carefully loaded them in sight of all.

Lark squinted at his challenger. He was certainly thin as a stick and homely as a hog. Was he a better lover? What the hell difference did it make? He had a pedigree. No doubt Sophie had already notified Iola von Schreck.

How he wished he could go at Routledge as he'd gone at Edgar Bell before the nullification elections, using a hired assailant. Of course the man had failed, but that wasn't the point. Lark was never involved.

The seconds summoned the contestants. Simms Bell said, "We have agreed that you will walk away from each other while Mr. Prickett counts aloud up to ten. On the tenth count you may fire at your pleasure. Is that satisfactory and understood?"

The adversaries nodded, never speaking or making eye contact. The fog was lifting, tinted by pale lemon-colored light. An unseen horseman cantered by on the road as the duelists took positions back to back. Routledge's second called out, "Ready. *One*."

Lark began to whimper. Folsey turned away in shame. As the count proceeded, Lark's fear became unbearable. When he heard *"Nine,"* he spun around and fired. There was a snap, a spurt of sparks; a misfire. It counted as his shot. Routledge calmly aimed his pistol. Moaning, Lark bolted toward the river.

Routledge's ball stopped him, hurled him down with a gaping wound in his side. When the seconds examined him, they agreed that the wound was probably fatal.

★ ★ ★

Lark lingered a full day and a night. At half past eight on the morning of the second day, he sent for Folsey. The young man appeared in his father's draped and darkened bedroom wearing soiled linen and smelling powerfully of gin.

Even in his last extremities Lark remained a dandy. He wore a French-style bed coat, bright red velvet, decorated with gold braid, as was the brimless cap of purple velvet. A gold tassel dangled from the cap.

He motioned his son to a bedside chair. Even that minimal exertion produced excruciating pain. "Where is your sister?"

"Sleeping, sir. The doctor's dosed her full of laudanum. She's almost lost her mind over this."

"Women are that way." He hated to ask the next question, but he burned to know. "Have you had any messages from your mother?"

"No, sir."

"She is not permitted to attend my funeral, understood?"

"Yes, sir."

Lark coughed. His stale breath flickered the flame of the candle, the only light in the hot, sour room. "Folsey, give me your hand."

Dry as paper, his fingers clasped his son's. "Listen closely, this is very important to me. In my life there is one great endeavor in which I failed. Sometimes I was too busy. Sometimes the opportunity was missing. You must pick up the burden. I want you to swear that you will."

Folsey gulped, nodded.

"You must avenge our family. Hampton Bell mocks and opposes all that is sacred and vital to the preservation of Charleston. His sluttish sister up North promotes nigger rebellion and nigger equality. Both for what they are, and for what Edward Bell did to my father, the surviving family must be punished. You must carry out the punishment, even if it takes years."

"Pa, I will if I can."

"I must have more than a *perhaps*. I must have your assurance. I've asked little of you in your lifetime. You're a clever boy but you do nothing with it. You will inherit a sizable fortune. In return I require a promise that will travel with you until it's fulfilled."

Silence. Lark's fingers constricted. "Folsey?"

Folsey feared rather than loved his father, but tears flowed anyway. "What can I say except yes, Pa? Yes, I promise. I'll see to it. Even if it takes years."

51

Reunion

In 1844, while the cloud of slavery darkened over the land, Americans read England's poet laureate, Wordsworth, and bizarre tales by a new Southern author named Poe. They flocked to the American Museum in New York to see General Tom Thumb and Phineas Barnum's other wonders. They filled theaters and concert halls for a new kind of entertainment: white men singing and dancing in blackface. Alex attended one performance of the Virginia Minstrels, whose star, Thomas Rice, brought down the house portraying a character called Jim Crow. Some of the tunes were infectious, some of the jokes amusing, but she thought the whole idea of minstrelsy mocked Negroes.

Senator John Calhoun sat in the cabinet again, serving as John Tyler's secretary of state. The Baptist church tore apart over the slavery issue and formed Northern and Southern conventions. A similar schism loomed in the Methodist Episcopal Church when the general conference ordered the bishop of Georgia to give up his slaves or his bishopric.

Slave catchers prowled the North. The case of *Prigg v. Pennsylvania*, decided in 1842 by the Supreme Court, let owners recover runaways under the 1793 Fugitive Slave Act, no matter what the law of an individual state stipulated.

President Santa Anna of Mexico let it be known that annexation of Texas would be construed as an act of war. Calhoun nevertheless negotiated the treaty to bring a vast new slave state into the Union. Abolitionists decried the treaty and deplored talk of a war to defend it. Henry Clay, Whig, and Martin van Buren, Democrat, each lost a presidential nomination because of public statements favoring Mexico's position. The autumn election gave the White House to dark horse Democrat James Polk of Tennessee.

Alex's eminence in the antislavery movement was now unquestioned. Her name, in large type, dominated posters and handbills, and she typically appeared last on a program. That was the case in December, the week before Christmas, when she returned to New York for a rally at the Broadway Tabernacle, where she'd first sung "A Better, Brighter Morning."

She shared the program with a handsome, articulate black man from New Bedford, Massachusetts, Frederick Douglass. He told her privately that he'd been born with the name Bailey. He'd changed it to foil slave catchers. "I expect they're still looking for Bailey. I ran away from Baltimore six years ago."

"How old were you?"

"Twenty. They'll have to kill me to take me back."

Alex was but three years older than Douglass. Sometimes she felt ten times that. She walked with a slight limp. In cold weather her right leg ached and she used a cane. Three anonymous men had waylaid her outside a church hall in Pittsburgh. Two held her while the third swung a lead pipe. "That's for Garrison and the all the rest of you white niggers who want women to behave like whores."

★ ★ ★

The Broadway Tabernacle at Worth Street had opened its doors as New York City's first Congregational church in 1838. The main hall seated four thousand. Tonight it was three quarters full. Alex played and sang a new ballad called "North Star." She was into the second stanza when a face in the front row of the gallery caught her eye. She was so startled, she forgot the next line. She recovered and smiled at Reverend Drew. After the program he rushed through the crowd to greet her.

"How grand to see you, Miss Bell."

"It's a pleasure for me as well, Reverend."

He held her hand longer than necessary. "I was speaking to the good people of Greenwich last night. One of them showed me an advertisement for this event." He was more gaunt than she remembered. His Byronic hair was streaked with white; wide swathes of it swept over his ears, a curious winglike effect.

"I'd be honored if you'd have supper again. Perhaps this evening?"

"I would enjoy that," she said, hardly thinking before the words rushed out. She remembered an obligation. "Oh, no, I can't. I promised to take supper with Mr. Douglass."

"My loss. He's an eloquent orator."

"Still quite nervous about speaking, but he feels he must. He's writing a memoir about his escape from Maryland. He says it may put slave catchers on his trail, but he won't be deterred. A brave young man."

"As regards supper, I don't accept defeat easily. The Tabernacle is holding an antislavery fair tomorrow. Might we take it in together?"

"I'd be delighted," she said. Later, she thought she'd sounded altogether too eager.

☆ ☆ ☆

He called for her at her hotel on lower Broadway. Soon, by mutual agreement, they were on a first-name basis. They toured the armory hall decorated with Christmas candles and greenery. Ladies of the sponsoring society offered a huge array of treats for sale—mince pie and brown betty, deviled oysters and hot pretzels, pralines and fudge and honeyed popcorn balls. Alex and Drew enjoyed apple dumplings and hot cider, then strolled on to the booths selling merchandise. She bought a packet of needles imprinted with the words PRICK THE CONSCIENCE OF THE SLAVE MASTER. Drew bought a bundle of quills labeled TEN WEAPONS OF TRUTH. Engraved portraits of Garrison sold briskly, as well as pirated editions of Mr. Dickens's *A Christmas Carol* and painted Toby jugs sent by an antislavery group in England. As usual at these events black patrons were almost as numerous as whites.

Afterward Drew took her to an expensive restaurant on nearby Duane Street. Three elderly musicians played a lugubrious version of the new hit "Buffalo Girls, Won't You Come Out Tonight?" Candles on the table reminded her of their first evening together, but there were differences. Although his smile was no less winning, there was a new gravity about him. Each found that the other had changed.

"I can't criticize you any longer for championing the cause of women, Alexandra. The scales fell from my eyes two years ago, when my uncle Nicholas died. After the funeral my dear Aunt Bea confessed to me that for years, when Uncle Nick drank heavily, which was often, he abused her. He took offense at the slightest thing, and he beat her. It was always concealed from outsiders. I never saw a hint of it when I was a boy. Aunt Bea suffered it because she thought it was a wife's duty. Last

May she remarried, a much finer man. I no longer think highly of my uncle."

"I've discovered something myself, William. What you said about the woman issue increasing the anger of audiences, especially of men— it's true. I won't abandon the message, but I've paid a price. I've been spat on, hit by flying brickbats, cursed with every foul word in English and a few in foreign tongues."

That brought a smile, for which he quickly apologized. "No need," she said. "You notice that I don't walk as well as I should." She touched the lacquered cane lying on an empty chair; told him about Pittsburgh.

"Another time, in Baltimore, a man who objected to the idea of women being free accosted me and burned me with his cigar." She laid her left arm on the tablecloth, palm uppermost, to show a round red scar on her wrist.

"Please know that I'm not complaining. I pay the price gladly. I only want to say I've learned how right you were that night. Sometimes all the madness and hatred seem too great a burden. Then I catch myself and know I must go on."

"I drove you away that night in Dayton," he said. "I regretted it as I've regretted few things in my life. I vowed that if we met again, I would do all I could to promote a different ending."

He paused a moment. "Our work is necessary, and moral, but as you say, it can burden the soul. Sometimes it's fearfully lonely." How well she knew. Years of solitary living, travel on grimy trains, hard beds in cheap hotels, had made her a virtual recluse.

"Men and women can draw strength from each other, Alexandra. You say you're compelled to go on. So am I. I would like to propose that at some time in the future, we go on together. That is, if you could entertain the possibility."

She was stunned, flattered, not a little thrilled. "Let me think a moment. I'm not accustomed to such frank declarations."

"I'm not accustomed to making them. I've only done it once before, with my late wife, Filomena."

"May we have some fresh air? I'll try to find the right words to answer you."

"Yes, of course. Waiter."

Outside, they discovered a soft snow falling. Alex pulled the hood of her plain gray burnoose over her head. Encountering a slippery curbstone, Drew took her arm. "There may be ice underneath." He didn't let go.

The evening was windless. The lights of New York gleamed prettily behind the falling snow. She savored the smell of evergreen boughs decorating lampposts and storefronts. A sleigh full of children went by, bells on the team ringing brightly. The city, which could be so ugly and raucous, had a peaceful, almost magical quality, and for the first time that she could remember, she found falling snow beautiful.

"You asked that I consider the possibility of the two of us going on together in some fashion."

"Yes."

"I can say that I'll happily entertain the possibility."

"Oh, marvelous. I hardly dared hope—"

"Wait. First, everything must be open between us." Under a street-lamp she drew her arm from his, threw back the hood of her burnoose so that he could see her face. Snowflakes drifted against her forehead, pleasantly icy.

"I must tell you about a man I knew in Charleston. A man I loved, as Shakespeare says, not wisely but too well. His name was Henry Strong."

☆　☆　☆

Ten months later Alex and William Drew exchanged marriage vows before a judge in Cleveland, Ohio, where both were speaking on the same program. Alex kept her own last name.

The Years Between
1842–1863

Early in May 1846 a Mexican army invaded Texas. General Zachary Taylor met the enemy at Palo Alto and Resaca de la Palma and hammered them back across the Rio Grande. Congress declared war, against fierce opposition from Whig members.

The war was not universally popular. Many condemned it as imperialistic, undertaken solely to add a new slave state. While Gen. Winfield Scott was advancing on the Mexican capital, Drew and Alex took part in a protest in New York. Two hundred marched, arm-in-arm in ranks of ten. Crowds along Broadway waved small American flags and cursed and spat on the marchers. Stones and bottles flew. A paving block thrown from a roof struck Drew's shoulder and drove him to one knee. He was dazed and bruised but otherwise unhurt.

From that day Alex detected a worrisome change in her husband. He was no less considerate, no less ardent and satisfying as a lover, but he grew somber. She hardly saw him smile, let alone laugh. He spoke of armed conflict between North and South as a certainty and pondered what would follow such a war.

He spent more time reading his Bible. The word *forgiveness* became part of his daily vocabulary. He reminded Alex and others that at Golgotha, Christ had asked forgiveness for those who crucified him. " 'For they know not what they do.' "

Alex argued the point. She felt the slave masters knew very well what they were doing, and why.

★   ★   ★

In one of those small miracles of human behavior, Folsey Lark underwent a sea change. It came about because he liked poker, a game new to the country in the 1830s. He played it poorly, especially when he drank. One morning he woke to discover he'd lost fifty acres of his best land to a man widely suspected of being a sharp.

Sick and wobbly, Folsey hurried to the office of the family attorney, elderly Theophilus McCrady of Broad Street. McCrady examined the note Folsey had signed. "Ironclad." He proceeded to tongue-lash his client.

"Come to your senses, Folsey. Your father, my lifelong friend, left you valuable income properties. If you persist in neglecting them, throw them away while in a drunken stupor, as you apparently did last night, I will call on my friends in the state judicial system. It's rather a closed club, you know. I can easily have you declared incompetent. I'll see that a conservator is appointed to manage your affairs."

"That's an empty threat," Folsey retorted.

"Then test it, sir. Test it, by all means."

Folsey retreated a bit. "I can't have someone running my life. I won't."

"Then you had better change course."

To the amazement of McCrady and those close to Folsey, he did. He controlled his drinking and gambling. Like Lydia Bell before him he called on friends to help him learn to be a better steward of his inheritance. If he wasn't as driven as his father, he was shrewder; some said more devious. Folsey never forgot the promise made at Crittenden Lark's bedside. He supposed he would fulfill it someday, but he was in no hurry.

Folsey preferred the bachelor life. Even so, he had needs. He formed a liaison with a handsome nineteen-year-old mulatto, Adah Samples. He kept her in a small house above Boundary Street. She was a beautiful creature, her waist tiny, her breasts mature and full, her throat long and graceful. Her smooth skin reminded him of amber. No one thought badly of Folsey for taking a free colored woman as a mistress. Indeed, he received compliments on his taste.

He lavished expensive gifts on Adah. At the end of their first six months together, he gave her a turban of yellow velvet with yellow-dyed aigrettes, imported from Paris. She loved to show it off when they went driving. His gentleman friends referred to Adah as Folsey's yellow bird.

Adah's parents were delighted to have their child cared for by a wealthy white man. Adah was an intelligent young woman and proved to be a steadying influence on Folsey.

★　★　★

Gibbes Bell was smitten with the ripe good looks of Folsey's younger half-sister, Snoo. Among the young men of Charleston he was far from alone in this, but Snoo favored him because of his family name. In 1847 they were married, over Ouida's protests that Gibbes was lowering himself.

Folsey's social standing was immediately improved, and a friendship cemented between the two men. Gibbes was one of those who counseled Folsey as he evolved into a successful businessman.

Though he now had a wife, Gibbes often daydreamed of his cousin Alex, "that damned woman." The phrase was attributed to his friend and political mentor, bearded and balding Robert Barnwell Rhett of the *Charleston Mercury*. Rhett's paper was the South's loudest voice clamoring for dissolution of the Union.

Gibbes hated Alex because of her betrayal of Charleston, her carnal dalliance with the dead freedman, Strong, and her lifelong rejection of Gibbes's advances. At the same time he could never rid himself of a desire to bed his cousin once before he died.

★　★　★

The Mexican War ended in 1848. Under the peace terms the United States gained vast new territories, the richest prize being California. In July, Alex traveled to Seneca Falls, New York, for a convention organized to discuss and promote women's rights.

She returned filled with zeal for the cause. She showed Drew sketches of some unusual feminine styles in a magazine for women, *The Lily,* published by Mrs. Amelia Jenks Bloomer.

Drew looked askance. "Trousers worn with a skirt?"

"A short skirt, as you can see. Why not, William? Mrs. Bloomer says it's hygienic. Conventional skirts drag on the ground and pick up mud and heaven knows what else."

"This Bloomer woman designed the trousers?"

"No, but people call them bloomers all the same."

The exchange was friendly. She and Drew often disagreed but without rancor. Theirs was a good marriage, though both were saddened by their inability to conceive a child while Alex was young enough. They never raised the issue of which of them was responsible. In quiet moments they held hands and spoke of what it might have been like to be parents.

✹   ✹   ✹

Upstairs at H. V. Hill's boardinghouse near Capitol Hill, John Calhoun died on March 31, 1850. He was sixty-eight.

For weeks he'd been too feeble to reach his Senate desk. Others read his speeches for him. Calhoun had suffered tuberculosis for years. His son John junior, a physician, wrote down the cause of death as "catarrhal weakness."

The South grieved. Ouida Hayward was inconsolable. She carried an engraving of Calhoun with her everywhere; she even took it to bed. Dr. Hayward was thankful they'd long ago moved into separate bedrooms.

Ouida blamed "race-mixing Yankees" for Calhoun's sad end. Her rambling fulminations frightened her twelve-year-old son, Calhoun Bell Hayward, named for the great man. Dr. Hayward resorted to careful euphemisms when he spoke to his son about his Ouida's increasingly fragile mental state.

A steamer brought John Calhoun's body to Charleston, accompanied by representatives from the Congress. The city gave him the largest funeral procession in living memory—scores of marchers, military units, an honor guard of prominent citizens accompanying a funeral coach modeled after Napoleon's. Ham and Jim Petigru joined the honor guard out of respect for Calhoun's long service to the nation.

Calhoun lay in state at City Hall, then was buried in St. Philip's churchyard. Ham considered it an irony when one remembered Calhoun scorning the city as frivolous and debauched. Calhoun's widow, his second cousin Floride, came from a family with strong Charleston connections; she wanted him to rest there. Boundary Street was renamed to honor him.

Ham and Petigru agreed that Calhoun had been a brilliant man, an accomplished politician, and a bulwark of the Union in his early years. But he'd squandered his talent, energy, and a good part of his adult life on a narrow, almost morbid defense of slavery.

"Standing forth in vindication of it," Petigru observed, "with never a word about its oppressive nature or a wish for its demise."

* * *

Friends of William Drew in Richmond sent him a chilling document: remarks copied down from an earlier exchange between Calhoun and Senator Mason of Virginia. Calhoun had stated his belief that the Union would be dissolved.

"I fix its probable occurrence within twelve years, or three presidential terms. The mode by which it will be done is not so clear. The probability is, it will explode in a presidential election." For once Drew found himself in agreement with the South Carolinian admirers and even some detractors still called the Cast Iron Man.

* * *

In 1850 Alex saw one of her great goals realized. Congress abolished slavery in the District of Columbia. Her happiness was tempered by a new fugitive slave law that strengthened the law of 1793 and thereby increased the danger for Negroes who risked flight to the North.

Although Drew counseled forgiveness after a war that he, too, believed was inevitable, he remained a militant activist. He joined half a dozen other men who traveled to Saybrook, Connecticut, to surround the jail where a captured slave had been imprisoned.

Before the abolitionists could batter the door open, an armed mob surrounded them. The would-be rescuers fell back and scattered into the night. The mob overran the jail, dragged the Negro out, and hanged him from a nearby oak. The incident left Drew with more bruises and a painful sense of failure.

Alex's eyes had been opened long ago to the hatred of colored people throughout the North. Incidents such as the one in Saybrook, while they didn't excuse similar ones in Charleston, proved that sins of intolerance weren't unique to her native state or the South.

* * *

In February 1855 Alex and Drew left New York City on a train bound for Rochester, where they were to appear with Frederick Douglass. Douglass joined them at Poughkeepsie. He'd spoken there the night before.

Freezing rain fell, glazing whatever it touched. The interior of the passenger car was infernally hot near the wood stove at the front, but frigid where they found seats at the rear. Alex could feel the hostility of passengers watching Douglass.

From her reticule she took a copy of Mrs. Stowe's novel *Uncle Tom's*

Cabin. In 1852 the book had become an international sensation. For all of its melodrama and stereotyping it was a powerful indictment of slavery. She was reading it for the second time.

When the train reached Albany, two burly men stomped into the car. They glared when they saw Douglass. They took seats two rows away, whispering together as the train left the depot.

Suddenly the larger of the two men appeared in the aisle next to Alex. His companion passed him to open the door, blasting the passengers with cold air. The first man hooked a thumb toward the open platform.

"Niggers to the rear car. This one's for white people."

Douglass frowned. "I beg your pardon?"

"You heard me, brother. You better go along if you don't want trouble."

Drew stood up. "No one's moving except you, sir." He made the mistake of emphasizing it with a poke of the man's lapel. The man drove his fist into Drew's belly.

Alex and Douglass jumped up. The man grabbed Drew's shoulders, pushed him out the door. On the icy platform Drew flung a punch as the train swayed. He slid sideways, his knuckles only grazing the other man's jaw. The man countered with a blow that drove Drew against the low rail of the platform. He slammed his palms into Drew's chest. Drew tumbled over and fell between the cars. Alex felt the bump of the wheels. "Oh, my God. *Stop the train*."

It took precious seconds for the brakes to seize and hold on the cindered rails. Drew's mangled body lay on the track behind the last car. The two men jumped off and disappeared, never to be caught or identified.

★   ★   ★

Drew lay in a hospital ward in Albany that night. Alex held his chilly hand; he wasn't entirely coherent. Shortly after 2:00 A.M. he roused to whisper, "Alex?"

"I'm here."

"Alex, do you love me?"

"I love you. Don't you know that?"

"Do you love me as much as you loved Henry Strong?"

"Just as much, yes."

A ghost of his old, brilliant smile fleeted over his face and was gone. He could barely speak. "I beg you to forgive me."

"Oh, my dearest. There's nothing to forgive."

"Yes, there is. Forgive me for . . . leaving you." His hand slipped from hers.

"William?"

Silence.

She rushed into the aisle. "Matron." She had lost her first love when she was twenty. Now, twenty years later, she'd lost her second.

★ ★ ★

She buried her husband in Roxbury, Massachusetts, beside his mother and the Reverend Justus Drew. Drew's murder—she considered it nothing less—put new steel in her. She continued to speak and sing her freedom songs with a ferocity that reflected the growing anger and strife in the nation.

The 1854 Kansas-Nebraska Act had effectively nullified previous compromises on expansion of slavery. The new law allowed territories awaiting statehood to decide whether they would come into the Union slave or free. Kansas became a battleground. An abolitionist named John Brown led savage attacks on the proslavery men. Groups throughout the South raised money to combat the free-soilers.

Armed volunteers traveled to Kansas to join the fight. Alex read of a Beaufort contingent, the South Carolina Bloodhounds, taking part in the looting and burning of Lawrence, the territory's free-soil capital. An antislavery broadside carried a sketch of the palmetto flag flying on a Lawrence hotel.

In May 1856 Charles Sumner of Massachusetts rose in the Senate to condemn the situation in "bleeding Kansas." His oration included an attack on Senator A. P. Butler of South Carolina, full of sexual references. Sumner accused Butler of taking as his mistress "the harlot, slavery."

A relative of Butler's, Congressman Preston Brooks of the Edgefield district, reacted by stalking into the Senate with cane in hand. He fell on Sumner and beat him senseless at his desk.

Northern papers called Brooks a monster. The South hailed him. Ouida sent a draft of a hundred dollars for the congressman's legal defense fund and contributed to a group of women who commissioned a silver loving cup engraved with Brooks's name and the words *Heros et Martyr*. She came home one afternoon with a scrap of lacquered wood wrapped in her handkerchief. Breathlessly, she showed it to her husband and her son.

"It's a piece of the cane Congressman Brooks used on Sumner. Folsey Lark's friend Marvin Rayburn sold it to me for ten dollars. His relative in Washington guaranteed its authenticity."

Xeno Hayward struggled to be patient with her. "Ouida, Marvin Rayburn is a charlatan. A wood shop in Summerville makes those 'authentic souvenirs.' Rayburn is profiting by duping people."

"Liar. *Liar.*" She threw the wood at Hayward and ran up the stairs, sobbing. In her haste she dropped her glasses and broke them under her shoe.

Hayward and his son exchanged looks of defeat. They heard Ouida crying and ranting for an hour.

✯ ✯ ✯

In 1857 Chief Justice Taney of the Supreme Court issued his decision in the case of a slave named Dred Scott. Scott had followed his owner, an army officer, from Missouri to free soil in Illinois and then Wisconsin. When Scott's owner died without manumitting his slave, Scott sued to gain his freedom.

Taney's decision said Scott could not seek redress in Federal courts because slaves weren't citizens, nor had they ever been. A slave was property, no different from a milk cow or a hunting dog.

Alex threw the newspaper in the fireplace of the Washington flat she'd shared with Drew. Slavery was destroying the country. Some months later an obscure former congressman and army veteran named Lincoln expressed it tellingly in a widely reprinted speech. He said that a government half slave and half free could not endure, a house divided against itself could not stand.

✯ ✯ ✯

In 1859 John Brown of Kansas raided the government arsenal at Harpers Ferry with the announced purpose of arming a slave revolt. The nation's foremost soldier, Robert E. Lee of Virginia, led troops from Washington to capture Brown, who was tried and hanged that December. The North had its own hero and martyr.

Brown's failed uprising raised ghosts of Saint-Dominque and Denmark Vesey in Charleston, where Democrats met in April 1860 to choose a national slate. The hotspurs, Gibbes prominent among them, demanded a platform endorsing protection of slavery in new territories. The favored candidate, Senator Stephen Douglas of Illinois, would have none of it. The rancorous convention adjourned after fifty-seven ballots and no decision.

Party regulars reconvened in Baltimore two months later and there nominated Douglas. The separatist radicals put up John Breckenridge of Kentucky on a platform incorporating their demands. Republicans met in Chicago and named Abraham Lincoln as their candidate. Lincoln's views on slavery were not widely known, making him the least controversial candidate.

With the Democratic vote divided Breckenridge had no chance, Douglas only a slightly better one. Gibbes and his crowd saw Lincoln's victory as a signal. With "the black Republican" in the White House there would be no accommodation. The time had come for the action proposed and argued about for two decades.

In December 1860 new rumors of Negro unrest swept the city. Gibbes locked his town house and took Snoo to Prosperity Hall. Ouida followed with her son after Dr. Hayward refused to go. Gibbes then rode up to Columbia, joining twenty-two other Charleston men, the largest delegation at the recently called secession convention.

A smallpox outbreak drove the delegates back down to the coast. On December 20 Gibbes sat in the hall of the St. Andrew's Benevolent Society on Broad Street. The vote for the Ordinance of Secession was unanimous. The delegates adjourned to Institute Hall that evening, to sign the document. Charleston celebrated with bells and horns, music and torchlight parading. The national flag came down, replaced by the palmetto flag.

Ten other states quickly followed South Carolina out of the Union. The Confederacy established its capital at Montgomery. The new government demanded the surrender of all federal arsenals and forts in the South, most particularly Fort Sumter. In March 1861 a new military commander arrived in the city. General Pierre Gustave Toutant Beauregard was one of the many West Point graduates who resigned regular army commissions to serve the Confederacy. A handsome, vain Louisiana Creole, Beauregard charmed the ladies and assured the gentlemen that Sumter would soon be theirs.

Lincoln refused to surrender the harbor fort. He warned that the fate of the nation was not in his hands but in those of his fellow countrymen. Gibbes insisted that Abe the Ape was maneuvering the South into the role of the aggressor, but he welcomed it. Weeks of tense standoff culminated at 4:30 A.M. on April 12, when Beauregard's shore batteries opened fire on Sumter. After a thirty-four-hour bombardment Maj. Robert Anderson surrendered and prepared to evacuate his garrison. The riven Union was at war.

Charlestonians were jubilant, as they had been on secession night. A tiny minority, including Petigru and Ham Bell, muttered about the folly of taking up arms against the more populous, industrialized North. Most of their contemporaries saw a bright vision of plumed cavaliers galloping off to a short war, ninety days or less. The North had its smoky factories and foundries, its plodding masses of white wage slaves, but the South had cotton on its docks and in its fields—cotton needed by mills across the Atlantic. King Cotton would force diplomatic recognition of the Confederacy in England and Europe. Gibbes was confident of it, Folsey less so.

"I advise you to put your money in gold and bank it in the Bahamas. What do we owe the bastards in Montgomery anyway? You see how they snubbed us. There's not a single Carolina man in the Davis cabinet. Jeff Davis is arrogant and bullheaded. Because he went to the Point and served in Mexico, he thinks he knows more about soldiering than anybody else. He'll drive us down, you mark me."

Testy, Gibbes said, "I thought you supported a war."

"I do, absolutely. Because a smart man can use it for profit."

Gibbes resisted a sally about Folsey's hypocrisy. Later he decided there might be something in the remark about Jeff Davis of Mississippi. The former United States senator and secretary of defense was not well thought of in Carolina. General Beauregard despised him. Gibbes would watch and await developments.

✯ ✯ ✯

Wade Hampton of Millwood Plantation on the Congaree was the third in his family to bear the same illustrious name. He was a state senator from the Richland district and a planter who worked three thousand slaves. After Sumter, Hampton resigned his seat and rapidly raised a mixed force of voltigeurs, cavalry, and horse artillery, the Hampton Legion. Dr. Hayward volunteered as a medical officer, hurried north, and tended the wounded at Manassas, the first battle of the war. The Legion distinguished itself in the rout of Irvin McDowell and his army.

Ouida was indifferent to her husband's patriotism because she'd long ago become indifferent to him. She wasn't so indifferent to their son when he put on a uniform. Cal was a strong, forthright young man with sandy hair and Ouida's pale blue eyes. He seemed blessed with the best traits of his father and, happily, few if any of Ouida's.

Ouida adored her boy. She fell on her knees in prayer the night he announced he was joining up, full of zeal for the fight. "It's like being filled with the Holy Ghost the black folks preach about in their churches," he told her.

★　★　★

The Union blockade of Southern ports presented a rare business opportunity. Among the first to seize it was George Trenholm, who had risen from clerk to senior partner of John Fraser & Company. The firm was one of three interlocked trading houses based in Charleston, New York, and Liverpool. Trenholm offered the services of Fraser, Trenholm of Liverpool as financial agents and underwriters for the Confederacy.

While the Confederate ordinance department rushed to buy arms in England and Europe, Trenholm's Liverpool branch bought and shipped blankets and bolts of cloth, shoes and medicines—things formerly obtained from the North. Once through the blockade at Charleston, the cargoes were auctioned for sums that more than offset the risk of losing a ship to a Union broadside.

Folsey and others saw the opportunity. Folsey organized Palmetto Traders, sold shares to raise $200,000, and sent a man to Hamilton, Bermuda, to buy an old schooner. "As soon as we auction our first shipment," he explained to Gibbes, "we'll have credit we can use to borrow more money and build a better, faster ship." Gibbes had taken Folsey's advice and sequestered funds offshore. He invested $40,000 in Palmetto Traders, becoming the second largest shareholder.

The schooner *Caribe* eluded blockading frigates and gunboats and darted into Charleston under a pale new moon. Her captain brought her through Moffit's Channel with Sullivan's Island lying close on the starboard side. Moffit's was one of two harbor channels navigable by heavy shipping. Continually shifting sandbars that defied charting ruled out entry any other way.

As Folsey prophesied, the auction of *Caribe*'s cargo brought Palmetto Traders a profit of forty percent on its investment. Folsey rushed to Richmond, where the Confederate capital had moved in May of 1861, there to romance the ordnance department and secure government shipping contracts.

★　★　★

Unlike his partner, Gibbes remained a sincere and ardent secesh. Even so, he didn't step forward as Dr. Hayward and Cal had. He pleaded pressures of business and his age, forty-four. A female friend of

Ouida's insulted him by reminding him that Wade Hampton was nearly as old. "Are you a slacker, sir?"

Gibbes heard the canard indirectly as well, more than once. Although the thought of combat terrified him—it terrified any sensible man—he wrote Colonel Hampton, who was accepting replacements for those killed and wounded at Manassas. The Legion, already South Carolina's elite unit, was the only place Gibbes felt he could serve.

Confident of a favorable response, he bought two smartly tailored uniforms, kissed Snoo good-bye, and caught a train for Virginia. He took with him an elderly house Negro named Oliver to be his valet in the field. Many in the Legion had done the same.

At Petersburg he bought a fine stallion. He searched out the Legion's winter camp, presented himself to the commander, and received a captain's commission. By then he found his valet an encumbrance, so he sent Oliver home. The man ran off to the Union lines, he heard later.

Some in Charleston expressed surprise when Gibbes distinguished himself on the Peninsula in the spring of 1862. In a series of battles Joe Johnston and Bob Lee drove McClellan's army back from within six miles of Richmond. Gibbes fell at Seven Pines, grievously wounded. Infection set in. Surgeons sawed off his left leg below the hip. He survived and was discharged honorably, though he hobbled about with a clumsy wooden limb hinged at the knee.

He received a hero's welcome—banquets, parties, a citation from the mayor. Ouida hated Yankees all the more for what they'd done to her beloved brother, but she was wildly proud of him.

Dr. Xeno Hayward had met an inglorious end on the Peninsula. During the Seven Days, with his orderly shot dead by a sniper, he took over a field ambulance carrying three Confederate wounded. He was driving to the rear on a desolate road when he heard someone cry out in the underbrush. He pulled off and hunted until he found the wounded man—a boy, actually, wearing the bloodied uniform of a Union regiment.

Hayward lifted the boy and carried him back to the sandy road. He approached the ambulance from behind, the boy heavy in his arms. Their combined weight detonated a buried Yankee torpedo. One of the wounded inside the ambulance reported the incident.

When Ouida heard, she refused to grieve or even shed a tear. "It was his fault. He should have let the Yankee die."

She was far more concerned about Cal, from whom she heard nothing. But he'd never been one to write letters. In the midst of news of ti-

tanic battles and appalling loss of life, Cal's silence filled Ouida's days
and nights with worry and fear.

☆   ☆   ☆

In the autumn of 1862 the North had a new anthem to replace "John
Brown's Body." People sang and marched to verses by Julia Ward Howe
set to an old hymn tune Alex had first heard when she was a child. The
melody, played on a wheezy pump organ, had issued from a tiny Negro
chapel she and her father were passing on the Savannah highway.

Nothing she'd written in the last few years could compare with "The
Battle Hymn of the Republic." She couldn't help a shameful stab of jeal-
ousy, or a certain sense that her time had passed.

☆   ☆   ☆

During the late summer of 1862 Folsey left Wilmington, North Carolina, on a packet bound for Liverpool. At a shipyard on the Mersey he
supervised the outfitting of the company's new vessel, christened
Charming Adah. She was steam powered, built for speed and capable of
eighteen knots. She had a shallow draft and a low, narrow silhouette.
The Merseyside shipyard painted her fog-gray, the preferred color for
befuddling enemy lookouts at sea.

Folsey had a contract to carry British Enfield rifles, cartridges, powder, and Blakely rifled field guns for Gen. Josiah Gorgas's ordnance department. "Our own cargo will be aboard too," he'd assured Gibbes
before he departed from Charleston. "I'm thinking of Belgian lace,
plenty of fancy dry goods for dresses, some ladies' corsets from Paris if
I can get them. Oh, and French champagne. I'll save a crate for us."

In the midst of writing a speech he'd been asked to give about his exploits on the Peninsula, Gibbes snapped at his partner. "I don't want to
hear about it."

Folsey laughed. "Fine. You just sit back and grow rich in a state of
ignorance. I'll handle the rest."

☆   ☆   ☆

Of all Union prisons the most feared was Fort Delaware on Pea
Patch Island near the head of Delaware Bay. Confederate soldiers
prayed they would never be sent there.

Pea Patch Island was no more than a muddy shoal. Its two large prisoner compounds stood on the northern end, away from the original fort
buildings. In September of '62 there came to the officers' barracks Capt.

Richard Riddle, late of the Congaree Mounted Rifles. He had ridden with Hampton against John Pope's Union army at Second Manassas, another Confederate victory.

Richard Riddle was fifty. He looked not merely thin but cadaverous. Long hair brushed his collar, white-streaked and unkempt. His catlike brown eyes with their curious gold speckling were sunken in dark hollows in his face. He was greatly depressed by his new home, a flimsy shed with cracks showing between the pine boards and a heavy infestation of bedbugs, lice, mosquitoes, and flies, not to mention the occasional snake.

He'd enlisted in Columbia, even though he had little respect or sympathy for the loudmouthed nabobs of the Low Country who'd promoted the war. He was cynically sure most of them would manage to avoid any direct encounter with the enemy they reviled. He put his profitable freight business in the hands of his wife, Loretta, and went off to war anyway.

In Hampton's Legion he rode and fought for months without a scratch. Then, at Second Manassas, a sharpshooter's ball killed his horse and threw him into brambles, where enemy soldiers captured him as he tried to fight his way out.

On Richard's third day at Fort Delaware a corporal was singled out for torture by the hated men of the 157th Ohio National Guard who policed the prison. The corporal was hung up by his thumbs for forty-eight hours, his toes inches from the ground. When his right thumb burst, he was cut down, but he was too weak to survive. Richard couldn't believe such brutality. The fort's commandant, Colonel Schoepf, not only encouraged his guards to abuse prisoners, he occasionally watched for his own amusement.

Even worse than Schoepf was the second-in-command, a captain who strutted about with a hickory club, his back protected by two Ohioans carrying bayoneted rifles. The captain liked to harass the lines of men at the reeking sinks, which prisoners were allowed to use only at night. The captain beat any man who took too long at the trench, or displayed what he called "improper attitude." One night the captain fancied he saw something offensive on Richard's face. He called him out, ordered him to kneel, and beat him. Richard writhed in his top-tier bunk all night.

Each barracks was subdivided into rooms called divisions, named according to the home state of the inmates. There was no South Carolina division at Fort Delaware; Richard's division was identified as "Mixed." For weeks he met no one from home.

Then a young lieutenant appeared, wearing a bedraggled gray uniform and kepi Richard recognized. Richard guessed him about twenty-five. Richard hobbled across the narrow aisle as the new arrival threw his thin blanket into an empty bunk. Fort Delaware issued one blanket or one overcoat for the winter but not both. A lot of good either would do, given the gaps in the pine walls.

The young lieutenant couldn't help gawking at Richard's face. Purple and yellow bruises spread from forehead to jaw. Richard had trouble articulating; his lip was badly swollen. "Carolina?" he said.

"Yes, sir, Captain. Hampton's Brigade. The infantry. After the Peninsula we were put in Hood's Texas Brigade under Colonel Gary."

"Old Bald Eagle Gary," Richard mumbled. "I was with Hampton's horse. They transferred us to Tom Rosser."

"We never met in the field, sir."

"No, we didn't, but there were a thousand men in the Legion. I could say welcome to hell but I expect hell's a lot more pleasant than this place. Where did they catch you?"

"Sharpsburg."

"Word is, that was a hell of a fight."

"Slaughter. Not much advantage gained by either side. Lee had to run away in the night. Like a whipped dog, those are the words my captors used."

"I'm forgetting my manners." He extended his hand. "Richard Riddle, from Columbia."

"Calhoun Bell Hayward. Charleston. Pleased to know you, Captain."

Richard scratched his chin. "A long time ago I met a fascinating Charleston girl named Bell. Her father was an attorney. My father hoped to do business with him. Edmund, Edgar, something like that."

"Edgar Bell. You could be speaking of Alexandra, my mother's first cousin."

"That was her name, Alexandra." He sat on the edge of Calhoun's bunk. He remembered the sail in Charleston Harbor; the girl's expert handling of the skiff; his callow efforts to make her like him. "I fell in love with that girl on the spot. She wouldn't pay me any mind. Not too surprising, since my face was blooming like a rosebush. Does she still live in Charleston?"

"No, she left. Went up North."

"Too bad for Charleston."

"She's well known. Speaks a lot on behalf of liberating the colored. You never saw her again?"

Richard shook his head. "When I was twenty-two I married a fine woman named Loretta."

"You have children back home?"

"We had two boys. The oldest, Joe, died of scarlet fever. Richard junior drowned, swimming where he shouldn't have. Losing both of them just about broke his mother's heart. Mine, too, I'll admit." He watched a plump rat scurry across the aisle. "Anyway, glad to have another Carolina man for company."

The young lieutenant glanced around, then bent closer to whisper. "Say, I've some money they didn't find. Possible to buy anything from the guards?"

"Most anything small enough to fit in your pocket."

"I've developed quite a taste for whiskey. Staying sotted's the best way to survive this misbegotten war."

"Not the best way to keep a clear head, though."

"Begging your pardon, sir, have you ever had a man die in your arms? A good soldier, young, decent—never kept a slave and didn't believe in it but he fought for the cause anyway. He was only three months married when a stray shot killed him. It came from our side. Hanged if I need or want a clear head to remember this cursed war every waking hour. The object is to forget."

"I understand, but—"

"You Goddamn traitors, shut the fuck up." The sudden yell startled them. Standing, Richard banged his head on the bunk above. A corporal, one of the Ohio guards, grabbed his collar, then Calhoun's.

"You sons of bitches, we don't permit whispering and plotting."

The young lieutenant began, "We weren't—" The corporal smashed his nose with a club. He bled all over his gray blouse. Both officers were ordered outside, where the corporal made them climb up on barrels with the lids missing. A crowd of guards gathered.

"All right, you two slave-fuckers, hold these." Guards handed up sizable logs to Richard and Calhoun. "Now, you birds balance there and stay put for two hours. You fall off or drop the logs, punishment's doubled."

After an hour Richard felt his arms might break. He constantly teetered on the barrel's rim. When the pain became too great he pictured Loretta. He survived the rest of the punishment that way.

☆ ☆ ☆

The sanguinary war ground on, its cost in lives and money and sorrow greater than anyone had imagined, especially the dashing young men and blithe young ladies who'd stood on the Battery and cheered and sung as the first star shells exploded over Sumter. Names of distant places that few had heard of were spread in headlines and written on the butcher's bill. Lincoln shuffled and reshuffled his high command, searching for a general who could win. Lee gambled with an invasion of the North that climaxed in three days in July 1863, at a small Pennsylvania market town called Gettysburg.

At that same time reaction to a new military draft incited riots in New York City. Negroes fled from the rioters, mostly poor whites blaming them for the draft. The rioters torched Negro cottages and hovels and hung their owners from lampposts. Troops fresh from Gettysburg arrived on the cars and helped quell the violence, leaving large sections of the city a wasteland of smoldering rubble.

In Washington, Alex read about the riots with a consuming sadness. The white bigotry she'd found throughout the North, bigotry that had killed her husband, inspired a strange and paradoxical homesickness for Charleston.

On a sultry night in late July she carried an oil lamp to the door to answer a knock. On the landing she discovered a small whiskered man whose boots smelled of the barnyard.

"Miz Bell? Got this for you." He handed her a crude envelope made of brown wrapping paper. She recognized the handwriting.

"It come through the lines," the courier added.

"How?"

"Don't know. I just messenger it from down the Potomac a ways."

She tipped the man and sat down in her best parlor chair with the lamp turned up full. Westward over Virginia a thunderstorm shot lightning bolts across the sky. The letter was written on the front and back of two prescription blanks.

Dearest Sister,

I apologize for the crudity of this epistle. Paper, together with every familiar necessity, is in short supply thanks to the war. So desperate are the newspapers, they print on stock of any color. For a time the Mercury *appeared on a fuschia sheet!*

But it is not my purpose to write an essay on the crumbling Confederacy, whose end is inevitable now that the great powers of Europe have refused to recognize our rump government. My purpose is to apprise you of a situation with our Mother.

She has failed rapidly during the past month. One is not sur-

prised, since she recently observed her seventy-third birthday. Candidly, I expected her to succumb before this.

Despite poor health she has somehow kept a core of hardiness all these years. Now, however, I fear her passing is not far off. The doctor who attends her concurs. If you wished to see her a final time, you would need to hasten home.

I realize the near impossibility of your doing so. People do not cross the lines as easily as letters that travel by the busy, and costly, underground mail service. I only share the information because I felt you would want to know. Any decision in the matter is entirely yours.

Earnestly wishing for your health and well-being, I remain forever

Your loving brother,
H.B.

BOOK THREE
CITY OF ASHES
1863–1866

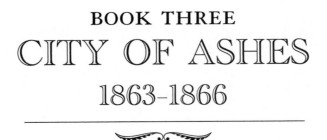

Sowing the wind was an exhilarating chivalric pastime. Resisting the wind is less agreeable.

> Civil War diary of
> George Templeton Strong, a New Yorker

The sins of the people of Charleston may cause that city to fall; it is full of rottenness, everyone being engaged in speculation.

> Gen. Josiah Gorgas
> Chief of Confederate Ordnance,
> 1863

The truth is, the whole army is burning with an insatiable desire to wreak vengeance upon South Carolina. I almost tremble at her fate, but feel that she deserves all that seems in store for her.

> General Sherman to General Halleck,
> 1864

A city of ruins, of desolation, of vacant homes, of widowed women, of deserted warehouses, of weed-wild gardens, of miles of grass-grown streets. . . .

> Sidney Andrews,
> newspaper reporter, 1865

52

The Blockade Runner

The morning after Alex landed at Nassau, New Providence Island, she called on the Henry Adderly Company, shipping agents for the Confederacy, and explained her need to reach Charleston. Adderly's man suggested Capt. James Jolly.

"A piratical sort, but he ain't under contract to the Richmond government. Sets his own schedule. He's in port with *Osprey*. This time of day you'd likely find him at the Royal Victoria, drinking champagne." Alex wondered about a master who imbibed at ten o'clock, but she couldn't be choosy. She thanked the man and set off for the hotel.

The war had transformed Nassau from a sleepy Royal Navy coaling port to a rough boomtown. Despite the hour sailors crowded grog shops, while others slept off binges in garbage-strewn alleys. Officers wearing Confederate gray mingled with merchants, stevedores, and a multitude of strolling whores, white, black, and shades in between. A seaman mistook Alex for one such. A whack of her cane sent him packing.

Alex was forty-eight, still slender, with erect posture she maintained at some cost. She wore a front-laced whalebone corset to relieve pain in her back. Her Washington doctor attributed the pain to neuralgia, a popular catch-all diagnosis. No one would have guessed she suffered, seeing her march along so straight and tall.

She wore a simple pearl-gray tunic with Turkish pantaloons under a short skirt; Mrs. Bloomer's hygienic costume. An Indian-patterned shawl woven in Paisley, Scotland, draped her shoulders. A wide-brimmed straw hat shielded her face from the August sun. After winters in the North she relished the heat.

The piazza of the Royal Victoria had a splendid view of the busy piers, Hog Island, and the sheltered harbor between. The harbor was crowded. Steamers without a berth anchored in the blue water; cargo lighters darted between ships and the shore. Alex had never seen so much baled cotton. Northern papers said Confederate monetary instruments were largely worthless, but the South still traded cotton for arms, food, and medicine.

She found James Jolly easily. Resplendent in blue and braid, he sat with a spyglass at his eye. A champagne flute and a long brown cigar smoldering in a dish lay at hand. Jolly was stout, florid, perhaps ten years her junior. Alex introduced herself and soon discovered a common ground. Jolly was a Conch, a native of the island, but his forebears had emigrated from South Carolina in the exodus of loyalists after the Revolution.

The captain offered her champagne. She declined; he insisted on ordering ginger beer with a few slivers of ice floating in it. Alex explained about her mother. "You are sailing to Charleston, are you not?"

"Regrettably, ma'am, yes. Captains with good sense are making for Wilmington, but the owners insist I go to Charleston once more. Do you know the Union has mounted a huge campaign from Hilton Head, and marched north to capture the coastal islands?"

She said she'd read of it, including the sensational failed assault on Battery Wagner on Morris Island in mid-July. A Negro regiment, something new in the Union army, had stormed the battery at night and been thrown back with tremendous loss of life. The regimental commander, a young Boston Brahmin named Shaw, died with his men. Instead of being given a proper officer's burial he was flung in a trench among his black soldiers. The idea of Negroes in uniform enraged and frightened Southerners.

Jolly said, "The Yankees want to bury Charleston. Cradle of secession and all that. They've floated torpedoes in the harbor and set picket boats and ironclads patrolling outside the bar. If a solitary signal light shows on Sullivan's Island, their batteries open up. Running in there is dangerous."

"Nevertheless, Captain, I must go, at all hazards."

Jolly's unwavering bonhomie annoyed her. "Understandable, ma'am, but there are other difficulties. *Osprey* is a River Clyde passenger steamer. We pulled out all the cabins so she carries more cargo. There's no place a lady could stay safely and comfortably." He snapped his fingers at a black waiter, ordered more champagne. "Excepting my cabin."

"How much would you want? Fifty dollars?"

"In these circumstances, ma'am, two hundred fifty. In gold."

She had the money, but there'd be scarcely anything left if she paid his price. She decided she loathed Captain Jolly, so genial and unsubtle in his greed.

"I only have American currency," she said.

"The bank down the road will be happy to exchange it. They do take a sizable fee."

It was an effort to control her temper. "Done."

"Well, then"—he saluted her with his flute—"I'll be happy to hang my hammock with the crew. Are your sympathies with the South?"

"Does it matter?"

"Not since we're doing a cash transaction. I was merely curious. We'll clear for Charleston soon as I fill the bunkers with anthracite. Doesn't smoke like soft coal, you know."

"I don't know, Captain," she said in a frosty tone. "I'll take my things to the ship this afternoon."

"At your pleasure, ma'am." Alex left her ginger beer untasted and marched down the piazza. A parrot in a cage in an open window screamed, "Grog, Goddammit, grog," to the amusement of loungers watching the tall blond lady pass by.

☆ ☆ ☆

She hired a porter to carry her steamer trunk but kept the canvas banjo case on her shoulder. They walked along by huge open-sided warehouses stacked with crates marked COMBUSTIBLES and ROYAL ARMOURY ENFIELD ENGLAND. *Osprey* was a sidewheeler with two short masts, two large paddle boxes, and two rakish stacks. She was painted a dull sea-green. Alex said to the porter, "Please take the trunk to the captain's cabin. I'll be aboard shortly."

She'd spied some large hogsheads that looked familiar. She'd seen them off-loaded from the ship that carried her from Philadelphia. The hogsheads bore new stenciling. PRODUCT OF BERMUDA. The Philadelphia ship hadn't called at Bermuda.

She examined a lading tag. CONSIGNED TO PALMETTO TRADERS CHARLESTON. Illegal cargo bought in the North? She shook her head. There was no end to the contemptible profiteering on both sides.

✯ ✯ ✯

Osprey's manifest listed the neutral port of Havana as the destination for its goods. The young Bahamian supercargo told her it was a subterfuge blockade runners used in case of capture. Alex shared Jolly's small cabin with two padlocked strongboxes, the captain's personal cargo. He freely named the contents—quinine in one, morphine in the other. "Either will sell for a hundred dollars an ounce, if not more."

They sailed on the dawn tide, running northwest through the Bahamian archipelago, deserted islands of sand and scrub. Ship's rations consisted of sea biscuit and salt pork by day, and for supper a watery fish chowder, soggy macaroni, and corn dodgers, little cakes the crew slathered with a fiery ketchup. At twilight all hands received a ration of gin and water. Jolly promised a champagne-and-oyster supper if they reached Charleston without incident.

Sanitary facilities were primitive. Alex was allowed ten minutes alone in the reeking head in the morning, another ten minutes at night. As for her daily bath, it was out of the question. She passed the time reading *Silas Marner* and a recent issue of *Harper's Monthly* containing a sympathetic article about her brother's friend James Petigru, dead this past March. *Died of heart trouble and sorrow,* one of Ham's letters said. Ham's faith in the unpopular Unionist beliefs he and Petigru shared had never wavered.

She had to draw her knees up to sleep in the bunk, which only confirmed her long-held opinion that she was too tall for most everything in the world.

✯ ✯ ✯

In the sunlit waters of the Gulf Stream, Jolly sent a lookout to the foremast crosstrees. The lookout earned a dollar for every sail sighted, but if someone on deck saw it first, it cost the lookout five. Twice they spied a ship of the Union's Gulf squadron out of Key West. Jolly immediately changed course, his escape helped by *Osprey's* dull paint and low profile.

The sun flashing off the blue-green sea bathed Alex in delicious warmth. Whatever perils and hardships waited in Charleston, there was also warm weather. Her neuralgia and her injured leg troubled her less. In a burst of confidence she threw her cane over the side and watched it float away.

She'd taken off the coarse netting that held her chignon, let her hair out like a gray-streaked banner. Crewman watched, puzzled. Alex laughed, leaning on the rail and feeling an unjustified giddiness. She couldn't help it. She was going home.

☆   ☆   ☆

The run to Charleston took three days, covering more than 480 miles because of Jolly's zigzag course. A knock roused Alex late on the third night. She held her muslin gown against her breasts and opened the door a crack. It was the supercargo, with a lantern.

"Beg pardon, ma'am. Captain asked that I wake you. We'll be making the run within the hour."

A thrill ran through her. "How are conditions?"

"Tide will be right but the moon's up and the clouds are clearing. Looks like some rain building in the north. We'll be in an exposed position for several minutes. Best to secure yourself in here."

"I prefer to watch from the deck."

"It wouldn't be safe."

"I insist. Considering what I paid, I deserve a good show."

"Then please stay out of the way, and be quiet. Captain flogs any man who so much as lets a far—makes a noise."

"Thank you. I'll get dressed."

☆   ☆   ☆

On deck the engine-room hatches were covered, the binnacle hooded. Speeding clouds glowed with an inner light from the hidden moon. The night air was heavy with the familiar damp of the low-lying coast, the faint tang of decay. Ahead, ship's lanterns lit the horizon. The light clusters were widely spaced. The blockade squadron was waiting for them.

Alex went forward between crates lashed down to deck cleats. It was still dark, although daybreak was near; a paleness marked the horizon astern. The clouds cleared long enough for moonlight to reveal the lookout in the crosstree above her. Five minutes later the moon vanished behind a rampart of rumbling storm clouds.

Jolly issued a muffled order at the helm. The engines slowed. Lightning glittered in the clouds, thunder came and, almost immediately, rain. Alex put her Paisley shawl over her head. *Osprey* plowed through the wind-roughened sea toward a gap between the lighted ships. In the distance she glimpsed scattered lights in the city. Her stomach hurt.

Another bolt of lightning lit up a three-masted steamer lying about a thousand yards off the port bow. The lightning shimmered on her iron-plated hull. A smaller vessel shot from behind the steamer and turned seaward to intercept *Osprey.* "Monitor closing fast," the lookout called above the hiss of rain.

A trail of sparks rose from the steamer. Suddenly an umbrella of white light opened, turning the raindrops silver. "That's *New Ironsides,*" someone yelled. There was no longer a need for stealth, only speed.

A red eye blinked on the steamer, followed by a roar. Bells rang; *Osprey* veered to starboard. Alex clutched the mast as a shell streaked across the bow and blew a geyser from the sea. A second rocket went up, illuminating the monitor bearing down on them. Forward of its turret a Union seamen readied the bow gun. Someone hailed them through a trumpet. "This is the Union monitor *Catskill.* Heave to or we'll sink you."

Jolly's response was to shout, "All ahead full."

A sudden grinding and scraping of the keel tilted the deck to port. Sand dunes and sea oats rose from the dark in the next lightning flash, alarmingly near the starboard side. *Osprey* was running close to Sullivan's Island. There was shouting and frantic cursing at the helm, then a sudden jolt; *Osprey* ran aground on a sandbar.

The engine driving her starboard paddle whined. The vessel shuddered. Just as the monitor's bow gun fired, she leapt free. The shell narrowly missed the pilot house and exploded onshore. Alex silently congratulated Jolly, as though she belonged to his crew. At that moment *New Ironsides* fired again.

The cannonball clipped the foremast. The upper third toppled down on the port side. Alex flung herself toward the starboard scuppers. The lookout's body plummeted, striking a crate, bouncing off, and landing on the deck with a sickening pulpy sound.

The broken mast had speared one of the hogsheads she'd examined in Nassau. Brine gushed out. A glistening slab of salt pork slid onto the deck.

The rain squall swept out to sea. Dawn light was breaking on the coastline and Charleston Harbor. Soaked and bedraggled, Alex peered at Fort Sumter off the port bow. Two rounds from the fort fell well astern as Captain Jolly screamed down the engine-room tube for more speed.

Osprey took a hit from *New Ironsides.* The cannonball hulled the stern and threw wood and iron skyward along with body parts. A moment later they were out of range, making for the Cooper River side of the peninsula.

Trembling, Alex saw another ironclad loom near Castle Pinckney. Jolly shouted, "It's *Chicora*. She's friendly. We're safe."

53

Ravaged City

Jolly greeted the captain of *Chicora* through a speaking horn. The vessels passed on their port sides, *Osprey* listing badly. The supercargo ran down to Alex. "Miss Bell, are you safe and sound?"

"Yes, but not that poor boy. Can you help him?" Her hair was sticky on her forehead, her shawl and dress soaked through. The supercargo bent over the lookout.

"Alfred's made his last run. He was a good lad. Not yet seventeen."

Osprey struggled through the river roadstead clogged with anchored ships, then swung toward Middle Wharf. Jolly went in too fast and reversed engines too late; *Osprey*'s prow rammed the wharf, damaging pilings and swaying the pier head. The captain reversed, then warped in more slowly; *Osprey* tied up near a group of ragged blacks waiting to off-load the vessel.

Captain Jolly caught Alex as she went below. "I regret the inbound passage was harrowing."

"No more so than you predicted, Captain. Thank you for bringing me home."

He touched his forehead and turned away, no trace of jollity left on his ashen face.

✳ ✳ ✳

On the pier she asked an elderly Negro about a cab. "Oh, no, ma'am, they's precious scarce, 'specially this time of morning. I can stow that trunk for you. Later maybe you can get some good soul to move it where you need it."

"All right, thank you."

"You from around here, ma'am? I seem to know your face."

"Yes, I am. I've been away a long time."

"I fear you won't hardly recognize Charleston no more. These are terrible times. Just terrible."

She trudged across East Bay with her banjo on her shoulder. A familiar pain spread in her lower back. She scored herself for throwing her cane away in a moment of unwarranted confidence.

She walked west on Hasell Street. The morning was quiet until the sudden faraway *crump* of enemy artillery broke the silence. As she reached Meeting Street, a bell tolled six. She recognized the beautiful sonority of Great Michael, but where were the others? Usually all eight rang the hour. And why was the church steeple wearing a coat of black paint?

To the south along Meeting she saw a panorama of change and ruin so great, it hardly resembled the same scene remembered from childhood. First there was the fire damage, in what Charleston called the burnt district. This she knew about from Ham's letters, but the reality was profoundly shocking. Familiar buildings were gone, leaving empty lots with jagged sections of blackened walls standing like gravestones amid military tents.

The Great Fire of 1861 had started on the night of December 11, near the very intersection where she'd crossed East Bay. Fanned by gale winds, it had advanced to Meeting, and south, all the way to Tradd Street, where the late Mr. Petigru's house burned to the ground with others. The fire swept along Queen Street to the Ashley before it exhausted itself next morning, having consumed nearly six hundred homes and buildings. Ham said most of the burned properties hadn't been rebuilt. No one knew how the fire started.

Of course, as always, her brother had written, *our good citizens blame arson perpetrated by slaves or resentful freedmen. We have feared the Negro for so long, when disaster strikes, the public mind can conceive of no other cause or culprit.*

She walked down Meeting in a daze of disbelief. Rats and wild dogs foraged in the gutters and alleys. Ragged children, white and black, appeared from nowhere, ran along beside her, tugging her arm, begging for rice. She gave them all the coins she had.

The beautiful old Circular Congregational Church had disappeared, and Institute Hall, where the secession ordinance was signed. The Mills House remained, and Hibernian Hall, and St. Michael's with its ugly black steeple. The randomness of the fire was everywhere evident. The fine hotel designed by Robert Mills was untouched—General Lee had watched the fire from its roof, Ham said—but directly across Meeting lay several burnt blocks where soldiers camped. She hadn't expected such a great military presence; the tents crowded every open space. Men crawled out in their underwear, scratching themselves, lighting cook fires. One pulled his crotch and shouted, "Hey, how much for a song and a hump?" His companions laughed. Alex glared.

She heard drumming and bugling from several directions. A moment later she darted back to avoid being run down by a horse-drawn artillery limber. At Broad Street she nearly collided with a dog-cart phaeton that turned the corner too sharply. The elderly driver reined his horse, brandished his whip. "Woman, you almost caused an accident."

"Streetwalker," sniffed the lady seated beside him. The couple looked familiar. DeSaussures? Mouzons? One of the elite families, anyway. People who might remember her. She cut the confrontation short by giving them an unmerited apology.

Once across Broad, she looked back. The phaeton still sat there, the white-haired lady turned on the seat, pointing and chattering at her husband. Alex had no desire to announce her return, but it appeared that she might have little say about it.

54

Ham

She walked beneath the stately trees of lower Meeting Street. Dust lay on the dry leaves; the city had a parched and airless feel. Weariness was clutching at her, slowing her steps. Sudden cannon fire reverberated across the harbor. The abruptness of it unnerved her. She could imagine what it did to the people of the city.

At South Battery great mounds of earth rose in what had been the public gardens. Soldiers and Negroes swarmed over the mounds with shovels and picks. Mules dragged a sledge carrying a great iron gun guarded by artillerymen. Toward East Bay, Alex saw similar batteries under construction.

She turned left to the familiar house. Its run-down appearance horrified her. Swathes of mildew discolored the exterior. The gate was scaly with rust. Inside the garden the flowers were gone; knee-high weeds had claimed the lawn. A section of the garden wall had collapsed, the bricks fallen in an untidy heap. Only the great live oak remained as she remembered it.

She knocked on the mildewed door on the piazza. The still air carried the curses and complaints of the workmen sweating in the hot sun. The door opened; there stood her brother, his finger marking the page of a law book. He'd come at last to the reality of old age, the look he'd carried since childhood. He was round-shouldered, his hair long, his striped trousers baggy, his vest dusted with ash. He would be forty-nine now, but he might have been seventy, so badly did his flesh sag on his sallow face.

"Oh, God. I so hoped you'd come, if not for Mother, then for me. Oh, sister." They fell into each other's arms, hugging fiercely.

He wiped his eyes. "Come in, come in. It's heaven to see you. Did you arrive by ship? Was it dangerous? You're beautiful as ever." It made her laugh.

"Nonsense, I was never beautiful. How is Mother?"

"Weak, but stable."

"Is Dr. Baltus still attending?"

"Yes, though he can barely totter. Every day I wish Xeno Hayward hadn't marched off to war and met his Maker. Baltus is old school, doctrinaire. He sweats Mother. He insists she take castor oil in molasses. It's futile. She's given up."

"Can I see her?"

"She usually sleeps till late morning. Are you hungry? Come in the dining room." She followed him, pausing briefly to look at Joanna's portrait. Someone had kept the canvas clean. The rest of the house was in appalling condition. Dust lay in the corners and gleamed like a coating of dark talc where sunlight struck the floor.

A small library of law books littered the stained dining table. Stubs of strong-smelling cigars lay in a Wedgwood saucer. "Do you still have house people?" she asked.

"No, I freed them, as you did Maudie."

"Dear Maudie. Do you know where she is?"

"I don't. She might have left the city."

"Who takes care of the place?"

"A man named Rolfe. He belongs to Judge Porcher's widowed daughter Letty. She hires him out by the day."

"Does he cook?"

"Sometimes. I fry up some bread if he's away. Neighbor ladies bring an occasional dish for Mother. She has no appetite. I have to empty the dish before I return it."

"So you and Mother are alone in this mausoleum with all those reb soldiers in town. Some of them look positively vicious."

"The new Charleston mobocracy. Since they arrived to defend us, household robberies have increased tenfold, as have assaults on women."

"What do you have to defend yourself?"

He blinked. "Why, nothing. I believe in the law, not weapons."

"My trunk's at Middle Wharf. I still have grandfather Edward's pistols."

"Do you know how to shoot?"

"I can learn," she said emphatically, thumping herself into a chair.

He removed an empty plate from the table. "Would you like coffee? It's mostly corn and okra seeds and chicory root, but it's better than none."

He returned from the kitchen with a chipped mug and slices of a coarse, strange-looking bread. "Made from boiled pumpkin and a little corn meal. Rolfe forages grains of corn from the feeding troughs of the cavalry. As you can see, we are living like potentates in the glorious Confederacy. Marion Marburg has a German word for all the substitutes. *Ersatz.*"

For the next two hours questions and answers flew back and forth between them, long after the oddly flavored coffee was drunk and the peculiar bread eaten. At the end she said, "I'm afraid I was recognized by an elderly couple on my way here."

"Then you must be careful. You're well remembered."

" 'That damned woman'?"

"I'm afraid so."

"Hardly a surprise. Tell me about the rest of the family."

"I avoid cousin Ouida. She's unbalanced and everyone knows it. I do encounter Gibbes occasionally. He gets about reasonably well despite his wooden leg. He's married to Folsey Lark's sister. Gibbes's mother, Bethel, lives with them. She must be nearly seventy-five. Gibbes has become very successful bringing arms through the blockade for the government. He and Folsey own most of a firm called Palmetto Traders." Her reaction startled him. "You know it?"

She described the mysterious hogsheads shipped from Philadelphia through Nassau; told him about the brine pouring from the broken cask and slabs of what she took to be salted pork. "I doubt its destination was the Confederate commissary department."

Ham picked a bread crumb from his plate, savored it on his tongue. "Then I am disappointed in our family hero, although, with Folsey's involvement, not entirely surprised."

She asked about the military situation. "Perilous," he said. "Admiral Dahlgren's flotilla controls the offshore waters. General Quincy Gillmore marched up the coast with God knows how many thousands. A British journalist came through the lines the other day. He said Gillmore's building a platform in the marshes capable of bearing the weight of a monster gun that can throw shells into the city. I expect they let the man come over with the story in order to scare us. They've painted St. Michael's steeple—"

"I saw."

"—supposedly to make it less of a target for artillery spotters. Ironic, your arriving on the eve of another calamity. Charleston besieged again. Grandfather Edward did the same thing. Is this family cursed?"

"Sometimes I can believe it."

"I must be honest with you, Alex." His pale hand fluttered over the law books. "I've been preparing for a legal defense that will likely bring down the wrath of the white citizenry."

"How so?"

"The tower of the old city jail presently houses seventy-three soldiers from the Fifty-fourth Massachusetts. That's the colored regiment that failed to take Battery Wagner. In theory the soldiers are prisoners of war, entitled to be treated humanely and exchanged, but Governor Bonham demanded that Beauregard turn them over to the civil authorities and Beauregard caved in. South Carolina will try the soldiers as slaves in rebellion, which amounts to a death sentence. A courageous colleague named Nelson Mitchell stepped forward to defend them. I'll be seconding him when it goes to trial."

"You feel it will harm your reputation?"

"What reputation? The Bell name may still be respectable, but after years of friendship with Jim Petigru I am barely tolerated. I'm not unhappy about it, mind. I only tell you because it adds a measure of risk for anyone living under this roof."

Alex sat up straight despite the pain in her back. "Well, brother dear, I'm damned if I'll leave after all the trouble it took to get here. Can Rolfe fetch my trunk? I want those pistols."

☆　☆　☆

At noon she ventured up to the second floor. It smelled of mold and some sickly odor that might have been liniment. It needed airing and cleaning. After she had a long sleep, she'd get to work.

Cassandra's room was black. Alex opened a shutter a few inches. Her mother lay under too many blankets. Alex drew off all but one. She stroked Cassandra's brow gently.

"Mama?"

Cassandra roused. "Who is it?"

"Alex, Mama."

Spidery fingers explored her hand. Recognition came slowly. "Alex? My daughter Alex?"

"Yes, Mama. Come home to see you. I've been so worried about you."

A feeble smile. "Ah. Now I know it's Alex, Alex worries about everyone." The tip of her tongue passed across her colorless lips. "Can you stay a few days?"

"As long as you want, Mama."

"I am so glad you've come. So glad. Times are hard. Good people killing each other. So glad," she said again, the sound faint as wind through pine boughs. She fell back to sleep. Alex was undone. She closed the door and bolted downstairs.

There she sank down by the wall, flung her arms over her head. Days of anxiety, of holding everything inside, erupted in great gulping sobs. She grew incoherent. "William, I need you. Henry, come back. I'm not strong. God, I'm so weak, please make me strong again. I hate this war. I hate the killing. I hate everything."

Ham poked his head out the dining room door, a cigar clenched in his teeth. He thought of kneeling to comfort his sister but reconsidered. He closed the door and left Alex to purge her grief as best she could.

55

Under Fire

Alex came home to South Battery on the morning of August 12, 1863. The cannon she heard were rifled guns dug into the sand of Morris Island, lobbing shells at Fort Sumter to set the range. She had more immediate worries: the condition of the house, meals for the family, care of Cassandra. She began sitting with her mother for at least an hour every day.

Ham introduced her to Rolfe, a light-brown man with dark-brown freckles and a grumbly disposition. Ham had warned her of Rolfe's fondness for a tipple. Alex advised him to stay sober or Letty Porcher-Jones would be hiring him out to someone else. "Do we understand each other?" Rolfe muttered that they did.

Alex and Rolfe set to work in a fury of sweeping and dusting, scouring and waxing. Rolfe scythed down weeds while Alex scrubbed floors on hands and knees. By the following Monday, August 17, the place looked reasonably habitable again.

That same day Union batteries began steady bombardment of Fort Sumter. More than nine hundred rounds flew over the harbor to smash the fort's brick walls. The cannonading made Alex edgy. Would they train their great marsh gun on the city? People lived in dread of "the Swamp Angel," Ham said.

★　★　★

Dr. Nigel Baltus called to see his patient late that day. The Bell family physician resembled an ancient gnome. His eyes had long ago lost their sparkle, and his mouth was a cave filled with gold nuggets. Alex immediately confronted him:

"No more sweating or purging my mother."

"Do you want her to die?"

"Frankly, I think the treatment is hastening it."

"Then I leave the case in your hands, madam. This was once a respectable and revered family. No longer. Everything they say about you is true. Good day and be damned to you."

★ ★ ★

The barrage continued Tuesday, when Alex set out for a shop in an alley above City Market. She wore a plain gingham skirt and the straw hat whose broad brim helped hide her face. She'd put away her bloomers so as not to draw attention to herself.

She showed one of Edward's pistols to Omar Lorenzo, proprietor of the gun shop. He curled his hand around the barrel; a finger nicked the spring release and the bayonet leapt out. He sucked a thin stripe of blood on his fingertip. "Wicked piece of work. English. Around 1760, I would say. You wish to sell it?"

"I wish to fire it. I need powder and ball, and instruction."

"The latter can be had readily enough. Powder and lead are impossible to get."

"I'm told you can buy almost anything in Charleston if you pay enough."

The shopkeeper smiled as though they shared a secret. He turned a key in a wall cabinet, brought out two sets of lead knuckles. In a melee outside an Indianapolis meeting hall she'd been hit with similar knuckles made of brass.

"These came my way from a brawl down in Fernandina. I can melt them down. Come back Friday and I'll be ready to give you a lesson. Leave the piece with me till then."

"It had better be here Friday."

"Oh, it will be. I know who you are. I can't afford to have your brother hail me into court for larceny. I have mouths to feed."

He wanted a hundred dollars Confederate. She bargained him down to sixty. She borrowed the money from Ham. His younger partner, Argyll Buckles's nephew Cedric, grudgingly agreed to the loan. Ham took the money from the cashbox of Buckles & Bell, replacing it with a promissory note.

*　*　*

Cassandra showed more animation every day. She encouraged her daughter to keep the windows open for fresh air. She said that when she felt a bit stronger, she'd like to attempt the stairs and visit the garden.

Friday, in a secluded yard behind the gun shop, Lorenzo set up a straw bale. He displayed a lead ball in his palm. He'd molded a dozen.

She watched attentively as he loaded and primed the pistol. Then he stood behind her, reaching around to position her arms. "Take aim, but it's well to avert your head in case of a misfire. A slow and careful shot is better than one that's too fast and off the mark." She disliked having Lorenzo thrust his hips against her but endured it until she fired the round.

The recoil rocked her. The ball buried harmlessly in the bale. "One more?" he suggested.

"Yes, but I prefer to try it alone." He stepped away, visibly disappointed.

She paid him, stowed everything in her reticule, and set out for home along Church Street. She wasn't confident that she could be an expert marksman, but she felt she could load the old pistols and use them at close range in an emergency.

*　*　*

The Union barrage continued; a gun boomed every ten minutes or so. Mortars and Parrott rifles, coehorns and British Whitworths poured out their fire, abetted by the guns of ironclads and monitors. They hammered Sumter and also Battery Wagner, to keep the defenders crouching in bombproofs, unable to get to their artillery and return fire. The noise gave Alex fierce headaches.

General Gillmore sent a note into the city demanding surrender of Fort Sumter and Confederate positions on Morris Island. He threatened to fire on Charleston if refused. Beauregard didn't receive the note immediately. Around half past one on Saturday morning Alex was jolted from sleep by a stupendous explosion. She ran into the hall. Cassandra cried out. Alex called back to say all was well, though clearly it wasn't.

Ham stumbled out of his room in his nightshirt, candle in hand. "They must have fired the Swamp Angel."

"They're attacking civilians."

"Under the rules of war they have the right. The city's fortified and garrisoned. The docks are points of entry for munitions. And this is the most hated place in the Confederacy."

They sat downstairs for the next hour. Alex asked about an eerie white glow in the south. "Calcium lights," Ham said. "Illuminating the Confederate batteries so the guns can find them. Union engineers work under the lights to advance the trenches."

Two more shells detonated in the city, the last no more than a few blocks away. They heard the whistles and bells of a fire company. Ham pulled on trousers and boots and ran to Meeting Street. He returned to say buildings were burning in Price's Alley. "Incendiary shells. They explode and scatter Greek Fire."

The sixteen rounds that struck Charleston before dawn brought uneasy quiet. General Beauregard replied to General Gillmore's note with a scathing refusal. The city braced for more shelling.

☆　☆　☆

Alex wrote a short list of items for Rolfe to look for at the City Market. Some farmers still brought produce into town. She wanted to buy dates or, as a substitute, dried persimmons. She wanted an Irish potato; barring that, a sweet potato. She wanted milk if it wasn't too heavily watered, and any green vegetables available. They were scarce; Cedric Buckles's wife grew flowers and herbs to cook as substitutes.

Rolfe held out the list. "Can't read this here. Mistress never taught us. Agin the law."

"Rolfe, you'll be a free man when the North wins the war. Abraham Lincoln promised it in his proclamation last winter."

"Yes'm, we heard what Linkum done."

"To survive you'll need to read and write and know your numbers."

"Who going to hire a teacher for this nigger? What I do with old Linkum's freedom anyway? I can't eat it. I can't carry it in a sack. Ain't no good to me at all. You want to tell me that list out loud?"

The exchange haunted Alex. How many thousands lived in dread of emancipation because they weren't prepared for it and didn't even know how to begin?

☆　☆　☆

Ham visited the city jail to interview prisoners with Nelson Mitchell. The lead defense counsel was a thoughtful, slow-spoken man, well regarded in the community. A few naysayers whispered that he was a secret Unionist, but there was no evidence.

Of the captured soldiers, two dozen had suffered no wounds. They insisted they had never been slaves, though of course this was to be expected, and they could offer no proof. At the end of the long day, Ham came home with a doleful report:

"They're a dispirited lot, and not solely because of the danger they're in. They believe the army betrayed them. Promised them the same pay and enlistment bounties given to white men, then reneged. At Battery Wagner they believe they were thrown in the front ranks to spare the white soldiers. One man said his captain warned him that if he objected or balked, he'd be shot in the back. Others verified the story."

"But the state is going ahead with the prosecution?"

"Yes, though now it's a two-edged sword. Lincoln has issued an order saying that if any Negro soldier is killed in violation of the rules of war, one of our soldiers will be executed."

"Can you and Mr. Mitchell save the lives of those men?"

"A moot question. Mitchell is adamant on one point. He insists the situation is too highly charged for us to risk mounting a defense based on the main issue—whether the men are soldiers or insurrectionists. We need another strategy."

"Which is?"

"Unknown. We're still searching."

★ ★ ★

Saturday the attack on the city resumed. In late afternoon Folsey Lark held court in the Mills House bar. He'd lately returned from Richmond, where he'd solidified new contracts by plying army purchasing agents with smuggled champagne and Virginia whores. Certain Charlestonians called Folsey a codfish aristocrat—a man of no breeding who made his money from trade. He didn't give a damn. His critics were pretentious bluebloods living in poverty.

A new round came screaming in every few minutes. The hotel lobby was full of guests running about in panic. In the bar liquor and fine cigars promoted a cheerful complacence. Folsey struck up a conversation with a German military observer, Count von Ravenstein. As soon as they heard the next shell arriving, Folsey exclaimed, "I'll wager fifty that it won't hit us."

"Ja, done, but if you lose, how will you collect?"

They watched the ceiling. The shell passed over, exploding somewhere to the north. Von Ravenstein produced a wad of Confederate notes, counted the bluebacks onto the bar. Folsey saluted the officer with his glass.

Applause greeted a surprising arrival, Gen. P.G.T. Beauregard. He was a stocky man, with brilliant dark eyes and elegant mustaches. His headquarters was just down Meeting Street in the James Simmons house. He marched in with his aide, Col. Tom Jordan,[6] close behind. The two officers sat at a corner table with a white-whiskered gentleman Folsey recognized as a prominent cotton broker. They seemed to be arguing over a sheet of figures, Beauregard puffing his cheeks and shaking his head repeatedly until the broker pulled out a pencil and wrote another figure that produced smiles and handshakes all around the table.

Beauregard was a Creole, the privileged child of a Louisiana sugarcane plantation. He'd gone to West Point, served in Mexico, and resigned his army commission when war broke out. He was beloved in Charleston because he commanded when Sumter fell. People called him the first Confederate hero.

He wasn't so favored in Richmond. His reputation had suffered after the Union victory at Shiloh Church in '62. When Gen. Albert Sidney Johnson fell on the first day, Beauregard assumed command of the army and that evening failed to press the attack. He was condemned for bad judgment, cowardice, and worse. Richmond whispered of Beauregard hiding in his tent, paralyzed by a temporary insanity.

The army retreated to Corinth, Mississippi. An infected throat and general debilitation sent Beauregard home on sick leave, ostensibly on the advice of doctors. He left Braxton Bragg in charge. He thought he carried out the transfer of command properly, but Davis construed his unauthorized departure as dereliction of duty and took the Army of the West away from him.

More than fifty of Beauregard's friends in the Confederate Congress petitioned Davis to restore him to command, on an equal footing with Lee. Davis would not. He sent Beauregard back to Charleston as commandant of the Department of South Carolina and Georgia. Beauregard's dislike of the president became something close to hatred.

✶ ✶ ✶

[6]Jordan, Beauregard's longtime right hand, helped establish the Rose Greenhow spy ring in Washington in 1861. See Part Two of *On Secret Service*.

Beauregard said good-bye to his civilian guest and worked his way down the bar, shaking hands. Folsey bowed to him. "General. This is indeed a pleasure."

"Mr. Lark, sir," Beauregard said, returning the bow.

"I hardly expected to encounter you in a hotel."

"A business matter to be settled. I'll not skulk at headquarters. I prefer to move about, show the citizens that we aren't intimidated by Gillmore's cowardly attacks."

"Allow me the honor of offering you and Colonel Jordan a whiskey." Beauregard nodded agreeably. Because Folsey liked to drink at the Mills House, he supplied the bar with contraband bottles at reduced prices.

"I hear you have a relative newly arrived from Yankee country," the general said. "An interesting creature, I'm told." Although married, Beauregard openly admired and flirted with women. In Charleston he could do it without hindrance; his second wife, Caroline, was ailing in New Orleans.

"You must mean Alexandra Bell. I'm only related by marriage. My half-sister is married to my partner, Mr. Gibbes Bell. He and Alexandra are cousins. She's from one of the old Charleston families. She left because of a scandal. Took a fancy to a freedman and had quite a hot affair until a few gentlemen of the town objected and put a stop to it. I have it on good authority that up North, she offered herself to niggers at every opportunity."

Beauregard took a moment to twist a point on his thick mustache. "Then perhaps I should not make her acquaintance."

"That'd be my advice. She's a tramp, probably diseased. I wouldn't have her if she offered herself with a sack of gold between her legs."

Folsey's loud remark generated laughter in the smoky bar. "Thank you for the counsel," Beauregard said.

Another shell flew over, landing nearby with a detonation that shook the chandeliers and rattled glassware behind the bar. Folsey toasted the general. "Here's to your courageous defense of our city, sir." He tossed off his whole glass; Beauregard took a single sip.

Folsey had already enjoyed several rounds. A warm, enveloping confidence overtook him as Beauregard and his aide left the bar. Spreading canards about Alex Bell was pleasurable and could be interpreted as honoring his promise to his father. Best of all it placed him in no personal danger.

✷ ✷ ✷

Early Sunday morning Ham and Alex went to the attic, opened a round window, and looked through a telescope at Fort Sumter. The flag of the Confederacy still flew, but large sections of the wall had been blown down, the rubble falling to form rough slopes leading to the water. Alex expressed dismay over the concentration of Union ships offshore.

"You know you can leave whenever you wish," Ham said.

"Abandon you and Mother? Not at a time like this."

Sunday evening was quiet. The air was tainted with the smell of fires. Alex sat in the shadowy garden, softly picking out "The Blue Tail Fly," President Lincoln's favorite. Rolfe had gone home to avoid curfew trouble, but before that he'd sat on the piazza for half an hour, listening to the banjo. For once he smiled.

A carriage rolled up in the street, an ornate coupe rockaway with shiny carmine paint. A large letter *B*, scrolled and gilded, decorated the side panel below the glass window. The Negro driver tied the dapple gray to the ring block and opened the door for his passenger. Alex saw, at the gate, a square-toed ankle boot and a striped trouser leg jut from the carriage.

The driver reached up to help Gibbes Bell alight. What effrontery, to call after all that had passed between them.

56

Alex and the Hero

Gibbes appeared nonchalant as he approached the gate. He didn't look the least bit like a victim of wartime shortages. Fancy black braid edged the lapels and pockets of his gray frock coat. His black cravat set off a vivid scarlet waistcoat. He was as stylish as a London nob.

He tipped his stovepipe hat. "A warm welcome to you, cousin. I wanted to hasten over the moment I heard you'd returned."

"I imagine half the town knows by now."

"Oh, all of the town. Those who matter, anyway. Hester Mouzon identified you. Might I come in?"

He'd unnerved her by appearing unexpectedly. She opened the gate Rolfe had oiled and scraped free of rust, led him to a garden bench. His left foot tended to drag slightly but he seemed unbothered. Heroism and commercial success had given him a confidence and polish lacking in his youth.

"How is your dear mother, may I ask?"

"Improving, thank you."

"Delighted to hear it," he said as he sat. "We must all have a social evening soon, circumstances permitting. They say the infernal Swamp Angel blew up during last night's bombardment. Trouble is, the Yankees won't miss it, they have guns aplenty."

Alex took the other end of the bench. Gibbes set his tall hat between them and they exchanged brief histories. She'd been widowed in 1855.

He offered appropriate condolences. Simms Bell had passed away five years before that; she returned the condolences. Simms had divided his property between his children but left Sword Gate to Gibbes. Ouida was a war widow. Gibbes had settled her in a town house adjoining his on Legare Street. She spent a great deal of time at Prosperity Hall, he said.

"I understand you distinguished yourself on the Peninsula," Alex said. "Were you decorated?"

"Oh, no, the government can't afford medals. They established a roll of honor for each battle. My name's on the one for Seven Pines." He clasped his soft manicured hands between his knees. "Alex, I say this with all sincerity. I know I behaved badly toward you heretofore, and I regret it. I'd like to heal the breach. I'll start by reassuring you that I had nothing to do with the death of that young buck, Henry Strong."

"It's good of you to say so, but I'm afraid your actions at the time suggested otherwise."

"Maybe you saw what you wanted to see. For years I've hoped we could put the incident behind us." *Not likely,* she thought. "They say you're a tub-thumper for the black abolitionists, like those Grimké women. I hear tell you wear trousers too." Smiling, he looked at her breasts, so obviously, she couldn't fail to notice. He seized her hand. "Damn if I don't still admire you in spite of it."

Rigid, Alex said, "How is your wife?"

He jerked his hand away. "Doing well, doing well. Since we seem to be getting personal, may I say that I hope your brother won't persist in defending those niggers posing as soldiers?"

"It's his decision. I happen to agree with it."

Red-tinted shadows of evening covered them now. A salt crow scolded them from the live oak. Gibbes clapped and shouted "Hah" and the crow flew away. "Naturally you do," he said.

That angered her unreasonably; she attacked. "I saw some strange cargo on the ship that brought me here. Casks of salt pork, sent through Nassau but loaded at Philadelphia. The casks were marked care of your company, Palmetto Traders."

"I don't know a blasted thing about salt pork, I'm only an investor. I'd have to ask my partner, Mr. Folsey Lark."

"Ask him, then. Ask him why it's all right to profiteer when children are walking the streets of Charleston, starving. Or don't you see them? Do you practice looking the other way?"

He leapt up and loomed over her. "This is intolerable. I come here with the kindest of intentions and you insult me."

A vein beat in his throat. She fisted her hands in case he hit her. *Murder is murder, nothing cancels that,* she thought. She held her tongue.

"By God, Alex, you're as arrogant as ever." He put on his hat and rushed to the gate as fast as his bad leg allowed.

At the carriage his driver took his arm to assist him; Gibbes shoved the man away, pulled himself inside, and slammed the door. The last thing she saw was the golden *B* disappearing in a cloud of red dust.

She'd been a fool to lose her temper with him. She might not meet him face-to-face again, but she feared she hadn't heard the end of their quarrel. For the first time since sailing into Charleston she appreciated the danger of her position.

When Mitchell's turn came, he introduced depositions in which each of the defendants swore to his place of birth and his status as a freedman before the war. Two had signed their statements; two had made their mark. Ham rose to call a key defense witness, the warden of the city jail.

"Warden, kindly cast your thoughts back to the hour when the first captives from the Fifty-fourth Massachusetts Colored Infantry regiment were brought into Charleston and incarcerated. What was their appearance at the time?"

"Some of 'em were pretty damn—uh, pretty bedraggled and bloody."

"What were they wearing?"

The warden threw a nervous, almost apologetic look at the prosecutors. His reply was barely audible. "Uniforms."

"May I ask you to repeat that, sir?"

"Uniforms. They were wearing Yankee uniforms."

"You testify to that unequivocally?"

"I was there, I ought to know."

"The uniforms were taken away from them?"

"Taken away and burned."

"Thank you, Warden. I have no further questions."

When Mitchell rose to present the defense argument, the chamber had heated to an intolerable level—this despite a somber gray rain dripping down the windows. Mitchell began quietly. He helf the pages of his text but he knew it so well he never looked at it.

"May it please the court. The matter before the court today is one of great consternation and import for the defendants whom we represent. It is also of great consternation and import for our young country, as how you decide this case will signal to the world how the Confederate States of America, the newest member of the community of nations, conducts its foreign and military affairs."

In the back row where half a dozen reporters sat, pencils flew.

"One may make the argument that the issue before the court is a relatively simple matter of answering two questions. Are the defendants entitled to prisoner-of-war status? Or, because they bore arms and, as my learned colleague asserts, because they have black skin, are they deemed to be insurrectionary slaves by legal presumption and, thus, to be put to death?"

One of the prisoners, Kirk, swayed sideways, eyes glazing; his comrade next to him held him up.

"The gravamen of the complaint against the defendants rests on the legal presumption that they are insurrectionary slaves because of their color, and, simultaneously, because they bore arms in the recent engagement at Battery Wagner. Under the rule of law, however, a legal presumption is no more than a proposition which stands only so long as no other credible evidence supports a contradictory conclusion. Where other credible evidence is presented, the presumption fades away. In this case there is credible evidence that allows the court to draw a contradictory conclusion."

Ham's shirt, sweated through, clung to him like wet rags under his old coat. The sound of the rain tormented his nerves. The chief judge scowled as he made notes.

"Testimony in this court has clearly established that defendants wore the uniforms of Union soldiers, only to be stripped of those uniforms when they were incarcerated. As to previous conditions of servitude, if any, there is no evidence of it whatsoever—no evidence as to who their masters were, if indeed they had masters at all. My learned friend the attorney general is correct when he says that, under state law, color may be considered prima facie evidence of the status of slavery, but this evidence is rebutted by the aforementioned uniforms."

Hayne and Aldrich exchanged side glances; smugly, Ham thought. Mitchell paid no attention.

"Further, were the defendants slaves, one would believe that at least one master might have appeared to lay claim to such valuable property. No such claim has been made. Has not, then, the weak presumption arising simply from color failed logical scrutiny?

"If the court believes it must determine whether defendants are prisoners of war or insurrectionary slaves, I would urge that the legal analysis favor a finding for prisoner-of-war status. But I am also a realist. I recognize that such a finding may well be unenforceable in the current wartime environment.

"We have heard much in recent weeks about President Abraham Lincoln's declaration of 30 July stating that if any Union soldier is executed in violation of the rules of war, Northern forces will retaliate in like manner. Frankly, Mr. Chief Judge and members of this honorable court, when weighed against that declaration, the overwhelming measure of logic and prudence calls for this court to abstain from making a rush to judgment in favor of insurrectionary slave status. Any such hasty decision may well escalate the tragic loss of lives we are already suffering in the current conflict. Many brave Confederate boys languish in Union jails and stockades. Therefore I respectfully urge the court to consider another course."

In his small, precise hand, Ham wrote on his tablet. The courtroom was silent save for the rain and the ticking of a large clock. He reversed the tablet on the table so Mitchell could glance at it. He thought he detected the tiniest smile on Mitchell's face when he read the message.

The Beaufort Nine are here.

Perhaps the judges sensed it too; their expressions of vague hostility had melted into blandness; even, in the case of the chief judge, frowning attention to Mitchell's argument.

Mitchell turned his back on Hayne and Aldrich and spoke more strongly. "The matter before this court goes to the heart of how the Confederacy conducts its foreign and military affairs. I say that because the provost marshal's court is a civil court from which there is no right of appeal. Therefore a finding in this matter is final, and so, in reality, makes foreign and military policy. Under circumstances where issues of this magnitude must be addressed, I submit they must be addressed in a nonjudicial forum."

Ham thought he heard one of the reporters in the back row say, "Jehosaphat." The chief judge rapped for order and threatened to eject anyone else who spoke. Hayne was scowling at Aldrich, as though co-counsel was responsible for the sudden change of atmostphere.

"The great Virginian, Chief Justice John Marshall"—Ham could almost feel an electric charge in the room at the mention of the legendary jurist—"who shaped enlightened common law thinking just after the turn of the century, opined that the judiciary should not entertain political questions. Marbury versus Madison is the seminal case in this regard, and Chief Justice Marshall's opinion is most persuasive. It lays the foundation of the political question doctrine.

"Political questions are properly committed to the legislative and executive departments of government and surely, questions of international and military affairs are the most political of all political questions. For this reason, honorable members of the court, I submit that you have no alternative but to let the *political* arms of our government deal with this matter which is so fraught with international implications."

Ham's eye moved from judge to judge and what he saw relaxed his body to the point of limpness. On all five faces, in varying degrees, he detected relief.

"Thus," said Mitchell, rising on tiptoe, "I implore this honorable court to enter a finding of lack of jurisdiction in a nonjusticiable political question." Grandly confident, he gave the panel a respectful bow. "I thank the court for its patience and indulgence." He picked up his coattails as he took his seat, his face relaxed, untroubled.

After deliberating for an hour, the five judges declared lack of jurisdiction and dismissed the case.

Mitchell and Ham drove to the jail in a rainstorm, fortified with celebratory rounds of bad whiskey. Mitchell scrambled up the slick steps of the gallows built for the Negroes in the jailhouse yard. Hatless in the downpour, he made a trumpet with his hands. "Gentlemen on the third floor. Can you hear me? You will not stretch hemp, you are recognized as United States soldiers. You are safe."

A couple of civilians in first-floor cells screamed oaths at Mitchell while black hands reached through the bars two floors above. The Negro prisoners shouted thanks and praise. Ham reeled home to South Battery in a blurry state of triumph.

☆   ☆   ☆

Military tents were everywhere in the city, from Battery Ramsay at White Point to Washington Race Course. Drunken soldiers roamed at night with few to stop them; policemen had gone to the army. Singing, cursing, and occasional gunfire disturbed the Bell household into the small hours.

Although shelling grew desultory, the bombardment of Charleston had touched off panic. Like the Children of Israel fleeing Pharaoh's army a good part of the white population shifted north of Calhoun Street, out of range of the siege guns. The post office moved, along with medical dispensaries and many law offices including Buckles & Bell. Civilians with sufficient money boarded trains for Columbia or Charlotte, while poor people settled in squatter encampments on open ground beyond the northern defense lines. Alex and Ham agreed they wouldn't leave the house until they felt it necessary.

Gradually Alex caught up on events in wartime Charleston. She heard of a fabulous submersible attack boat named the *Hunley*. Cooper Main, one of the Mains of Mont Royal plantation, had something to do with its development. Alex had met Cooper Main at a levee years ago. He was a paradigm of Southern courtesy, and yet much like her brother: intelligent, iconoclastic, no blind follower of majority opinion.

She learned that seven of St. Michael's bells had been taken down and sent to Columbia for safekeeping. She heard about Robert Smalls, the daring slave pilot of *Planter,* a Confederate patrol boat. One night when the white officers were ashore, Smalls had put his wife and children aboard and sailed out to the Union blockade, and freedom.

Rolfe helped Alex hitch the mare to an old dog cart Ham had bought from a man who used it to hunt. The slatted box beneath the seat still smelled of dogs. She set out for the Strong house. She was astonished when she saw Marion Square. It was chockablock with army tents, lean-tos, and shelters made from packing crates. Cook fires fouled the morning air. Crude stalls served as curbstone shops.

Signs everywhere announced temporary offices. On the corner of Meeting and Henrietta above Calhoun, a canvas banner on a two-story house identified CRESCENT BANK—MARBURG BOOKS. The Marburgs had been family friends for years. She must call.

A Union shell landed south of Calhoun, over toward the Cooper. Fiery smoke billowed above rooftops. People on the street took notice but appeared unworried.

Alex turned onto John Street; memories of Henry and his family came flooding in. When she stopped in front of the house, a mangy hound darted out to snarl and snap at the mare. Hamnet Strong's courtyard was littered with garbage, old saddlery, broken furniture. In the doorway of what had been Hamnet's shop, a woman sat on a tub, her dark brown breast bared to suckle a baby. A white youth in the ragged remains of a butternut uniform hobbled outside on a crutch. He shouted at Alex. "What you staring at? Go back to your Goddamn champagne parties."

She understood the anger. Ham had described the parties and balls that had continued until the onset of the siege. "The elite went mad trying to pretend things were normal."

At an upstairs window a white woman emptied slops into the dirt near the nursing mother. Disgusted, Alex turned the dog cart around. Charleston's troubled past almost seemed attractive when measured against the present.

★ ★ ★

She called on the Marburgs next day. The bank was transacting business from flimsy tables in the parlor. Stacks of books filled the dining room. One small table held copies of the *Deutsche Zeitung*, Charleston's German newspaper. Marion Marburg and his wife received her on the upstairs landing, amid furniture arranged to imitate a parlor. All the bedrooms were occupied, Mrs. Marburg explained.

Marion Marburg, grandson of the Hessian soldier and present head of the family, was in his late thirties. He had his mother's tawny coloring and the characteristic carroty hair and blue eyes of the family, but not the usual stoutness. He reminded Alex of a long-legged heron. And he was tall, one of the few men Alex could talk to without looking down.

Marion and his wife, Esther, of the Charleston Cohens, had four sons at home: Joshua, Isaiah, Daniel, and Malachi, all under twelve. A fifth boy, Jeremiah, had died in a typhoid epidemic. Daniel and Malachi raced around the upstairs while Esther served tea brewed from the leaves and twigs of yaupon holly. "It has a poor taste. I'm so sorry," she said with a sigh.

Marion's oldest sister, Helena, had turned into a gray-faced spinster. In Helena Alex saw a reflection of herself: a lonely middle-aged woman slipping downhill to the grave. She was relieved when Helena excused herself and went downstairs to watch over the books.

As for Marion's other sisters, Sophia was in Chicago, married to a rabbi. Margaretta had died of childbed fever; two daughters and her husband, superintendent of a gunpowder factory, resided in Augusta. Gerda, the youngest, was in Paris, studying painting. "Living a Bohemian life of which her mother strongly disapproves," Marion said.

Malachi and Daniel fell out the door of a bedroom, pounding each other as they rolled on the carpet. Marion leapt up, spilling tea on his trousers. "Boys, stop that instantly." They did, but each blurted an accusation of the other. Marion sent them off with a promise of punishment later. Wistful Esther sighed again. "Living with four boys is taxing. The oldest bullies the next youngest, and so on down the line. If only we had one girl to set an example of gentility."

"*Where am I? Where is everyone?*" The cry made Alex jump. Marion whispered, "My mother."

"Naomi? Oh, may I say hello?"

"Alas, she wouldn't recognize you. She came into her dotage prematurely. She requires constant care." When Naomi wailed again, Esther disappeared into a bedroom.

Alex and Marion discussed the war. He thought Jefferson Davis dictatorial and inept. "The Confederacy's going bankrupt because Davis and the Congress refuse to tax the citizens. The war is financed with bonds whose worth steadily declines. I know the secretary of the treasury, Mr. Memminger, he formerly practiced law here. He is a weak man, and stubborn. That is a particular failing of us Germans. Early in the war Memminger had an opportunity to sell cotton for a massive infusion of capital. He would not do it, but he had no alternate plan. At that time I began moving gold to Bermuda."

"Because the South will lose?"

"Inevitably. I would hasten the day if I could. This is my city. I love it as my father and grandfather did, but I'm not blind to its errant ways and fatal mistakes. The war, fomented on these very streets, began with foolish illusions. Now it goes badly, and human nature reigns. We live amid frightened politicians and coldhearted buccaneers. Sorrowful times. It's grand to have your company again, but are you sure you want to remain in Charleston?"

"This is my home," Alex said. Which wasn't an answer. She didn't have one.

★　★　★

Toward dawn on October 1 a volley of gunfire and a crash of glass brought Alex and Ham downstairs at a run. In the ground-floor office a jar stuffed with flaming rags had set fire to the oval rug. Choking on the smoke, brother and sister rolled up the rug and smothered the flames. Ham threw the carpet out the broken window and craned around to see the facade.

"They fired at least six rounds into the house."

"A reprisal for defending the soldiers?"

"I would say yes, but Mitchell's had no such trouble."

"Then who would do such a thing?"

"I'll write one name at the head of the list. Folsey Lark."

"Because of the trial?"

"Perhaps, but I don't think so. Something happened between our families long ago. I'm not sure what it was, but I've known for years that the Larks feel great enmity toward us. Folsey is dangerous because he's duplicitous. At heart I think he's cowardly—he never dirties his hands but hires others. He and Gibbes are alike in that respect, though I consider Folsey the more violent of the two. You might load one of those pistols."

"Already done. It's underneath my bed."

They exchanged bleak looks. If they hadn't been isolated before, they were now.

★　★　★

On the night of October 5 a fifty-foot steam-driven boat crept out of the harbor. Most of *David*'s hull was submerged. A torpedo bobbed at the end of a ten-foot boom on the bow.

David approached the Union ironclad *New Ironsides* and rammed her. The explosion sent up an immense geyser of fire and water. *David* was swamped but managed to steam away to safety. The disabled iron-clad had to withdraw from the blockade. Charleston enjoyed a brief euphoria and contemplated an amazing new kind of warfare.

☆　☆　☆

A week later Cassandra woke from an afternoon nap and said she'd like to see the garden. Alex helped her comb her hair and tie the ribbons of her robe. Cassandra was pale but cheerful as she clung to Alex and took the stairs one deliberate step at a time.

Rolfe was weeding in the garden. He snatched off his cap. "Afternoon, ma'am," he said to each of the women. He'd listened to Alex playing her banjo twice more, asking politely each time. Music was mellowing him ever so little.

"What a glorious day," Cassandra said. And it was: mild and dry, with light airs off the harbor to dispel insects. Sulphur butterflies sailed in and out of shafts of light falling through the branches of the live oak. Any child of the Low Country could tell from the sun's altered position that winter would soon come calling.

Alex settled her mother on the garden bench. "If you're not warm enough, I'll fetch a blanket."

Cassandra smiled. "Always worrying. I'm very comfortable."

"Then I'll work a bit. I'm planting four-o'clock. You don't wait years for the blooms."

"*Mirabilis jalapa*. In my time we called four-o'clock the Marvel of Peru because of so many colors from a single plant. I shall sit here next year at this time and enjoy the beautiful blooms."

Alex was delighted by her mother's good spirits. She pulled up her skirts and set to work with a trowel, looking up frequently to check on Cassandra. In half an hour she had all the seedlings planted where they would catch the sun. Cassandra had fallen into a doze, reclining against the iron bench with her mouth open. Time to take her upstairs. Alex brushed dirt from her skirt, stepped to the bench. "Mother?"

Her hand flew to her lips. She felt for a pulse. Cassandra's heart had stopped.

58

The Good Seed

Snoo Bell sent a slave to deliver a maudlin letter of condolence, written on the back of wallpaper. From Ouida they heard nothing. Cassandra went to her rest beside Edgar in the shadow of St. Michael's black steeple. Above the steeple clock, a hundred and fifty feet in the air, lookouts with telescopes kept watch on Union activity around the harbor.

Few attended the burial: the Marburgs and their unruly sons; Cedric Buckles and his wife with an infant in her arms; the widow Letty Porcher-Jones; a handful of tradespeople and two elderly ladies Alex didn't know. Of the sparsity of mourners Ham said, "She lived too long. Most of her friends have died."

Alex was uncomfortable in a boned corset and layers of crinoline under a heavy dress of black bombazine. The crinolines were hooped from the knees down. The steel rings hit her legs at every other step. A Negro seamstress had sewn the mourning garb. The price amounted to banditry, but Alex couldn't bury her mother wearing Mrs. Bloomer's pantaloons. She was not that disrespectful of the traditions of death in Charleston.

Great Michael tolled as the gravediggers threw the first shovels of earth on the casket. The solemn moment was disturbed by a company of old men marching by, accompanied by a thumping bass drum. Gaudy letters painted on the drumhead identified the GEN. HAGOOD CITY GUARD. The decrepit volunteers sang, but not in unison. *"Hurrah, hurrah, for Southern rights hurrah."*

Ham drew Alex aside when the mourners had gone. "You're free now. There's nothing to hold you here. I can manage by myself."

"I admit I've been thinking about it."

He put on his tall hat. Slender and stoop shouldered as he was, he resembled Lincoln. He slipped his arm around her waist. "I know you despise this place."

It was true, yet in a small and contradictory corner of herself it wasn't. Coming home had awakened good memories along with the bad. The suffering she saw around her, the suffering of ordinary people of both races, tore her heart.

＊　＊　＊

They arrived at South Battery to find a funerary wreath of sweet grass, painted black, nailed to the door on the piazza. Ham touched the wreath.

"Paint's still wet. This was not sent in sympathy."

When he found Rolfe he said, "Burn it."

＊　＊　＊

It was sullen, uneducated Rolfe who planted the seed. It took root and grew in the teeming streets, where growing numbers of black refugees roamed alone or in ragged families. They huddled in alleys with their few possessions carried in sacks or wrapped in rags. They crowded rat-infested tenements near the Cooper River piers, sometimes ten or fifteen to a room, Alex heard. Were they freedmen or runaways? Did it matter? All their eyes had the same look of hunger, bewilderment, and fear.

One grizzled grandfather approached Alex with a child on his shoulder. The child sucked her thumb and hid her face. What Alex took to be rat bites marked the little girl's arms. The old man showed Alex a cardboard square with an address scrawled on it.

"Ma'am, can y'all read this? We been walkin' from Walterboro four days and Addie's near to dyin'. They say food's to be had at that place."

Alex gave directions. The old man's effusive thanks touched her. That night she opened her small trunk, lit a candle, and withdrew her late husband's Bible. To justify the risks he took, he'd often quoted Christ's words in the thirteenth chapter of Matthew: *He that soweth the good seed is the Son of man.*

She closed her eyes and prayed for guidance, as she hadn't prayed in a long time.

☆ ☆ ☆

Next evening she and Ham sat down to supper together. Candles were reflected on the surface of the table she'd cleaned and polished. The meal consisted of greens with a few precious bits of pork mixed in, and what Ham called secession bread, a stone-hard loaf baked with rice flour. She revealed her idea while they ate.

"I would teach a few Negroes privately. Teach them their letters, and rudimentary reading. If I could help only a handful, it would be a start."

"A start down a very hazardous road. Why do you want to do such a thing?"

"Someone must. Can you imagine what it would be like to be free but unable to read a simple contract, or a circular offering jobs?"

"Dear sister. Your idealism will get you killed one of these days."

"There are worse ways to leave this earth. William taught me that."

"We know we have enemies in Charleston. Wouldn't you rather go back to the North?"

"Sometimes I would, but there's no longer a need to preach abolition, the Union's fighting a war for it and it will come. I could be useful here."

"Where would you conduct such a school?"

"Why not Bell's Bridge? It's virtually shut down."

"And dilapidated."

"I'll find money for repairs."

"I can't dip into the law firm's cash box again."

"Let me worry about it."

"Can I possibly dissuade you from this?"

"No."

"Then you might ask Marion to give you a loan. He didn't send all his gold reserves to Bermuda. I do wonder whether you can find pupils. Wouldn't Negroes be too frightened of punishment if you were discovered?"

"Surely some are braver than others."

"You do have a stubborn streak," he said, not unkindly. "I retire in defeat."

"Thank you. Charleston will fall one of these days, and the Confederacy. We'll have to put this country back together."

He didn't argue with that.

☆ ☆ ☆

To lure Rolfe she sat in the garden picking out a slow version of "All Quiet Along the Potomac Tonight," a Union song; a lot of Southerners liked it too. Presently Rolfe appeared in the twilight shadows, almost without a sound. He'd been repairing the mare's stall in the small stable building. "All right if I sit a while and listen, ma'am?"

"Yes, if you first allow me to tell you about an idea I have."

Cautious but curious, he sat down on the piazza steps.

"It's a school. I want to teach a few of your people to read, to prepare them for the jubilee."

Rolfe chewed his lip. "We talked 'bout this before. Nigger could get punished bad for trying to read."

"That's true. We'd keep the school secret from everyone, even owners like your Miss Letty."

"Cost money, this school?"

"No." Her callused fingertips brushed the strings, the notes softly ringing in the air. A whippoorwill vanished into shrubbery to nest for the night. "Would you come to the school, Rolfe?"

After a silence: "Guess I would if you let me."

She jumped off the bench and ran to him. "You'll be my first pupil." She pulled him into a hug.

Perplexed and alarmed, he quickly separated himself. He didn't know what to make of a white lady touching him. Alex ran back to the bench to give him another song. He asked for "Lorena." Soldiers and families on both sides liked the sweet, sad ballad. She played and sang it for him as the evening darkened.

59

Conversations at a Grave

At that same hour the President of the Confederacy was far from Richmond, touring the war front. He'd gone first to Tennessee, to settle differences between two of his generals, Bragg and Longstreet. From there he traveled on to north Georgia, Alabama, and his home state of Mississippi. In early November his private train brought him to Savannah, then South Carolina.

Jefferson Davis hadn't visited Charleston since attending Calhoun's funeral, nor had his popularity increased there. If anything, the opposite was true; a substantial and vocal anti-Davis faction existed in every state of the Confederacy. Beauregard's disaffection was well known, and the animus of Robert Barnwell Rhett, publisher of the *Mercury*, was constantly on view in the columns of his newspaper. Rhett had never gotten over his rejection for a cabinet post. He characterized Davis as "perverse and incompetent," not to say "vindictive, arrogant, and egotistical." Because of Davis's West Point credentials and military experience in Mexico, Rhett said he thought himself a better strategist than his generals, including Lee.

Artillery on the Neck fired salvos to salute the presidential train when it was still a good way off. A friendly depot crowd, largely white, waved handkerchiefs and placards with messages of welcome. The November air was cool, ripe with autumn smoke and the eternal stink of the mud flats.

When the President stepped down from his car, General Beauregard greeted him with formal politeness. He joined Davis in an open carriage, the first of four in a procession guarded by cavalry and followed by a German band blaring "Dixie's Land." Few remembered that the South's anthem was written as a Northern minstrel tune, or that Lincoln Republicans had marched to it in the campaign of 1860.

The carriages traveled slowly south along Meeting. Large crowds shouted and clapped. Bunting and flags decorated buildings even in the burnt district. The carriages arrived at Broad and Meeting. At least a thousand people waited under garlands of laurel strung above the intersection. Alex was in the crowd with her brother and Marion Marburg. She drew hostile looks from a few who recognized her.

Alex had only seen pictures of Jefferson Davis. In person she found him unimpressive. He was a pale, cadaverous man with a tuft of chin whiskers, a high forehead, and fair hair going gray. His black suit was ordinary and looked cheap. She'd read that he was a veritable museum of maladies: neuralgia, malaria, an ulcerated cornea, and heaven knew what else. When the President turned his head to acknowledge one section of the crowd, sunshine striking his left eye made it glisten like a milky marble.

Davis spoke from the courthouse steps. Beauregard stood stiff and resplendent behind him; the double row of buttons on his cadet-gray tunic shone. He stared at the back of Davis's head as the President began his address.

Davis commended Charleston's military defenders, and its citizens, for resisting the enemy onslaught. He praised Maj. Stephen Elliott, commandant of Fort Sumter, who stood next to Beauregard, his military chapeau under his arm. The general was frowning at the sky.

"Charleston must not and I believe will not be taken by the enemy." Applause. "Were it to prove otherwise, I trust yours will be the glory that I desired for my town of Vicksburg upon her surrender. I wished for the whole to be left a mass of rubble." A hush then; he was speaking of the end. The unthinkable.

"Alas, it did not happen. Charleston's fate must be different. If there should be a tragic outcome to your struggle, you face a choice. Will you leave Charleston naked prey for Yankee spoilers, or a heap of ruins?"

A man shouted, "Ruins." A woman near the courthouse steps echoed it. "Ruins." Soon the crowd was clapping and chanting. *"Ruins, ruins, ruins, ruins."* Alex didn't join in, nor did her companions.

At the conclusion of the speech the crowd disbanded and the President moved to his carriage. General Beauregard said good-bye and left with his aide, presumably to attend to duties. Marion said, "The general looked daggers at Davis, did you notice?"

"Davis didn't recognize Beauregard by name," Ham said. "Just that one reference to 'our commanding general.' I imagine the rift between the two just became a chasm."

The German band serenaded the carriage as it rolled away to King Street. Davis would stay at the home of former governor Aiken while inspecting Charleston's defenses. A well-publicized banquet was scheduled for the evening, courtesy of Palmetto Traders. Guests would enjoy boned turkey stuffed with truffles, baked and fried local oysters, tomatoes and peppers and other scarce vegetables, and quantities of Madeira "assured to be more than fifty years old." Mr. Folsey Lark and his partner, Mr. Gibbes Bell, had been mentioned along with the menu in every newspaper but the *Mercury,* which printed nothing about the event. Marion planned to attend the banquet with Esther. Ham wasn't invited.

Alex walked with her brother and the banker as far as City Market, then left them. She wanted to think about what needed to be done at Bell's Bridge.

She strolled east to Church Street, then turned south again, past a work crew filling a shell crater. She didn't notice a large coach stopped opposite St. Philip's until she was almost upon it. The coach, shiny black with three glass windows on each side, was a conveyance of someone wealthy. She'd seen similar ones in Washington; they cost five hundred to a thousand dollars.

A Negro held the horse's headstall and watched the sky as though expecting a fatal round to come whizzing in at any moment. Alex greeted him with a nod and a smile. Inside the iron fence of the burying ground someone was speaking. She recognized Ouida, kneeling beside a Spartan grave, a rectangle of brick with a small marble slab laid in the middle.

Ouida's enormous hooped skirt, white once, was yellowed by time. So were her white mesh gloves and a white half-veil that reached the tip of her nose. Springy English curls, long out of fashion, dangled below her ears. Scarlet lip rouge and an excess of face powder gave her a grotesque, clownlike look. Rimless oval pince-nez lay against a round chain holder pinned to her bodice.

Alex spoke softly to the driver. "I know that lady. I knew her husband too. Did they bring his remains back from Virginia?"

"No, missus, he's buried up there someplace. That grave belongs to Mr. Calhoun."

"John Calhoun?"

"Yes'm. Mistress comes here least once a month."

Dogs yapped in the distance. Clearly vexed, Ouida shook her finger at the unresponsive person under the sod. Alex shivered and started away.

"Cousin? Is that you?"

Ouida came out the gate sideways, her immense hoops tilted up to ease the passage. She pulled a fine gold chain from the holder on her bosom, set the pince-nez in place. Her watery blue eyes enlarged behind the lenses. "I hardly expected to find you still in Charleston."

"I have things to occupy me." Alex spoke carefully, pleasantly, so as not to excite or antagonize her cousin. "I was very sorry to learn of Dr. Hayward's passing."

"He doesn't deserve sympathy," Ouida said with a toss of her curls. "He tried to help a Yankee and God punished him. The Yankees are devils. Lincoln is Satan."

"Ouida, I think it would be best if we didn't discuss—"

"I fear the Yankees have my son a prisoner. I've not heard from him in months. Every Yankee should burn in hell. They brought all this misery on us."

Alex couldn't help a retort. "The Yankees aren't solely responsible for the war. Charleston fired the first shot."

"And all you can do is gloat over what's happening to us."

"Look here, Ouida. I feel sorry for everyone in Charleston, including you. No sane person wishes suffering on others."

"You make me sick with your piety. How dare you come back to taunt and insult us."

"I'm doing neither. This is my home as much as it is yours. I came back because my Mother was ill."

"She deserved to die. She raised a Yankee whore."

Alex slapped her, then instantly wished she could roll back time and cancel the mistake. Ouida touched her powdered cheek. "I can have you charged with assault."

Sorrow melted Alex's anger. "Oh, Ouida. Haven't you vented enough hatred for one lifetime?"

"No, not yet. Mr. Calhoun says you and your kind must never be forgiven. You want to destroy the South with your insufferable righteousness. He told me that today." Ouida's high, hectoring voice attracted attention from passersby. The Negro driver, torn between mortification and fright, looked wildly up and down Church Street.

Ouida picked up her skirts and swept to the coach. The driver jumped to the box, jerked the whip from its socket, and flicked the croup of the horse.

That evening Alex described the encounter to Ham. "You called her unbalanced. If she talks to someone who's been dead since 1850, she's more than that. She's a madwoman."

"Yes, that fact is widely recognized but largely unspoken. Ouida's wealth and position protect her. Best to avoid her."

"I fully intend to do so. My God, Ham, how many enemies do we have in this town?"

"Many more than I'd like. Care to change your mind about the school?"

A Union round crashed in the distance. "No. People like Folsey and Ouida don't own Charleston. It's our city as well as theirs. I won't run."

60

Prisoners

In the spring of 1863 Richard Riddle and Cal Bell hoped for parole from Fort Delaware under the cartel for general exchange of Union and Confederate prisoners. It was a man-for-man exchange, with tables of equivalencies for different ranks. Richard, a captain, was worth six privates, Cal, a second lieutenant, three.

In May their hopes were dashed. Largely at the instigation of Lincoln's secretary of war, Mr. Stanton, the cartel collapsed. Stanton and General Grant objected to continually resupplying the Confederacy with men likely to violate parole and return to the fight.

During the summer all Confederate officers in the North were loaded on the cars and moved to Johnson's Island Military Prison in Sandusky Bay, a mile from the shore of Lake Erie. A Union sloop continually patrolled in the bay with guns trained on the prison.

"Well, here we are again," soldiers liked to say when confronted with a circumstance no different from their last. The expression was never more relevant than when the two South Carolinians arrived at the prison compound. The same fierce winds blew through gaps in the barracks walls. The same Lincoln hirelings guarded the deadline. The same putrid rations—wormy bread, beans, occasionally some pickled pork—were distributed at noon, one meal every twenty-four hours. The same chinch bugs and grayback lice deviled unwashed flesh. The same sinks overflowed with waste and bred plump wharf rats. Prisoners caught the rats, skinned, and roasted them. Richard was damned if he'd eat rat. Cal said it was passable fare.

By this time Richard and Cal were no longer fresh fish but salt fish—prison veterans. On their second night at Johnson's Island muggers from the next barracks swarmed in to raid for possessions. It was a curiosity of prison life that guards often overlooked knives belonging to inmates. Richard kept a six-inch folding Bowie hidden in his pocket. One of the muggers got a feel of it, buried in his thigh. The raid ended abruptly.

Cards and dice helped pass the time. Richard never gambled. Surviving day to day was enough of a gambling game for any man. You wagered your stamina against smallpox, and pneumonia, and typhoid fever. If you lost, the good men who'd organized the prisoner YMCA carried your corpse away.

Northern winter closed down. The wind howled. The temperature stayed below zero for days. A wood-burning stove in each barracks did little to alleviate suffering at twenty below. Prisoners hacked up chairs and legs of bunks and fed the pieces to the stove. At night, when Richard put his canteen under his head for a pillow, the contents froze.

Thick ice on the bay drove the guard sloop away and encouraged escape attempts. Richard was asked to join one in late December. Wary of the leader's intelligence, he declined. It was well he did; three of the four who scaled the wall and fled across the lake came back in chains, hands and feet frozen. One died in the prison hospital. The leader had perished when his pursuers put two bullets in his back. They left him for the fish when the ice melted.

Richard had seen snow in Columbia, but never in such heavy quantities as fell on Johnson's Island in the winter of 1863–1864. He engaged in a new sport, snowball fights. His bones creaked, but his ferocity and his throwing arm quickly raised him to the rank of commander of the Blue Army. It took the field against the Red Army in exchanges of icy missiles that lasted two and three hours, until the warriors fell back, too cold and exhausted to continue.

A sadistic guard observed Richard and Cal's friendship, accused them of being lovers. Both of them considered it an insult to their honor. Southern men could be friends without that kind of thing, although there was plenty of it in the prison. Strange whispers and groans often disturbed the night.

Richard sharpened his folding Bowie on a borrowed whetstone. One bitter February morning the offending guard was found stiff in the snow with his startled eyes bulging and his throat slashed.

Questioned, Richard said he and Cal had played cards until dawn. Others in their barracks swore to it. Richard and Cal were spared transfers to an eight-room death house where convicted prisoners lived with a sixty-four-pound iron ball on a six-foot ankle chain until they were hung.

Richard went back to carving miniature soldiers. Cal was much better at whittling. His canoes and little sailing ships rigged with sticks and thread sold well as souvenirs in Sandusky shops. The money was returned to the prisoners by the fair-minded prison commandant. Cal spent his on whiskey smuggled in by the guards. He drank steadily, a sip at a time, from first light until dark. Richard hated to see it.

Richard lived for an end to the war and a return to his native state and his wife, Loretta. Then, God willing, he'd never have to look at another Yankee face, never have to speak to a Yankee or do business with one. He'd go home hating Yankees. Cal just wanted to go home to some better whiskey.

61

Dark December

Adah Samples took a colored-only car of the Northeastern Railroad up to Florence. Adah's mother, widowed in the summer, had gone to live with her brother on his farm. Adah was depressed to see so many people following the train on the road beside the right-of-way. On horseback and on foot, in buggies and wagons, they were fleeing the endangered coast for Columbia or Flat Rock or some other refuge.

Adah, in her late twenties, was handsomer than ever. She had a resolute eye and a ripe body men found desirable. It belonged to Folsey, though of late they'd hit a rough patch. Folsey was inattentive, short-tempered. Palmetto Traders had suffered a huge loss in October when the blockade runner *General Bee* broke apart in a coastal storm. The firm lost six hundred bales of cotton bound for Liverpool.

The blockade had all but closed Charleston Harbor. The one Atlantic port remaining open was Wilmington, North Carolina, a hazardous twenty miles up the Cape Fear River, past the Union guns at Fort Fisher. Lately Folsey spent all his time in Wilmington. He'd been there the past four weeks.

Adversity had a way of weakening and defeating some, but not Adah. Folsey's recent behavior only toughened her resolve to preserve the relationship. He wasn't the kindest of human beings, but he was a stallion in bed, and a richer man than she had a right to wish for. He might be pleased if she demonstrated her loyalty with a surprise visit.

After she left her mother at her uncle's farm, she went to Florence and bought a ticket for the eighty-mile trip on the Wilmington & Manchester. The ticket agent asked for $12.75. Adah calculated quickly. "Fifteen cents a mile. That's outrageous."

"Tell it to Jeff Davis. What's a nigger got to say about it anyway? There's one coach, be sure you sit in the last three rows."

From the separate shanty reserved for Negroes she watched workmen piling fragrant sacks of coffee beans on a flatcar. Blockade bounty, surely. Her train arrived. Five miles up the line she asked the conductor why they were traveling so slowly.

"Can't go more'n fifteen miles an hour. Track's all run down. Can't be repaired, mills that made rails make armor plate now. South's falling apart. You be careful in Wilmington, missy. Meanest city in the Confederacy these days." He squeezed her arm and bumped her breast with his knuckle. "I like that pretty yellow turban."

They arrived after dark. The Wilmington waterfront was unattractive and noisy, the piers crowded with ships, and the streets full of refuse and wandering sailors. Downriver, along the east shore, low clouds glowed red. Saltworks, Folsey said; the kettles boiled day and night to evaporate seawater.

Groghouses filled the night with raucous voices and tinkly music. A poster advertised Sunday cockfights. Adah climbed steep and muddy Market Street to the boardinghouse where Palmetto Traders rented rooms. She carried her portmanteau up one flight, shivering with anticipation as she raised her yellow glove to knock. Telltale noises stayed her hand.

She wrenched the knob, threw the door open. Light from the hallway gas mantle revealed a naked woman prone on the bed, her hips elevated; Adah couldn't see much more than her enormous white hams. Folsey knelt behind her, jaybird naked except for his favorite tasseled Hessian boots.

"Told you to lock the damn door," the woman said.

Folsey snatched his spectacles from the bedside table. Folsey was forty-seven, his soft good looks fading, his blond hair thinning. He peered at Adah through large square bifocals with ugly cement lines where the lenses joined.

"What in Christ's name are you doing here?"

"I wanted to surprise you. Obviously I did."

"There's an empty room two doors down. Wait for me there."

She stamped her foot. "I will not. You said you loved me, Folsey Lark. In July you said we'd be married."

"Well, I say a lot of things. I'm damn mad about this, Adah. You have a lot of brass, stalking me like some damn spy." The woman covered herself while Folsey stamped across the room, his shrunken manhood dangling.

"I reckon it's time we called a halt. Go on home to Charleston. Haul your things out of the cottage. I get back and find you still there, I'll burn it down around you."

More angry than frightened, Adah fairly spat at him. "Bastard. That's all you are, a no-good cheating fickle white bastard."

The woman giggled; even Folsey was amused. "I do claim certain parts of that title, yes. Now get out of here before I hurt you."

Adah stood fast. Folsey took a menacing step, raised his voice. "I said go."

She ran down the stairs. On lower Market Street she rented a room at a seedy colored hotel, bolted the door, and threw herself on the bed. She cried awhile, then roused at the sound of tapping at her door. A rough voice whispered in some strange language. Sailors from all over the world gathered in Wilmington.

"Whoever you are, you'd better leave me alone. I have a gun." Evidently her English communicated; he went away.

Adah sat up, rubbed her eyes. This would pass. Folsey had clipped her tail feathers but not forever. She'd survive, without charity from her uncle and her mother. The yellow bird would fly again, see if she didn't.

☆ ☆ ☆

"Oh, there's a nigger watching the house," Ouida cried.

She stood by a window of the sitting room at Sword Gate. Gibbes had sent a trustworthy slave to bring Ouida to town for Christmas eve. She hadn't visited Charleston since meeting Alex. Gibbes had convinced her that going to Mr. Calhoun's grave was unsafe; Union shelling of the city had resumed.

Snoo rushed to Ouida's side. "Please be careful with the candle, dear." Ouida held it too near the draperies, and her hand shook. At least she was wearing her glasses.

Snoo lifted the drapery for a clear view of Legare Street, where weeds grew and broken glass lay like scattered diamonds. Ouida whispered, "It's Virtue, I know it. His left ear's missing." She lived with the memory of Lydia's body crushing her to the heart-pine floor, the warm blood bathing both of them. Ouida still washed her hands and face several times a day.

Snoo gently pried the candle from Ouida's fingers, blew it out. "Look again, dear. It's just a boy, with both his ears." And already gone into the night.

With a vague, helpless gesture Ouida said, "But I was sure. I dream of him all the time, you know." Twice, she thought she spied her mother's slayer lurking on the grounds of Prosperity Hall. Each time she sent slaves to catch the man, and each time they came back to hesitantly say they'd found no one. Not even footprints. Ouida reacted by calling them liars and locking herself in her room.

Snoo settled Ouida in a chair by the Christmas tree, a volunteer cedar cut from the sandy soil of Malvern. Snoo had decorated the fluffy branches with ribbons, popcorn strings, white mistletoe berries, and an engraving of Robert E. Lee in place of a star. She offered Ouida a plate. "Have some of my special fruitcake, dear." The wartime cake was made with dried cherries, dark-blue whortleberries, and watermelon rind. Ouida hated it.

Gibbes came in with a bag of striped candy sticks, surely from one of his ships; there was no candy in the South. He presented each woman with a set of silver-chased Parisian hairbrushes, then showed his small gift to himself, a box of imported fishhooks and sinkers. "The niggers can go down to the harbor and catch us a char or a porgy for dinner." Few people fished in metal-starved Charleston anymore; hooks and sinkers couldn't be found.

A houseman served snifters of brandy. It was French, not the vile ersatz made with sweet potatoes. Sipping it calmed Ouida. They saw her up to bed at half past nine, then sat on a love seat glumly discussing her mental state. They agreed that the only remedy for it was a continuing supply of spirits and opiate tonics.

Shortly before 1:00 A.M. violent explosions shook the house. Gibbes flung himself out of bed. "The damned villains are firing at us on Christmas." Under the door a ruddy light shimmered. He pulled on his fine London dressing gown of orange silk. "Snoo, wake up, there's a fire."

He ran with the gown flapping around his bare ankles. He discovered Ouida in the lower hall, an old woman's lace-trimmed cap pulled down low on her forehead. She had another candle, and no glasses. The Christmas tree was ablaze.

"It was an accident, Gibbes. I heard a noise. I stumbled."

A burly houseman ran from the pantry where he slept. "Luke, fetch a bucket of water," Gibbes ordered. "Then go into the street and sound the alarm."

Snoo came down in a robe of vanilla-colored brocade. Gibbes threw the bucket on the fire. Not nearly enough. In Legare Street, Luke hallooed and shouted while Gibbes pulled furniture away from the fire. Smoke thickened. One wall had already caught, devouring a Watteau reproduction Snoo prized. Gibbes, Luke, and another houseman kept a bucket brigade going until the fire company arrived. By then the ceiling was burning, and two walls and part of the floor.

Gibbes, Snoo, and Ouida retreated to a safe spot while the firemen dragged their hose through the front door and pumped water. All the volunteers except the man in charge were colored, replacements for whites gone off to fight. At least the Charleston Negroes were performing a useful service instead of taking advantage of the wartime confusion. Half the slaves at Prosperity Hall had run away. At Malvern every last one was gone, making it necessary to close the house.

The water brought the fire under control, then put it out. In the dining room Snoo wept over the smoke and water damage. Ouida wandered aimlessly, getting in the way but never apologizing. Gibbes caught the arm of the white fireman.

"I know you."

"Yessir, Mr. Bell. Corporal Plato Hix."

"The Peninsula," Gibbes said with a sudden pained look, quickly gone.

"That's right, sir." Plato Hix was a stout chap with a round, bland face and large dark eyes. He seemed nervous. He showed his right hand, stubs of scar tissue instead of a thumb and index finger. "Took a ball at Seven Pines and couldn't rightly fire a musket afterward. They sent me home." He touched his forehead and turned away.

A few minutes later he returned to Gibbes and said, "Fire's out. Believe it's all right we go now."

"Our people will clean up in the morning." He saw no point in thanking the colored volunteers for doing what they were supposed to do.

Hix said, "They fired on St. Philip's tonight. Scored a hit, I seen it when we ran over here."

"Damn Yankees have no respect for the house of God. No respect for anything, including holy days."

"Yessir, seems so, don't it?" Plato slipped out the door, his boots splashing in the water escaping over the sill.

★　★　★

Trudging beside the pumper, Plato Hix thanked his blessed Lord that he'd managed to keep his composure with Mr. Gibbes Bell. He knew a secret about that gentleman, a secret so dire, he'd shared it with no one, not even his wife, Mary. If Mr. Gibbes Bell only knew how he'd trembled when the fire company was called to Sword Gate.

From the Peninsula he'd traveled all the way home to Charleston, a long, arduous journey on foot, because Mary and their two little ones waited there. Mary was a free mulatto woman of good character, though poverty and the difficulties of marriage to a white man had worn her down and blurred her good looks.

A comet's tail of sparks streaked overhead. The shell crashed into a wall of St. Michael's and exploded; they had another fire to chase. A hell of a Christmas, sure enough. Old Charleston couldn't stand many more like it.

62

1864

"Can you cut one of these from a piece of wood?" Alex showed her pencil sketch.

Rolfe jutted his lower lip. "Looks like a paddle to beat on somebody."

"Nonsense, it isn't nearly big enough. This is drawn to size."

"Then what is it?"

"A hornbook, a very old way of learning your letters. They're pasted here." She touched the large vertical rectangle with a narrower handle at its lower edge. "Usually there's a thin piece of deer or elk horn to protect the letters, but we'll have to do without that."

Reversal of Rolfe's sullen air was immediate. "Know just where there's a scrap of cypress. Have it done for you late today."

On a precious square of writing paper wheedled out of her brother, Alex inked the alphabet, three or four letters in each row. She separated a wafer of sealing wax from a letter of Drew's, one of many she'd saved. She thought he'd be pleased to see it used this way.

Rolfe brought her the cypress paddle as the January sun was going down. She melted the wafer and dripped wax on the corners and the center of the wooden rectangle. She pressed the paper in place and held it. You couldn't buy glue, not even for postage stamps, which had all but disappeared.

Rolfe studied at the homemade hornbook. "I seen all those letters in

Miss Letty's newspapers, but I don't know what they are or how you s'posed say 'em."

"You know more than you think. Pull up that footstool." Seated beside her, he watched as she pointed. "This is the letter *a*." She sounded it. "Say it." He did. "This is the letter *b*. Like the bee that stings. Say it." He did. Her work had begun.

✯ ✯ ✯

In the attic she found a boyhood slate of Ham's and a little muslin sack of crumbly chalk. Among the offerings in the dining room at Marion Marburg's house she discovered a worn copy of *McGuffey's Eclectic Primer*. Reverend McGuffey taught at Miami College in Oxford, Ohio. A Cincinnati firm printed his series of instructional readers, literally by the thousands; parents, teachers, and the clergy approved of their moralistic approach. Children learned to read with uplifting poems and stories that inspired proper behavior. She asked Marion's sister Helena to watch for a *First Eclectic Reader* as well as a *New England Primer*, an older but no less popular beginner's text.

Little cargo had come through Bell's Bridge in the last two years, and none since the preceding autumn. Planks spongy with rot sank under her feet when she went to inspect. The old storage sheds for rice and indigo were too large for her purpose. So was the scale house. The small kitchen building was ideal. She opened the rusty padlock and immediately stepped back, fanning the air to clear the fetid smell. Squirrels had gnawed through the eaves to make nests of twigs and Spanish moss. Her own Augean stable.

She and Rolfe labored for a week, sweeping and scrubbing, then applying a watery whitewash to interior walls. At one point Rolfe looked like a white-face minstrel. When Alex held up a scrap of mirror, he laughed with great glee. He'd done well with his instruction in a short time. He knew his alphabet and could sound out simple sentences from McGuffey's primer. *It is so. On we go. I am he.*

As soon as the kitchen building was furnished with an assortment of rickety chairs and wooden boxes, and Ham's slate and chalk, she went prospecting for other students. Marion Marburg's elderly cook had twin nephews, fat little boys named Washington and Jackson. The cook's husband won their mother's consent and dragged the reluctant nine-year-olds to Bell's Bridge one evening. He sat in a corner during the first hour-long lesson. He thwacked heads when either twin showed inattention or disrespect. The following week the boys came back without the older man.

At the end of every lesson Alex sang and played the banjo. The boys liked the music as much as Rolfe did, especially "The Camptown Races." The instruction took hold gradually. One evening Jackson, the quicker of the twins, surprised her by running in and exclaiming, "I know where they sell beer. *B-e-e-r*. I read the word on a sign, what do you think of that?"

Alex flung her arms around him. "I think it's wonderful." How re-markable and thrilling—almost forty-nine, and she finally had children to teach.

☆　☆　☆

All this went on against the continuing drumbeat of war. Fear and privation stalked Charleston. Empty bellies growled louder; resentments grew, directed chiefly at the government. A letter in the *Mercury* called for President Davis's impeachment. A dozen people wrote letters sec-onding the idea.

The area below Broad Street was a wasteland of mostly abandoned houses and lightless streets unsafe after dark. Beauregard's artillery, his "circle of fire" defending the harbor, did nothing to forestall Union bombardment, which occurred at all hours. Alex seldom slept a night without interruption. While the guns boomed, she lay with her hands tightly clasped on her breast, wondering if they should have moved out long before.

In February the iron attack boat *Hunley* sank the Union's screw steamer *Housatonic* offshore, only to sink itself, all hands lost. The Confederacy's submersible warfare program ended on the bottom of Charleston Harbor.

Late in the month a screaming shell dug a crater directly in front of the house. Two artillerymen in the White Point battery died. Alex and Ham agreed they should go. Marion Marburg helped them find and rent a small house on Chapel, a block west of the Northeastern Depot. Alex, Ham, and Rolfe moved essential furniture north of Calhoun Street in a borrowed wagon, then returned to nail the shutters closed and block the downstairs doors with X's of foraged lumber. The well-loved house, so full of memories, looked sad and disfigured as they drove away.

☆　☆　☆

In the West, Lincoln found a commander who could win. He named U. S. Grant general-in-chief. A constitutional amendment abolishing slavery passed the Senate. Beauregard left Charleston, called to duty in Virginia as fighting there intensified. He gladly fled what had become, in his own harsh phrase, the Department of Exile.

Grant fought at the Wilderness, Spotsylvania, Cold Harbor, heedless of the number of men lost. Ham said Grant used regiments and battalions the way a smoker used matches. Marion Marburg observed that the North had many more match factories than the South, and Grant knew it.

In May gallant Jeb Stuart fell at Yellow Tavern. William Tecumseh Sherman thrust out of Chattanooga to hammer Joe Johnston in Georgia with a hundred thousand effectives. Off Cherbourg, France, the Union sank the South's legendary commerce raider *Alabama*. The newly organized National Union party nominated Lincoln for President and an unknown Tennessee tailor, Andrew Johnson, as his running mate. The South's faint hope lay with the Democrats, who called Gen. George McClellan out of retirement to run on a so-called peace platform.

The scorned treasury secretary, Memminger, resigned. Too late, cynical gentlemen said, and lit their cigars with Memminger's currency. The exotic Confederate spy Rose Greenhow returned from England via Halifax and drowned trying to row ashore at Wilmington. In the heat of September, John Bell Hood evacuated Atlanta and Sherman marched in. Lincoln won reelection on November 8. A week later, Sherman's great war machine lurched into central Georgia.

Horrific tales of plantations set afire, valuables plundered, wives and sweethearts raped, reached Charleston's trembling elite. A rabble of white and black men followed Sherman's army. When this horde passed by, they left weeping women and terrified children and, where great houses had once stood, only brick chimneys. People called them "Sherman's sentinels."

On December 21 Gen. William Hardee ordered his troops to evacuate Savannah and retreat north across the Savannah River. Hardee had replaced Gen. Robert Ransom as commander of the military district of Florida, Georgia, and South Carolina. Ransom had replaced Gen. Sam Jones, who had replaced Beauregard. Every man was a West Point graduate.

Sherman telegraphed Abraham Lincoln to present him the city of Savannah as a Christmas gift. It was evident to all but the blind that the South's defeat loomed.

✶　✶　✶

Christmas. At Prosperity Hall a meager fire of fatwood and pine cones burned in the cavernous hearth of the great room. Tall windows framed a gray-green world: palmettos, oaks, and pines lashed by heavy rain; wet Spanish moss fallen on the lawns like so many clipped gray beards. A northwest wind whipped up foam on the Ashley. Ouida peered at the rushing river, disconsolate. "Where is my boy? What have they done with him?"

"You'll find out soon enough," Gibbes said from the divan, where he sprawled with a cigar. Palmetto Traders no longer generated income. In November the partners had overridden minority shareholders and sold the company's last ship. Gibbes continued to spend as though nothing had changed. He was sliding toward poverty with the desperate fatalism that was now epidemic in the Low Country.

"How will I find out?" Ouida wanted to know.

"Sherman's in Savannah. The end's coming. Then it will all sort itself out."

Ouida's eyes enlarged behind her spectacles. "Will Sherman come this way?"

"Only time can answer that," said Folsey as he strolled in with a bottle of port and wineglasses. Folsey's face had grown even more pale and puffy from indulgence. He'd installed a new white mistress in the Charleston cottage, but he never brought her around. He traveled everywhere with an adolescent waif named Kaspar Helios, whom he'd picked up from the streets. He called Kaspar "my little Greek boy." Ouida thought there was something sinister to that but didn't care to imagine sordid details.

"Dinner yet?" Gibbes inquired of his partner.

"Soon. Your wife's tending to it with Kaspar's help. Care for port, Ouida?"

"Oh, heavens yes, I'm freezing in here."

Ouida took the glass with a trembling hand; wine spilled on her satin skirt. She drank like a parched traveler in the desert. Her spectacles reflected the popping fire. "They say Sherman did terrible things to women."

Gibbes said, "Actually, I understand he issued orders prohibiting such. But of course he has all those bummers, those damned camp followers he can't control. They do the damage."

Ouida held out her glass for more. "They want to destroy Charleston, don't they? God knows what will become of us."

"We're certainly in for a bad patch if Sherman marches up the coast," Folsey agreed. "However, there's always the possibility that he'll spare us. He served at Moultrie twenty years ago, when he was a mere lieutenant. Painted watercolors, they say. Read some law. Got along famously with people, and loved the city."

Gibbes snorted. "A more likely influence on General Sherman's decision will be the present condition of Charleston. Why waste men and matériel attacking wreckage?"

Ouida shuddered. "Whatever he does, the niggers are sure to rise up. The Yankees will encourage it. We'll be Africanized."

"Now, there's a pretty term I haven't heard before," Gibbes said. Seeing Ouida's agitation, he hurried to her side and hugged her. "Don't worry so. We'll protect you."

From his perch on the harpsichord bench Folsey said, "Frankly, I'll be glad to see peace restored. I don't mind doing business with Yankees if there's profit in it."

Gibbes shot him a look. "We've been friends a long time, Folsey, but I take extreme exception to that remark."

"Why? We made a pile of money with the help of certain gentlemen from New York and Boston."

"Not with my knowledge or consent."

"But you didn't mind using the money to buy fine clothes and set a decent table." When Gibbes turned red, Folsey raised a placating hand. "Let it pass."

"I will not. Ouida's right, the Yankees want to Africanize the South. They've already destroyed our economy and butchered our finest young men. I may have to bow my head before them, but do business with them? Swear loyalty to their government? Never."

Folsey saluted with his wineglass. "Spoken like a hero." Gibbes thought he detected sarcasm.

Ouida's hands clenched. "I'd kill every last one if I could."

"By God, I believe you're serious, sister. You should have been a soldier."

"I still may be. There are ways."

At that moment Snoo sailed into the great room trilling, "We are ready."

She pulled up short, wondering what she'd interrupted. They all looked so grave. The fire snapped in the chilly silence, then subsided, leaving the forlorn sound of the rain.

★　★　★

They dined on deer meat. One of the housemen too old to run away had shot and dressed the buck. Snoo personally prepared rabbit from a German recipe. Dinner concluded, they played whist. Gibbes saw his partner cheating but said nothing; he was used to it.

After two hours Folsey excused himself. A servant brought his carriage around. It was a phaeton with a standing top and side curtains rolled down against the rain. Kaspar was already inside, feet on a charcoal warmer. The boy's feral eyes darted everywhere, though he never looked at anyone directly.

On the piazza Folsey slipped into his hooded coat of green wool tweed. "I didn't mention this earlier because your sister is too excitable. My friend Rex Porcher-Jones, the judge's grandson, he's picked up rumors of some kind of secret school teaching niggers to read."

"In Charleston?"

"Rex believes so. He doesn't know where it is or who's behind it."

"We must find it, put a stop to it."

"My thought exactly. I'll make inquiries. When we have reliable information, we can take steps."

Gibbes leaned against a white column, puffing a new cigar while Folsey took the reins and swung the phaeton down the oval drive into the river road. Gibbes had a suspicion about the person who might be responsible for such a school. If he was correct, he'd take enormous satisfaction in moving against it. He and Folsey would hire others to act for them and render appropriate punishment.

But the end for Charleston came too soon for them to accomplish it.

63

Freedom of the City

As the Union artillerymen advanced their works, shells began to land north of Calhoun Street. Alex and Ham subsisted on small portions of boiled rice and pieces of corn bread with mold scraped away. Both lost weight, until they resembled, as Ham put it, "A prime pair of bean poles."

Sherman was in Carolina. Rumors about his route of march swept the city with the regularity of the tides. He was on the road to Charleston. No, he'd veered toward Columbia. No, Charleston. "Clever strategy," Ham said. "Neither place dares send relief troops to the other."

At Bell's Bridge, Alex tutored her pupils two evenings a week. Rolfe had quietly recruited a young man named Clem, who belonged to a neighbor of Letty Porcher-Jones. Clem's brain was quick, more than compensating for a bad stammer. Clem brought his sister Cora, ten years older. She cooked at a tavern; she was the slave of its black owner.

The pupils were a mixed lot. Rolfe was the brightest, but each one's progress gratified Alex. Fat Cora walked, moved, and thought slowly. Yet there came a moment when her eyes filled with a ravishing light of understanding and she put three letters together in her head and whispered, "Cat?" Alex almost wept.

January became February. The same harrowing tales they'd heard from Georgia reached them again: farms burned, railroad tracks torn up, a wide black scar of scorched earth left behind when the Union horde passed. Sherman struck Branchville, Orangeburg, crossed the Congaree. So he wanted Columbia after all.

Friday, February 17, Ham rushed to Chapel Street at two o'clock. "Hardee's evacuating all the troops, I have it on good authority."

Alex set to work cleaning and oiling Edward's pistols. Her fingers moved slowly, so as not to accidentally spring one of the under-barrel bayonets. She was careful to scour out the priming pans; Lorenzo the gunsmith had warned her that even a slight residue of burned powder would suck up moisture from the humid air and likely cause a misfire.

Keeping the pistols on half cock, she carefully loaded dry powder and ball. She'd bought an old powder horn from a junk dealer; some long-ago marksman had carved it with the words *Josiah Biggs, His Horn*. She wondered whether he'd shot at the British or only small animals and waterfowl.

To the slow beat of snare drums General Hardee's ragged regiments marched out by way of the Neck beginning at dusk. Alex and Ham watched the sorry exodus on Meeting Street for a while. Never had she seen so many soldiers reeling along out of step and plainly drunk.

Sleep that night was impossible. Hardee wanted to leave nothing useful to the enemy. The Confederates burned and sank ironclads in the harbor, blew up the magazine on Sullivan's Island, set fire to stores of cotton and rice hauled to public squares. The night sky lit with a continual red fireworks whose noise gave Alex another headache. "Walpurgis Night," Ham muttered.

By midnight a dozen fires were burning across the peninsula, fanned by a nor'east blow. Refugees streamed past the Chapel Street house in the small hours, jamming the already crowded Northeastern Depot in hope of finding space on a last train out.

Dawn came. Gritty eyed and hungry, Alex sprawled in a parlor chair, one pistol in her lap, the other at her feet. Ham walked in from a visit to the depot. "It's insanity. They're practically killing each other to get at a few sacks of rice."

"And the Union soldiers?"

"No sign of them, but they can't be far away."

"Ham, let's go home. I'd rather protect the other house."

He agreed. Shortly before eight Alex slung her banjo case on her shoulder and they set out. She carried the pistols and powder horn in a croker sack. Smoke stung her eyes and made breathing difficult. From the Ashley to the Cooper fires ate away at rooftops.

They walked toward Meeting against a flow of people still hurrying to find a train. Suddenly, behind them, an explosion blew the depot into the sky and sent the refugees into screaming retreat. "There was a sizable powder cache next to the depot, maybe something set it off," Ham said.

Coming on the Bell house for the first time in weeks, she blanched and said, "Oh, my God, what happened?" One of the front gables was gone. Wedged in the hole, a curved piece of iron reflected the smoke-veiled sun. The big rifled guns along South Battery had been blown apart. Similar iron fragments lay in the sandy street to the east.

The two of them ripped down the boards nailed across the piazza door, opened shutters. Alex was thankful to find Joanna's portrait unharmed. While they worked, Union troops of the 52d Pennsylvania Volunteers marched into Charleston singing "John Brown's Body." Color bearers carried the American flag and a banner blazoned with the word LIBERTY.

Black people crept into the street, terrified at first, then dancing and cheering when they saw that the two dozen soldiers were Negro. At Broad and East Bay a white officer, one Colonel Bennett, received the city's surrender from a deputy of the mayor.

From the garden Alex heard a brass band play "Hail, Columbia." The music unsettled her in a peculiar way. The citadel of slavery had fallen, justly punished for its sins. For years she'd wished for nothing else. Yet she felt no joy, only weariness, and a formless sorrow. Her injured leg ached again.

By midafternoon two civilian wagons reached South Battery. Men unloaded bulky cameras and clambered over the ruined guns, exposing glass plates to make a photographic record of Charleston's defeat.

Alex thought it prudent to hide one of Edward's pistols behind books in the front office. That night she and Ham slept on pallets there. She left her banjo leaning against the wall on the first stair riser. She hadn't ventured up to the dank and dusty second floor, or the attic, to inspect the roof damage. She'd do that in the morning.

Before she could, the liberators came.

★ ★ ★

There were four, three Negro privates, young and cocky, and a white lieutenant. They stomped up the steps from the garden and pounded the butts of their revolvers on the door. One soldier used his gun barrel to break an inset of ornamental glass. Alex heard the crash and ran to the hall.

Revolver in hand, the lieutenant stepped into the hall. "Stand fast," he said when he saw Alex with her pistol on full cock. "Put down that piece. I won't ask a second time."

He seemed so young to be so fierce. In his twenties, turnip nosed but otherwise not bad looking, with a short growth of blond beard. His dark-blue sack coat was dusty and stained, the brass buttons tarnished. His forage cap showed the gold-embroidered eagle of the infantry. His weapon was a .44 Army Colt from a belt holster. Alex didn't want the confrontation to end in bloodshed. She laid Edward's gun on a side table.

"Now move away from it."

She did as he ordered. The officer touched his cap. "Second Lieutenant Francis Wurtz, Company D, Twenty-first U.S. Colored Regiment. We're going house to house to declare the freedom of the city. Any niggers on the premises?"

Ham stood behind Alex, uncombed hair falling over his forehead. "No, sir, we own no slaves," he said, emphatically and truthfully.

The lieutenant indicated the pistol on the side table. "We're authorized to confiscate weapons and search for contraband."

Alex's eyes burned with resentment. "What exactly is contraband?"

"Whatever we say it is. Don't interfere. Boys, go to it."

The soldiers bolted like jackrabbits, two heading upstairs, one to the dining room. The fourth grabbed the case on the stair and pulled out the banjo. Alex ran at him, pounding his shoulder. "Leave that alone."

He cursed her, went up two steps, away from her. Alex held out her hand. "Give me that." The soldier swung the banjo by its neck, smashing it on the newel post. Wood snapped; broken strings twanged. She hurled herself at him again. The lieutenant grabbed her from behind, bent her arm so that she dropped to her knees.

"That's no way to act, woman. Show us you're glad to see us." Grinning, he hauled her up, pulled her against him for a rough kiss. His beard scraped her skin. She tasted tobacco on his wet tongue.

Ham leapt on the lieutenant. The soldier who'd broken the banjo dragged him off and pistol-whipped him twice. Ham staggered, blood running out of his hair and dripping from the tip of his nose. The soldier kicked his shin. Ham fell, landed hard on his chest, gasping.

Alex heard crockery break at the rear of the house. She darted past the lieutenant, almost reached the front office where she'd hidden the other pistol. "Damn you, woman, come back here." Wurtz fired a round. The ball tore splinters from the doorjamb. One nearly nicked her eye.

"I'll put the next one square in your back if you don't behave."

"For God's sake do what he says," Ham pleaded, on his knees and blinded with blood.

A soldier ran down the stairs with pieces of her clothing. "Whole lot of this upstairs. Mighty fancy, Lieutenant." He stuck a pair of Alex's cotton drawers on his head, the legs dangling like white braids. He curtseyed to Wurtz and wiggled his rear like a dance-hall soubrette. The lieutenant laughed.

One of the soldiers relieved himself against the wall at the back of the hall. Another returned from the kitchen with an armload of dishes. Alex froze when he stopped in front of Joanna's portrait. "Who this be?"

The lieutenant shrugged. "Some old secesh whore. Leave it, nobody would buy such a thing."

The looters carried off a strange assortment of prizes: dishes, a rocker, a set of brass andirons, and the pistol from the hall. The books in the front room didn't interest them and no one thought to search behind them. Alex stood trembling, her arm around her brother. She felt violated.

She had long ago been purged of certain illusions about people. The North was not a community of angels, and color didn't confer sainthood on an entire race. Even so, she'd risked herself willingly on behalf of Negroes. Now she saw them behaving like animals, desecrating her family home as she was certain they'd desecrate her once-beautiful city. For a brief, feverish moment she was a Southerner again.

On the way out Lieutenant Wurtz paused to say, "You and all the other secesh in this sinkhole of treason are whipped. Better remember that, and show some respect, or it'll go hard with you."

She met his stare, silently defiant. Then she spat on his boots.

His bearded face turned ashy. Alex ducked her head as he aimed his Colt. At the last moment he pulled the barrel up, firing three times at the ceiling. Pendants on the chandelier splintered. Glass and plaster dust fell.

"Old bitch," he said, and stalked out behind his men.

She had a presentiment then. The surrender wouldn't bring a true peace, only more hatred. What astonished her was the ferocity of that hatred within herself.

Later that day Union ships in the harbor fired a hundred-gun salute to celebrate Charleston's fall. An onshore wind carried the smell of gunpowder through the open windows. Alex bent over her ironing with a continuing sense of foreboding.

64

Celebration and Reunion

Brigadier General Alexander Schimmelfennig arrived from Morris Island to put the city under martial law. Marion Marburg admired the general because he was German, an émigré who had fled after the failed revolutions of 1848, as Gen. Carl Schurz and other Union officers had. The wheel of history came around: the general set up headquarters in the Miles Brewton house on King Street, the British headquarters in Edward's day.

The stars and stripes replaced the Confederate flag on public buildings. In the attic Ham found an American flag he'd hidden in '61. He climbed a ladder and hung it on the piazza to the left of the garden steps.

Black soldiers worked alongside Charleston volunteers to put out the last fires. Confederate uniforms were banned. General Order Number 8 required all residents to take an oath of allegiance. The military evicted the *Courier*'s editorial staff and brought in Northern journalists; Schimmelfennig wanted "a loyal paper."

On Sunday, Ham and Alex went to church. Because St. Michael's and St. Philip's were badly damaged, communicants from both congregations worshiped at St. Paul's on Coming Street. A rumor buzzed through the pews that Colonel Bennett had ordered the rector to offer a prayer for Abraham Lincoln. Reverend Howe prayed instead for "our fallen comrades who made the ultimate sacrifice." Schimmelfennig ordered the church closed.

The streets teemed with black field hands and Confederate deserters, more every day, homeless and hungry. At the request of a friendly city councilman Ham joined a committee charged with locating any existing stores of rice and grain and distributing them to the needy. The wealthy had escaped to the countryside. Gibbes and Ouida were gone from Legare Street, but thuggish white youths stood guard at their town houses. Empty dwellings were still being looted, or invaded by squatters.

In March, schools reopened. Seven were operating by the end of the month, under a new superintendent of abolitionist persuasion. Alex decided Washington and Jackson belonged in a regular classroom. She took them to school herself. She was sent to a second-floor room presided over, surprisingly, by stout and gray-haired Letty Porcher-Jones.

"How grand to find you here, Letty."

"I was a teacher before I married. Many of us have come back to help."

"I don't see any white pupils on this floor."

"Whites downstairs, colored up here, that's the rule. The Negro may be free, but he will never be our equal. Are these boys from the school you've been conducting in secret?"

"You know about that?"

"My son, Rex, sniffed it out. He followed Rolfe one evening and spied on you. Rolfe is an honest colored man. When I confronted him about his absences before curfew, he confessed."

"And you didn't report it to anyone?"

"Nor did I punish him. It was apparent to me months ago that the slaves would have their freedom. I am not a complete ninny, Alexandra, or heartless. I know they need education to survive. What you're doing is worthy, if dangerous."

"I thank you for your understanding."

"Do you expect to continue teaching?"

"I must. I have pupils too old for public school. May Rolfe continue to attend?"

"How can I deny him? He's a free man."

"Fine. I plan to move the class to our house. We have more space, and there's no longer any need for secrecy."

"I wouldn't be too sure. I have no control of Rex now that he's grown. He and many of his friends despise anyone sympathetic to the colored." Old echoes of Ham's warnings stirred. "Also, yours is a special case."

"Because of the work I did up North?"

"Yes. Take my word. People have not forgotten."

☆   ☆   ☆

Heavy rain moved in from the Atlantic that night.

Alex happened to glance from a downstairs window just as dark was settling. Amid the abandoned South Battery gun pits and half hidden behind a weedy mound of earth, a solitary figure stood with an umbrella. A Negro, that much was evident, but whether man or woman, she couldn't tell in the poor light. The watcher wore a patchwork blanket like a shawl.

She lit a candle, carried it to the window, looked out with the light falling on her face. It had the desired effect: the watcher saw her and hurried away to Meeting Street, skirts trailing in mud puddles.

A woman, then. But who?

☆   ☆   ☆

On March 29, Wednesday, Charleston Negroes celebrated the jubilee with a huge parade led by mounted marshals wearing red, white, and blue sashes, and a "Liberty Car" carrying thirteen girls dressed in white to represent the original colonies. The band of the 21st Colored Regiment provided music.

Companies of soldiers and sailors marched. Standing at the curb a block below Marion Square, Alex saw 2d Lieutenant Wurtz pass by, saber at his shoulder. He spied her in the predominantly black crowd, silently articulated a filthy name for a woman.

Hundreds of Negro tradesmen marched—carpenters, coopers, ironworkers, tailors, butchers. Schoolchildren marched. Letty Porcher-Jones struggled to keep up with her class, which included Washington and Jackson. Jackson waved a placard declaring SLAVERY IS DEAD.

Going home, Alex was twice forced off the sidewalk by aggressive blacks. The second time, one of them cursed her. After a flare of anger she realized she should expect such behavior in the aftermath of sudden freedom. She needed to be tolerant for a while.

☆   ☆   ☆

On April 9, at Appomattox Court House, the curtain fell on the last act of the war. A few Confederate forces remained in the field after the surrender. Jeff Davis was at large, having fled Richmond, where huge fires, deliberately set, destroyed records of his government.

In Charleston the victors quickly planned a symbolic celebration. Major General Robert Anderson, who had surrendered Sumter in '61, would return to the city on Good Friday, April 14, to raise the American flag.

Friday dawned a bright blue day. Every ship in the harbor broke out flags and patriotic bunting. By eight o'clock rowboats and skiffs, shrimp boats and steam barges were ferrying guests across the three miles of water to the fort's rubble-strewn landing stage. The brick fort was a ruin. Three of its five sides had been blown down by bombardment. Second- and third-floor interiors had disappeared entirely.

Ham and Alex went over at ten. The skiff's owner pointed out a U.S. mail steamer, *Arago,* anchored outside the harbor bar. She carried more than eighty dignitaries from New York, including Anderson and his daughter; the President's secretary, Mr. Nicolay; the Reverend Henry Ward Beecher, who would present the day's oration; and Alex's friend Garrison.

Alex and her brother landed and made their way into the fort's one-acre floor. Ham pointed out a well-dressed black man he identified as Robert Vesey, Denmark Vesey's son. Born a freedman, he'd survived his father's reputation and prospered as a self-taught contractor and architect.

Robert Smalls, now attached to the Union navy, piloted his side-wheeler *Planter* into the harbor and transferred to a ferry barge. People cheered when he walked down a dirt ramp from the fort's parapet.

Starting at eleven a transport vessel brought the guests from *Arago.* They joined army and navy officers on a platform decorated with baskets of greenery and wicker arches surmounted by a gold eagle. Alex pressed through the crowd to reach the monkish Garrison, older now, but still possessing the hot eye of a warrior. They greeted each other warmly. She said, "This must be a proud moment for you."

"For almost forty years I fought the sin of sins. I knew a day like this would come, but often I wondered if I would live to see it. Your poor city has reaped the whirlwind, Alexandra."

And still may, she thought.

"I'm speaking to the congregation at Zion's Chapel tomorrow. Please come."

"I will," she said as they parted.

She guessed that three or four thousand had gathered on the hard benches by the time the program began at noon. After the invocation and opening ceremonies, Anderson and a sergeant who had taken the flag down in '61 stepped forward carrying a large leather mailbag holding the flag struck in '61. Anderson was a gaunt and wrinkled Kentuckian with stiff gray hair that reminded Alex of Calhoun's. He drew a paper from his pocket, consulted it, then frowned and put it away. Without notes he spoke briefly and movingly, concluding, "I can only say to you that I thank Almighty God I have lived long enough to perform this last act of duty to my country."

Noncoms attached the old flag to the halyards of the 150-foot staff. Anderson seized the rope and pulled. A wind had come up; it unfurled the flag, thirty-six by twenty feet, riddled with shrapnel holes and ripped by the weather. The sight brought a roaring ovation.

Others took a turn: Gen. Quincy Gillmore, Garrison, Reverend Beecher. When the flag reached the top of the pole, six cannon on the parapet fired in sequence, ear-pounding detonations that touched off a hundred-gun salute from ship and shore batteries. The cannonading went on for half an hour.

Beecher experienced difficulty with the whipping wind. His hat blew away. He was forced to grip the pages of his speech with both hands. Before the war he'd been burned in effigy in Charleston; now he spoke of reuniting the nation. He pleaded for universal education of Negroes. He praised the President and accused "the cultured and unprincipled ruling aristocracy who wanted to maintain their power at any price. They wrought the destruction so tragically on view in this once beautiful city."

The day, if not necessarily Beecher's oration, was a triumph. Alex returned home weary but happy. That night the assassin Booth shot Lincoln at Ford's Theater.

Word of the President's death on Saturday morning wasn't telegraphed to Charleston until after Alex set out for Zion's Chapel, a large colored church on Calhoun Street. Walking along Meeting a block above City Market, she came on one of the many vendors who had set up little stands around the city.

The vendor was a colored woman, dimly seen except for a gaudy red-and-yellow turban. She sat on her haunches in a shaded recess in the stucco wall. A dozen small brown nutcakes and some benne-seed cookies were laid out on a box in the sunshine. A palmetto whisk drove off hovering flies.

Alex paid less attention to the woman than to her companion, a white boy. Perhaps eight or nine, he had stubby legs, thick arms, a round Nordic face, and white-blond hair badly in need of barbering. He stepped in front of Alex, played an Irish air on a mouth organ, and did a little heel-and-toe dance. She dropped coins into an old straw hat at his feet.

"Very good, young man. What's your name?"

"Bob." He slitted his blue eyes as he spoke. There was a teeth-gritting tension about him. He didn't smile.

"And your friend?" Alex turned to acknowledge the woman in the dark recess. She couldn't have been more stunned if the earth had opened.

"*Maudie?*"

"Yes'm, Miss Alex, it's me. They call me Maum Maudie down Grahamville way."

"Heavens above. What are you doing here?"

"Trying to keep from starving, me an' Little Bob." She emerged from the dark alcove and they embraced.

Tearful, Maudie said, "I knew you were back, I heard people say so. I went to call but I was too scared to knock on your door."

"Were you the person I saw watching the house?"

Maudie nodded. "Little Bob, say how do to Miss Alexandra Bell. She owned me when we were girls, but she set me free."

Alex shook hands with the cheerless boy. Maudie said, "I found him wandering after the fighting at Honey Hill 'way last November. Georgia militia was trying to stop Sherman, but one of 'em killed Bob's widowed mother right on her doorstep, a stray shot. I took him in."

There were age lines on Maudie's face, patches on her shapeless dress, blisters on her bare feet. A long crescent scar marred her left cheek. "How did you get that?" Alex asked.

"Bad man I was married to, he cut me. Only did it to me once. I sharpened up my rice hoe and next time, I gave him better'n he got. Never saw him again."

"You're so thin, Maudie."

"Thought there might be more food here than in the country. I was wrong." Maudie waved her whisk over the cookies and cakes. "Woman over by the east docks rents me her oven. Sometimes what I pay her cancels out what I make selling. Still, a body's got to try."

"Do you have shelter?"

"A blanket and my old umbrella. We sleep wherever we can."

"We'll remedy that. You two are coming home with me, no argument."

Little Bob shot a look at Maudie, as though their bubble of sudden good fortune might pop at any second. Alex clapped and beamed. "We'll be a family again, Maudie. Oh, we have so much to catch up on." She clasped Maudie's hand and silently asked Mr. Garrison to forgive her for missing his speech.

65

Ruins

Johnson's Island paroled its prisoners in the late spring. South Carolinians were released last, as a punitive measure, after they took the oath of allegiance. Richard tasted the humiliation for days, bitter as gall.

He and Cal had each lost nearly thirty pounds during incarceration. Both had beards down to their chests, Richard's mostly gray.

They rode boxcars south to Cincinnati. As they chugged into the rail yard, a private died before their eyes, shaking with ague and calling for his mother. Two other rebs converged on the corpse, eager to lift a fine Kerr revolver, five-shot .45-caliber double-action, probably stolen. Richard got to the dead boy first. He kicked the men to drive them back, shoved the Kerr in his belt with glee in his flecked eyes. He found ammunition in the dead boy's pockets.

They ferried over the broad Ohio and walked through the grassy meadows and green mountains of Kentucky, border to border. They survived on berries and roots, fish or rabbit they caught. They drank from springs or raided wells at night. They didn't call at farmhouses, never knowing which side a farmer might have taken in the divided border state.

One afternoon while Richard fished in a creek with a string, a bent nail, and worms, Cal borrowed his revolver. He held up a storekeeper in a nearby hamlet, relieving him of a quart of corn juice from a local still. Richard had given up trying to talk Cal out of his destructive habit of liquoring himself day and night.

In east Tennessee they stole two horses and saddles from a livery barn. "Don't let it trouble you," Richard said as they rode away. "In this part of the state they loved the Union." Cal conducted several more raids on crossroads stores and each time returned with some kind of whiskey. He called it his crutch.

The closer they came to Carolina, the more Richard's spirits improved. He knew Sherman's army had ridden across the state like the Mongol horde and overrun Columbia in February. But after so many months of loneliness and worry, he had to believe all was not lost. Loretta would be waiting for him, they would pick up their lives together, and he would set his wagons on the road again.

He was unprepared for the extent of the destruction. He and Cal rode through a burned belt maybe twenty miles wide; there, instead of farmsteads, only chimneys remained. Fences lay like broken matchwood. Weeds covered abandoned fields. Rails on the Charlotte & Columbia had been heated and bent; they stood like so many steel pretzels, fantastic images against the sky. "Sons of bitches," Cal kept saying, swigging from his bottle and ready to fall out of the saddle. "Sons of bitches."

Union patrols passed by but didn't bother them; in North Carolina they'd exchanged their uniforms for pants and work shirts taken from a storekeeper at gunpoint. And there were many others wandering: soldiers with an eye missing, a leg amputated; black men and women, faces bewildered, clothes bizarre. Some of the women wore gray army jackets, the men flour-sack shirts or coats cut from carpet. Few had shoes.

☆　☆　☆

After the Union army appeared on the heights south of Columbia, a brief period of shelling had followed. Frightened merchants and householders rushed into the main street, Richardson, with bales of cotton they'd hidden in yards and storerooms; they feared the shelling would ignite it. Sherman ordered a stop to the bombardment before that happened, but the cotton stayed in the middle of the street, stretching for blocks.

The enemy marched in to the strains of "Yankee Doodle." Drunken soldiers, principally from Howard's XV Corps, ran riot. They pillaged relics in the State House, threw turpentine on the street cotton and set it on fire. It was great sport until a brisk north wind turned to a gale. Two thirds of the town burned.

* * *

Richard's foreboding returned as they rode into the midland hills, once so verdant and pleasing to the eye. In Columbia homes were gone or reduced to looted wreckage. Where gardens had bloomed, only blackened earth showed. Trees had caught fire and fallen on once-shady avenues, amid rubbish and broken furniture.

Richard's heart beat fast as he and Cal jogged down Gervais Street under a hot white sky. Cal pointed out a cannonball lodged in the west wall of the State House. They turned up Richardson Street, passing demolished hotels and office blocks, then rode west again on Laurel, past the fallen armory on Arsenal Hill. There the street sloped toward the Congaree, where Richard's freight yard had occupied an entire block at Laurel and Gist. From the hillside he saw that his business no longer existed. Pens and barns for his mules and oxen, the small office—all gone. As if to mock him the black shell of one freight wagon leaned on two charred wheels in the main yard. He could still smell burned wood.

Was any of the stock penned somewhere? Loretta would know.

They rode back to Wheat Street, below Gervais. Near the river he and Loretta had built a five-room house. It had burned to the foundation. There wasn't a human being to be seen, only some rooting pigs.

Piers jutting up like giant tombstones were all that remained of the Congaree River Bridge. Richard and Cal boarded a five-cent ferry. They had no money, so the ferryman drank from Cal's supply of rum.

In the shantytown on the west bank Richard tied his horse in front of a ramshackle house with daisies growing in the dooryard. "A man named Simon West lives here. He worked for me."

"I'll wait," Cal said, throwing a leg over his saddle and uncorking his jug.

Richard fanned himself nervously with his hat, knocked. A dried-up woman with a naked infant on her shoulder came forward through sour-smelling shadows. "Mr. Richard," she exclaimed. He touched his forehead politely.

"Dora. Is Simon about?"

"Simon"—as she said his name the tears came—"you don't know? Oh, I guess you wouldn't. Three weeks after Sherman left, we had smallpox. Simon died."

"Dora, I'm so terribly sorry. I saw the freight yard."

"God curse those fiends for what they did."

"Do you know where I can find Mrs. Riddle?" Cal's horse neighed fretfully. Dora West's silence and her evasive eye gave the answer. "Oh, my God. Not Loretta."

"The pox carried off so many." She wept again.

He felt faint. He couldn't control a tic in his right eyelid. The miles of walking and riding, the months of hoping and yearning—for nothing. With some effort he found his voice. "Was she properly buried?"

"Simon tended to it before he fell sick. She's in the Lutheran churchyard down the road."

"Thank you. If there's anything—" He broke off. What could he do for her, or anyone? All that was left to him was a weapon and abiding hatred of those who'd reduced his city and state to ruin.

Trying to mount, he missed the stirrup twice. When he swung up, Cal offered the jug. Richard shook his head.

"I'm mighty sorry, Richard. I heard what the lady said."

"I want to see the grave."

"I'll ride down and wait at the ferry."

Richard turned his horse's head. "All right," he said, starting up the rutted road in the pitiless afternoon glare.

✫ ✫ ✫

Good-hearted Simon West had carved a grave marker from a slab of pine. He'd scribed LORETTA FLOWERS RIDDLE into it, though without a birth date. It said just "—1865."

Richard knelt in the shade of tallow trees whose leaves rustled in a sultry breeze. He clasped his hands to pray, couldn't; even his thoughts were locked into numbness. He stayed at the grave for an hour, until his tears were exhausted. His rage would never be.

✫ ✫ ✫

Near the West Columbia ferry dock, within sight of the fallen bridge, they found an inn. They bargained for space in the barn in return for chopping wood and slopping pigs. Richard noticed every window in the ramshackle inn building propped open with a stick. He asked the landlord about it.

"Hell, we give up all the window weights so's they could make bullets. Damn lot of good it did. I hope Jeff Davis suffers plenty when they catch him."

"They did, a few weeks ago, down in Georgia. Man up Gastonia way told me. He said Davis tried to escape in a woman's dress but I can't believe that. They took him to prison in Virginia."

"Not good enough. Ought to crucify him," the landlord said.

At sunset Cal borrowed Richard's revolver. He returned in an hour with three dollars in Yankee greenbacks. "No trouble at all. Strangers don't argue with Mr. Kerr. Let's have ourselves a meal. There'll be money left over for more popskull."

"Why do you drink so much? It'll kill you."

"What's to live for?" Cal said with a shrug.

After a pork chop and greens and some passable beer in the deserted taproom, he was less gloomy. "You plan to stay in Columbia, Richard?"

Richard stared at his knuckles. "There's nothing here. I saw where my insurance agent had his rooms, downtown, opposite what's left of Hunt's Hotel. The agent may be gone, and I'm damned sure the insurance company's gone. I won't even ask, not without Loretta."

Cal laid a nail-bitten hand on Richard's sleeve. In the wan lamplight he looked the older of the two; his nose was red. "You can't just hang up your fiddle. Come on down to the coast with me. Change of scene. Maybe a fresh opportunity. We've been through a lot together. We're friends. That's something to hang on to."

"Guess it is," Richard said, uncertain.

"Come along, then."

Richard nodded.

★   ★   ★

They reined in at a road junction deep in live oaks and pines. "Yonder's the road to my mother's place on the Ashley. You're welcome to stay with us."

Richard decided against it. Cal had talked a lot about his mother, Ouida Hayward, whom he didn't like very much. He lumped her with his Uncle Gibbes and all the other Low Country aristocrats who had provoked a bloody war they were incapable of winning.

"Thanks, but I don't want to take charity. I'll ride on down to the city. It can't be worse off than Columbia. Maybe there's work for able-bodied men."

"Well, if we don't see each other at Prosperity Hall, I'm sure we'll meet in Charleston. I can stand Mama only so long. Guess it isn't her fault, she saw my grandmother slashed to death before her eyes."

They shook hands. Richard turned the horse down the south road, leaving Cal at the junction with a new bottle in hand and a sad, lost look on his face.

"Got to start over," Richard told himself, as though he could make it happen merely by saying it. "Got to start over."

66

Alex and the Stranger

In the weeks following the surrender two hundred hired laborers cleared the streets of rubble and garbage, weeds and broken glass. A committee of Charleston gentlemen that included Marion Marburg traveled to Washington to present the new president, Andrew Johnson, with suggested names of an interim governor. Johnson's presidential order of May 20 granted amnesty to all but fourteen classes of Confederates. Ham belonged to none of them. He gladly signed the loyalty oath.

The scourge of Carolina paid a visit to Charleston. Ham was thrilled to be invited when General Sherman took tea with Jim Petigru's frail widow, Amelia. Ham said the general resembled a storekeeper more than a soldier. He was mild spoken and courteous, expressing regret for the damage done to a city he remembered favorably from his younger days.

"But he never apologized for what he did elsewhere," Ham said. "He quoted General Halleck, who told him the soil of Carolina should be salted so no more secession crops would grow. I'd say Sherman heeded that charge. He'll be cursed forever around here."

★　★　★

Few young men could be seen in the city; young women in weeds were ubiquitous. A Northern actor-manager brought back theater at Artillery Hall on Wentworth Street; soldiers, freedmen, and white civilians sat together in uneasy familiarity. As the weather warmed, attractive mulatto ladies attached themselves to Union officers who squired them along South Battery on Sunday afternoons. People of color had been forbidden to walk there before the war.

Charleston streets were a Union-blue sea. Alex found it wonderful that black men were wearing the uniform, though the Negro soldiers were openly sneered at. They in turn didn't hide their anger, or their authority.

* * *

Maudie and Little Bob moved in. Maudie shared Alex's bed. Little Bob curled up on a pallet at the foot. Alex didn't mind the crowding; it lent a sense of renewed life to a house long shadowed by the menace and despair of war.

Maudie blended into the daily routine as though she'd never been away. She volunteered to cook, but she was quite clear about how she would do it: taking turns with Alex, as an equal.

Alex found Little Bob something of a puzzle. He was a polite boy but withdrawn, seldom saying more than a few words unless asked a direct question. Even then his answers only hinted at inner feeling. When she asked if if he liked Charleston, he said, "Pretty big place. No room to run."

She tried to be affectionate but quickly realized that the boy didn't want to be touched, let alone hugged or kissed good-night. He was most relaxed in the evening, when Alex played the old harpsichord and Maudie kicked off her straw slippers and danced barefoot with Little Bob clapping. They sang together—"Kingdom Coming" and "Tramp! Tramp! Tramp!" and "Go Down, Moses" and "Marching Through Georgia," a new anthem not heard publicly in Charleston. Little Bob had a sweet boy's tenor he used effectively when they sang "Tenting Tonight." Ham never took part in the impromptu musicales but often looked in, smiling and nodding pleasurably.

Alex moved her classroom to the dining room of the house and searched for new students. The class grew to seven. Her pupils were a spectrum of the social upheaval produced by emancipation and the occupation.

Rolfe now earned wages from Letty Porcher-Jones. Clem lived on the streets, choosing to beg rather than work for his former master. His sister Cleo was one of those frightened of her new independence. By drawing an X—she couldn't as yet write her name—she entered into a labor agreement with the black tavern keeper who had owned her. At Ham's suggestion Cedric Buckles examined the agreement while Cleo waited nervously in his client chair.

"These terms are unconscionable, Miss Cleo. The man took advantage of you. You have all but signed yourself into slavery again, and for an indefinite period of time."

" 'Least I know where I am, don't need to wonder and worry all the time," Cleo said.

The first of Alex's new pupils was white, a volunteer fire brigade captain named Plato Hix. A quiet sort, though he seemed perpetually unhappy, as though carrying some invisible burden. He could read simple English and print short words in stiff, blocky letters, but he wanted to improve his vocabulary and learn proper penmanship. Alex said neither study fitted her plan for the class, but she stole a few minutes occasionally to teach him what she could.

Arthur Lee, barely out of his twenties, drove a night soil wagon; unpleasant work, but it paid. He told Alex that whatever she taught him would be taught in turn to his eleven children.

Aunt Mary-Margaret, toothless and frail, claimed to be seventy-five. She was determined to read, though she declared she had no intention of reading anything but Scripture. Alex added a King James Bible to the small shelf of books she used in class.

Jewel, nineteen, was the illegitimate daughter of a light-skinned prostitute; she made no secret of it. Jewel's mother pushed her to the class, wanting better for her child than a life in the cribs. Jewel was the slowest pupil, probably because she constantly veered between obedience to her mother and an urge to rebel. Alex feared that no matter how hard she tried, she would lose Jewel eventually.

✯ ✯ ✯

One evening before class Ham dashed into the house with a bloodstained napkin knotted around his head. "For God's sake, what happened?" Alex exclaimed.

"The white soldier boys prefer the old secesh crowd to all the black freedmen wandering about. I stumbled into a fracas between soldiers and some colored. Brickbats flew and I caught one."

Before she could commiserate, he rushed on. "I have news. I was at the Mansion House for two hours, entertaining a new client." The Mansion House was a venerable old hotel on Broad Street, lately reopened. Ham dropped two law books on the office table and pulled off his boots. At fifty-one, though gaunt and gray, he seemed in better spirits than at any time since Alex's return.

"Mr. Maxwell's from Boston. A speculator in commodities. He came down by steamer to buy cotton and rice futures."

"A Yankee doing business here? That's a hopeful sign."

"Ah, but there's more. Maxwell knows three other investors who will be here within a month. They've already reserved at the hotel. South Carolina may be on her knees, but she still has valuable goods in her barn. I think we should fix up Bell's Bridge. Get ready to reopen for business."

"That's a fine idea. What if I go there tomorrow and inventory what needs to be done?"

He seized her waist and danced her around. "Hurrah. Maybe we can wash the red ink off the books of Buckles and Bell at last."

Alex was wide awake before dawn. With a shawl over her shoulders, moving as briskly as she could with her aching leg, she arrived at Bell's Bridge just as the sun rose out of the sea and painted the inner harbor. Her presence at the end of the pier attracted gulls. She held up her empty hands as she had long ago. They squabbled and swooped over her, then flew off. She laughed and inhaled the old, intoxicating perfume of the harbor, a mingling of mud and salt and summer air not yet heavy with dampness.

Using a pencil and a precious block of paper from the law office, she started a list of the most urgent repairs. Half the roof of the first storage shed had collapsed. She opened the padlock using Ham's big ring of keys. Inside she found the roof debris and an infestation of rats that ran over her shoes as they fled.

At the second shed her mouth rounded in silent surprise. The padlock chain hung in two pieces, filed through. She had an uneasy feeling that she might not be alone on the pier.

She rolled the door back on its noisy wooden wheels. Someone grumbled, "What the devil?" She couldn't see the interloper in the dark. She stamped her foot.

"Who is that? You're trespassing. Come out this instant."

"Woke me up, woman."

"What do I care? Show your face."

Slow steps brought him to the light. He was a man of middle years, lean and strong-looking. Half a dozen Carolina wrens could have nested in his gray beard and shoulder-length hair. He'd slept in his clothes, overalls and a ready-made shirt, faded gray. A blanket full of moth holes draped his shoulders.

"This is private property," she began.

"You forgot to post a sign saying so."

"Don't quibble with me, sir. You got in here illegally. Collect your things and go. If I catch you on the premises again, I'll have the city police arrest you."

The man blinked against the light; his large brown eyes had a curious familiarity. Recognition came to him suddenly. "You're Miss Bell. You took me boating once, from this very pier. We sailed out to watch them building Fort Sumter."

Stunned, she said, "Why, that's right. Your father brought you along when he called on my father." She couldn't recall his name, though.

"Your father the attorney," he said. She caught a whiff of something sour on his clothes. He offered his hand; at least that was clean. "Richard Riddle."

His handclasp was warm, strong. "I do remember." She remembered much more: his terrible complexion; the lovelorn looks he threw at her that afternoon, and how haughtily she had dismissed him.

"I plead guilty to the charge of breaking in. I didn't have a penny left, or anywhere to lay my head. I was walking down East Bay when I saw this place and remembered it. It looked deserted, so I got hold of a file, never mind how."

"You don't live in Columbia any longer?"

"No. While I was coming home from prison in Ohio, my house and my business were destroyed by Sherman's vandals."

"You were in the army, then."

"Congaree Mounted Rifles. At Second Manassas I was captured by those Northern bast—our Northern foe," he corrected with a slight coloration in his cheeks.

"Well, I suppose I can let you stay until we start repairing the wharf. Are you employed?"

"I drive a garbage wagon back and forth to the marshes. Pays thirty cents a day. That's how I eat."

"You're one of the city street cleaners?"

He nodded. "Won't last forever, but I'm lucky to have any kind of job. So many don't. They offered me a helper, a colored fellow, but I said no. I didn't fight for those people, and I don't propose to work with them."

For a moment or so they had conversed amiably; now he was hostile again. "Mr. Riddle—"

"Captain Riddle, if you don't mind."

"The war is over, sir."

"Not for me. I lost everything. I lost the dearest woman in the world to smallpox."

"Your wife? I'm terribly sorry. And I'm sorry things are so difficult for you, but—"

"Difficult for the whole state. They say we lost over twelve thousand men. Sherman burned and pillaged like a madman. I should have expected that, I spent a couple of years with his verminous colleagues. I'll never forgive the Yankees for what they did to us."

"I would remind you that South Carolina started the war."

"Whose side are you on? I thought you were Charleston born."

"I am, but I'm trying hard to be an American again, as we all should."

"Oh, spare me your pious cant, Miss Bell. I'm a damned rebel and I've earned the right to stay that way. I'll clear out. Send you a new chain when I can afford it. Good day." He rolled the door shut in her face. It banged the frame; termite dust drifted down.

Alex was furious. Riddle was the kind of stiff-backed Carolinian whose militancy had brought on the war, and the very conditions he railed about now. She stuffed paper and pencil in her pocket and marched up the pier. She'd finish the inventory another time.

☆　☆　☆

When she came back next morning, true to his word he was gone. The shed had been swept out, as if no one had trespassed.

Remembering William Drew's passionate advocacy of forgiveness, she wanted to feel sorry for Riddle. It was difficult; she disliked him intensely. Yet that night he visited her in her dreams, his odd speckled eyes glowing as he touched her hand and whispered words she couldn't understand. She awoke with her nightdress twisted between her legs, damp with perspiration.

She dismissed the dream as a late symptom of the midlife change that had tormented her with dizzy spells, night sweats, and erosion of her patience and good temper. Riddle was a recalcitrant lout.

She lit a candle and sat down to brush her hair in front of Cassandra's oval mirror. She plied the brush hard, painfully tearing out tangles, angered by her confusion and by what she saw in the glass: long tresses more white than blond; a childless woman of fifty with a roof over her head but little else.

Alex hated self-pity, but at 3:00 A.M., it came easily. She threw the hairbrush on the floor and rested her head on her arms while the candle burned down.

67

Ouida's Tea

Cal stumbled down the stairs at half past ten. Ouida's boy had been home four weeks. The first few days were a delirious ecstacy of reunion; Ouida wept frequently. At first she neither understood the meaning of Cal's whipped look nor clearly heard his bitterness. Then, as she awoke to the changes in him, a battle began. Sometimes it was a skirmish of glares and pouty silences, sometimes a frontal assault of angry words. This morning he seemed benign, if bleary eyed.

"Good morning, Mama."

"In the name of heaven, cover yourself." Cal wore only a pair of drawers. His hair was uncombed, his hairless chest bright with sweat. They were into the hot season, without a single house slave to cool the white masters with fans.

"You've seen me with less on than this," he said. " 'Least I hope you swaddled me once or twice when I was a babe. Give us a hug."

"Stay away from me. You smell like a groggery. Where do you get liquor?"

"There's plenty to be had if you know where to look."

"How do you pay for it?"

"Cards and dice, Mama. Sometimes faro. I learned skills in the army. Anything for breakfast?"

"Do you think I'm a nigger cook you can order about?"

"No, but far as I can see, there isn't another cook at Prosperity Hall, nor a washerwoman, nor anybody else to do for us."

"Dear Lord, what ever brought this on? What happened to you?"

A muscle in his throat quivered. "I'll answer you the way I answer anybody who asks, Mama. The war happened. You and your Goddamn friends happened, the ones so eager to send boys off to fight, though they'd never go themselves, oh, no. Old men issue orders, young men die. It's a tradition, isn't it?"

"The Yankees did this," Ouida moaned, kerchief at her eyes. "I'd kill every Yankee on earth if I had the power."

By then he'd left the hall for the kitchen. She heard him knocking about, dropping a pan, breaking a piece of crockery, spewing his filthy oaths. That he should have come home a wastrel, a burnt-out wreck, broke her heart. What they had done to him demanded punishment.

✮　✮　✮

In the soggy July heat Gibbes walked the fallow fields at Malvern. Once indigo had flourished here, and cotton. The weedy desolation mocked him; reminded him of his straits. All the money earned through Palmetto Traders had been spent. His Confederate bonds were worthless. So, it seemed, was his land.

He and Snoo had moved out to Malvern because he loathed the sight of all the strutting soldiers and, as Snoo put it, "The streets are so niggery anymore." Gibbes had to drive the coupe rockaway himself, with Snoo and their luggage inside. The coach's glossy carmine paint had faded and grown dull. Bits of the gilded *B*s on the side panels had flaked away.

Leaving the city, they'd passed the site of the old Fairgrounds Prison, now a burying ground for the blue-bellies. In May, Union fanatics had celebrated some sort of memorial day at the cemetery. Gibbes had leaned over and spat at the graves as they rolled by.

✮　✮　✮

Gibbes's fine cambric shirt stuck to his back and belly. Gnats deviled his neck. Little triangular burrs attached themselves to his pant legs as he walked. Leaving the field, he sat down beside a magnolia, weighted with unhappiness. His finger traced in the dirt, the same two letters, *OW*, over and over.

In the war's aftermath resistance had hardened within Gibbes. He refused to take Andrew Johnson's oath, even though he fit none of the excluded classifications. He hadn't been a high-ranking officer of the Confederate army or navy. He no longer possessed $20,000 in liquid assets. Even so, he was damned if he'd swear loyalty to the Constitution and obedience to the laws of the nation. On Independence Day he had refused to show the stars and stripes at Malvern.

The North poured out a poison stream of propaganda about equality for the freed slaves. It was sponsored and promoted by a powerful clique of extreme Republicans bitterly opposed to Johnson's generally moderate reconstruction plan cast in the forgiving mold of Lincoln's program. He'd be a dead man before he'd go along. Top to bottom South Carolina's situation was intolerable. But what to do about it? Damned if he knew.

He traced O W again, then scowled and scuffed it away with his boot. He walked into the silent house. He presumed Snoo was napping. They lived without servants, forced to do all the chores themselves.

On the river porch he picked up a *Mercury,* now filled with Yankee flummery and precious little news. He rocked in a rocker, swore at the midges and mosquitoes, flipped the pages for items of interest. He found just one. The recently appointed provisional governor, Benjamin Perry, had called a special election of delegates to a convention in September to write a new state constitution.

Election?

The idea was so simple and obvious. If true sons of Carolina were to keep the state out of the hands of the white radicals and the black-hearted niggers, those patriots must launch a new war, a secret war whose soldiers appeared outwardly docile and cooperative.

He dragged himself upstairs, his hands on the bannister pulling, his artificial leg thumping the risers. "Snoo?" He burst into her bedroom, where she sprawled behind gauze curtains hung from the four-poster's canopy. She'd put on a thin summer gown for her nap, not expecting interruption. He could see her sex and the round, rosy breasts that had first attracted him.

"Snoo, wake up, I want to tell you something." He batted the curtain aside, flung himself down beside her. She murmured and frowned in her sleep. "I'm going to run for office. Help write a new state constitution. You hear me, Snoo?"

Gradually her eyes focused. "No. Tell me again."

He did, a step at a time. First, the special convention; he'd campaign to be a delegate from Charleston. He knew he'd win; influential friends

Alex introduced Maudie, who was polite but plainly puzzled by Richard's presence. Richard set the lamp on a hall table, where it illuminated Joanna's painted face. Without asking he went to the dining room and blew out the other lamp. He returned carrying his slouch hat.

"Guess it's pretty obvious someone doesn't like you, Miss Bell."

"I expect it's the teaching they don't like."

"Well, I don't like it much, either, but I wouldn't register my opinion with a cowardly attack."

"I owe you for all you've done, Captain."

"Hardly, ma'am. I didn't catch the shooter."

"But you pulled Bob and me out of a tight place tonight. I'd really like to do something in return."

His gaze held hers. Little Bob sat on the staircase, not understanding the meaning of the looks passing between them. Nor did Maudie. Alex felt a strange, pleasant quiver in her breast.

"Well, now." He cleared his throat. "I did enjoy our conversation, even though we disagree pretty fiercely. You could let me call on you so we could talk some more." Before she could reply he said, "I don't know anybody else in Charleston except one person, you see, and he's out in the country a whole lot of the time."

The response that sprang to mind was *How flattering*. She held it back, though her tone was cooler when she said, "Of course I understand what you're saying. You're most welcome to call, Thursday excepted. I hold class Thursday night."

"Thank you. Honestly never expected I'd ask to spend time with a Yankee woman."

"Captain Riddle, you know I was born and raised in Charleston. I am not a Yankee woman."

"Well, not on the outside, anyhow." He tipped his hat. "Good night, Miss Bell. You, too, ma'am. Be sure to lock your doors. When I'm settled at the street railway company, I'll come by for a chat and another piece of that fine cheesecake."

"Maudie baked it," Alex said.

He walked off in the night. Maudie stamped her foot. "Will somebody kindly tell this child what in the devil is going on?"

Ham arrived a few moments later and asked the same question.

☆ ☆ ☆

Next morning Alex returned to Prioleau Street, where she climbed the stairs of a squalid tenement. She introduced herself to Plato's handsome but haggard wife, a mulatto. No wonder they had to live in such a dismal place.

Giving her name eased the woman's apprehension. "You're his teacher," Mrs. Hix said. Alex asked why Plato had left the class. The woman didn't know. Where might Alex find him? The woman told her.

The Mansion House hallway smelled of cigars and overflowing spittoons. She found Plato buffing the brown brogans of a man reading Horace Greeley's *New York Tribune*. Plato refused to meet her eye.

Alex sat on a hall bench to wait. The man flipped a coin to Plato, leaned sideways, and squirted tobacco juice into the spittoon next to the chair. The juice hit the rim and spattered Plato's hand. Plato wiped it on his leather apron. The man left with no apology.

"You decided not to stay with the class, Plato?"

"Been way too busy." Not the real reason, she suspected.

"You're a good student. Will you come back at some later time?"

"No, can't do that. But thanks for all you done."

"You're welcome. Put your writing to good use." Disappointed, she turned away.

"Miz Bell." She waited. Nervous fingers tapped his trouser seam. "You're related to Mr. Gibbes Bell of Legare Street and Prosperity Hall, that right?"

"He's my first cousin."

"Thought so. Just wondered. Mr. Gibbes is a fine man." The insincerity was apparent.

A new customer arrived and took the chair. Plato squatted on his box, bowed his head. The man's odd behavior troubled her. She knew him as a quiet sort, but not anxious, or secretive. She hoped nothing was wrong at home.

70

Secret War

Gibbes campaigned in barrooms, parlors, law offices, and at small gatherings at Sword Gate that Snoo arranged. His vision, his promise, was simply stated. "A white man's government, for white men, by whatever means are necessary."

He faced no serious opposition. Most of the elite gentlemen of Charleston wanted nothing to do with reconstructing South Carolina in any way that would mollify the radicals in Washington. They missed the point. Gibbes was following what he saw as the only clear path to recapturing control of the state. Along the way compromises, and dissembling, would be necessary.

Only a third of the city's electorate cast votes in the election. Some Low Country precincts skipped it entirely. Gibbes hired a jobless veteran to drive the rockaway and traveled to Columbia in relative comfort. On September 13 over a hundred delegates convened at the First Baptist Church, an imposing Greek revival building on Hampton Street that the fire had miraculously spared, even though buildings close by had burned.

The convention repealed the 1860 secession ordinance, then took up the issue of slavery. James Orr, a well-respected former congressman and speaker of the House, warned that Washington would never withdraw troops or seat a congressional delegation unless slavery was fully and clearly repudiated. The majority fought off an effort to compensate slave owners for financial loss and restrict Negroes to manual labor; here, Gibbes was on the losing side. The convention declared slavery and involuntary servitude abolished, never to be reestablished.

Gibbes stood with the majority in refusing to accept and consider a memorial on suffrage submitted by blacks from Charleston. Suffrage in any form wasn't on the convention's agenda, though this deliberately defied the Northern radicals.

The celebrated war hero Gen. Wade Hampton declined an offer of the governorship. James Orr was put forward as the convention's choice. Andrew Johnson approved Orr's candidacy and the convention's other actions. An election was called to organize a new General Assembly. Gibbes campaigned as he had before and easily won a seat in the House.

✳   ✳   ✳

That same month brought a new military commander to Charleston. General Daniel E. Sickles was one of the nation's more prominent, not to say lurid, public figures. Gibbes knew about him because "Devil Dan" had fought at Seven Pines, the battle whose very name tortured him.

Like Gibbes, Sickles had an artificial leg, the result of a stray cannonball at Gettysburg. The general was too important to have his amputated leg thrown away with others in a bloody basket; his was preserved and presented to him. He placed it on display in an army medical museum.

Sickles's career was something even a nickel novel writer would hesitate to imagine. A Tammany lawyer and Democratic congressman, he'd figured in a famous prewar love triangle. A nephew of Francis Scott Key had involved himself with Sickles's wife, Teresa. The cuckolded congressman shot Philip Barton Key to death in a public square in Washington. Promptly arrested, Sickles engaged Edwin Stanton to represent him. Stanton got him off with a plea of temporary insanity, a defense never used before.

Clerics and prudes deplored the murder and the acquittal, but many admired Sickles for defending the sanctity of marriage. That was not something he respected outside of his own house, however. He continued to drink and womanize openly.

When war broke out, he raised New York's Excelsior Brigade and commanded it bravely, though some said he almost caused Union defeats at Chancellorsville and Gettysburg. Through friendship with Grant and Lincoln he was given command of the Military District of

South Carolina in September 1865. He left his reconciled wife, Teresa, and his adolescent daughter in New York and traveled to Charleston, where he surveyed several mansions for an appropriate headquarters. He chose 33 Charlotte Street, a brick home built by a prosperous planter named Thomas White. The White residence was serving as a hospital. Sickles threw out the staff and patients and moved in.

He publicly declared friendship with the South and Southerners. Few in Gibbes's circle believed him, even though Sickles distributed food to the poor. Rumors of the general seeking out and entertaining local beauties began to circulate. It was whispered that no chaste woman was safe in his presence.

Richard Riddle encountered Sickles accidentally. The Charleston Railway Company had laid new tracks on Calhoun Street and partway down Meeting. Richard drove a car on the line six days a week. Making the turn south at Marion Square one afternoon, he was surprised when a short, middle-aged, bulldoglike officer with a drooping mustache dashed after the car and jumped aboard. He was even more surprised to see two stars on the officer's shoulder straps.

"Take me as far as you're going." The officer's speech had a juicy quality because of the cigar clenched in his teeth. Richard took an instant dislike to the man.

"You'll have to put out your cigar," he said.

Sickles's eyes closed to slits. "Do you know who I am?"

Richard guessed, but he said, "I don't know and I don't care."

"I am Major General Sickles, commander of this district."

"That may be. Doesn't change the fact that smoking on the cars is against company rules."

"You don't say. Well, sir, you may consider the rules suspended for the next half hour, or until I leave the car, whichever comes first." Astonished passengers watched Sickles haughtily turn away and take one of the wicker seats. Richard seethed but did nothing; prolonging the dispute would almost certainly land him in a cell, and he'd had a bellyful of that.

The conductor who had witnessed the exchange approached the general timidly. "Sir, the fare."

"I ride free."

The conductor wilted. "Why, that's right, of course you do." Sickles folded his arms, gazed out the window, and continued to enjoy his smoke. Richard yanked the overhead cord and clanged the bell furiously, even though there was no one on the rails ahead of him.

★ ★ ★

Slowly the city emerged from the tribulation of war. Each week a few more vessels called at the port. Rebuilding began, the largest project being the Northeastern Railroad depot rising on the ruins of the old.

The city faced a debt of over $5 million but nonetheless went forward with necessary improvements. Shell-cratered streets were paved. Sidewalks were built, with the addition of thick wooden curbs to protect them from damage by carts and drays. The mayor announced a program to illuminate over two hundred streets with gas lamps. He also dedicated the new street railway; aging William Gilmore Simms read an ode written for the occasion. Simms's prewar popularity was a memory. New York publishers had abandoned him because of his unrelenting defense of slavery.

Retail merchants moved back to King Street. Marburg's sold books again. The Crescent Bank renovated and reopened its damaged quarters on Broad. Buckles & Bell rejoined the Chamber of Commerce. Ham thought it prudent to designate Cedric Buckles as the official representative. A few diehards would let no one forget Ham's friendship with Petigru the Unionist.

While plantations stood idle for lack of workers, Charleston's reviving business climate lured Northern speculators. Several brought contract work to the law firm, improving its cash position. Repairs at Bell's Bridge went forward in a mood of optimism.

One notable speculator arrived on the ramshackle right-of-way of the Northeastern line, alighting from his opulent private car at the edge of the depot construction. Brevet Brigadier General Adoniran Huffington was a red-bearded Yankee of great physical stature and reputation. He bragged of friendship with Lincoln's first secretary of war, Simon Cameron. Both men had risen from the cesspool of Pennsylvania politics, and it was through Cameron that the general, as he insisted on being addressed, got his army commission.

Huffington had distinguished himself, if that was the right term, at Chantilly, Virginia, in 1862. After the Union defeat at Second Manassas, Huffington's 14th Pennsylvania Reserves took ninety rebel prisoners at Chantilly. None survived the first night of captivity. A rebellious lieutenant serving under Huffington, who was still a colonel at the time, called it a massacre, vicious and intentional.

Huffington trumpeted his innocence, blaming excessive zeal of "loyal subordinates" he refused to name. The Committee on the Conduct of the War examined Huffington's case and found him innocent of wrongdoing. Those who hated "Bloody Ad" said cronies in Congress had arranged for him to be absolved. The stigma faded quickly; he was breveted the following year.

By the summer of 1865 Huffington had established himself as a developer and builder of railroads, with headquarters in Pittsburgh. Two local banks financed him. Each held a one-third interest in his company; the general controlled the other third of the shares.

Huffington wasn't a man to blend quietly into the Pittsburgh scene. He stood out in any crowd and always ducked his head to enter a room. He was a family man with eleven children—he'd buried three wives to reach that number—and a devout Presbyterian who prayed publicly at every opportunity. His tiny black eyes intimidated lesser men. He was famous for shouting at those who opposed him.

The general's agents roamed the South looking for ruined railroads that might be gobbled up cheaply, repaired, and restarted at a profit. The agents brought him surveys, inventories, and faded news clippings about the moribund Greenville & Columbia, a line of some 145 miles, with short branches to Anderson and Abbeville.

Huffington recognized a prime opportunity but knew he needed the cooperation of the state government. A liberal corporate charter, state approved, was mandatory. Support must be assured by the state's purchase of stock and its guarantee of corporation bonds. Arriving in Charleston, the general cast about for local citizens who could forward his cause. His eye fell on Folsey Lark.

After several interviews Folsey was invited to join the inner circle of the Carolina Railroad Development Company, or CRDC. Huffington promised a seat on the board if Folsey performed satisfactorily. Folsey didn't mind being sneered at as the scalawag lapdog of a carpetbagger. He'd been called worse.

He traveled to Columbia to attend an organizational meeting of what Huffington termed his apostles, a group of venal pols, bureaucrats, and free agents whose job it would be to win the cooperation of "those whose friendship we will unhesitatingly reward." The target list included not only legislators but also the attorney general, the state auditor, the treasurer, the land commissioner, and chairs of the House and Senate Committees on Railroads. Folsey was assigned legislators to cultivate and was also given $3,000 to rent and furnish a luxurious caucus room where some of the proselytizing would be done.

Huffington convened the meeting of his apostles in the unfinished caucus room located on Richardson, three blocks from the State House. The room smelled of new paint, and the windows were raised to get rid of fumes. The noise of saws and hammers and planes was constant. Folsey had supplied an assortment of chairs and benches.

The general held forth, stomping up and down in his heavy boots and waving and gesturing like the most flamboyant of preachers. Few men frightened Folsey, but the general did. If he could judge from the faces of the eleven other apostles, his reaction was not unique. It took two hours for Huffington to reach his impassioned conclusion.

"The old Carolina system of living and working failed, gentlemen. The old system is dead as Jeff Davis's chances for enshrinement in the Confederate pantheon. This state can no longer survive with a posture of artificial self-sufficiency and isolation, nor can it ignore the fast-flowing tide of national, not to say global, industrialization.

"We are on the cusp of a fantastic profit, in which we all may share. Once we achieve our goal, I shall dedicate myself with equal vigor to reaching another, also for our mutual benefit. I shall apply my sweat and my capital to becoming United States senator from this fair state. Yes, I am of the North. Yes, I fought against your kith and kin. But our white skin makes us brothers again. Like you I am sickened at the thought of Carolina becoming another Liberia.

"Some will oppose us openly. Others may work secretly. We must and we shall foil them all. Smite them with every ounce of our God-given strength. To do that we must humbly call upon Him whose guidance and support is essential if we are not to fail. On your knees, gentlemen. Let us pray."

He dropped to the floor with a colossal thump, clasped his hands, and awaited similar action from the apostles.

Some knelt immediately. Folsey was slow, aghast that he'd gotten mixed up with a religious fanatic. He was the last person seated, more out of shock than protest. When Huffington turned those tiny eyes on him, Folsey almost broke his kneecaps joining the others.

Huffington prayed for twenty minutes, at peak volume. Folsey squeezed his eyes shut, wondering if he should sever himself from the group. The general surely wouldn't condone the abandoned private life Folsey led and enjoyed.

"O Lord," Huffington cried, "grant thy blessing to our righteous cause. Bring confusion to our enemies. Crush and destroy any who stand or speak in opposition to us. Aid and abet our just undertaking, which will shower the white race of Carolina with monetary and spiritual blessings beyond reckoning. All this we humbly and prayerfully ask in the name of thy beloved son Jesus Christ, He who died on the cross for our sins, amen." When the apostles failed to echo it with sufficient volume, Huffington flashed his murderous eyes and roared, *"Amen."* Folsey fairly screamed it, his face red with strain.

A few days later he returned to Charleston, and Kaspar, still harboring doubts about working for a moralizing hypocrite like Bloody Ad. Those doubts were eventually overcome by a phrase of Huffington's that he couldn't get out of his head.

At his first meeting with Gibbes, Folsey described the general's unsettling combination of ruthlessness and religiosity. Gibbes was amused. "Not exactly your kind of fellow, is he?"

"No, but he offered all of us something tremendously tantalizing. In his words, we're on the cusp of a fantastic profit. You'd like to get your share, wouldn't you?"

Gibbes agreed that he would.

"All right, then. Friend to friend, what's your vote worth? Name your price. We'll pay it."

☆　☆　☆

Richard visited the Bell house at least once a week. For several evenings he and Alex played Beast, a simple card game she remembered from childhood. He complained that it was too simple and taught her two-handed poker. Alex didn't know the game; she'd never played cards with Drew. It wasn't that he considered it immoral, as many clerics did. He thought card games were frivolous time-wasters. Alex quickly caught on to the hierarchy of poker hands. She bluffed frequently, with success.

She enjoyed Richard's company, although they hotly argued the state of the nation and the motives and programs of the Johnson administration. He didn't bring up her teaching, but he challenged her beliefs in other ways. One night as they relaxed in a wooden swing Ham had hung on the piazza, he said, "What do you think of a black person and a white person marrying?"

Anguishing memories of Henry Strong rushed in. She had never spoken his name to Richard; she'd mentioned her marriage to William Drew only briefly. "I see nothing wrong if two people love each other and are willing to withstand the inevitable public scorn."

"But aren't Negroes inferior?"

"That's what we were taught, Richard. Inferior, lazy, dishonest—I heard it over and over when I was growing up. Some are that way, I suppose. Some white people as well."

"Could you love a black man?"

"Why not?"

"Because it isn't natural."

"Really? Did the Lord come down on a cloud and inform you of that personally?"

"By God you're an exasperating creature." His laughter softened the complaint. She turned toward him in the shadows.

"Richard, you're carrying a lot of old ideas, like a hundred-pound sack of stones on your back. Put down the burden. Think in new directions. It's a new day."

"Not one that I like very much."

"If you keep trying to march into the past, you'll only be miserable. Change comes like the tides or the periods of the moon. You can't stop it. You must accept it, live with it."

He grabbed her hand. "Time to get out the cards."

They both looked down at his fingers twined with hers. Alex suddenly felt vaporish. His embarrassment was evident. He withdrew his hand.

"I'm sorry. I was forward."

She smiled to put him at ease. "I say it again. You're a true Southern gentleman."

"Which, according to you, is not so good."

She rose from the swing. "Let's play poker."

It was odd that she liked him even though she couldn't tolerate many of his ideas. The complexity of human behavior confounded her once again.

71

Confessions

In November, Gibbes took the rain-soaked roads back to Columbia. The General Assembly met on the grounds of South Carolina College, the Senate in the library, the House in the chapel. Members ratified the Thirteenth Amendment, a sour pill to swallow. Gibbes spoke of the need to remember the chameleon, adept at changing its color to protect itself. He urged patience and a fixed eye on the goal: a white man's government for white men.

Governor Orr appealed to the legislators to establish rules to protect the thousands of former slaves roaming the state, lost in a society they couldn't understand or deal with. "It is our humanitarian duty," Orr said.

With a nod and a wink Gibbes and his colleagues set about reestablishing elements of slavery in the name of protecting the Negroes. New statutes referred to as the Black Codes did offer a few sops to the freedom of persons of color, defined as all those having more than one-eighth Negro blood. The Codes permitted Negroes to sue and be sued in the courts, testify in cases personally involving them, and enter into legally recognized marriage contracts with others of their race. Interracial marriage was prohibited. "To avoid an inevitable descent into miscegenation—the white race mongrelized out of existence," Gibbes declared in a speech from the floor.

The Codes said Negroes could work only as farmers or servants unless they bought an expensive license and paid special taxes. They could not own guns, the exception being one fowling piece allowed to a farmer. The death penalty was mandated for murder, housebreaking, assaulting a white woman, or stealing a horse, mule, or baled cotton.

Servants could not leave the employer's premises without permission. Whipping of adult servants was permitted if proper judicial papers were obtained first. Whipping of servants under eighteen could be done at the master's discretion. The terms *master* and *servant* appeared frequently in the Codes, along with a statement that Negroes *are not and never shall be entitled to social and political equality with white persons.*

Alex was furious when she read about the Codes in a newspaper. Richard thought the new laws served a useful humanitarian purpose. They quarreled over it and parted angrily at the end of the evening. Two days later he brought her one of Joel Poinsett's crimson-leafed plants to make amends. She was touched. Richard's meager salary on the city railway surely didn't allow for such extravagance.

The visits resumed, though not without continued controversy. "Did you own slaves?" Alex asked after a hand of poker. She had a pile of twenty wooden matches in front of her. She'd reduced him to four. Rolfe had nailed temporary boards over the shot-out window of the dining room.

"One, at the freight yard. An honest man and a hard worker. Loretta wouldn't have a house girl. Said it was wrong."

"Did you ever think of freeing your man?"

"Loretta suggested it before I joined up. Never did it. Jacob disappeared while I was up North. Look, I wasn't one of your damn Low Country grandees running a hundred or two hundred slaves. There weren't many like that in the whole state."

"Enough to hold power and preserve the system."

"I don't think owning just one slave is—"

"It's the same as owning a hundred or a thousand, Richard."

"Lord, why do I take this punishment?"

"Because you're a decent man, and I think that down deep inside something tells you I might be right."

"Cut the cards."

Alex hated the way he clung to old ideas, yet she wanted to continue seeing him, to chip away at them, and honor Drew's plea for forgiveness of enemies, difficult as that was sometimes. There was also another, more emotional reason she couldn't admit to anyone. She liked the recalcitrant rebel more than she should. She wondered why a middle-aged woman had night thoughts that properly belonged in the head of an adolescent girl.

★ ★ ★

A military messenger delivered a cream-colored envelope from General Sickles's headquarters. It contained an engraved invitation to attend the general's Christmas levee at the newly reopened Mills House.

"How on earth did he get my name?" Alex wondered.

"Cedric, probably," Ham said. "He and Mrs. Buckles are going. You know Sickles has an eye for charming ladies. I'll be happy to escort you and protect your virtue." She laughed and swatted his nose with the envelope.

"We might have a good time, Alex. The town's very tense. Awash with rumors of a Negro uprising at Christmas."

Alex shook her head. "Every year. Will it ever end?"

★ ★ ★

A week before the levee Richard took her to see a traveling dime museum and menagerie set up in a tent near the Ashley. The menagerie consisted of a llama, an ocelot, and an old lion in a cage who yawned and refused to rise off his haunches. The museum featured a one-armed albino woman who folded paper into clever animal shapes, a small dolphin lethargically swimming in a wooden tank, a glass blower, and a magic show presented by one Mr. Nostra Nostradamus. It was a tawdry affair, but she enjoyed herself.

Walking home through the mild December night, she mentioned General Sickles's invitation. Richard whipped off his slouch hat and slapped it against his leg. "You mean you'd actually hobnob with that man? Not only is he a Yankee, he's a drunkard and a lecher."

"I have no direct evidence of that. I'd like to meet him."

"I met him on the horse car and I can tell you he's an arrogant toad. I wouldn't come within ten yards of him."

"So there's no possibility that you might escort me?"

"What? Are you ragging me? I ought to turn you over my knee and swat the foolishness out of you."

She separated her arm from his. "That wouldn't be advisable. I'm not some spineless thing you can order about. You're getting very dictatorial, Richard. I don't like it and I don't understand it."

He stopped by the stucco wall of a darkened house. "Oh, you don't? Why do you think I trot around to your house like a puppy? I like you, and I shouldn't, because you don't like me, what I am or what I was. But I still come back for more. I don't want that little Yankee viper to lay one finger on you."

"Why, you sound jealous of General Sickles."

"You bet I am, woman." She gasped as he pulled her into a clumsy kiss.

The pressure of his mouth, the tobacco scent of his skin, stirred her unexpectedly. She slid her left arm around his waist. They kissed for nearly a minute under the bright December stars.

When they broke the embrace, she patted her hair, though not a strand was out of place. "Richard, I am fifty-two years old. I don't need this kind of complication in my life."

"You think I do? Don't know what's come over me."

Perhaps the same thing that had come over her with unexpected stealth: she cared for him. He aroused feelings that she thought had died with Drew. They walked homeward in tense silence. Near South Battery he stopped again.

"I tell you, Alex, this is the most confusing damn situation I've ever lived through, except maybe the war. Poor Loretta in her grave, and I'm carrying on like a lovesick boy."

"Lovesick?" Her legs wobbled.

He turned away, his profile visible against lights of a steamer crossing in front of the ruins of Sumter. "You heard me."

She took his hand.

"I'm flattered, Richard, but I don't want you to feel guilty about your wife because of me. We can go on as we have, just being friends."

He shook his head. "It's too late for that. I've got to ask—do you want me to stop calling on you? If you do, say so."

She remembered his kiss; how good it felt after all the long, lonely years.

"No, I don't."

"I can't change my ways."

"Don't be too sure," she said, and kissed him again.

The kiss left her warm and fulfilled. She hummed "A Better, Brighter Morning" as they approached the garden gate. A provost guard on horseback trotted by, saw they were white, touched his cap, and rode on. After a quick peck of Richard's cheek she darted inside. She was in terrible trouble, and so happy, she covered her mouth and giggled.

72

A Blackmailer Intrudes

For the second time in less than a hundred years, Charleston was an oc-cupied city. Nearly 7,500 U.S. Army officers and men garrisoned South Carolina. Some residents made plans to emigrate to Latin America. Brazil offered farmland at twenty cents an acre; in Vera Cruz bands greeted arriving expatriates with "Dixie's Land."

The Johnson government refused to seat the state's newly elected congressional delegation. Delegations from other Confederate states were similarly turned away. Alex declined the invitation to General Sickles's levee, without regret. She and Richard had crossed a boundary by admitting more than casual interest in one another.

The next boundary was intimacy. She confessed to herself that she wanted to make love despite fears that she was a dried-up old woman. She never spoke of this to him, or even hinted. The consequences for both of them were unknown and potentially hurtful. Loyalty to Henry and Drew deterred her as well.

For Christmas she bought Ham and Richard ready-made white silk shirts from a reopened King Street haberdashery. She snipped a tag from Richard's shirt that identified Brooklyn, New York, as its place of man-ufacture. Little Bob received a smaller shirt, with scant enthusiasm. Maudie liked her hand-painted flask of English scent.

Richard gave Alex a sweet-grass basket of things for the garden: grape hyacinth and crocus bulbs, small seed packets fashioned from newspaper. "I've marked them. Blue larkspur. *Portulaca sativa*—think that's how you pronounce it. Oriental poppy—didn't get many of those, they're dear. And this is pink alyssum. I was told the variety's uncommon."

"So are you. All this must have been frightfully expensive. You shouldn't have spent—"

"Don't tell me *shouldn't* at Christmastime. I wanted to give you something you'd like."

"Oh, you did. Thank you." She threw her arms around his neck and kissed him.

Ham surprised her with a Van Hagen banjo guitar. "Found it at Riley's junk shop. Looted from someone's home like most of his goods, I suspect."

She was thrilled. The banjo guitar incorporated features of both instruments. It was fretted like a guitar but had the banjo's short extra string on the side. Ham included a copy of *Frank B. Converse's New & Complete Method for the Banjo With or Without a Master*. Converse was a celebrated minstrel man. With good things to put in the ground and an instrument to play, Alex felt the world returning to a sunnier time.

The holidays passed without racial unrest. On New Year's Day, Sickles declared the Black Codes illegal and abrogated. Gibbes and his like-minded colleagues went into temporary retreat to await a new opportunity to further their cause.

✭ ✭ ✭

After New Year's the dreary winter of dark skies, dank air, and fitful spits of rain settled over the Low Country. Papers announced that the National Savings Bank and Trust Company planned to open a Charleston office, competition for the Crescent. Meanwhile, Folsey and other gentlemen with cash carried on a brisk private loan business, charging interest of twenty-five and thirty percent.

New firms opened: a sash and door company; a factory that stamped sheet tin into milk pans and bucket bottoms; a seed-pressing firm marketing a substitute for linseed oil. Small enterprises like these set the city's commercial machinery in motion again, but labor, like capital, remained scarce. The Chamber of Commerce sent an agent abroad to promote South Carolina to potential immigrants in Ireland, Germany, and Scandinavia.

Northern steamship companies resumed service. The New York &

Charleston line signed an agreement to dock its steamers *Champion* and *Manhattan* at Bell's Bridge, and Ham hired a new superintendent. The man's unfortunate name was Wofford Crawford. He answered to Slim because he was not. Tubby, bowlegged, and in his late thirties, Crawford was a veteran of the Charleston Light Artillery and a lay preacher in a breakaway Baptist sect. He didn't hide his scorn for Charleston's sybaritic style of life. Crawford let the contract for a swing-out passenger gangway to be built on the wharf. The first steamer docked without it, unloading several more Yankee speculators lugging fancy carpetbags.

☆   ☆   ☆

Ouida lived in a constant state of near-hysteria over conditions at Prosperity Hall. Gibbes rode out there at least once a week to attempt to soothe her. He couldn't count on her son to do it. Calhoun remained a burned-out sot.

Gibbes's humanitarian missions met with little success. Ouida remained Ouida, her hair perpetually disheveled, her clothes tattooed brown by an iron clumsily applied. Her spectacles trebled the size of her irises.

"Gibbes, I can't endure this. Mama never taught me to cook or sew. Every time I drive my buggy to the crossroads, all I can buy are root vegetables or weevily biscuits. I hate that swarthy storekeeper too. I'll bet he has nigger blood."

"I wouldn't be surprised. The Pertwees have been marrying and mingling in the Low Country for years."

"But what am I to do? I wasn't raised to conduct myself like a scullery maid."

"Neither were scores of other women of your station and breeding. They survive. So must you."

"Oh, Gibbes, I don't think I can." Wailing, she tore off her glasses and ran from the room. She blundered against the newel post as she fled upstairs. Gibbes sighed, bereft of any serviceable solution to his sister's problem.

☆   ☆   ☆

To the office of Buckles & Bell one dark day in late February came a shabbily dressed man with two fingers missing from his right hand. He introduced himself as Plato Hix and asked to see Mr. Hampton Bell, Esq., please. Ham took the visitor to his gloomy office; at midday it had the look of twilight.

Hix sat fiddling with his soiled gray kepi, under a charcoal portrait of James Petigru done at Ham's request. "Sir, I've read of you in the papers. You're the good lawyer that got those nigger soldiers off, aren't you?"

"I was one of the attorneys, yes. Mr. Mitchell was lead counsel."

Out of Hix's pocket came an envelope pasted together from stiff paper. Ham saw the words *Property Mr. & Mrs. P. Hix,* and an address on Prioleau Street, written in a poor hand.

"Like to hire you to keep this for me, sir. How much would you charge?"

"What you're requesting isn't exactly a regular legal service, Mr. Hix. The Marburg bank can give you a locked box."

"No. I come to you because your name's Bell. It's an old and good name, even if some of the Bells aren't so—" He bit off the sentence. " 'Scuse me."

"You were saying?"

"No, sir, never mind."

Ham tapped the envelope. "What's in this?"

"Private information, is all." Ham had heard the truth shaded and evaded in court testimony many times; he heard it again in Hix's answer.

"Why do you require someone to take care of it?"

" 'Case anything happens to me, sir."

"Your life's been threatened?"

"Oh, no, sir, no." Despite the chill in the office Hix was sweating. "It's just a family matter, but there could be some trouble over it. I wrote down some facts about it 'till it's all settled."

"The contents of the envelope are secret?"

"Yes, sir."

"Mr. Hix, I appreciate your confidence in me, but I can hardly take money for stowing an envelope in our safe. I'll be happy to do you the favor at no charge. Just be sure to come back and claim it when this family matter is resolved."

On his feet, Hix exclaimed, "Yes, sir. We'll have it settled soon, a week at most. Then I'll be back. God bless you, sir." He grabbed Ham's hand and shook it violently.

Ham wanted to open the envelope, see what could throw an apparently law-abiding man into a state of nerves. He suppressed his curiosity and placed the envelope in the firm's black iron safe.

★   ★   ★

A freakish thunderstorm with a mixture of snow and rain struck the coast. The snow melted as it fell. Plato Hix trudged through the foul weather wearing his kepi and a secondhand poncho, vulcanized rubber on muslin. Some unknown reb had painted a checkerboard on it. Even protected this way Plato was soaked when he reached Prosperity Hall.

Gibbes Bell and a woman he introduced as his sister received him in the parlor. "Yes, ma'am, we met that time fire broke out on Legare Street." The woman stared at him, silent and hostile. Plato's poncho dripped on the fine Turkish carpet. The woman huffed and left the room, her spectacles riding low on her nose.

"Please excuse my sister, she's not herself," Gibbes said. "I remember you very well. Hix, wasn't it?"

" 'S right, sir. Plato Hix. I looked for you at Malvern, then came here."

"We're visiting my sister for a day or two. My wife went on to Savannah to shop." Gibbes invited Hix to sit. He didn't like this man, or the surprise visit.

"I surely hate to disturb you, sir. I just got no choice. I have two head of children to look after and I can't hardly do it. Times are hard."

"If this involves money, I don't make loans. My friend Mr. Folsey Lark might accommodate you."

Lightning painted the room white; thunder hit close by. Several heavy limbs crashed on the brown lawn. Little flames danced on the trunk of a live oak split in half.

"Please hear me out, sir. I was on the Peninsula in eighteen and sixty-two. Wade Hampton's Legion. I fought at Seven Pines, sir, like you did. Like Major Wheat, who died there."

Tiny jewels of sweat gleamed on Hix's forehead. Gibbes's heart pounded. He ran his hand down his thigh, clamping hard on the cup of his artificial leg.

"A lot of men died at Seven Pines, Mr. Hix. I don't take your meaning. You'll have to state it more clearly."

"I saw Major Wheat die, sir. I figure that's got to be worth something. I'm sorry to come to you like this, but I can't let my wife and youngsters starve."

A long moment passed, the only sound the rush of rain off the eaves. Gibbes wanted to attack the man, knock him down, batter him senseless. He smiled and stood.

"I understand what you're saying. I'm sure we can settle this to our mutual satisfaction. Take off that slicker. Be comfortable. Would you care for a hot drink?"

"Why, sir, that would be welcome. I came through a mighty lot of cold rain to get here."

"Sit back and I'll ask my sister to brew us a pot of her special herb tea."

He left. Plato wanted to clap his hands and whoop.

☆ ☆ ☆

Two hours later Gibbes dragged Plato Hix out of the house by his collar. The tea had done its work; Hix was unconscious. He'd be dead within a few hours, depending on the strength of his constitution. Ouida hadn't hesitated to fix the tea once Gibbes explained that the man was a dangerous intruder demanding money and threatening violence if he didn't get it.

Hix's boot heels dug ruts in the muddy ground. His head lolled. *Heavy son of a bitch,* Gibbes thought. When night fell, he'd bury Hix way out in the brush at the edge of the property. No one ventured there.

Cold and drenched, he pulled Hix into the stable. The dying man moaned. Gibbes's fine bay, Trajan, neighed and kicked his stall. Gibbes stroked and soothed the animal, but Trajan kept tossing his head. He nipped at Gibbes's hand. Gibbes leapt away, almost losing his balance because of his stiff wooden leg.

Rain pelted the roof shakes, leaking through in several places. Gibbes propped Hix against a post. He found rope and wrapped it around Hix and knotted it. He had little fear that Hix would have the strength to attempt an escape, or even waken, but he took no chances. Certain events on the Peninsula on the last day of May 1862 could never be revealed to the world.

He stepped back, wet gray hair straggling over his forehead. His coat was ruined, his trousers muddy, his boots soiled by stepping in horse pies. Hix breathed so lightly, it was barely audible. Gibbes heard a horse, ran to the stable door.

"Oh, sweet God." Up the lane from the river road galloped a bare-headed and bedraggled Cal Hayward.

☆ ☆ ☆

Cal ducked his head as he rode into the stable. Even with the odors of wet hay and manure and horseflesh swirling, Gibbes smelled the whiskey.

Cal threw his leg over the saddle and dropped to the ground. He staggered, a silly smile on his face. "Whoops." He belched. He saw Hix. "Who'n hell's that?"

"Some tramp. I went off to the crossroads store for an hour and when I came back, I found him in the house, in this condition. Where've you been?"

"Charleston. What's wrong with him?"

"He's poisoned. He'll die soon."

"*Poisoned?*"

Gibbes hissed and gestured for quiet. Cal ignored him. "Who poisoned him?"

"I'm sorry to say it was your mother, with some of her oleander tea. She admitted it to me. She had some notion he was a Yankee."

A remarkable transformation occurred then. Cal's eyes cleared. He stood without weaving or wobbling. "Why would she do something terrible like that?"

"You know how she hates Yankees. She tried using the poison once before, with a Union officer who stopped by. I prevented her from serving him the tea. Today I was too late."

Cal lost control, screaming, "What are you telling me? *What are you telling me?*"

"That we have to bury him as soon as he dies, and never tell a soul. I don't think you should blame your poor mother too much. She's not right in the head and we both know it."

"That sure-God doesn't excuse murder."

Gibbes didn't answer. The rain abruptly slowed, dripping through the shakes, forming puddles. Thunder rolled distantly as the storm moved out to sea. Plato Hix's head sagged lower on his chest. He moaned again. Trajan kicked the stall, a sound loud as gunshots.

73

Ouida's Fall

Gibbes and Cal buried the dead man. They spoke only when necessary. A sharp northwest wind was blowing as they finished. They trudged back to the great house under thousands of remote and icy stars. Ouida met them with a lamp. "Be careful of that," Gibbes said. She wasn't wearing her glasses.

"Where have you been? Where did you come from, Cal?" Neither answered her. Gibbes brushed by and headed for the liquor decanters in the sitting room. Cal started upstairs after an intense look at his mother, whether of anguish or censure, Gibbes couldn't tell.

The house oppressed him with memories of Hix. He slept fitfully, disturbed by Cal ranting and throwing things about in the next room. Once he heard Ouida tapping at Cal's door, speaking in a faint, imploring voice. Cal yelled something. She went away.

Gibbes rose before dawn, woke his sister, and told her that he felt a need to join Snoo in Savannah. He saddled Trajan and took the road to the Ashley ferry. The bridge at Charleston, destroyed when the Confederates left, was not yet repaired.

Midmorning found him near Jacksonboro. He rode Trajan hard, as if fleeing pursuit. *This will pass,* he assured himself. *No one will find Hix and he'll be forgotten, he was a nobody. Cal won't incriminate his mother. The past will stay buried along with Hix and Owen Wheat.*

✷ ✷ ✷

The following night Ouida sat in the sewing room with a flag draping her shoulders like a shawl. It was the glorious Confederate battle flag, designed by dear General Beauregard—thirteen white stars in a cross of St. Andrew on a red field. Formerly the flag had waved over the door of Ouida's Legare Street town house, an emblem of her pride and patriotism. It was made of cheap material, thin and brittle, but she loved it and wanted it close to her.

Reflections of the lamp wick shimmered in her spectacles as she tried to sew a new hem on a threadbare petticoat. Age had weakened her eyes; she stabbed her middle finger with the needle. Tears flowed. "I don't know how to do this, I'm not meant for this, it's servant's work." She flung the bloodstained petticoat into the shadows, threw the needle and thimble after it.

She heard Cal's heavy tread and confronted him at the foot of the stairs. He wore a straw planter's hat, a bedraggled gray cape, and reeked of rum. Like a prosecutor she pointed at his leather satchel.

"What's that? Where are you going?"

"Back to the city."

"Who are you visiting?"

"I'm moving out, Mama."

She reacted as though he'd smashed her face with his fist. "*What?* Am I hearing this? What do you mean, moving out?"

"Just that. I wanted to leave without disturbing you."

"So I'd be frantic when I woke up and found you were gone?"

"I left a note upstairs."

"Oh, very considerate, Calhoun Hayward, very considerate of your poor impoverished mother. How do you propose to take care of yourself in Charleston? And don't give me sass about cards and dice."

"I'll work. You must have heard of work, Mama. Most of the world does it."

"Don't sneer, I hate that. Tell me why you're doing this." He stared dumbly, his face a study of pain. She shrieked at him. "Answer me, damn you."

Her cursing made him blush. He could admit only half the truth: "There's a woman I'm seeing, but I can't see her if I'm moldering away in the country." How could he look his mother in the eye and call her a murderess?

Ouida clutched the flag to her breast. "Who is she? I demand that you tell me."

"Her name's Adah. With an *h*."

"Adah with an *h*, an *h*." Ouida paced on the heart-pine floor. "I don't recognize the name. She can't be from one of the old Charleston families or I'd know her. She must be a newcomer." She pressed her palms to her white-powdered cheeks. "Dear Lord. She isn't the daughter of some swinish carpetbagger, is she?"

Cal seemed to gather himself. "She's colored. A beautiful, intelligent—"

"Colored? You're infatuated with a *nigger*? My God, what did the war do to your mind?" She paced again, wildly excited. "It's the liquor, all the liquor you pour into yourself. Only a drunken sot would take up with—"

"Mama, this is ugly. Please don't say any more. I'm going. I'm sorry for you, sorry you're poor, sorry you're alone, but I won't stay here and rot away imagining things that might have been. We were deluded, Mama. Deluded and arrogant. We had no chance to win the fucking war."

"Oh, you vile, filthy creature." She threw her spectacles. They hit the leg of a table, cracking one lens into a star pattern. "You can't do this. You're betraying me. You're betraying our family, all we ever stood for."

"That's gone. That was yesterday. I'll write you soon. Good-bye."

He lifted his bag and strode past her, trailing fumes of rum. The door closed. Ouida covered her eyes. "Oh, God, why me? Why me?"

She stepped toward the table to find her glasses. She couldn't see where they'd fallen. Her left shoe crushed both lenses.

Sobbing, she knelt and groped. She found the frames, felt the lenses crumbling in little pieces. She twisted the frames, hurled them away, cursing again. She lurched up and ran to the sewing room with the flag clutched against herself.

The lamp was a dancing blur. She navigated toward it but misjudged the distance. Her knee bumped the three-legged taboret, overturning it. She reached to catch the lamp, too late. The lamp struck the hardwood floor. The chimney and the oil reservoir broke. The oil soaked the carpet fringe and ignited.

Ouida tried to beat out the flames with the flag. The brittle cloth caught fire. She cried out, stumbled backward, and lost her balance. She fell against a window, shattering it. She lay on her back, a huge nail of pain in her spine. She'd impaled herself on broken glass.

She clutched one of the draperies. Rings snapped; the smoldering curtain came down, smothering her. She flung it off. The more she writhed, the worse the pain was. Flames quickly consumed the flag, the drapery, spread across the valence to the other side of the window.

"Calhoun. Calhoun, son, where are you? Help me."

Frightened as a child, she lay still, watching the light grow brighter, panting in the intense heat. The fire ate the dingy wallpaper, the faded carpet, the unpolished furniture, engulfed the discarded petticoat. She whimpered, "Calhoun."

Her hair began to burn, a bright helmet of flame.

☆ ☆ ☆

Cal took the Cooper River Road. A half mile beyond Mont Royal, the plantation belonging to the widow Madeline Main and her late husband, a faint rosy glow appeared behind him. Because of the serpentine curves in the road, and his swift gallop toward the city, he never saw the light of the fire that destroyed Prosperity Hall and his mother with it.

74

The Letter

Newspapers reported the destruction at Prosperity Hall. Instead of a great estate Gibbes now owned burnt timbers, rubble, and outbuildings. Alex took no satisfaction from it.

Ouida's accidental death stunned Alex and generated pity and sympathy not felt for years. Ouida had to be considered family in spite of her aberrant behavior. Ham called her entire life "unfortunate."

Gibbes arranged for Ouida's funeral to be held at St. Philip's, perhaps to distance himself from his relatives. Richard offered to accompany Alex. She kissed him, thanked him, and said it wasn't necessary. Ham would be with her.

Few attended the service. Over the years Ouida's extremes of temper and opinion had driven off her friends. Gibbes and Snoo sat in a front pew, Folsey Lark across the aisle. Cal wasn't with the family.

A half-dozen elderly black people were scattered in the gallery. Maudie was among them, with Little Bob at her side. He wore his Christmas shirt and a cravat Maudie had sewn. Negroes were seen less and less in Charleston's white churches. Ham said they no longer wanted to worship where they had during slave days. They were breaking away in large numbers to found their own congregations.

The whole affair depressed Alex. Because of the weather the nave of St. Philip's was gloomy. The organist's renditions of "Abide With Me" and Bach's "Come, Sweet Death" seemed to deepen the mood of melancholy. It was evident the rector hardly knew Ouida; his remarks included few personal details, and many bland generalities about cleansing sin and putting off sorrows of the flesh. She was thankful when "Jesu, Joy of Man's Desiring" rang out and the mourners rose to leave.

Stepping into the aisle ahead of Ham, she spied Cal in a rear pew with a handsome woman, a light-skinned Negro. Alex saw Gibbes stare stonily at his nephew. There was little doubt as to why.

The mourners gathered under a canopy in the churchyard as rain fell. After the coffin went into the ground, Alex approached her cousin and clasped his gloved hand.

"A terrible thing to happen to anyone, Gibbes. It was an accident, wasn't it?"

"We assume so. A peddler passing by the morning after the fire found her, without her glasses."

"You know you have my sympathy."

"Thank you, I'm sure of that." Stiffly polite, he might have been talking to someone he barely knew.

How terrible he looked. Thin, and sallow, almost jaundiced. He struck her as a man distracted, as though by a wasting disease. She felt sorry for him until he raked her with a look reminiscent of his old, lustful self. She took her brother's arm and left.

On Church Street she saw Cal under a big black umbrella, hurrying away with his companion. "Who is the woman, I wonder?"

Ham said, "I surely can't tell you. From the way she's clutching on, I assume their relationship is more than casual. Folsey must be acquainted with her. He gave her murderous looks in the churchyard. Thank heaven Ouida isn't here or we'd have had a riot on our hands."

✷　✷　✷

At the end of ten days, which was three days longer than his agreement with Plato Hix called for, Ham withdrew Hix's letter from the office safe. He went to the headquarters of the Charleston police and spoke with one of the detectives recently hired. The detective said he knew of no reports of an accident or foul play involving someone named Hix. Ham braced himself for a visit to Prioleau Street.

He loathed the mixed neighborhood where poor law-abiding blacks were forced to live amid the city's worst riffraff. Half-naked children, white, blue-black, brown, and yellow, played around the stoop of Hix's tenement. Ham stepped over the reeking street drain, ignored the grimy children with their hands out, and went up the dingy stair, his leather document case clamped under his arm.

The staircase swayed alarmingly; the risers felt soft as cheese. A grimy windowpane leaked light from above. And the smell! Ham pressed a clean handkerchief to his nose and mouth. Why did a white man choose such a dismal address when, for the same money, he could rent in a less odious neighborhood? The moment Mrs. Hix answered his knock, he understood. Plato Hix had married a woman of mixed blood. Attractive once, perhaps, she was round-shouldered, haggard. Her expression said Ham's arrival boded no good.

He tipped his tall hat as a rat scurried by his toes. "Mrs. Hix? Hampton Bell. I'm an attorney."

"Yes?"

"I have a letter your husband deposited with me. He asked me to keep it secure while he attended to some personal business. He said he would reclaim the letter within a week but he's failed to appear, so I thought it my duty to call. Is Mr. Hix at home perchance?"

"Ha'n't seen him for days."

"Will you allow me to come in?" She stood back, though reluctant.

The apartment consisted of two rooms. Amid an assortment of battered furniture a boy of five or six sat on a scrap of carpet, turning the pages of a cloth picture book. The rear room served as a combination sleeping area and kitchen; a girl, younger, slowly stirred a spoon in what appeared to be a bowl of corn meal mush. One small window admitted the flat's wan light.

Mary Hix pushed the boy. "Shoo, Benny, go sit with your sister." She lifted a damp lock of hair off her forehead. "I'm real sorry for the way the place looks. Plato don't make a lot of money blacking boots. You can sit there." She indicated an old sofa with a block of wood propping up one leg.

"Much obliged." Ham took the seat, the leather case resting on his knees. "Do you know how I might locate your husband?"

"No idea. Day he left, he said he had business in the country, and we'd be a whole lot better off soon as he took care of it."

"You haven't seen him since then?"

"No, sir, nor heard from him. I'm half out of my mind worrying."

"I can imagine. I visited police headquarters before coming here. They have no information."

"I thought of going to the police but I know they don't much want to help"—she faltered—"people like me."

"Did your husband say anything else before he left? Anything that might offer a clue as to his whereabouts?"

In the rear room the girl flicked her spoon at her brother. He wiped a gob of mush from his cheek and yanked her hair. Mary Hix screamed, "You behave, both of you, or I'll blister your behinds." She twisted her soiled apron. "I'm so sorry. You were asking . . . ?"

"Do you recall anything that might suggest where we could find Mr. Hix?"

"He did mention a Mr. Gibbes Bell. Same last name as yourself. Is he a relative?"

"A cousin. We're not close. Please go on."

"Plato said if anything happened to him, it would be Mr. Bell responsible."

"Those were his exact words?"

"Not exact, maybe, but I remember the sense of it."

Ham felt a tightness in his throat, a nervous spasm in his stomach. Mrs. Hix's statement was alarming but legally useless. Even with corroboration the testimony of a colored woman against that of Ham's highly regarded cousin would carry no weight with the police, or any court in South Carolina. He believed the same would hold true if Mrs. Hix were poor white.

"I'm scared something's happened to Plato, sir." She wasn't alone; Ham was envisioning a figure crumpled in an alley, a body floating in a river. He opened the brass clasp of the case.

"This is what your husband left in my keeping. As you see, it's addressed to you."

Mrs. Hix took the letter, fingered it, as if not sure of its purpose or meaning. "I wonder, would you be able to read it for me?"

"If you prefer." He retrieved the letter quickly, not wanting to embarrass her by forcing her to say she was illiterate. He inserted a finger under the flap, removed the sheets of cheap paper covered with bad handwriting. He scanned the first few sentences. "My God."

"Sir?"

"It concerns the war. Allow me to read it silently first."

He went swiftly through the unparagraphed document. When he finished he was thoroughly unnerved. Surely it was a tissue of falsehoods. But if so, why write it? No adult who thought clearly, reacted rationally, would fear such a wild story. Even setting aside Gibbes's status in the community, a prosecutor would not give credence to the letter without supporting evidence, or another witness.

"There's nothing here to help us locate your husband. What the letter contains is nothing short of . . ."

Ham wet his lips. How to tell her? The only way was straight out.

"An accusation of murder," he said.

★ ★ ★

Rather than read the letter aloud he summarized it in careful, evasive language appropriate to a courtroom. By the end Mary Hix was crouched on a stool and weeping. "That man, your relative, he must've killed Plato for writing it all down."

"I urge you not to repeat that charge to anyone. It's unprovable based on this letter. For your own safety I advise you to keep silent while I consider what, if anything, might be done." In truth he hadn't a glimmer of what to do, other than throw the letter back in the safe and wish to God he'd never seen it.

She promised to heed him. He fled down the swaying stair. In Prioleau Street it was raining again, a hot, soggy drizzle. At Buckles & Bell he laid the letter on the blotter and stared at it, wishing the words would disappear or magically reveal some hidden, innocent meaning.

At home on South Battery that evening he showed Alex the letter and explained how he'd come by it. He and Alex sat together on a Hamnet Strong settee. "I fear this was written for purposes of blackmail. Mrs. Hix as much as confirmed it. I likewise fear Hix is no longer in a position to realize his expected financial gain. I suspect he may be dead."

Horrified, Alex reached for the scrawled sheets. "Let me read it, please."

75

Seven Pines

This is a true and honest statement of Corpral Plato Roscius Hix CSA. I never ment to see what I seen that day in 18 & 62, sometimes I wish God scald my eyes so I did not. I never saw any body white or nigro scairt as bad as Capt Gibs Bell.

In the spring of 1862 General Joe Johnston fought and retreated, fought and retreated, in front of George McClellan's army on the Peninsula. The strategic withdrawal took Johnston to the outskirts of the capital, and had two objectives: to give Richmond time to strengthen defenses, and Johnston time to find favorable ground for a decisive engagement.

Gibbes reached the headquarters of the Hampton Legion two days after a skirmish at Eltham's Plantation. Federal troops disembarking from boats in the York River were driven back in brief action. Gibbes shuddered when he heard that the Confederates lost "only" forty-eight men, with another forty-six taken prisoner.

The Legion was now part of the division of Brigadier-General William H. C. Whiting, a West Point engineer who at one time worked on the defenses of Charleston and Morris Island. Hampton had been given command of an entire brigade the preceding October but had yet to receive formal promotion.

Gibbes reported to Maj. Owen Wheat of the brigade staff. Wheat was a large barrel of a man with pale, frosty eyes, unruly gray hair, and a single star on his collar. He received Gibbes's salute and papers, kept him at attention while he packed and lit his pipe.

"Let us be candid, Captain. We both know what secured your commission. Social position, connections, not experience. Well, I'll not soothe you with fantasies. A battle is the devil's own business. Imagine the worst and you're but a tenth of the way to reality. Further, your company is now about fifty-percent replacements, green striplings mostly. First time they see the elephant, they may run. As an officer it's your duty to stop 'em. I am intolerant of cowardice." Gibbes's bowels were churning.

"The Legion fought bravely at Manassas. On the Warrenton Turnpike we found ourselves in the thick of it. Never had I imagined such a continuous rushing hailstorm of shot, shell, and musketry as fell around and among us. Those of us who survived constantly wonder how it happened. I don't say this to alarm you but to prepare you." Gibbes didn't believe him. Wheat probably took sadistic pleasure in frightening his subordinates.

"Lieutenant Frank Adams will introduce you to your men. You may keep that fine horse you tied outside, but as of now you're in the infantry. Look on the bright side. Combat presents many a sudden opportunity for promotion."

It did not surpriz me that Maj W. & Capt B. come to a bad end, they did not like each other, all the men knew it. I never seen much of Capt Bell in Virginnia since he led one compny and I marched in another. But soljers talk and I heard the capt was not liked by his men either, they could tell he didnt care for plain folk & had got his rank becaus of who he was. Nor did he like the Army life but had joined up like some others so as not to be looked down on. That was not true of all officers esp Gen Hampton who was a brave and true fighter for the Cause. At 7 Pines he took a ball in his foot while in the saddle & refusd to dismount but made the surjun extrack the ball right there, in the stirrup so to say.

First Lieutenant Frank Adams had been a schoolteacher in Branchville. First Sergeant Oliver Burks owned a small cotton farm in Richland County. Both knew how to march, which Gibbes did not.

A few men in the company carried outdated muskets, but most were equipped with .69-caliber percussion rifles stamped with the name of the Palmetto Armory of Columbia. First Sergeant Burks drilled the veterans and their clumsy replacements while Gibbes observed, finding confidence to take over just days before the war engine roared to life.

Camp duty was miserable: scant rations, muddy bivouacs, nearly constant rain. Gibbes slept badly, haunted by Wheat's ominous words about battle. Wheat harassed and criticized him at every opportunity. He let Gibbes know the reason:

"I did not volunteer to fight this war so Low Country gentlemen like yourself could put on plumed hats, mount fine horses, and trot off to glory. Frankly, I despise you and your kind. Although in a minority, you maneuvered the rest of us into an armed quarrel over slavery. I am not a slave master and never have been. I own a tobacco warehouse in Florence. The men who work for me receive wages, not whippings and cast-off shirts at Christmas. I long ago decided Carolina would be a whole lot better off if we shipped all our colored to Connecticut or some benighted province like Iowa and learned to dirty our hands with honest toil."

"Sir, with respect. Isn't this war all about the right to own property, niggers included?"

"Your war, sir. I'm fighting for the land I possess. The patch of ground where I was born and still reside. I'm here because I don't want some gaseous Yankee politician telling me I can't spit into the wind if I choose. I'm no student of the philosophies of government"—though prating like one, Gibbes thought—"but it seems to me that if I have freely entered into an agreement to form a union, I should have the privilege of withdrawing from that union if and when it no longer comports with my beliefs. In other words, Captain, I am not fighting for your right to beat your niggers at your whim, I am fighting for a separate and independent Confederate republic." Wheat waved his corncob, leaving traceries of blue in the air. "Dismissed."

☆ ☆ ☆

While the Confederate government prepared for the worst, burning records and readying an escape plan for President Davis, Joe Johnston prepared to fight. He would strike McClellan's advancing right wing to prevent linkage with 40,000 reinforcements, including a division of McDowell's, that would give Little Mac 150,000 effectives at the gates of Richmond; a two-to-one advantage. As it turned out, McDowell's advance was a feint; he was soon countermarching to Fredericksburg.

The swollen Chickahominy River split McClellan's army. Three corps, Sumner's, Porter's, and Franklin's, held the north side, two more, those of Keyes and Heintzelman, the south. Incessant spring rain had created a muddy maze of new streams, tributaries, and ponds.

On May 30, Friday, south of the river, Confederate reconnaissance showed Silas Casey's division strung across the Williamsburg Road about a half mile west of the junction known as Seven Pines. Casey's left extended south of the road, into White Oak Swamp, while his right ran north for about a mile, to the Fair Oaks station of the Richmond & York River Railroad. Divisions of Couch and Kearny backed up Casey's line.

After dark a violent storm brought down rain at the rate of three or four inches in two hours. The rain continued through the night, flooding roads and low places. Johnston's attack started on Saturday, hours behind schedule due to road conditions and costly misunderstandings of orders by Longstreet.

Whiting's Division had the task of watching the Union right. At dawn Saturday they prepared to march from Richmond to Fair Oaks on the Nine Mile Road, a distance of six miles. Rain, mud, and General Longstreet's division breaking camp at the city's Fairfield Race Course hampered their progress. By one o'clock they were scarcely two thirds of the way to their objective.

In the afternoon improvised bridges allowed units of Sumner's corps to cross to the south side of the Chickahominy. Scouts discovered this and Whiting rushed three brigades, Hampton's, Pettigrew's, and Hatton's, to repel Sumner; Hampton's brigade was on the left. Gibbes would later say that when they advanced, they found hell without Satan.

★ ★ ★

It was already past five in the afternoon when they neared the Federal lines in an enveloping womb of dripping trees and watery sinkholes. They advanced in standard formation, two skirmisher companies out in front, then the main line, and two companies behind it as reserves. Gibbes's was a flanker company, at the left end of the main line. Bayonets were fixed, although Frank Adams said they were seldom used. "They're more to frighten than kill."

Given the thick woods, intermittent rain, and a rising ground fog, it was hard to recognize comrades even a few feet away. Uniforms were muddy; gray might be blue, and vice versa. Men carried their rifles over their heads as they passed through standing water of uncertain depth. The forest grew darker. Less than two hours of daylight remained.

Gibbes made a brave show of flourishing his straight infantry sword as he sloshed knee-deep across a newly channeled stream. "Forward, men, forward, we'll meet them any moment." He was mortally afraid. Whistles and warbles echoed eerily in the wood. Whether they were bird calls or signals, he couldn't say.

Far away to his right rebel yells and a rattle of shots signaled Hatton's men engaging. Then, directly ahead, a rifle cracked. Gibbes saw the spurt of flame. Near him Frank Adams cried out and sank into shallow water. A bullet had cleanly drilled the center of his forehead.

Exploding shells set damp tree limbs to sparking and smoking. The distant artillery threw grapeshot as well, filling the air with hissing metal that felled four more men. Sumner's bluebellies opened up across their entire front; sheets of flame leapt out. "Forward, forward!" Gibbes screamed himself hoarse, walking backward, flourishing his sword. More men dropped. The company's ranks disintegrated as soldiers wheeled and ran to the rear, leaving their rifles in the mud.

Another shell landed twenty yards away. Gibbes cringed and covered his head against a rain of earth. No sooner had he uncovered than a ball tore his gray sleeve. He peered down at the hole in the cloth and lost control. His bowels released. He ran with the others, away from the hail of enemy fire.

About half past 6 we met Sumner's boys in the woods where you could hardly tell who was friend or enmy. Men sank to their bellies in water, shot or just stumbling, they screamed and yelled like scairt babes. Formations broke, compnys melted together, everything was crazy. I must have went the wrong way for I found myself amongst men I never saw befor. A ball hit my hand and I fell in a crick bleeding bad. I climbed out and held fast to a tree trunk. More men ran away, wild eyed, one was Capt Bell.

What little courage Gibbes possessed deserted him in that mad flight. His stinking trousers sagged, shaming him. He lurched out of a water hole, slipped, and fell on his face, trembling and sobbing. A familiar voice boomed in the murk. "Form details, form details. Those unhurt prop the wounded against trees so they don't drown."

Gibbes told himself to get up, run; he recognized that voice. He wobbled up on one knee, only to collapse again. The dusk was deepening. There were few men anywhere near him. He couldn't stop crying.

A hand yanked his collar, flung him on his back. Major Wheat's livid face dripped sweat and rain. "You rotten coward. I saw you bolt. I wagered you would, first time I laid eyes on you."

Gibbes groped for his holstered revolver. Wheat slapped his hand down, then pulled his own short-barrel revolver, an imported Tranter. "You'll hang for this, you son of a bitch."

Wheat's hand must have been slippery; he fumbled with the revolver grip. Gibbes seized Wheat's wrist in both hands, wrenched the revolver loose. Wheat's eyes popped. "You yellow toad, you don't have enough guts to—" Gibbes fired into Wheat's mouth, blowing off the back of his head.

I was in pretty bad pain after they got my hand. I hung on to a tree trunk not 5 yds from where Capt Bell shot the maj. in cold blood but he didnt see me, he was looking out for himself.

The man who could have destroyed Gibbes's life lay motionless, eyes open, a little blood dribbling from his mouth, black as licorice. The gloomy woods were full of red flashes, yells from both sides, shell bursts, men running or lying hurt and pleading for help. Medical corpsmen rushed to the rear, carrying wounded in blankets sopping with gore.

Gibbes left Wheat and splashed down into the water, moving not to the rear but toward the guns. *Not too far, not too far,* he thought as the hissing and snapping of bullets and buckshot grew louder. He stopped on a muddy slope. When he believed he was unobserved, he gritted his teeth, aimed Wheat's revolver to his left thigh, and fired.

His leg buckled. He stifled a scream. He reached behind him and dropped the revolver into black water, where it sank. He threw his own sidearm after it. He couldn't remember losing his sword, but he didn't have it. He shouted into the rain. "I'm hit. Over here, I'm hit."

A corpsman soon reached his side. Gibbes's left trouser leg was dark with blood, his mind hazy. The corpsman smelled Gibbes and winced. Duty compelled him to take hold of Gibbes's arm.

"No, son, no, see to the major first," Gibbes said. "He's back there. I think they killed him."

Then he fainted.

*God strike me if I lie, I saw the Capt shoot the majr, run a little
ways, & put the pistol to his own leg. I expec he wanted to look
like he took a wound from the enemy but he outsmarted him self
because I heard later that the gangreen set in & the surgeons
took his leg. So they sent him home. I hung on the tree til they
put me on a litter. While I was passed out they sewed up my
hand with the fingers shot off. They sent me home & in
Charleston I learnd everyone said Capt Bell was brave at 7 Pines,
he was a hero. I saw him run. He was scairt bad or worse than
any of the rest of us, if he wasnt then tell me why did he do murder & cover it up? Both sides say they won that day, Yankees call
the battle Fair Oaks, our side 7 Pines. This is my truthfull acount
of what I saw there in Virginnia in May 18 & 62.*

76

Storm Rising

"Despicable," Alex said when she finished reading. "Sham heroism, and murder to cover his cowardice."

"Assuming we can believe Mr. Hix's testimony," Ham said. "I see no reason not to do that. Old Tom Bell, from all I know of him, was common as a pin, and never pretended otherwise. But ever since Adrian and Lydia, position and reputation have been of colossal, not to say paramount, importance on that side of the family." An acerbic smile. "Of course that remains a tradition in certain quarters of town, doesn't it?"

"What's to be done with the letter?"

"Nothing, unless you wish to expose our cousin. Which assumes it could be accomplished using a document whose contents can't be corroborated or amplified by the writer. I continue to suspect Mr. Hix has left us."

"Gibbes?"

"One can only suppose."

She shivered. If it was true, their cousin was responsible for three deaths, counting Henry Strong and the colonel named Wheat. Surely he deserved punishment, but she didn't want the responsibility.

"I won't want to attack him, Ham. He's deceitful, and a libertine along with everything else, but it isn't my place to conduct a public hanging."

"Then that finishes it. Almost. There is still one person to whom the existence of the letter is critical. We ought not guarantee him total immunity. The letter returns to the safe at Buckles and Bell."

★ ★ ★

In April 1866 President Johnson declared the rebellion in South Carolina over. Some occupying troops were withdrawn from the state, but an ample number remained to annoy the Charleston populace, especially with the intemperate and dogmatic Sickles in command.

On Alex's birthday Richard brought a gift, a fine old bracelet of Mexican silver, and a proposal of marriage. Alex clucked over the bracelet's suspected cost to avoid facing the other issue. Privately she could admit she loved him, though with serious reservations.

"Richard, I'm not sure we could get along, feeling so differently about many things."

"Aren't there issues we can set aside?"

"You mean race, and the course of the state and country? No, I can't. Nor should a husband ask it of a wife."

They sat on the old bench in the sweet-smelling twilight garden. His flecked eyes brooded. "Then you're refusing me."

She touched his hard brown hand. "For the present I am."

"There's hope of a reprieve?"

She didn't know. "May we go inside? I'm chilly."

★ ★ ★

Mary Hix somehow found money to buy a small burial plot. One balmy afternoon Ham accompanied her to inspect the empty grave dedicated to her husband. Mary had decorated the grave in a way often seen at poor Negro cemeteries: a scattering of small stones, black and white and rust-red; chips of green and purple bottle glass; shards of a blue vase.

Benny scuffed his shoe in the dirt. Little Abby whined about needing a toilet. The Atlantic breeze pushed Mary's hair across her face like a veil. "We'll never find him, will we, Mr. Bell?"

"I would think not."

"Then what's to be done? Plato told me who—"

"Mrs. Hix, the man your husband named can't be reached by the law. Don't torture yourself wishing it otherwise."

"It isn't right," Mary exclaimed. "It isn't right that someone's above the law."

"But, alas, that is often the case." Painful to have to say that on a spring day with clouds of innocent white flying in the brilliant blue sky.

"It isn't right," she repeated furiously as they left.

☆   ☆   ☆

If Charleston was a phoenix, Alex thought, the creature was still mostly buried in the ashes. Too many houses remained roofless and windowless. Too many buzzards scavenged in the open-air markets. Too many reeking street drains overflowed. Too many cow yards threw the stench of dung on the warm wind. Too many barrooms, bordellos, and tenements replaced abandoned homes and shops along East Bay.

Too many street confrontations between loitering blacks and whites reached the flashpoint of violence.

To buffer herself against the restless, unhappy state of the occupied city, Alex cultivated her garden. She planted seeds and bulbs Richard had given her; sheared off the tops of her fast-growing *Fatsia japonica;* thinned the white blossoms of the star jasmine twined on the piazza railings. Little Bob helped, smiling when he got down on his knees with her. His stubby fingers made the dirt fly.

Ham came home with stories of the Union League of America organizing Negroes into political clubs, taking advantage of what he called "the Negro's anxious state of locomotion."

"The League men say their purpose is honorable, their operation aboveboard, but I hear that some of them use low tactics to frighten members. They don't want what's best for the colored man, they want votes for the Republican party. They want to vote Negroes like herds of cattle."

Alex devoted three nights a week to her school. Four new pupils had heard of it and come to her door.

Alice Van Epps, forty, wanted to emigrate to Liberia, there to teach African children. Operatives of the African Colonization Society were actively recruiting in Charleston. Nearly three hundred men and women had already signed up to go.

Twin brothers, Jo and Jim Davies, were in their twenties and trained as masons. Jo kept a fat plug of tobacco in his cheek but conscientiously went outside to spit. Where others saw ruins, the brothers saw opportunity. Mayor Gaillard's council had recently passed "An Ordinance to Aid in Rebuilding the Burnt District and Waste Places of the City." It established low-cost loans for anyone who rebuilt with brick. The brothers wanted to start a small brickworks. They realized they had to read, write, and figure if they were to do it.

Bo Bethea, a shrimper in his fifties, came simply because he felt inadequate without literacy. Bo verified the stories of Union League intimidation. "After we gave a password and pledged allegiance to the flag and sang songs, we had to kiss a Bible and swear to elect only true Union men. They said if we didn't, they'd report us to the President and he'd take away our freedom, we'd be slaves again. Could that be, Miss Alex?"

"Never, and they're wicked to say otherwise."

Passing through the dining room, Ham said, "Don't get exercised, sister. That's politics. Always has been, always will be."

★   ★   ★

Gibbes remained in the city during the spring. He had no desire to visit boarded-up Malvern or the ashes of Prosperity Hall. He'd abandoned both places to the weeds and wild pigs, despairing of ever seeing another penny of profit from the land.

Home life was not pleasant. Snoo was constantly in a state, unable to find a colored cook who knew how to prepare a dish unless it swam in fat. Colored laundresses broke buttons on Gibbes's fine shirts and ironed them brown. The hired girls almost laughed in Snoo's face when she reprimanded them. She wept frequently and learned to swear.

A copy of the *Rural Carolinian* chanced across Gibbes's desk. One of the editors, a Col. D. H. Jacques, described *stimulating and invigorating reports concerning deposits of phosphoric rock recently located along the Wando River. Small samples have assayed in a significant way. We have long known of marls rich in calcium carbonate in our tidal rivers, but phosphoric deposits, if present in quantity, could presage a brisk new industry, providing farmers with less costly fertilizer than the Peruvian guano presently employed.* Gibbes snipped out the article and saved it in a drawer. Perhaps his river property wouldn't be worthless forever.

In Washington the damned demagogues of the radical Republican party wanted a constitutional amendment to guarantee the franchise to Negroes. The amendment would be submitted to the states in June or July. Northern papers said representation in Congress would be denied any state refusing to ratify the amendment. Gibbes took up his pen and wrote a letter for circulation among his more affluent constituents.

We will never allow this outrage to become law in our state. Would any rational white man desire that Negroes, a people steeped in ignorance, crime, and vice, should go to the polls and elect men to Congress who are to pass laws taxing and governing them? The Negro is utterly unfitted to exercise the functions of a citizen. We shall protest and resist this upheaval of the social order, for it seeks to place an ignorant and depraved race in power and influence, above the virtuous, the educated, and the refined.

Over brandy, Folsey criticized Gibbes's screed. "Empty words, friend."

"Why do you say that?"

"Because your own relative continues to teach niggers to read and write and think themselves perfectly fit to vote. And you do nothing about it. It doesn't go unnoticed. You may never win another election."

☆　☆　☆

Richard found Cal a job at the horse barn of the Charleston City Railway. Cal swamped out stalls, carried hay, and didn't seem to worry about his status or lack of it. His disposition improved; he whistled and hummed. The only negative Richard observed was Cal's familiar habit of sneaking drinks in the daytime and lingering too long in grog shops after dark.

Cal and Adah lived in rented rooms in one of the mixed streets above Calhoun. On a warm Tuesday in May he reeled home later than usual, half past ten. He found Adah waiting in the tiny parlor, her arms crossed on her breast. A whiskey bottle stood on an otherwise empty table.

"Sorry 'm late," he began, reaching for her.

"Stay back." Adah's eyes were fiery. "I know you still hurt because of the war and your poor mama, but that's no excuse for a man ruining himself."

Cal's bleary smile vanished. He wiped his sleeve across his mouth. "I could use a swig of that bottle."

"Take it. I set it out so you could make your choice."

"Choice? What're you talking about?"

"The drinking or us. You can have one or the other."

"What the devil do you mean, 'us'?"

Adah slowly uncrossed her arms and lowered her hands to her belly.

"Oh Lord, Adah. Merciful God, you're going to have . . . ?"

"Yes, but I won't bring up a child with a father who's a sot. You have to marry me, Cal, and you have to forswear the whiskey, except maybe a toddy at Christmas, or I'm leaving you."

"Adah, Adah." He flung his arms around her, buried his mouth in her neck. Her emotional carapace crumbled; tears splashed her cheeks, and his. He picked her up and tenderly carried her to their bed.

Cal Hayward was not seen in Charleston taprooms after that night.

★ ★ ★

The *South Carolina Leader,* a new paper favorable to Northern opinion, praised Alex's school in a long article. The mayor, Peter Gaillard, visited to observe an evening class and chat with the students. General Sickles, he of the glorious mustachios and lecherous eye, spent a similar evening. He managed to bump into Alex several times, caressing her arm or patting her shoulder while apologizing floridly.

Perhaps the most interesting visitor was a Negro whose skin was the color of old ivory. Tall and thick around the middle, he had an unconsciously grand air and flawless grooming. Alex noticed a high gloss on his nails.

Francis Cardozo was a Charleston native, the product of a liaison between a Jewish gentleman and a mother who was part Indian, part black. Education at the University of Glasgow and a London seminary had prepared him for the Presbyterian ministry. He'd held a pulpit in New Haven for a time. After the war he'd returned to help reopen the schools.

"Our lives run parallel, Miss Bell. We both came home to our native city."

"There are powerful attractions in Charleston, Mr. Cardozo. I ran away from them, but I couldn't escape them."

"I'm greatly interested in what you're doing here."

"My little academy is a very small effort to attack a very large problem."

"But most significant because it's a private initiative. All of your students are Negro, am I correct?"

"I had one white chap. He only stayed a short time."

Cardozo studied the improvised classroom from the hallway. "I have a theory on education. I believe the most natural method of removing race distinctions would be to allow children, when five or six years of age, to mingle in school together. Children don't know hatred."

"That's a laudable vision, Mr. Cardozo." And one that she found too daring for easy accomplishment, at least in her lifetime.

* * *

June brought summer's wet again, the kind of weather that stifled breathing and made the skin glisten. Nerves grew strained; tempers were inflamed. Maudie saw a waterspout dancing in the Atlantic. Hurricane season was upon them.

Grumbling thunder woke Alex on her sodden pillow three nights in succession. Next evening at dusk, while she worked in the garden, a carriage stopped at the gate. She was startled to see Gibbes's coupe rockaway, its peeling carmine paint coated with dust. A mule had replaced his handsome gray.

Alex slipped behind the great live oak and peeped out to watch him approach the gate. Ham hadn't yet come home to supper; Maudie had taken Little Bob to a magic lantern show. She was alone in the house and sharply aware of it.

Gibbes looked old, but he was decently dressed, in the traditional summer outfit of a Low Country gentleman—white frock coat and trousers, starched white shirt with black cravat, no vest.

He rang the little bell at the gate. She wanted to hide, but conscience wouldn't allow it. She stepped from behind the tree and went to greet him. Unsightly sweat rings darkened her gray dress beneath her arms.

"Why, Gibbes. This is unexpected." As had been the unhappy visit after she returned.

He swept off his broad-brimmed planter's hat, a gesture she thought too flamboyant by half. His sangfroid astounded her. He'd called her arrogant when he welcomed her home and she rebuffed him, but to judge from his smarmy smile, it might never have happened.

"Forgive the presumption of an unannounced call, cousin. I have something important to discuss. Might I come in?"

"The house is hot as an oven. Why don't we sit in the swing?"

"As you wish." He held out his hat so she would precede him to the steps of the piazza, then followed with the peculiar jerky gait caused by the wooden leg. Clouds covered the sky, but it was no cooler. Brief gusts of wind blew dry leaves from the live oak; offshore, another storm muttered.

77

Storm Breaking

Gibbes heaved a great sigh as he sat. His white trouser leg stuck out stiffly; his shoe tip touched the jasmine twined on the railing. He'd fortified himself with Dutch courage; Alex smelled the whiskey.

She sat down, careful to leave space between them. He pushed with his crippled leg and the swing moved, *creak* and *creak*.

Out of his sleeve came a soiled white handkerchief. He fanned his face. "Smells like rain." Another wind gust raised dust from a patch of bare ground. "Is your brother here?"

"He'll be home any minute."

"Or maybe he won't," he said with that sly smile she remembered too well. She braked the swing with her foot.

"May we talk about the reason for your visit?"

"Simple enough, cousin. It's your nigger school. You know I hold an elected office. The voters of my district—white men, need I remind you—are angered by what you're doing. They come to me because you and I are related. They want something done."

"Why should that be? Down at Penn Center white teachers are helping black people learn. My little classroom's no different."

"Oh, but it is. Those women on Lady's Island migrated from the North. They're part of the locust plague this state is suffering. No matter how you deny or denigrate it, you're a Southerner."

"I'm an American. So are you."

His left hand dropped on her leg. "You haven't changed one iota, have you?"

"Nor have you. Take your hand away."

"When I'm damn good and ready. The school—"

"Will not be closed. I believe that ends our discussion." She jerked her knee so his hand slipped off, then bolted up. Temper reddened his face as he lunged from the swing. He yanked her by the arm. She'd have fallen if she hadn't seized the swing chain.

"I'll have my way about the school, and maybe I'll just have my way with you." His fingers went to his flies; he began to unbutton.

"Christ knows you've denied me for years, always acting holier than a nun. Come here." He hooked an arm around her waist, brought his mouth toward hers. She wrenched her head aside, heard the sound of the gate closing.

"Hallo, who's that?" Ham called. He came quickly across the garden and up the steps. Gibbes stepped back. Both Ham and Alex could see the undone buttons. Ham scowled. "Well, now. Seems I interrupted something unpleasant. I'm entitled to an explanation, Gibbes."

"He wants the school shut down," Alex said.

Ham hooked thumbs in the pockets of the black vest that made him look like an undertaker. "Not exactly the explanation I was after, but you should know better, Gibbes. You have no right or authority to ask for such a thing."

"Don't be so fucking smug. I have friends. I have ways of accomplishing what I want done."

"Get off this property."

"A pleasure. I've said my piece. If you don't do what I ask you're damn fools."

He shot a look at Alex as he jammed his hat on his head. Ham was between Gibbes and the steps. He didn't move. He shoved Gibbes's chest. "Just a minute. It would be a mistake for you to pursue this. We have possession of a letter written by a man who fought in the Hampton Legion. The man saw you at Seven Pines, the very hour you received your wound. His letter contradicts what everyone believes about you. If it became public, it would damage, or should I say destroy, your reputation as a war hero."

Silence. The wind rushed in again, scattering fallen leaves. The air was pregnant with rain, but only a few large drops fell. Gibbes acted like a man bludgeoned.

"I don't know a thing about any such—"

"The letter was written by a soldier named Plato Hix. Are you familiar with him? It seems he's dropped out of sight mysteriously."

"I demand to see this letter."

"No. It's locked away where no one will find it unless we direct them to it."

Lightning painted the garden white; thunder rolled over the harbor. Ham leaned against a post with his arms folded while Gibbes struggled for words. All he managed was "Goddamn you. Goddamn you both." He crushed his hat in his hand and elbowed Ham out of the way. The capricious wind lifted the skirt of his white coat as he fled, struggling to button his trousers.

The street gate clanged. The wind died. Ham said, "He's guilty as hell, isn't he? And of more than one murder, I'd stake a hundred dollars on it."

Alex rested her cheek on his shoulder. He hugged and held her until her trembling subsided. "What next?" she said.

"Nothing good, surely. I'm glad we didn't mention Mrs. Hix knowing about the letter. Who knows what he might do to her?"

☆ ☆ ☆

The room was half shadow, half brilliant lamplight. On George Street torches streamed by, borne by hallooing men. Folsey heard a distant popping of gunshots, then a police whistle.

The last of the smoking torches passed out of sight. The crash of the kitchen door made Folsey jump. Gibbes appeared, disheveled and perspiring.

"Hell of a time to pay a call, my friend."

"Can't help it, the matter's urgent."

Folsey lifted a pale hand toward the window. "What's all that racket outside?"

"Niggers amok again. One stabbed a white man at Tradd and Meeting last night. That set it off."

"Didn't know. I rode in from Columbia this afternoon."

"The rioting's worse tonight. I need a drink."

Folsey put on his bifocals and poured two whiskeys. Gibbes gulped all of his, then said, "It's time to go after them. Civic disorder provides perfect cover."

Folsey peered over his spectacles. "Go after who?"

Gibbes glanced at the open door of the library. "My cousins. They've tossed me on the griddle, never mind how, and they're going to fry me if I let them. I have to get rid of them."

Folsey sipped from his glass. "You know it's my ambition and obligation to rid the world of both of them, but this is a poor time. For one thing, my bones always warn me about bad weather. There's a big blow coming."

"A double distraction. I want you to do it now, Folsey. I can't risk a delay."

"It's impossible. You've got to understand my position. I'm allied with Huffington. I can't afford to be involved in—"

Gibbes yelled at him. "You won't be involved in a damn thing if you don't do what I ask. People overlook sin in the dark but not sin in the daylight. Huffington won't associate himself with a pederast. He'll shun you like poison if he hears about that boy you keep upstairs. I'll collect my voting money, but your fantastic profit, as you call it, will go aglimmering. You won't be able to get your foot in the door of a privy."

Folsey gritted his teeth so hard his jaw trembled. "You bastard, you wouldn't—"

"Indeed I would, sir. I'm desperate. Give me your answer, right now."

It took Folsey the better part of a minute to calm down. "Suppose I say yes. Could you guarantee I'd be able to take care of both of them at one time?"

"Yes, leave it to me. I'll arrange it so they're at South Battery this time tomorrow. If things misfire, we'll delay to the following night, and every night thereafter till it's done. How many men do you need to help you?"

"I won't be directly in the picture, you understand. It'll take at least two besides Slope. You pay for them, every penny."

"Agreed."

Heat lightning washed the windowpanes. A policeman's rattle sounded nearby. Folsey reflected again, then managed a wan smile. "Well, you've got me. I suppose I might as well get it done. Grandpa William, who no doubt is roasting in hell, will be happy to see it, and my father too." Gibbes knew about Folsey's deathbed promise and had often speculated that Folsey never meant to honor it in his lifetime if he could avoid it.

Folsey refilled their glasses, offered a toast. "Here's to the end of unwanted trouble, then."

"Unwanted cousins," Gibbes said. "And Grandpa William and your father resting peacefully at last." He smiled. Folsey didn't.

* * *

At five-thirty next morning Gibbes left Snoo snoring and went to his desk. He lit a candle and composed a note to be delivered to the attention of Hampton Bell when the law firm opened.

This is an acknowledgment that you have persuaded me on the issue recently discussed. I will call at your house tonight, half after eight o'clock, to explain my decision. It is is my hope to effect a lasting truce so we may henceforth go our separate ways in peace.

He signed his initials and rang a small brass handbell. His hired manservant, Desmond, tore into the room.

"Mr. Gibbes, why you ring the bell so hard? You sick?"

In a high state of excitement Gibbes said, "No, I'm feeling good. I am feeling wonderful. Here is what I want you to do."

78

In the Storm

The day remained dark, with occasional spits of rain. By four o'clock the wind was blowing steadily off the ocean. Heavier rain fell after six, when Ham arrived home dripping and grumbling. "Nasty out there. I wonder if we're in for more than a soaking."

Maudie answered. "Yes, sir, I do think so."

Alex listened to the rain hammering the windows. "Too early in the season for a hurricane."

"God don't watch the calendar," Maudie said. She patted Little Bob, who'd taken refuge at her side. "Tide was low about three. Be high in three hours." When a tropical disturbance made landfall at high tide, the storm surge was that much more dangerous.

"Please take Bob upstairs," Alex said. "Find a secure spot to stay if things get bad." Maudie led the boy away. "What about our visitor? Do you think he'll come?"

Ham sat at the dining table, peeling off wet stockings. "If it's important to him, and I think it is, I expect he'll try."

By seven the wind was howling across the Battery, shaking doors and rattling windows. A knock sent Alex to the piazza. There she found Richard, wrapped in an oilskin poncho with his hat dripping rain. "I came soon as I finished work. You'd better batten down for this."

She touched his hand and gave him a warm look as he stepped inside. Ham appeared, said, "We should nail up the shutters on the water side." Richard volunteered to help.

It was a struggle to plant a ladder, but fortunately the wind pushed it directly against the front of the house. Richard had to raise his voice to be heard. "You take the ground floor, I'll go up." He scooped nails from a tin can, bit down on the heads of half a dozen, and climbed.

Wind continually swayed the ladder. He needed one hand to hold a shutter closed while he drove nails. Rain half blinded him, but he managed to secure the first window, climb down, and move the ladder. When the upper windows were done, he helped Ham finish a last one on the ground floor, then called retreat. Before they had a firm hold on the ladder, the wind picked it up and sailed it down the street. They heard it crack, saw rungs fly off. Ham started after it. Richard restrained him. "Leave it for later."

In the house they peeled off wet clothes; Richard made do with some of Ham's, which were rather too tight for him. Alex served them whiskey toddies. A loud clatter drew attention to the ceiling. "Shingles," Ham said. "Let's hope it doesn't tear off the whole roof." Carolina hurricanes had a habit of doing that. Even a relatively small storm could wash away great stretches of low-lying shore and flatten entire buildings.

Ham finished his toddy. "We're expecting a visitor soon."

"I can leave," Richard said.

"I don't believe he'll come in this weather," Alex said. In the kitchen, wind blew the door open so forcefully the window shattered, raining glass. They heard more roof shingles ripping away. The relentless wind and rain got on Alex's nerves. She wished she could hide in a shell, turtlelike. They sat at the dining table toying with the empty toddy mugs and wondering how much worse it would get.

* * *

About twenty past eight a black depot wagon drawn by two mules turned the corner at Meeting and drew up opposite the house. Bundled in a greatcoat, scarf, and derby, Folsey held the reins.

A side curtain lifted; three men climbed down from the back. Two were white, wearing dark coats and caps. The third man was a huge Negro with a slanting forehead and a prognathus jaw. Thin strips of light framed the closed shutters of the Bell house. "They must be in there," Folsey said. "Get it done before the storm gets worse."

The black man said, "Aye. Boys, keep your pieces dry 'till we're under cover." He reached under his coat to grasp a navy Colt in his belt.

He charged across the street, splashing through small rivers of rushing water. Sticks and uprooted plants flew through the air; a broken chair; three feet of picket fence. At the piazza door the big man pulled his navy Colt and signaled the others to do the same. One henchman, a chinless fellow, snickered. "Goin' to be polite an' knock, are you, Mr. Slope?"

"They'll know we're here without that." Slope kicked the door with his heavy boot, smashing it off its hinges.

✳ ✳ ✳

Alex, Ham, and Richard huddled in the front office. They'd run out of conversation and were waiting for the eye of the storm to pass. The sound of the door breaking brought them to their feet. A powerful draft blew out two of their three lamps.

A man holding a stubby revolver leapt into the room and fired a shot. Ham staggered, blood flowering on the sleeve of his shirt. Richard had no idea who the intruders were, but their intent was plain. He flung a stool at the shooter. The man batted it down. Richard lunged at him and took the stubby revolver by force.

The man jabbed his thumb in Richard's eye, clawed his face. Richard put the revolver to the man's belly and blew him backward into the shelves. Flailing hands tore down books that covered him as he lay moaning.

In the hall a second white man hesitated. An immense Negro with a Colt revolver pushed him aside. The black man had simian features made all the uglier by his insane grin. Richard threw a chair at him and charged.

The black man sidestepped, tripped him. Richard sprawled face-down on the floor. The man kicked his head twice. Richard rolled onto his back, dizzy and retching.

"You next, missy." The black man aimed into the office. Alex lunged sideways. The gun roared; she crashed against shelves opposite those where the first assailant had gone down. A sudden memory made her fling books aside, reach through the gap, and pull out Edward's pistol hidden there.

The black man set himself for another shot but the Colt jammed. A touch of Alex's finger released the spring bayonet under the pistol barrel. Crouched low, she ran at the Negro and thrust the point into his thigh. He screamed and swung at her with the barrel of his Colt. It grazed her ear, hurt her shoulder. Striking upward, she drove the bloody bayonet into his throat.

The Colt clattered at his feet. A red stream spouted from his neck, splashing her dress. The Negro fell into the hall and lay on his side, thrashing his legs as he died.

The third man, the chinless one, ran for the door. Somewhere in the house more windows broke. Richard snatched up the Colt, and chased the fugitive.

Stinging rain made it almost impossible to see. Wild with panic, the man couldn't get the gate open. Richard came up behind him and put a bullet in the back of his knee. The man toppled into a bed of palmettos.

Richard heard a steadily mounting roar in the harbor. He pried the gate open, saw the depot wagon etched in a lightning flash. The driver hauled on the reins, attempting to turn in water already half a foot deep. Richard had seen the driver around town but didn't know his name. He brandished the Colt. "Get down from there."

The driver lashed the mules. Richard aimed; the Colt jammed. Out of the harbor rose a wall of water twenty feet high. It struck Richard and the wagon, lifted them, and hurled them toward the house. Richard nearly drowned as he tumbled over and over inside the tidal wave. Then the wave passed, leaving the house leaning crookedly on its foundation. The storm surge submerged the house next door, then found other paths, roaring along South Battery and flooding into Church and Meeting streets.

Richard lay limp against the house where he'd been thrown. The depot wagon was broken apart like matchwood. One of the mules lay on its side, braying in pain.

The wagon driver dragged himself from the wreckage. Confused, he ran the wrong way, through the open gate into the Bell garden. Richard struggled up and chased him.

Leaves and palmetto stalks flew in his face. A grinding sound made him look up. The wind lifted the great live oak out of the ground, its roots dragging up clods of earth. The old tree tilted slowly and fell. The wagon driver blocked his face with his forearm. The tree came down on both men.

⋆ ⋆ ⋆

Alex saw it happen. She jumped off the piazza the moment the live oak crashed, shaking the earth. *Oh, heaven, he's dead,* she thought as she clawed through broken branches. *Don't let him be dead.*

She dropped to her knees beside him. A medium-sized limb had fallen across his legs. Pushing, she was able to move it. "Richard?" She stroked his wet face, put her cheek against his lips. Breathing, thank God. Joyfully, she kissed him, then flung herself on him. He writhed and uttered a plaintive, "Oww."

Wounded Ham was calling out to her. "Over here. It's Folsey, under the tree trunk. His neck's broken. He's dead."

Alex slowly comprehended that. She and Richard lay half submerged in water flooding the garden. The rain soaked and chilled them; she didn't care. Holding him, she had never been so happy.

★   ★   ★

How they passed the long night without succumbing to hysteria, Alex couldn't clearly recall afterward. Images of certain moments were strung together like beads, but of the connecting thread, the times between, she had no recollection.

She remembered knotting a cloth around Ham's upper arm to stanch the blood. Treatment from a doctor while the storm still raged was an impossibility. Ham insisted he could survive until daylight, though his skin was the color of lard and his face a glistening mask of sweat.

Upset by the gunfire, Little Bob came downstairs crying. Alex succeeded in calming him, then extracted a promise that he wouldn't come down again until morning.

Richard was massively bruised; he hobbled. Even so, he was able to drag the bodies of the two attackers outside and leave them in the garden near Folsey. The man who'd fallen by the gate was gone.

Maudie swept up glass, mopped up water, and lit candles, trying to burn out the charnel-house stench. Blood drying on the heart-pine floor had turned it brown. Expunging the stains was a problem for another day.

Worst of all for Alex was the recurring picture of the bayonet stabbing into the Negro's neck. She had killed him, and the guilt tortured her. It would forever.

About six in the morning, the wind dropped to a whine. She and Richard and Ham met in the dining room to face the inevitable. Alex put it in words.

"The authorities have to be told."

"I know, sister, I know. Soon as I'm patched up, I'll take care of it."

"How will you explain it?" Richard said.

"Why, I won't. I'll plead ignorance. We were victims of a senseless, unmotivated attack. I can suggest it may have had something to do with my stand on certain issues, but I'll say it's only a guess. How can they prove anything to the contrary?"

"Why did that Lark fellow have it in for you?"

"Old family grudges. But it goes beyond that." Ham stared at the nails of his right hand. "I have a strong suspicion someone else sent those men. I'll address that issue, never fear."

Alex looked around the table. "Is anyone hungry?"

Richard said, "I am."

"I'll make coffee and fry some bacon."

By seven the storm had moved inland. Next door, the upper story of the Daws place was gone. Richard left for an hour and brought back a harried young doctor, who poured claret into Ham, gave him a broom handle to bite, and sutured his wound. Fortunately the bullet had passed through flesh without hitting bone.

Alex was washing the breakfast plates when Maudie found her. "There's an almighty big hole in the ground where that old tree was."

"I know."

"The roots pulled up something must have been buried a long time ago. You better come see."

79

Tom Bell's Secret

She drew her hands out of the basin of soapy water, dried them, and followed Maudie outside. An old iron box lay canted in the huge hole left when the tree fell. Most of the flood water had leached into the ground, leaving only a puddle at the bottom of the hole. The box was dented and badly rusted but otherwise undamaged.

"Let's find a hammer and chisel and see what's in it," Alex said.

The lock resisted for a while, but eventually Alex broke it open. Rust flaked away as she lifted the lid and discovered a package wrapped in wet layers of oilskin, lying in an inch of storm water.

Unwrapping the oilskins revealed two thick books. Carefully she opened the first, peeled the heavy pages apart. They were damp, especially at the edges, and spotted with mold, but the faded handwriting for the most part was readable. Her astonishment grew as she realized the books were diaries, written by her great-grandfather.

There was also an explanatory letter, heavy parchment folded and waxed shut. She broke the seal.

Before the city falls, as I am certain it will, I will hide a second cache, these volumes, secured in a strong box like the one holding my account books. I will bury it deepest of all, unknown to my servants or my son Edward. My son Adrian is not a concern. He has chosen to side with the enemy.

I hide these books so as to conceal certain facts about my father, who he was and how he sustained himself after he fled the foundling home in Bristol and ran away to sea in his twelfth year.

At some future time my father's history may not matter, yet I am troubled by a fear that it could besmirch my son's good name and harm his prospects, or those of his heirs. Reputation and pride of place are cornerstones of life as it is lived in Charles Town.

If what I do is wrong, I ask the Heavenly Father to forgive me. If I have unacceptably hardened my heart against my elder son, for that, too, I beseech the Lord's mercy.

Thos. Bell
4th April 1781

"Our name isn't Bell," Alex said to Ham and Richard when she showed the diaries several hours later. Ham's right arm was swathed in a sling with the tapes tied behind his back. Grumpily, he said, "Then what is it?"

She struggled against an urge to giggle. "Greech."

"Greech?" Ham said, as though tasting tainted meat.

"According to this diary Tom Bell's father's name was Sydney Greech. When he came to Charleston he was a fugitive. He'd been a crewman on a ship captained by a man named Stede Bonnet."

Richard said, "Who would that be?"

"They called him the gentleman pirate," Ham said. "One of the sea rovers who plagued this coast in the early seventeen hundreds. The most famous was Blackbeard Teach. He and his bully boys strutted up and down the streets of Charleston terrifying the citizens. As for Bonnet, an expedition headed by Colonel William Rhett caught him and his shipmates where their vessel was careened in the Cape Fear River. Brought 'em all to Charleston in irons."

"Not all," Alex said. "Not Sydney."

Ham nodded and went on. "Bonnet himself managed to sneak out of jail, but he was apprehended on Sullivan's Island and hanged. They hadn't invented the gallows in those days so he was swung off a cart, slow strangulation. Legend says he went to his death carrying a bunch of posies. A gentleman to the end."

Alex took up the story. "Sydney Greech avoided the same fate by running off and disappearing into North Carolina before Bonnet was captured. It's all written down in Tom's fine hand." She couldn't restrain a burst of laughter.

Ham was severely vexed. "Do you find it funny that the founder of this family wanted to conceal unsavory facts about an ancestor?"

"The founder of this family?" Alex said through a storm of tears and giggles. "The founder of this family was a lowborn thieving buccaneer with a stripe of yellow down his back. If only they could have known, Lydia and Simms and Ouida, living their pretensions and fighting like dogs to defend their grand reputations."

Ham sniffed. "I would say the contents of that box demonstrate that our revered forebear wasn't entirely free of pretensions, as we have always believed. He wanted to be thought of as a person of substance, not a pirate's whelp."

Alex hugged herself and rocked. "Oh, it's delicious."

"Does the book say why Greech called himself Bell?" Richard asked.

Alex wiped her eyes. "No, Tom's confession omits that detail. Maybe he liked the sound of it. We'll never know."

"Well, it's all very droll," Richard observed. "Pretty damn typical of Charleston."

No one disagreed.

80

Settling Accounts

Two days later Ham sent a formal note to Gibbes, asking him to call at the law office. Gibbes didn't reply for three days, then turned up unexpectedly one afternoon.

Wearing an appropriately somber sling of black cloth, Ham shut the door with his good hand. "So we won't be disturbed." There was continual racket in the street as carts carried away storm debris. A dozen houses had been blown down and nine people were dead, including a child drowned in the tidal surge.

"I am severely pressed for time," Gibbes began.

Ham's thick head of hair was nearly white, enhancing his air of rectitude. "I won't waste words. You'll recall the letter mentioned in a previous conversation? It rests in that big safe in the outer office. Lest you have an urge to act rashly a second time, heed this. If anything untoward occurs involving me or my sister, or anyone in our household, the letter goes to the authorities, as well as to every newspaper in Charleston, Columbia, and Greenville. With it goes my sworn statement endorsing its validity based on meetings conducted with Mrs. Mary Hix. Should you have some lunatic idea about destroying this office, copies of the letter have been placed safely elsewhere. With that made clear I have this to say to you. You had better resign from the legislature, on any pretext that will save face." Gibbes began to sputter and interrupt, but Ham wasn't through. "You must resign and never stand for office again, or I promise your reputation will suffer a sharp decline."

"By God, you've got more gall than—look here, you forget who I am. Your cousin. Would you stoop to blackmailing your own flesh and blood?"

"Cousin you may be, but you're a damned murdering bigot too. You tried to have us killed"—Gibbes opened his mouth again; Ham immediately raised his hand, palm toward the visitor—"kindly spare me the pious denials."

"I know what's behind this. Your beastly love of the Goddamn niggers."

Expressionless, Ham said, "That is not at issue. You've heard my terms."

Gibbes chewed his lip. "Supposing I do what you and your do-good sister want. Nothing will change. We will take back this state anyway. Drive down the colored and keep South Carolina in the hands of white men."

"We'll see."

"What a smug little worm you are. You really think you can thwart me?"

"I do. I know who and what you are. I also know full well that one less of your kind won't dam the flood, but it will certainly remove a few drams of poison from the stream. That is all I have to say."

"But—"

"There is no appeal, Gibbes. I bid you good day."

★　★　★

Gibbes spent the remainder of the afternoon in the saloon bar of the reopened Mills House. He saw a number of acquaintances but declined to join them. He retired to a corner with a bottle of Kentucky's finest and proceeded to drink himself into a stupor. He seethed and raged. He was trapped.

Gradually the alcohol calmed him, and he considered the standoff Ham had effected. His cousin was, if nothing else, a man always true to his word. If Gibbes resigned his seat, his reputation would remain intact. He could then continue to work behind the scenes to help reclaim the state for its rightful owners. When he left the hotel after seven, he was in somewhat improved spirits.

He swung his stick almost jauntily as he walked along Legare Street in a state of hazy confidence. Near Sword Gate rain began; nothing like the torrents that had come with the hurricane but enough to raise a murky mist. Lamps gleaming in the ground-floor windows shed welcoming light on the small front yard. He happily anticipated the food he'd tell Desmond to prepare.

And after supper, the report. He'd received it late that morning and was eager to read it more carefully. The report dealt with an assay of soil samples from Prosperity Hall. The hired geologist said there was great promise of phosphates, in quantity, in his land along the river. If that proved true, new wealth was not a chimera but a real possibility.

Someone stepped from behind a large elm planted on the curb a few steps beyond his gate. A woman heavily draped in a hooded talma approached. "Mr. Bell?"

"Yes?"

"This is for my husband." The woman emptied a small silver pistol into his face and chest.

Gibbes collapsed against the iron gates, dying as he slid to his knees. His vest left scarlet swathes on the wrought metal. The woman threw the pistol over the fence into his yard and ran.

Gibbes's killer was never found. Mary Hix and her children moved out of the state.

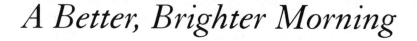

81

A Better, Brighter Morning

Of all the departed ones who had been connected to the Bells by blood or marriage, Folsey Lark was mourned least. Scarcely a dozen attended his funeral: Rex Porcher-Jones and some other cronies; three former employees of Palmetto Traders; a strange moony-eyed boy who sat alone in a rear pew, snuffling and wiping his nose. Snoo was too distraught and stayed home.

The authorities attributed her half-brother's death to unknown causes, the most likely being association with evil companions. General Huffington publicly denied knowing Folsey. In private he insisted he'd always been suspicious of the man's character and had intended to cut short their relationship.

It was different with Gibbes. His funeral was a civic occasion. Hundreds of people crowded the nave and overflowed to the steps of St. Michael's when he was laid to rest.

For days Gibbes had been the subject of fulsome eulogies in the press. *An exemplar of Southern courage,* he was called. *A valiant soldier and patriot who put aside wartime animosities to serve and resurrect his city and his state.* Editorialists said his death was untimely. *We are confident he would have gone far, perhaps even to the highest forums of the capital of our reunited nation.*

Mayor and council members attended, and fellow legislators. General Wade Hampton rode down from Columbia to bow his mighty head in prayer. Snoo wept uncontrollably throughout the service. She swooned on the grass as the coffin was lowered and Great Michael tolled.

Leaving in their carriage, Ham and Alex exchanged confidences. "I felt a horrid hypocrite sitting there without an ounce of sympathy for him," Alex said. Ham admitted a similar lack.

"We no longer need the letter. Will you give it to me?"

"For what purpose?"

"It's time to bury the hatreds."

Ham hardly hesitated. "I'll fetch it home tomorrow. You're a wise woman, Alex."

She leaned back, closed her eyes. "But old. Old. Do you realize there's no one to carry on the family name?"

"I regret that I never married."

"You could still father a child. You're not Methuselah."

"But ever so set in my bachelor ways, alas."

"Then the Bells go silent."

She hadn't meant to say it that way, but it was appropriate. Ham responded not with a smile but a little sniff. When they reached home he took her gloved hand and helped her step down from the carriage. She used her cane again. Ever since the storm her injured leg had troubled her. Just another sign of fragile mortality, she thought in a moment of uncharacteristic self-pity.

The following night she and Richard walked arm-in-arm along the Battery. Ripples in the cobalt harbor were touched with the light of the setting sun. The air smelled of fish and the mud flats strewn with white oyster shells. The night of blood and horror might have been a fantasy.

She laid her cane against a waterside bollard and took the letter from a pocket in her skirt. He knew the whole story of it. He was silent as she tore the pages in half, then again, and a third time. She tossed the inky confetti in the air. The offshore wind carried it over the water, where the bits of paper attracted noisy gulls who left as soon as they found it inedible.

"Rest in peace," she said, "though I really doubt this part of the world will know peace for a long time, perhaps generations. Defeated people find it hard to forgive or forget. There's a gulf between the races not easily bridged."

"Not too big a gulf between us, I hope." After reflecting a moment he said, "I don't intend to drive horsecars the rest of my life. It may take five years, but I'm going to start another freighting company. In Charleston. I've come to like the place. I haven't withdrawn my marriage proposal."

She placed her hands on his shoulders. "Dear Richard. I've thought about that endlessly. We fought on opposing sides, figuratively if not literally. During the last years of my marriage to Reverend Drew, he used one word in regard to the end of the war. *Forgiveness.* That was the foundation of peace, he said. That was the first essential. I recognize his wisdom. So I'd like to make peace between us and accept your proposal."

He whooped. "Lord above." She touched his lips.

"If we marry, I won't change my beliefs, or hide them."

"I guess I'll have to put mine up against yours and see who comes out aces."

"Fair enough, my dear. I'll change your ways, see if I don't."

"I accept the challenge." He was beaming; she felt a sudden confidence that they could succeed together. She fell into his arms and shamelessly planted a long kiss, right there in front of God and everybody in the city of Charleston who might be watching.

"There is one thing," she said as they strolled home. "I want the Bell line to continue."

"Children? How—?"

"No, no, I'm far too old. I would, however, like to adopt Little Bob before we marry. He'd be ours, but I want to change his name legally to Robert Henry Drew Bell. Would you object?"

"Not a bit. Would he?"

She shook her head, more gray than golden now. "He and I had a long talk on the subject just yesterday. He likes our household, though he doesn't often say it."

"Then he's part of the family, and welcome."

They walked arm-in-arm. Richard glanced at Alex from time to time, admiringly. It moved him to say, "You should have been a general. We'd have won the damn war."

✯   ✯   ✯

Cal and his wife, Adah, called. "We're going to Chicago."

"While I can still travel," Adah said with a lowering of her eyes. Refined women, no matter what their station, didn't discuss pregnancy except with intimate friends and relatives, and then only in a kind of genteel code.

"It may be easier for us in the North," Cal said.

It wouldn't be, but they would learn that, and if they were strong, as devoted as husband and wife as they seemed to be, they would survive. So Alex said, "Yes, very possibly so. Blessings on you both."

☆ ☆ ☆

On the first of July, Maudie discovered an interloper in their kitchen. She brought the ragged youngster to the stuffy sitting room, where Alex was struggling to decipher small type in a newspaper. She had new spectacles.

"Must have sneaked in the back door. I found him stuffing some of my corn dodgers into his pants." Maudie was the soul of stern justice; she gripped the boy's arm like a policeman restraining a desperate criminal.

The boy was six or seven. His cocoa-brown face might have been winsome if it hadn't been so dirty. Alex had seen too many like him skulking or begging in the streets, the flotsam of the tides of war.

"What's your name, young man?"

"Micah John."

"Where do you live?"

"Up the Coosawhatchie a ways. I don't live there no more."

"Where are your parents?"

"Kilt when the white men burned our cabin."

"Who were they?"

"I don't know who they were."

"Why did they burn your house?"

"Looking for money. There wasn't none."

"Wasn't any," Alex corrected. The boy stuck out his lower lip. "Do you have brothers or sisters?"

"Nuh-uh."

"Any kin that you know about?"

"Off in Tennessee somewheres. Don't know their names."

She smelled the dirt and sweat on him. First thing she'd do was throw him in the zinc tub and scrub him down. She rapped her cane on the floor.

"Maudie, we can help this boy. Would you stay with us awhile, Micah? We can feed you and care for you."

"Just like you was his mother?" Maudie said with raised eyebrows. "Isn't Little Bob enough?"

"Stop that. I'm too old to be anyone's mother. Grandmother, well, that's a different story. From what I see of others, a proper grandmother likes plenty of children around her."

The boy frowned. "Who's Bob?"

"Another youngster who lives with us. You'd like him. I think he'd like you. What do you say, Micah? A warm bed, an equal share of our food—would that please you?"

Long seconds passed. "Yes'm."

"Let's be very clear, so you don't agree and later feel I wasn't honest with you. You'll have to work, we have a great deal of repairing to do and we don't keep servants. You'll have to do as you're told. I don't abide spoiled sassy boys who cry and stomp to get their way. If you don't want to obey, and carry your weight, we have to say good-bye."

There was no hesitancy. "I can be like you want, ma'am."

Alex's heart soared. She laid her cane aside, took his grimy fingers in hers. "Let's go back to the kitchen. While you eat, we'll get acquainted."

He smiled for the first time. She wondered how he'd like the name Micah John Bell.

☆ ☆ ☆

On the glorious morning of the Fourth, the hottest day of the summer so far, the five of them strolled beside the harbor. Few white people were abroad; they disliked the holiday because the freed slaves celebrated and paraded in the streets.

Distant music of a brass band drifted over rooftops shimmering in the heat. Maudie held hands with Micah John. Alex held hands with Little Bob. Richard trailed along behind in amiable silence until, unprompted, he suddenly stepped forward and took Micah John's other hand. Alex wondered whether he'd ever clasped the hand of a black person for other than a business transaction.

He saw her watching. Over the heads of Maudie and the children he responded with a smile of mysterious contentment. Away up Meeting Street the bells of St. Michael's, back from Columbia and hung in their rightful place, rang the hour.

So much to heal, Alex thought. So much to rebuild. So much to worry about. She laughed at herself. Cassandra would say she was the ideal choice for worrying.

They stood hand in hand gazing at the water, Richard, Micah John, Maudie, Little Bob, Alex. Gulls soaring, waves sparkling, boats bobbing, the bells chiming in St. Michael's steeple—how she loved it. The air was sweet with the eternal, unforgettable essences of Charleston: flowers, the salt sea, the mud flats steaming in the sun. Feelings of age dropped off like a burdensome cloak. A terrible time had passed for her beloved home. There was beauty before. There would be beauty again.

Afterword

Ever since I moved to the Carolina Low Country nearly 25 years ago, the fascinating, often bloody history of the region has held me captive. Beyond the borders of the state little seems to be known of this colorful past, save for awareness of a few scattered incidents of the Revolutionary and Civil wars, the firing on Fort Sumter perhaps being the most famous.

The history of the state is far more than a single mural of shells exploding in Charleston Harbor on an April night in 1861, or a vaguely imagined pageant of white-columned plantations, cultured women, harsh masters, and mistreated slaves, though all those existed. Most people are surprised to hear that more Revolutionary War battles were fought in South Carolina than in any other colony. John C. Calhoun's role in setting the intellectual and emotional foundations for secession during the nullification crisis is mostly known through textbooks, scholarly studies, and graduate seminars in history. The list goes on.

Years ago I decided that someday I would write about this unique and paradoxical part of America. When the time came, I began to see a prism that created a spectrum. The prism was one of the world's most charming cities, and the spectrum its daily life, beautiful and tranquil sometimes, but contentious and violent too. Thus the novel emerged.

Two historians with deep roots in the state started me thinking about the subject in detail. The first is named in the dedication: the late George C. Rogers, Jr., professor of history at the University of South Carolina,

Columbia. His *Charleston in the Age of the Pinckneys* is still in print and eminently readable. George and I corresponded often, met for lunch when we could, and became friends. Like my wife, Rachel, and me, George's passions included cruise ships and theater.

The second academic to whom I owe a great deal is Dr. Lawrence Rowland, now retired as professor of history at the University of South Carolina, Beaufort. In 1989 Rachel and I enrolled in Larry's class on South Carolina history from its beginnings to the War of Separation, as Southerners often called it at the time. The drama and excitement Larry conveyed, so unfamiliar to me then, resulted in a thick volume of class notes that I still depend on.

Although this book focuses on a particular city in a particular state, I would not want it to be considered "regional." That fate befell *Homeland*, a favorite of mine, when the publisher loftily decreed that "I see it as a heartland book," meaning Chicago, where most of the promotion money was dumped, largely ignoring the rest of the country.

Further, during the years of the story, South Carolina and Charleston impacted national affairs in a significant way. The reverberations of those years are still with all of us. In a book of essays on the West by Larry McMurtry, I came across a quote that speaks to the point. McMurtry quotes Patricia Nelson Limerick's *The Legacy of Conquest,* on the subject of the wars between Indians and whites:

"In truth, the tragedies of the wars are our national joint property, and how we handle that property is one test of our unity or disunity, maturity or immaturity, as a people wearing the label 'American.' " That is essentially what Alex tries to convey to her recidivistic cousin late in the novel.

Now for some notes about the text.

The fictional house built by Tom Bell between Church and Meeting Streets, on what was later named South Battery, is modeled on an actual house from the 1790s that still stands on the same street. Like Tom's it is a classic 'Charleston single house,' one room wide, two rooms deep, with the main door located on the piazza at the side, overlooking the garden. Tom Bell's house was different in that it was brick enhanced with stucco. He was one of those eighteenth-century Charlestonians "bragging in brick" to show his material success.

The drinking party from which Francis Marion escaped took place on March 19, 1780, some weeks before it occurs in the book. I moved it because it was too good to bypass.

The story of the red-coated monkey Colonel Balfour is almost certainly apocryphal, yet remains a part of the lore of Charleston's occupation by the British.

Evidence that British officers attended a so-called Negro ball exists only in a single letter from the period. One scholar whose judgment I trust speculates that the letter may have been American propaganda, designed to embarrass the enemy.

I advanced the confiscation and removal of the bells of St. Michael's by one year. They were later shipped to London as stated.

No records exist to positively identify the place Denmark Vesey was hanged in 1822. I chose the location that for many years had the greatest currency in Charleston oral history.

Angelina Grimké's *Appeal to the Christian Women of the Southern States* was published in 1836. I advanced the date by one year.

The July 1835 sack of the Charleston Post Office and subsequent rioting occurred as described.

Alex's speech in Dayton is adapted in part from Angelina Grimké's remarks before the Massachusetts State House in 1838. On February 21 that year she and her sister, Sarah, became the first women permitted to appear before an American legislature.

What might be described as the show trial of soldiers from the 54th Massachusetts Infantry Regiment (Colored) presents a fascinating historical mystery. We know that the state in the person of Governor Bonham wanted to prosecute and punish them as slaves in rebellion. We know the identities of attorneys on both sides. We know the trial's outcome. The five-judge panel, declining to handle what was obviously a hot issue, fell back on a time-honored evasion: lack of jurisdiction.

The mystery is, there seems to be no transcript, no record whatsoever, of the trial itself.

This was an irresistible challenge, but I must make clear that the trial as you have it in Chapter 57 is fiction, although the "Beaufort Nine" were real. Obviously Ham Bell wasn't involved. Nelson Mitchell's actual co-counsel was another well-regarded Charleston attorney, Edward McCrady.

Mitchell's defense argument, which led to the "no jurisdiction" decision was something I was not equipped to write. The argument woven through the scene was generously and very creatively drafted by John Napier, Esq., of Washington, D.C., and Pawleys Island, South Carolina. John is eminently qualified, being an attorney, a former U.S. Congressman from our state, and a former Federal Court of Claims judge. I appreciate his contribution, and gratefully acknowledge it here. (Let there be no mutterings about the kind of unacknowledged cribbing that has lately afflicted the field of historical scholarship.)

Although the soldiers of the 54th were spared death or reenslavement, they were not freed. They languished in Charleston jail until December 1864, when they were transferred to the wretched military prison at Florence, South Carolina. The end of the war found them in another prison in North Carolina. There they were released at last.

Looting of Charleston houses by African-American troops led by white officers took place in February 1865, as described, though it probably had less to do with race than with the centuries-old behavior of a conquering army.

In the Reconstruction section I have again adjusted the time of certain events for the sake of the narrative, though never by more than a few months. No significant events have been invented. Race riots, for example, did occur in Charleston in the summer of 1865 and again in 1866.

The use of oleander tea to poison Union troops is mentioned in literature but, so far as I know, not supported by evidence. Still, the idea is fair game for a story: oleander grows widely in the South, and its deadly toxicity is unquestioned. As recently as the 1980s a case of death from ingestion of oleander tea was reported in the *Annals of Emergency Medicine*.

The incident of "Devil Dan" Sickles and his cigar on the horsecar was reported in the *Washington National Intelligencer* in August of 1867, not 1865. Sickles's biographer, W. A. Swanberg, says the story is untrue but I included it because it beautifully represents Sickles's forceful, not to say high-handed, approach to military governance.

Some of Colonel Wheat's remarks about battle are adapted from a written account by a trooper of the Hampton Legion who survived First Manassas, and the war.

Gibbes's diatribe about the 14th Amendment is likewise adapted from statements published at the time.

Francis L. Cardozo spoke of black and white children going to school together more than eighty years before Dr. Martin Luther King, Jr., espoused the same dream.

Brigadier General Huffington is fictional, though inspired by a notable South Carolina carpetbagger, "Honest John" Patterson, who in 1872 succeeded in bribing his way to a U.S. Senate seat. The Pennsylvania Reserves are authentic, but Huffington's regiment, the 14th, is not. Pennsylvania Reserve regiments numbered 1 through 13.

Alex's lyric for "A Better, Brighter Morning" has a bit of a history. It was written a few years ago, during my year and a half of collaboration with lyricist Richard Maltby, Jr. (*Miss Saigon, Big, Ain't Misbehavin'*, et al.) and composer Charles Strouse (*Annie, Rags, Bye Bye Birdie*, et al.). We were all hard at work trying to hammer out a story line for a large-scale musical version of *North and South*, an ambitious project conceived by Richard's wife, Janet, who is a Broadway producer. The project is as yet unfinished (and may remain so).

During one of the sessions I remembered that solo singers and singing groups wrote and performed anthems for antislavery rallies. The Hutchinson Family Singers was one very famous aggregation; they appear briefly with fictional Virgilia Hazard in the novel.

I thought we should have a similar, historically germane moment in the show: a rousing song typical of such anthems, which were long on sentiment and fervor, if sometimes short on literary quality. I wrote the lyric at our place in Greenwich, tucked it away, but never showed it to Richard or Charles. They are, after all, theater luminaries with many Tony Awards between them. I didn't imagine the song would ever be useful in another context.

The infamous N word challenges a novelist writing about the past. During the years of the story the word was widely used, uttered even by the most well-intentioned people. To omit it would play false with history. I chose to use it.

A cavalcade of fascinating men and women passed through Charleston during the years of the story. One whom I wanted to fit in but could not was an eighteen-year-old army private from Virginia who served with his artillery battery at Fort Moultrie from November 1827 until December 1828. He had enlisted under the name Edgar Perry and had already published a book of poems. We know him as Edgar Allan Poe.

Another colorful personality I did not find room for, perhaps out of some subconscious concern that she might come to dominate the story, is Mary Chesnut, wife of James Chesnut, Jr., South Carolina soldier and politician. During the war Mary observed life in Charleston and, later, Richmond. She wrote about it in what became known as *A Diary from Dixie*. The diary is unmatched on several counts: Mary's keen perceptions, her lively prose style, and her unabashed bitchiness. Several editions are available, the best in my opinion being that edited by the historian Vann Woodward and published by Yale under the title *Mary Chesnut's Civil War*.

So many aspects of Charleston's past are so well documented, down to the design of garden gates and the knobs on furniture, that complete accuracy is very likely beyond the grasp of a mere mortal. To quote Dr. Arthur Schlesinger's introduction to the first volume of his study of the era of FDR, "The author will greatly welcome any corrections or amplifications for possible future editions." Address these to JJFICTION@aol.com. My office will then evaluate them.

As always, an incredible array of helpful people made the writing task easier at every step. I now thank them formally, though of course with the usual strong caution that they must not be held responsible in any way for what I have put on the page.

In Charleston: attorney and historian Robert Rosen, who, with unstinting generosity, shared his knowledge of the city's history, which he has chronicled in two splendid books; Daisy Bigda, Patton Hash, and Peter Wilkerson, all of whom were at the South Carolina Historical Society when the project was launched; also Nicholas Butler and Mike Coker at the Society's headquarters on Meeting Street.

In Columbia: Dr. Tom Johnson, director of the South Caroliniana Library at the University; Dr. Lacy Ford and Dr. Walter Edgar of the History Department; Catherine Fry and Barbara Brannon, director and managing editor, respectively, of the University of South Carolina Press; Patrick McCawley, reference archivist at the South Carolina Department of Archives and History.

In London: at the Middle Temple, Anthea Tatton-Brown, deputy under treasurer, and Lesley Whitelaw, archivist; also Hilary Hale and Barbara Boote.

Others who helped in ways large and small are Patricia Cornwell; Dordy Freeman; Herman Gollob; John Lawless; Gilbert M. Martin; Angela Wiggan Marvin; my grandson Hart Montgomery; Judi Murphy; Mary Oliver, archivist-curator of the Montgomery County, Ohio, Historical Society; Michael Renaud of Corel Corporation, Toronto; Dr. Lawrence Rowland of the USC/Beaufort, previously mentioned; and Dr. Stephen Wise, author and director of the Marine Corps Museum at Parris Island, South Carolina. Special thanks to Pat Falci, former president of the New York City Civil War Roundtable, for vetting a portion of the manuscript, and to Jeffrey Ward, who created the endpaper maps.

In earlier novels I have indicated my debt to the research facilities of the Thomas Cooper Library at the University of South Carolina, and to its longtime director, Dr. George Terry. George passed away in 2001 and is greatly missed. He was not only a trained historian and a superb library administrator, he became a close and valued friend. His death was untimely; he was only fifty-two.

Clare Ferraro and Louise Burke enthusiastically endorsed the idea for the novel when they were directly associated with Dutton. Clare's successor as publisher, my old friend Carole Baron, was similarly enthusiastic. I thank all of them, along with my editor, Doug Grad, his able assistant, Ron Martirano, and art director Rich Hasselberger. As a scarred veteran of advertising, I can offer fully qualified professional admiration of Rich's skill. He has created a striking and appropriate format for the jackets of my books.

Frank R. Curtis, Esq., of New York, my attorney and literary representative for more than twenty-five years, provided the usual stalwart support for the project.

And my wife, Rachel, again helped me through the inevitable struggle that accompanies the writing of a long manuscript. To her I renew my debt of love and devotion.

John Jakes

Charleston, Hilton Head Island, and Columbia, South Carolina

London, England

Greenwich and Chester, Connecticut

Maui, Hawaii

1999–2002

www.johnjakes.com

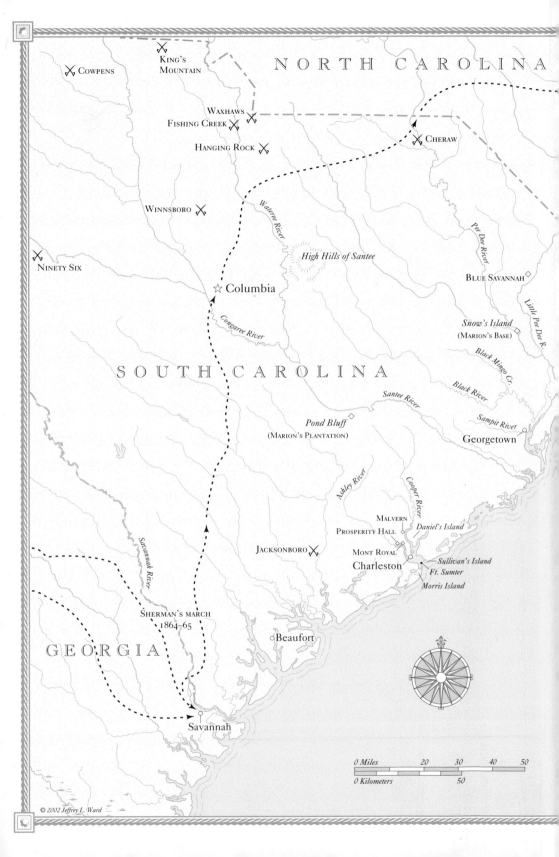

NORTH CAROLINA

⚔ COWPENS

⚔ KING'S MOUNTAIN

⚔ WAXHAWS
FISHING CREEK ⚔
HANGING ROCK ⚔

⚔ CHERAW

WINNSBORO ⚔

Watree River

High Hills of Santee

Pee Dee River

⚔ NINETY SIX

☆ Columbia

BLUE SAVANNAH ◇

Congaree River

Snow's Island
(MARION'S BASE) ◇

Little Pee Dee R.

SOUTH CAROLINA

Black Mingo Cr.

Black River

Santee River

Sampit River

Pond Bluff ◇
(MARION'S PLANTATION)

Georgetown

Ashley River

Cooper River

MALVERN
PROSPERITY HALL ◇
Daniel's Island

JACKSONBORO ⚔

MONT ROYAL
Charleston

Sullivan's Island
Ft. Sumter
Morris Island

Savannah River

SHERMAN'S MARCH
1864–65

◇ Beaufort

GEORGIA

○ Savannah

0 Miles   20   30   40   50
0 Kilometers   50

© 2002 Jeffrey L. Ward

About the Author

John Jakes is the bestselling author of *The Kent Family Chronicles, The North and South Trilogy, On Secret Service, California Gold, Homeland,* and *American Dreams.* His love and knowledge of American history are a reflection of his own heritage. His maternal grandfather emigrated from Germany in 1861 and settled in the Midwest. On his father's side he is a descendant of a soldier of the Virginia Continental Line who fought in the Revolution. He lives in Hilton Head, South Carolina, and Greenwich, Connecticut.